**Praise for the Regency Romances
of Allison Lane**

Kindred Spirits

"*Kindred Spirits* is a diamond of the first
water. . . . Regency fans can always count on
Allison Lane. . . . This book will be a strong
contender for best Regency romance
of the year!"
—Romance Reviews Today

The Rake and the Wallflower

"This lively, well-crafted story offers an
insightful look at the realities of Regency life
with a few surprising twists."
—*Library Journal*

The Notorious Widow

"Ms. Lane never fails to deliver the goods."
—*Romantic Times*

THE
MADCAP
MARRIAGE

ALLISON LANE

A SIGNET BOOK

SIGNET
Published by New American Library, a division of
Penguin Group (USA) Inc., 375 Hudson Street,
New York, New York 10014, U.S.A.
Penguin Books Ltd, 80 Strand,
London WC2R 0RL, England
Penguin Books Australia Ltd, 250 Camberwell Road,
Camberwell, Victoria 3124, Australia
Penguin Books Canada Ltd, 10 Alcorn Avenue,
Toronto, Ontario, Canada M4V 3B2
Penguin Books (N.Z.) Ltd, Cnr Rosedale and Airborne Roads,
Albany, Auckland 1310, New Zealand

Penguin Books Ltd, Registered Offices:
80 Strand, London WC2R 0RL, England

First published by Signet, an imprint of New American Library,
a division of Penguin Group (USA) Inc.

First Printing, January 2004
10 9 8 7 6 5 4 3 2 1

*Many thanks to the wonderful members
of the Beau Monde and the Regency loops
who collectively know everything
about the Regency period and selflessly
share that information with others.*

Marry in haste and repent at leisure.
—Old English proverb

Chapter One

May 20, 1814

*H*elen St. James awoke to cold, dank stone under her cheek and people murmuring off to her right. Where was she?

"—never saw . . . lengthy swoon." The voice belonged to a stranger.

A pounding head and overwhelming sense of danger kept her motionless. She was clearly indoors, though she dared not open her eyes to find out where. Instead, she sniffed—delicately.

Mustiness blended with the scent of wax candles. And something more—wine, perhaps? The combination was odd. Wine and stone might indicate a cellar, though cellars were usually lit by tallow lanterns. Yet even Audley's disused Tudor wing smelled fresher than this.

A second voice penetrated her fog. "—carriage sickness . . . nothing since breakfast . . . excitement too much . . ."

Her uncle, Sir Steven St. James.

Fear lashed her brain. Fury followed, burning away the fog. Steven was dangerous, and more cunning than she had expected. He'd tricked her by—

"I've seen many a bride swoon, but none who remained insensible for so long," insisted the first man. "I won't be a party to a deathbed marriage. Your man assu—"

Marriage. This must be that church on the edge of

London. Her last memory was of Steven ordering the coachman to stop. How long had she been unconscious?

Steven's hearty tone cut across the vicar's words. "It is merely weariness. The lovebirds are so eager to wed, they refused to postpone the ceremony a minute longer."

A snicker rippled from her left. Steven's son, Dudley. She was surrounded.

Helen barely controlled a shudder. Dudley made her skin crawl. Not because of his pockmarked cheeks and scarred forehead—or even his limp. She blamed no one for the ravages of time. It was the gleam in his eyes that she loathed. And his rapacious hands, his quick temper, his disregard for anyone weaker . . .

The whisper of a silk skirt approached, accompanied by a cloud of cloying perfume that obliterated all other odors. Here was yet another enemy—Maude Cunningham, who doused herself in chypre several times a day. Now exposed as Steven's mistress, she had served as Helen's maid since the day Steven turned off Tessa.

Helen stifled another burst of fury. Why had it taken her so long to realize that Maude was Steven's spy? If she'd paid attention, she might have escaped their clutches.

If only she hadn't been distracted!

Fate had played her a cruel trick, striking her mother with apoplexy at her father's deathbed and throwing the household into chaos. Steven had taken advantage of her inattention to insinuate himself into Audley Court— in flagrant disregard of his brother's will—by convincing her trustees to appoint him as overseer. By the time Lady St. James had died, Sir Steven ruled both house and estate, making Helen a prisoner in her own home, denied callers and forbidden to write letters.

She had still been reeling from that shock when Dudley arrived bearing a special license. Only her vicar's refusal to read services for an unwilling bride had saved her. But this vicar wasn't an ally. Sir Steven would not have stopped here unless a hefty bribe had convinced the man to ignore her objections.

"Wake her, Maude. She must have fallen asleep." Steven's irritation boded ill.

Helen concentrated on remaining limp—Maude loved

to kick. Until she could escape, she had to stay unconscious.

She had known that accompanying Steven to London
posed risks—he never acted without a reason—but she
hadn't expected him to spring his trap so quickly. Under-
estimating him could cost her everything. Her own plan
had been to slip out after dark and find her guardian,
Lord Alquist. But they'd stopped before reaching May-
fair. When she'd tried to flee, Steven had bashed her on
the head.

A pitcher of cold water suddenly drenched her face
and gown. Yelping, she surged to her feet, then cursed.
Doom was at hand.

"Excellent," said Steven. "I knew you were eager to
conclude the formalities."

Dudley laughed, reaching for her arm.

Shaking off water let her evade Dudley. Her eyes
darted about, seeking an exit. But the church was larger
than it had appeared from the carriage window. Its nave
could easily hold five hundred, so flight was out of the
question. As wobbly as she was, even Dudley could
catch her before she reached the door. And there were
more people to give chase than she'd thought. Steven's
secretary and Dudley's valet stood to one side, blocking
another avenue of escape.

Fighting was also useless. She could never defeat
five opponents.

That left guile. Steven's one weakness was contempt
for female intelligence.

She staggered, then clamped a hand over her mouth.
"I'm going to be sick!"

Maude and Dudley recoiled. Steven froze.

Helen met the vicar's gaze, then stumbled toward the
oversized chalice atop the nearby altar.

As she'd hoped, he didn't want her using his chalice
as a basin. Grabbing her arm, he hustled her along the
transept and shoved her into his study.

Helen locked the heavy wooden door as her eyes fran-
tically scanned the room. His desk held the parish register, open and ready to sign. A basin atop the low
bookcase explained why he'd dragged her here. Her
gaze skimmed past it, coming to rest on an open window.

"Thank God."

Hiking her skirts to her hips, she wiggled through the narrow casement, then nearly yelped when she landed in a rosebush. Thorns slashed her legs and gown as she struggled free. Other roses covered the walls enclosing this tiny garden. For one terrible moment she feared she must climb them. . . .

A rusty gate was tucked into the corner. Exhaling in relief, she sprinted for freedom. London might be dangerous for a woman alone, but anything was better than Dudley.

"How dare you ignore my summons for four days?" thundered Lord Hillcrest, his face purpling as he pounded on his desk.

"I wasn't at home to receive it." Rafael Thomas glared at his father. "I was attending Alquist's funeral—as you should have been," he added deliberately. "You should at least have sent condolences to his widow."

"Why? She schemed against me for years, undermining my authority, turning my family against me. . . ."

Rafe let the diatribe flow past him. If he withdrew deep enough into his mind, the words made no impact. Hillcrest's complaints never varied. Even the few that contained a grain of truth were pointless.

As he settled into a chair, Rafe wondered what the man wanted this time. They had been at odds for twenty-eight years. Hillcrest made impossible demands. Rafe ignored them. The pattern was too established to change, though a thread of hope wished otherwise.

"Pull your mind out of Lady Willingham's bed and pay attention," snapped Hillcrest, slamming a book down with a crack like thunder.

Rafe opened his mouth—Lady Willingham's obvious availability didn't interest him—but Hillcrest gave him no chance to speak. "You've sowed more than enough oats, boy. It is past time for you and Alice to set up your nursery."

Rafe rolled his eyes. For ten years Hillcrest had demanded that he wed Alice Pauling, but Rafe refused. Besides that he disliked Alice on her own account, her dowry included the estate adjacent to Hillcrest Manor.

Never would he consider living so near. Constant battles would destroy his sanity.

He much preferred London. Gossips might cluck their tongues over his latest conquest and shake their heads at past foibles, but the liveliest courtesans and most passionate matrons vied for his favors. Society hostesses kept him at the top of their lists, for his wit enlivened any gathering. Reformists courted his support against the day he would assume a seat in Parliament.

Marriage could wait until raking lost its charm—another five years, or maybe ten. But Alice Pauling would never be on his list of potential brides. His wife must share his interests and satisfy his libido, for he had vowed fidelity after marriage. She should respect his decisions and defer to his desires. And she must have a limited dowry—preferably no dowry at all.

Steadying his temper, he met Hillcrest's flinty eyes. "I will *not* wed Alice. I've refused this match for ten years. Nothing has changed."

"Of course you are marrying Alice." Hillcrest shook his balding head. "Pauling and I agreed to the match when Alice was born. You cannot jilt her. She loves you."

"I cannot jilt someone I never offered for," he snapped. "Forget this insanity. I won't wed the chit. She's timid, insipid, and hasn't two thoughts to rub together." Rising, he headed for the door. "I have plans for the evening, so if you will excuse—"

"Sit down!" Exploding from behind the desk, Hillcrest shoved Rafe into a chair.

Rafe stared at his fists while he fought to rein in his temper. This was turning into the worst confrontation yet.

The library had always been dismal, its austerity reflecting Hillcrest's character. But the ghosts of past confrontations made it worse. Here a young Rafe had endured unearned lectures and petty punishments. Here he had repudiated Alice again and again. Here he had declared independence by throwing his allowance in Hillcrest's face.

"I am appalled to claim you as my son," snarled Hillcrest, punctuating the words with his hands. "You are the worst excuse for a gentleman society has ever seen! A debauched, drunken gamester without an ounce of intelligence, a dissipated wastrel who has long since sacrificed honor on the altar of hedonistic impulse. Thank God your mother is gone. She would have wept to see what you have become."

"Don't drag Mother into this!" Rafe surged to his feet, removing Hillcrest's height advantage. He had learned long ago that arguing merely prolonged these meetings, but he could not sit silent while Hillcrest maligned his mother. "She protested this match from the moment you suggested it. Were she here, she would protest even more. She despised arranged marriages—and with good reason. Hers made her miserable!"

"Lies! You misunderstood everything about her. Her only reservation concerned Lady Pauling's weak constitution, so she counseled patience until we discovered whether Alice might share it. She would agree that you need a calm, sober wife to counter your wild ways. Your name has become a byword. Newspapers bulge with your scandals. Everywhere I go, men condemn your public drunkenness and reckless gaming. How many women have you seduced?"

"That is none of your business," Rafe snapped, though in truth he hadn't seduced anyone in years. He didn't have to.

"You *are* my business."

"No." It was time to stop caring that harsh words might alienate Hillcrest for all time. His hope for reconciliation was a fantasy. "I came of age seven years ago and answer to no one, especially a fool. You are worse than the most irresponsible gossip, accepting baseless speculation and wild exaggeration as truth because you are too stupid to know who to believe and too lazy to investigate for yourself." He kept his tone icy, though his knees shook and curses ricocheted through his head. Hillcrest was so sure of his own judgment that he refused to listen to evidence in Rafe's favor—as Rafe knew all too well.

"Exaggeration?" demanded Hillcrest, shaking his fist. "I can read, boy. As can society. The papers are full of your exploits."

"Most of them false."

"Enough, Rafe. Pauling will forgive you once you settle down—"

"I would never ask him to lower his standards so far." Rafe moved behind the desk so Hillcrest was farther away. "Nor would I associate with anyone who felt it necessary to do so."

"I said enough! He is dying and wants Alice wed before he goes. It is time to assume your responsibilities. The contracts have been accepted—"

"Not by me!"

Hillcrest raised his chin another notch, signaling increased implacability that hardened Rafe's resolve. "We will hold the wedding in three weeks. The betrothal announcement will appear in tomorrow's papers."

"No!" Betrayal. All the worse for being unexpected. Why would Hillcrest court the very scandal he abhorred? "You cannot force me into a union I repudiate."

"You have nothing to say in the matter. Pauling and I signed the settlements last week."

"*You* signed?" He glared, appalled at this newest evidence of disrespect. "I am of age and cannot be constrained by your signature. I have refused the connection a hundred times. A thousand times. Nothing has changed."

"Exactly. Nothing has changed. Pauling accepted your hand on Alice's behalf twenty years ago. Since you are dragging your feet, I've made all the arrangements. Your valet is closing your rooms and will arrive this evening."

Rafe's temper shattered. "You are worse than Napoleon, trying to force your will on others. But you'll lose, just as he did. I will never wed Alice. Your scheming will only create a new scandal for you to mutter over."

"How dare—"

Rafe grabbed the brandy decanter and headed for the door. "I'm leaving—permanently. If Jameson has removed so much as a cravat from my rooms, I'll have him transported for theft. Think about that next time you consider playing God with other people's lives."

"If you walk out that door, I'll leave every groat to a benevolent society. You'll never receive another shilling from me."

Rafe laughed. "A toothless threat from an impotent

tyrant. I haven't received a shilling from you in ten years, Hillcrest. Keep your money. I don't need it. As for Alice, if you want Paulus Grange so badly, marry her yourself. I refuse."

"If you leave, Pauling will sue you for breach of promise."

"Impossible." Rafe vulgarly gulped brandy from the decanter, then grinned as Hillcrest's face purpled. "Oh, he can probably sue you. But I signed nothing, and I promised nothing. Do you recall the part of the marriage service that requires a response from the groom? If you drag me to the altar, that response will be *Never!* Rather than accept Alice, I would marry the first girl I see. Lady or leper, princess or prostitute, it makes no difference. And that's a vow."

Still carrying the decanter, he slammed the library door and stormed from the house.

At least the groom had kept Caesar ready, as ordered. He hoped Jameson was as smart. Swigging brandy to dull the pain of this latest betrayal, he cantered down the drive.

By the time he reached the turnpike, the decanter was empty and the sting of incipient tears had replaced his fury. How could Hillcrest be so cruel?

Rafe shook his head. A better question was why he left himself vulnerable to Hillcrest's attacks. He ought to know better, yet he'd obeyed this summons, hoping yet again that Hillcrest might finally consider him worthy of respect.

Stupid. When would he accept that they would never be close? The battle lines had been drawn the moment an infant Rafe had showed a preference for his doting mother over his stern father. Nothing had changed. The price for his father's acceptance remained repudiation of the woman Hillcrest despised.

Rafe always refused.

Lady Hillcrest had been a saint, devoting her life to shielding him from Hillcrest's diatribes. It had been natural to protect her in turn. But Rafe's loyalty had further inflamed Hillcrest. Her death had changed nothing. Rafe must now protect her memory from Hillcrest's continuing attempts to turn her into the meek-mannered cipher he'd wanted.

He halted at an inn to refill the decanter.

If Alice had been different, he might have considered her, despite her dowry. But she was the antithesis of his ideal wife, having lifeless looks, a bland personality, and a mind incapable of original thought. Bedding her would be less exciting than watching wood decay.

He preferred women with spirit. Nothing heated the blood faster than a lively debate with a witty mind— especially when that mind was attached to a seductive body. And what better way to settle differences than a passionate romp in bed? It was the sort of relationship he enjoyed with his liaisons.

Remounting Caesar, he spurred toward town.

His first call must be on his solicitor. He had never actually studied how much authority a parent had over an adult child. Was he right that Hillcrest's signature could not bind him? Were there other ways Hillcrest could interfere with his life?

That newspaper announcement would create scandal no matter how it played out. A lady could break a betrothal, but a gentleman could not. He hated the idea of publicly denouncing his father, but that might be the only way to avoid ostracism. He would not wed Alice.

Escaping ostracism would not restore his credit, though. His reputation would convince many matrons that he had compromised Alice, then refused to wed her. His two-week absence from town might support such tales.

He cursed his reputation—and his own idiocy. Ten years earlier, his mother's death had triggered a month of debauchery and dissipation as he fought to assuage grief. That brief craziness had founded a reputation that haunted him to this day.

"There has to be a solution," he mumbled, wishing he could think clearly. He shouldn't have drunk so much brandy. Already his head felt muzzy, with swarms of bees buzzing in his ears.

He slowed Caesar to a walk as cobblestones replaced the rutted road. Five- and six-story buildings closed in on either side. A cacophony of clattering wheels, hooves, and shouts enfolded him as carts and carriages jostled for position on the crowded street, most headed for Blackfriar's Bridge.

He swayed. That second bottle had left him more well-to-go than he'd been in years. Dizziness nearly unseated him as he tried to shake away the spots dancing before his eyes. Venders vied for his attention, offering meat pies and fresh milk, flowers and rag dolls, apples and sex.

He squinted at the bony prostitute. She must be starving if she was plying her trade this early. It was barely four.

Tossing her the decanter, he swerved down a side street and out of sight. She could eat for a week by pawning the bottle, and he needed both hands free if he was to stay on his horse.

Cursing this latest stupidity, he squinted at a sign, then turned down another street. He'd drunk fast and deep, so the effects were still catching up with him. His body craved sleep, but he had to see his solicitor. Maybe Shipley could cancel Hillcrest's announcement. Surely the newspapers would cooperate when they learned that the notice was false.

An accident blocked most of the street, but he squeezed past and turned down Green Walk, a narrow lane skirting the wall surrounding Christchurch. Shipley's office stood opposite its rusty gate.

"Devil take it," he muttered, peering around as he dismounted. "Where'sh everybody?" People usually clogged the lane, including half a dozen boys seeking half-farthings in exchange for minor services. He needed one to hold Caesar, but today even the boys were gone. Probably to gape at the accident—or pick the pockets of those gaping at the accident.

He was leading Caesar to the nearest lamppost when the screech of rusty hinges knifed through his head. A woman charged from the churchyard, nearly knocking him over. His free hand caught her before she bounced into the filthy street.

"Oh!" The gasp was a husky contralto that snapped his nether regions to attention. "I didn't see— Ooh!"

Her second gasp was wantonly seductive. One hand slid down his chest while the other caressed the scarred cheek that fascinated so many of his conquests.

Another courtesan plying her trade early. But this one he would accept. And if she was half as talented as she seemed, he would keep her awhile.

"Very nice," he murmured, examining her wares. She was nearly as tall as he, her tawny lashes level with his mouth. Fiery curls framed a heart-shaped face containing the greenest eyes he'd ever seen. Nipples puckered by a dampened yellow gown distracted attention from its shabbiness.

Clever. Very clever. His fingers itched to touch, his lips to suckle. What a temptress! Circe herself could do no better. He'd hardened with astonishing speed.

Lust drove all thought from his mind. He wanted her. Needed her. If not for Caesar tugging on the rein, he would take her right now. Where the devil had everyone gone?

Business first, he reminded himself, recalling why he was here. Lust must wait, though he needn't postpone all pleasure.

Jerking her against him, he closed his mouth over hers, plundering her sweetness. His hand shifted to caress a breast already swollen with passion.

One shapely thigh rubbed his throbbing shaft as she swayed.

He lost himself in her taste, images tumbling through his head of fiery curls spread across a pillow, that wanton body pressing—

"No!" she gasped as his hand slipped down the front of her gown. She stumbled backward, shock blazing in her eyes.

It took him a moment to understand that his erection had startled her, and another moment to register that she hadn't kissed him back. . . .

He narrowed his eyes, clawing through the brandy fog to examine her again.

Her features were refined. A rose branch and several thorns clung to her skirt, explaining the snags. A reticule hung from one wrist. Her hair retained the imprint of a bonnet. She'd dashed through the gate as if the hounds of hell nipped at her heels. Was the terror now swirling in her eyes the cause of her flight or the result of his advances? She was probably a virgin.

Damnation! His loins still throbbed. But avoiding virgins was the one rule he'd never broken, not even during the madness of ten years ago.

"Pardon me." Though frustration bit deep, his apology was sincere, if a bit slurred. "I didn't expect to find a lady here. Why are you alone?"

A thud echoed across the churchyard, widening her pupils. "Please help me, sir. Can you direct me to Berkeley Square? My guardian lives there."

"What?" He knew he was drunk, but why was she in Southwark if she was seeking Berkeley Square? It was miles away on the other side of the Thames.

She inhaled, tightening her gown across that magnificent bosom and trapping his gaze on her pebbled nipples. His shaft pressed painfully against his pantaloons.

Words reverberated inside his head—*marry the first girl I see.* Marriage would be no hardship with this one and might solve all his problems.

"—uncle is forcing me to wed my odious cousin," she was saying in a very cultured voice. "I jumped from a window, but I won't be safe until I reach my guardian. Quickly, sir, before they catch me. How do I reach Berkeley Square?"

"How is it that your guardian lost track of you?" he asked absently, his eyes still trapped. His head whirled faster. Heat surged through his loins. *First girl . . . marry . . . princess or prostitute . . .*

"My uncle incarcerated me because he wants my estate. Please, sir. There is no time." Louder thuds echoed. She lowered her voice. "They will find me gone at any moment. How do I get to Alquist House in Berkeley Square?"

The name wrenched his gaze to eyes seething with desperation. "Lord Alquist is your guardian?"

She nodded.

"He died a fortnight ago," Rafe said slowly. "I just returned from his burial. Didn't anyone tell you?"

She swayed, blanching, one hand covering her mouth. "Dear Lord. No wonder he dared bring me to London.

What am I to do?" Muffled shouts joined the thuds. "He's coming. I have to leave. My trustees are with Formsby's Bank on Broad Street. Can you direct me there?"

The bang of a door hitting a wall signaled a broken lock. Voices shouted over one another.

"Gone!"

"—ought to wring her—"

"Damn the bitch!"

"—window—"

"—broken roses—"

Rafe's heart raced. Her problem was worse than his. Her pursuers sounded too angry for a rational discussion.

"I'll take you." He tossed her across Caesar's withers, then swung up behind her as curses flowed from the churchyard. "Stay low and hang on."

Spurring to a canter, he kept her head below the top of the wall so the men racing toward the gate would not see her. The moment Caesar cleared the church, he turned down a side street, then into a maze of narrow lanes.

"Who are you?" he demanded when they were out of sight, hoping conversation would distract him from another wave of lust—every stride ground her hip against his erection.

"Helen St. James, daughter of Sir Arthur St. James of Audley Court, Somerset." She flung an arm around his neck as he rounded another corner, plastering her against his body.

"The honorable Rafael Thomas, at your service," he managed. With her head pressed against his chin, her perfume engulfed him. Heliotrope, his mother's favorite scent.

Marry the first girl I see. She was certainly spirited enough.

In a bid to restore his reason, he ducked into an alcove between two buildings so he could put some space between them.

"Relax," he commanded, prying her fingers loose. "You are safe."

She released him, but his relief was short-lived. Now it

was her eyes that captured him, drowning him in their green depths. If only he had full control of his faculties! But his head spun worse than ever. Clatters and shouts from the street beat dully against ears awash in the rush of blood. He burned wherever she touched him. Her taste—

Gathering his few remaining wits, he forced his mind back to business. "We have a problem, Miss Shan-Sin"—he couldn't get *St. James* to roll off his tongue, so he settled on—"Miss Helen. I can deliver you to Broad Street, but the trip will take the best part of an hour. By then the bank will be closed. Is there anyone you can stay with until morning?"

"I have no acquaintances in town just now. My uncle has held me hostage since my father died last year. I planned to slip away tonight and find Lord Alquist, but you say he is dead."

"He was struck down by a wagon two weeks ago."

"Then what am I to do?"

Church bells chimed five.

It was far too late to seek Shipley's help. The solicitor couldn't reach one newspaper before it went to press, let alone the dozen that might have received Hillcrest's announcement. Not all of them were based in Fleet Street.

Dizziness spread to his stomach, which threatened to cast up the brandy. That reckless vow again screamed through his mind. *Marry the first girl I see . . . first girl I see . . . first—*

"You must marry me." The words shocked him, though he didn't reclaim them. It was the best solution for both of them. "It is the only way to retain your reputation. Spending the night together is bad enough. Leaving you alone would be worse. Without my protection, you will be ruined by morning—provided you live that long. London is dangerous."

"Marry you?" She choked.

He met her gaze. "I'm not such a bad bargain, Miss Helen. I'm heir to a viscount and considered a gentleman in deed as well as blood." At least in most circles. "Marriage will thwart your uncle. But we'll have to hurry. Doctors Commons closes soon."

"Doctors Commons."

Helen cursed the shock that froze her tongue. She stared at Mr. Thomas—the very drunk Mr. Thomas. His breath smelled strongly of brandy. His tongue was tied in knots. Green-tinged cheeks and blurry eyes confirmed his condition—foxed to the gills. At least he wasn't violent. She'd barely escaped a beating the last time Dudley had come home in his cups. While Mr. Thomas had been on the verge of ravishing her right on the street, she could hardly deny that she'd invited his advances. Since her refusal, he'd been a perfect gentleman.

He swayed. "We need a special license, Miss Helen. Doctors Commons is the only place to get one." Narrowing his eyes, he added, "You *are* of age, I presume."

"Twenty-two. Quite on the shelf."

"I wouldn't go that far." He brushed her hip, swirling heat into her stomach. Every touch had done that since she'd run him down. And that kiss . . .

He scrambled her wits, making the last hour seem even more unreal.

She hadn't seen him before crashing into him, then had been too stunned to back off—and not because of the impact. He was tall, dark, and hard. Very hard. And blazingly masculine, exuding power that demanded attention. Those muscular arms and shoulders needed no padding to fill his well-cut coat. His legs were equally fine. A curly-brimmed beaver hat pressed dark curls onto his forehead, reminding her strongly of Alex—

Wrenching her thoughts from the cad who had jilted her four years earlier, she focused on Mr. Thomas. Or tried to. It was hard to think through a pounding head and churning stomach.

His most surprising feature was the silver filigree that cupped his left cheekbone like delicate lace, reflecting the silver-gray of his eyes and adding intrigue and character to a face that might have seemed conventionally handsome otherwise. Before she'd realized her intent, her finger had traced that enticing scar. It was clearly old, for it blended smoothly into his skin.

Heat had seared her fingertips. Then his mouth had plundered hers, shutting down all thought. Not until she'd identified the hardest muscle of all had she come to her senses.

Thank God she'd pulled away. Another time she would have fled, but she was desperate. And he'd been her only hope. The narrow street had been quite empty, and his arms had seemed so very safe. . . .

Think!

Her ears buzzed louder than a beehive.

Rafael Thomas, viscount's heir. That was all she knew about him. Name and station. Why would he offer marriage? She tried to imagine, but Steven's blow had scrambled her wits.

Even with the scar, he could have anyone he chose, and he must know it. She could imagine women throwing themselves at his feet, for he exuded an aura that commanded her to touch, explore, and demand satisfaction. Every brush of his body strengthened the command. Every whiff of his scent urged her closer. Her hand raised—

Shocked at the images forming in her mind, she shook her head—and immediately regretted it as pain knifed through her skull.

Steven had halted the carriage as the church tower tolled four. So unless she'd been with Mr. Thomas far longer than she thought, she had been unconscious for half an hour. Concussions muddled thinking, which ought to prompt caution. If these sensual longings were a side effect, they might disappear by morning.

Yet Mr. Thomas was right. With Lord Alquist dead, she had nowhere to go. London was dangerous for a woman alone. With her lack of either money or maid, no reputable innkeeper would accept her. So he was her only hope. She should thank Fate that he was offering marriage rather than ruination. That alone indicated an honorable character. She could do worse—Dudley, for instance.

"Well?" he demanded.

Her hands twisted in her lap, but she nodded. "You have done me a great honor, Mr. Thomas. I will endeavor to make you a proper wife."

Relief was so dizzying that Rafe nearly fell off Caesar. *Marry the first girl I see.* "You might as well call me Rafe, my dear," he managed. "You have made me the happiest of men."

The declaration dealt a fatal blow to his stomach. Twisting sideways, he retched again and again, dredging up his very toenails. His betrothed—another spasm hit with the word—uttered soothing sounds, adding embarrassment to his discomfort.

Nearly a quarter hour passed before he headed for Blackfriar's Bridge and Doctors Commons, one arm wrapped securely around her as if fearing she might disappear.

Fool . . . fool . . . fool.

The charge battered his head with every step. What the devil had he done?

He was worse than a fool. This latest impulse might ruin him completely. What did he know about Miss Helen St. James anyway? She might be mad or diseased or incapable of intelligent thought. Anyone accepting such a ramshackle proposal must have something seriously wrong with her. She possessed an estate, uncommon beauty, and a vibrancy that demanded attention. So why was she unwed at the advanced age of twenty-two?

Yet it was done. Having given his word, he could not renege. And the match would end the fight over Alice once and for all.

But never in his wildest dreams had he expected this to be his wedding night.

Chapter Two

*H*elen suppressed another wave of dizziness as she pushed the last bites of beef listlessly around her plate. The little she'd eaten was curdling in her stomach.

Three hours had passed since she'd rammed into Rafe. Her head pounded worse than ever, making it impossible to concentrate. Surely this was a nightmare. Any moment she would awaken and—

"Is the food not to your liking?" Rafe asked.

The question cut through her rising panic. "It's fine." Transferring a sliver of meat to her mouth, she gamely chewed, surprised that he'd noticed her abstraction.

He was so drunk that he'd nearly fallen from his horse on Blackfriar's Bridge. The effort to hold him upright had increased her own dizziness and activated her conscience. By the time they'd reached Doctors Commons, it had been screaming—he had no idea what he was doing; wedding a stranger was insanely reckless; her best course was to cry off and find some other escape.

Yet honor had forbidden her to cry off. Alex had already tarnished her reputation. A jilt—even in such ridiculous circumstances—would worsen it. She couldn't do it.

Be honest, she admonished herself as Rafe picked at his dinner. *You expected someone else to call a halt.*

She blushed.

"Are you all right?" he asked.

How had he noticed? She could have sworn his eyes were on his food.

"Quite all right," she murmured. "Though it seems rather warm tonight."

Rafe's knife clattered to the floor. A dozen diners turned to stare as his gaze moved lazily over her body.

Embarrassed, Helen ducked her head. This was all her fault. She should have protested at Doctors Commons. She knew Rafe was too drunk to be competent. He'd leaned so heavily on her shoulder that she'd practically carried him into the building. Instead of dragging him inside, she should have demanded that he escort her to one of his society friends—there had to be many who would have taken her in. Or she could have asked about old schoolmates who might be in town. Marriage was an absurd solution. He could have protected her just as well by delivering her to whomever had taken over as her guardian—or to Alquist's solicitor, for that matter.

Now it was too late. Instead of protesting, she'd meekly accepted his offer, too desperate to think clearly. And Rafe had seemed safe. . . .

"Where is your trunk?" he asked, jerking her thoughts back to the dining room. "We must fetch it."

"No." She tucked her trembling hands under the table—his question revived her terror. "My uncle has it, but I must speak with my trustees before going near him. I doubt he will part with it anyway."

Surprise flashed across Rafe's face. "It is yours. No gentleman would keep it."

"He is no gentleman and can cause untold trouble. He has already convinced my trustees to violate trust provisions by setting him in charge of my estate. I must reach them before he can poison them further against me. Unless I'm waiting when the bank opens tomorrow . . ."

He nodded, lapsing into silence. A forearm propped against the table seemed to hold him upright, though she no longer trusted appearances—a lesson learned at Doctors Commons.

The moment she'd pushed open the archbishop's door, Rafe had straightened, walked inside unaided, and turned on his charm. He had an abundance of charm. The archbishop's clerk had nearly tripped in his haste to serve them. Helen had been too busy fighting off a swoon to protest.

Damn her for a fool. She knew that drunkards were notoriously single-minded, refusing to relinquish whatever idea was stuck in their befuddled heads. A neighbor had once tottered halfway to Taunton before sobering enough to question his mission. Thus she'd been the only one with any sense.

Not that she'd used it. She should have expected charm. Rafe was a London gentleman much like Alex— six feet tall, with the same dark good looks and blazing masculinity. Thus it followed that he also used charm to deflect attention from lies, dishonor, betrayal—

She wrenched her mind from the past. Rafe had not betrayed her. Charm made him dangerous, but only time would tell whether he used it to promote dishonor as Alex had done. So far, it had only promoted the plan she'd stupidly accepted.

He'd charmed the clerk into issuing a special license even though they'd arrived at closing time. Then he'd hustled her down the street, where he'd played the ardent lover for the rector's benefit. The man had been beaming when they left.

She'd been too surprised to protest. Not until Rafe whisked her into this hotel had she caught her breath enough to fear that Rafe, like Alex, used charm to glide through life with minimal discomfort. There was a reason why the law required waiting periods before marriage and why only the Archbishop of Canterbury could grant an exemption to that rule. Marriage was forever, so both parties needed clear heads. If they hadn't been so near his office . . .

"Drunken foolishness," she murmured, crumbling bread onto her plate.

"Did you say something?" he asked.

She shook her head—gingerly.

"What will you wear to the bank if you don't retrieve your trunk?" He remained stuck on her wardrobe. "You can hardly call on your trustees dressed like that—not if you expect them to take you seriously."

She glanced at her gown. She'd done her best to smooth snags and repair rips, but it remained ragged. "I will have to take that chance. You don't know my uncle."

"No. But I do know bankers. Tomorrow's first call must be on a dressmaker. Mademoiselle Jeanette is the best. With luck she will have something made up that can be fitted for immediate use. You can't arrive at the bank dressed like a beggar."

Stubbornness glared from his eyes, but he was right. She knew better than to offer men an excuse to dismiss her. Even those who knew she was conducting legitimate business often ignored her. Men scorned any female who ventured beyond the drawing room, so she would need every weapon at her disposal tomorrow, including a well-cut, dignified gown.

"Very well, but that means rising at first light."

He flinched, but returned his eyes to his dinner.

Raucous laughter erupted from a boisterous group in the corner. Four men sprawled in repletion. Their companion drained a tankard of ale, then slapped his thigh when his next comment drew more guffaws. They looked like poor merchants rather than gentlemen. It was a shock to realize that they fit the dining room quite well. She'd paid it little heed earlier, but shabby was the kindest description. Stains marred the wallcoverings. Mends dotted the tablecloths. The chairs were sturdy rather than stylish, and most needed refinishing. This was not a hotel that catered to society.

Helen dropped her head, unwilling to draw attention by staring at the other diners.

Rafe sighed. "I hope Jeanette can dress you quickly. If she has nothing made up—"

"All dressmakers keep mourning gowns on hand." She shrugged.

"I thought your father—"

"True. Mourning is past for him, but my mother died last month."

He eyed her gown, provoking a new blush.

"My uncle demanded that I wear yellow today." Which should have put her on guard, but she'd been too immersed in her own plans to notice—a mistake that might cost her dearly. "I will switch to half-mourning in deference to our marriage, but black will do for tomorrow."

"Of course. It might even aid you with the trustees."
His eyes gleamed.

His lack of questions seemed curious. He should be
demanding details of her estate and trust. Gentlemen
expected good dowries. Such silence raised alarms.

She quelled her sudden panic, for he was no fortune
hunter. There was no way he could know about her inheritance, which was why she'd accepted him. The exis-
tence of a trust would seem routine since unmarried
ladies could not own property. He knew she had an estate, so it must be in trust. He had no reason to expect more.

Her father had long feared that she would fall prey to
a fortune hunter who would incarcerate or even kill her
once he controlled her inheritance. Steven wasn't the
first to covet Audley and all that went with it. A dozen
others had sniffed at her heels over the years. Even a
sordid reputation did not deter the desperate. Her father's fears had mushroomed as his death approached,
prompting frequent warnings about men like Steven,
who had married wealth, then locked his wife in an asylum the moment she produced a son.

Helen knew of worse examples. Her closest friend had
been swept off her feet by a fortune hunter, accepting
his protestations of love as genuine. But a month after
their hurried wedding, Clara had fatally fallen from a
cliff—despite that she hated walking and never went out
alone. Charles had sworn through his tears that it had
to have been an accident, for Clara would never have
taken her own life. His insistence might fool the magistrate, who had done everything possible to cover her
suicide, but Helen knew it had been murder. Barely a
fortnight later Charles had wed a dowerless childhood
playmate, who gave birth to an eight-pound boy five
months afterward—a scant seven months after he'd
met Clara.

Nightmares had stalked her ever since—terrifying
dreams in which greedy hands threw her over cliffs,
shoved her into burning buildings, held her under icy
water . . .

At least she needn't fear murder with Rafe. Ignorant
of her fortune, he had wed her solely from chivalry. *I'll*

protect you, he'd vowed as they'd entered the church. *Your uncle can't touch you now.* It was a heartwarming thought. She'd been in charge for so long, with no one she could rely on to—

"Are you finished?" he asked, again interrupting her thoughts.

She nodded. Did he intend to spend the night here? He'd murmured instructions to the porter on the way in. Perhaps his rooms disallowed women.

The thought reminded her how little she knew of the world beyond Somerset. Though she'd lived in London as a child, the memories were hazy. Her mother's instructions for her aborted come-out had focused solely on the Marriage Mart and had described gentlemen only in terms of matrimonial prospects. Their lives remained a mystery. But greed was not the only trait she should fear. Some men were cold. Others brutal. A neighbor had reduced his wife to quivering silence by flaunting every mistress in her face while belittling her own charms to all and sundry.

She studied her enigma of a husband. Dishevelment stripped away his suave elegance, revealing a man who might prove dangerous if thwarted. For the first time, she wondered how he had gotten that scar. In lamplight, it gleamed brighter than ever. It might be too late for second thoughts, but that did little to steady her.

Rafe steered her toward the street. "My carriage should be waiting."

Carriage? But her voice wouldn't work. His touch was making her dizzy. His silvery eyes held an unmistakable spark—Alex had sported that same look on occasion. This was her wedding night. Rafe would expect her to—

Of course, he will, snapped her conscience. *Single-minded drunkards. The goal hasn't changed. If he hadn't recognized your innocence, he'd have taken you in the street. Just be glad he married you first.*

Her panic redoubled. If all he wanted was coupling, what hope did this union have? He would tire of her by the time he was sober. And when he discovered her reputation . . .

"Are you all right?" asked Rafe, sliding an arm around her shoulders.

"Tired. It's been a long day." Suppressing panic turned her voice wooden.

"Of course, it has. But you can rest soon. The fog is moving in."

He pulled a man's cloak from a plain black carriage and wrapped it around her. Its satin lining brushed softly against her skin.

Rafe settled her inside. Before she realized his intentions, he'd tucked her firmly against him, cradling her head in the hollow of his neck.

"Relax, sweetheart," he murmured. "We'll be home soon."

She wanted to ask where home was but knew her voice would shake. At least he attributed her tremors to cold, giving her time to exert control over her growing panic. She had walked willingly into marriage. Balking now could cause only trouble.

The coach bucked as a wheel hit a broken cobblestone, stabbing new waves of pain through her head. She bit back a moan.

Rafe's arm tightened.

Fainting was not an option. He had wed her to bed her. Denying him his rights, however inadvertently, could prove dangerous when he was drunk. But she could manage. Unlike Dudley, Rafe's touch raised desire. And even if he wanted nothing more, there was no reason to vilify his motives. Hers were no better. Against all sense, she had wed a perfect stranger to obtain protection against Steven's scheming and Dudley's lust. She could only pray that they could form an amicable partnership come morning.

To restore her receptiveness, she recalled the moment when Rafe had swept her into his arms. His kiss had stirred feelings she'd not experienced in four years. His tongue had darted into her mouth, exploring more boldly than Alex had dared.

Warmth swirled into her womb as if he'd again caressed her breast. She could almost feel his erection pressing—

Very good. Just keep your heart intact. It's the only way to survive the next betrayal. You know there will be one. *Men care for little beyond their own desires. Remember Alex's lies.* . . .

She nodded. Duty demanded that she accept whatever intimacy Rafe wanted. But while a marriage of convenience was a time-honored tradition that often led to love, she must not expect miracles.

Men were notorious for ignoring consequences when pursuing their desires and for abandoning old interests when a new diversion appeared. Alex wasn't the only man who had betrayed her. Her father had vowed to protect her, yet Steven had circumvented his arrangements in less than a week. Her trustees had sworn to uphold her father's wishes, yet they had leaped at the chance to remove Audley from female control. And despite being her guardian, Lord Alquist had not written once since her father's death, even ignoring her plea for help. So she could not count on Rafe for more than he'd already given. By morning, he might despise her.

Or she might despise him. Why had he offered for a stranger? Even oceans of brandy shouldn't wash away his duty to the title that would one day be his. Duty was ingrained from birth. Yet he'd offered, knowing nothing beyond her claimed breeding, which was considerably below his.

"We're home," Rafe murmured.

"Right." Heart pounding, she patted the handkerchief she'd pinned into a cap. What would his staff think? The irregularity of this match would raise eyebrows even among the servants. Thank heaven he had provided a cloak. It lent her some semblance of propriety.

But her spirits tumbled when she emerged in front of a shabby rooming house. He was penniless! Dear Lord. What had she walked into? She hadn't thought him a fortune hunter, but to a man with nothing, even the most marginal estate could beckon. Knowing that Steven was scheming for hers told him it was beyond marginal. Rafe would expect to own it outright now that they were wed. What would he do when he learned the truth?

Dizziness engulfed her. If only she could escape this nightmare . . .

*   *   *

Rafe inhaled, then let the air out slowly as he helped Helen from the carriage.

Married.

The reality had yet to set in.

The details were lost in the wine fogging his mind, but the license in his pocket was real enough. He had no idea whom the rector had found to act as witnesses, but everything had been done according to law, so the marriage was now immutable fact.

Not until Helen had stumbled on the church steps had he thought beyond the ceremony. Despite hurried repairs, she still resembled the street prostitute he'd first thought her. And if she hadn't had that thread—

Leave it to a female to retain her reticule while fleeing for her life. He nearly chuckled. But it was good that she had. Without needle and thread, the rents in her gown would have drawn unwanted attention. She'd also applied more of that enchanting perfume. He could hardly wait to reach a bed and—

He dragged his mind onto more prosaic matters.

If they'd ridden directly to his rooms, they would have met society denizens returning from the fashionable hour in Hyde Park—not the ideal way to announce their marriage.

Stopping for dinner had given him time to summon his carriage and had allowed society to disperse to evening entertainments, clearing the streets. Not that it guaranteed secrecy, he admitted as Mitcham emerged three doors down.

Rafe hustled Helen inside, praying they hadn't been spotted. Rumors that he'd brought a light-skirt home would make the inevitable scandal even worse. His reputation didn't need embellishing.

Which raised another problem. He had to warn Helen about the betrothal announcement.

She already had too many grievances—his assault on a public street, his insistence on marriage when she was too terrified to refuse, casting up his accounts . . . She must despise him, so how could he admit that the protection he'd promised her was meant to protect himself? He should never have embroiled an innocent in his war with Hillcrest.

But the deed was done. Easing her obvious nerves was tonight's concern. Tomorrow they must come to terms about the future. For better or worse, she was his. But it would be all right. Her easy agreement to his arrangements promised congeniality, unlike the constant warfare his parents had endured.

"Where are we?" she murmured as they mounted the second flight of steep, grimy steps.

"Maddox Street. My rooms are on the top floor."

Her foot slipped on a worn tread.

He bit back a curse. This was hardly a suitable place for a well-bred bride.

Keeping rooms on Maddox Street was as deceitful as the rest of his life. For most of its inhabitants, Maddox Street provided temporary shelter as their fortunes waxed or waned. Rafe was one of the few who stayed. He didn't belong here, but then he didn't really belong anywhere.

Ten years ago a top floor suite on Maddox Street had been all he could afford. Though a hand of cards with Portland had changed that, he'd kept these rooms. Now they were yet one more deceit atop the reputation he didn't deserve, the political aspirations he'd kept hidden, the wealth few knew he commanded. He should have moved out the day he'd come of age.

There had been little incentive, though. Where would he go?

He would never be satisfied with the life of idle pleasure enjoyed by other heirs to titles. And though he liked dabbling in finance, he would never be as astute as his man of business. Now he'd jumped into marriage with both feet, then done everything possible to disgust his wife.

"We'll find better quarters tomorrow," he promised.

She nodded.

It was only fair. His rooms were small and sparsely furnished—he spent little time here, often sleeping at the house he kept for his mistresses. With only one bed, he couldn't even offer Helen her own space. His staff consisted of a valet, secretary, and footman, but the secretary occupied rooms elsewhere.

Barnes must look for a town house tomorrow. Maybe

Priestley's place. Rumors claimed Priestley was rolled up and would have to rusticate for the foreseeable future. He might welcome an offer.

But Rafe's immediate concern was his wedding night. Desire had been building from the moment they had met. Even embarrassment hadn't dimmed it. Anticipation had made dinner stretch interminably. Now that he could have her, his loins strained for action.

He must break her in carefully, though, nurturing her passion so she experienced all the pleasure he could give. He prayed that his control was up to the task.

Helen's head pounded by the time they reached the top floor. She need spend only one night here, thank heaven. Once she dealt with her trustees, they could move to her town house.

Her father had let it since buying Audley, so she had no idea what condition it was in, but it had to be better than this. Chunks of plaster had fallen from the ceiling. Wall cracks were wide enough to see through. Several treads were so worn that she had to fight for balance. How a drunkard could live here without breaking his neck—

She bumped into Rafe when he stopped before a door. Her mother had once claimed that she thought too much, which seemed to be true. Her best course was to concentrate on the moment and let tomorrow take care of itself.

"We're here," he announced, urging her through the door. Two servants stood inside. "Helen, my footman, Paul, and my valet, Jameson. My wife, Helen Thomas."

She murmured greetings, but inside she quailed. No housekeeper. No maid.

One glance at the furnishings confirmed that this was, indeed, his entire staff. No one of means presented a shabby face to the world, thus Rafe must be destitute. The door opened directly into a sitting room containing only half a dozen chairs and a small chest. To her right was a dining room, to the left a bedroom. That appeared to be it.

Tomorrow's meeting with the trustees would be trickier than she'd feared. Lust for wealth could drive men mad—witness Steven. Rafe would be irritated enough to learn that Audley would remain under her control. Few men would stand for a wife who controlled the purse strings as well. So she must hide the full extent of her fortune until she knew Rafe better. Building the sort of partnership her parents had enjoyed would take time. Introducing contention too soon might doom the process.

He dismissed his servants and escorted her to the bedroom. "I will have to maid you tonight," he announced calmly.

"If you could undo the ties . . ." Her voice trailed off, for the mere thought of his hands on her back made her dizzy, which was good. A willing wife might mitigate his fury when he discovered the terms of her trust.

His hands moved seductively, with nary a fumble as he dealt with hidden pins and ties. Unlacing her stays, he teased beneath the edge of her shift. Heat flowed from the contact, flushing her face and building a fire in the pit of her stomach.

"That should do it." His voice had deepened. "I will be back shortly."

The door clicked shut. Helen frowned.

Now what? She had no nightgown, no brush, nothing with which to conduct her usual bedtime rituals. Searching her reticule didn't help. While it contained perfume and extra hairpins, she'd left her comb in her dressing case. Cursing, she laid her gown over the back of a chair, slipped her stays and petticoat beneath its skirt, then removed her stockings. She would have to sleep in her shift.

At least tonight should banish Alex from her head for all time. The cad had invaded her sleep for four years, prompting appallingly lascivious dreams. The cravings they incited were bad enough, but she was disgusted that he could slip past her fury. How could she melt into the arms of her betrayer?

Forget Alex, advised her conscience.

She prayed tonight would make it possible. Rafe exuded the same magnetic masculinity as Alex, so surely he could oust unwanted nighttime visitors.

She was finger-combing her hair preparatory to braiding it when Rafe returned.

"Very nice," he breathed, just as he'd done after she'd run him down. "I've never seen hair that color. Liquid fire." Moving behind her, he buried his nose in her curls.

Helen froze.

"Relax, my dear," he purred. "This will feel good. I promise." Hands slipped seductively down her arms, curving across her stomach. He nibbled the side of her neck, laving each bite with his tongue.

She leaned back, giving him more access. Her fingers stroked the sleeves of his dressing gown, not quite daring to touch the bare wrists only inches away.

His lips grew bolder, demanding surrender. The moment she gave it, he snuffed the lamp, then scooped her onto the bed.

She yelped as pain shot through her head.

"I won't hurt you, Helen." He pulled the sheet over them, providing welcome protection.

Helen's head throbbed where it touched the pillow, so she rolled toward Rafe. And froze.

He was naked.

Rafe forced himself to relax as Helen tentatively inched her hand toward his neck. He wanted nothing more than to bury himself inside her, but it was too soon.

He'd nearly exploded when he'd returned to find her in an almost transparent shift with her arms raised over her head like a Siren. Red-gold curls cascaded in silken waves to her waist. He'd wanted to take her where she stood. Never had he needed a woman this badly.

But she was innocent. He must be slow and gentle. Since looking at her threatened his control, he'd doused the light, confident that she would prefer darkness.

Surprisingly, the dark focused his senses, feeding desire and thickening the air until he couldn't breathe.

"Touch all you want," he murmured when she jerked her hand away. He traced the line of her jaw, then trailed down her shoulder and arm. Gossamer-soft skin. Tantalizing fragrance.

Leaning in, he kissed her, then moaned when she hesitantly met his tongue.

Slowly, he reminded himself. *Slowly. In and out. Nib-*

ble her lips. Ease your fingers toward the fullness of her breasts.

Her hand returned more boldly, scorching his skin as she explored his arm.

Damn, but he was hot. He deepened the kiss, brushing his thumb across a plump nipple.

She arched, gasping.

Passion. Pure passion. It burned as bright as the fire of her hair. Need exploded. He flexed his hips against her thigh, groaning as he slid against her soft skin.

Again she froze.

He fought for control. He had to make this good, stoking her passion until she craved release as much as he. Stroke by patient stroke he fanned the fires, easing her shift aside. Her nipples hardened to his touch. Tremors rippled under her skin. She stifled a moan.

"Let it out, sweetheart," he murmured. "I love to hear you."

"Rafe!" she gasped when he drew her breast deep into his mouth. "What—"

"That's right." He moaned with her, shifting so she could continue her careful exploration. His hand inched across her stomach toward her mound. "Beautiful."

As her passion rose, her touch grew bolder. Across his chest, then lower, building his need until he nearly screamed. Lovemaking had never felt this good. Her innocent caress burned hotter than any mistress's practiced touch. Her response pushed him higher than ever before, for it was wholly genuine.

He fumbled for her core, amazed at his clumsiness. He was far too close to completion. First he must relax her, prepare her for his entry . . .

She skimmed a finger along his shaft, then clasped it firmly in her hand. *Dear God!* He arched . . .

Helen gasped as Rafe thrust against her. He'd been doing wondrous things to her body, touching and kissing until she was panting and nearly incoherent. She explored him in turn, reveling in the differences between them.

He was hard and muscular, covered with silky hairs that raised sparks wherever they brushed against her.

Exploring lower, she passed a trim waist and firm buttocks, finally reaching his manhood.

Silk-sheathed iron. How could something so hard feel
so soft? So intriguing. So alive.

"God!" he gasped, arching again when she squeezed.
"Now— Need— Can't wait—"

His control snapped for the first time in years. He had
to have her. Had to thrust hard and fast and deep . . . .

Desperate, he dragged his thumb over her nubbin.

Helen screamed, digging her nails into his back. He
was driving her mad, but it wasn't enough. She needed
more. Much more. Writhing against his hand, she
fought for—

His tongue ravaged her mouth as he rolled, thrusting
her legs wide.

Her scream changed from passion to pain.

"Helen!" Rafe froze. He hadn't yet entered her, so
how could she hurt? "Helen?"

He pulled his hand from under her head. It was wet
and sticky.

Horror banished lust. He scrambled to light a candle,
then rolled her gently to her side and parted her hair.
A huge knot was topped by a jagged gash. Blood oozed
where his frenzy had reopened it. Older blood stiffened
the surrounding hair. Had she fallen trying to escape?

Covering her with a quilt, he paced the room, cursing.
There was every chance that when she woke, she would
be appalled to find herself wed to a stranger. Concussion
might even erase memory of the wedding.

At the very least, she would be upset. He'd forced her
into marriage at a time when she could not think ratio-
nally. Would she hate him? Had his impetuous proposal
trapped him in the very union he'd feared since he was
old enough to understand his mother's torment?

Cold seeped into his soul. He would never survive
such a marriage. He'd seen too much fighting in his
youth. There had not been a moment of peace at home.
Facing a similar future would drive him mad.

But it was early days to accept failure. He'd sworn to
protect her, so that was his immediate duty. How had
she been injured?

He tried to remember what she'd said after crashing

into him, but he'd been reeling from the brandy, furious at Hillcrest, and engulfed in lust. Nothing else had registered.

Damn! What the devil had he gotten himself into?

Chapter Three

May 21

Rafe awoke to a pounding head and a soft bottom nestled against his morning erection. Unwilling to open his eyes—which he knew from experience would cause pain—he kneaded his mistress's breast.

"Wake up, Lydia," he murmured sleepily. "I need your morning remedy." She made a potion that eased the effects of overindulging.

"Who—? What—?"

Not Lydia. This voice was sultry.

Rafe cracked his lids. The girl had scrambled away and now cowered against the bedpost, a quilt clutched to her chest. Red curls raged wildly over her shoulders.

Memory roared back.

Helen. His wife.

Sitting up unleashed Gentleman Jackson and his corps of pugilists to brawl in his head while Satan's slaves lashed his stomach into a stormy sea. Sunlight plunged daggers into his eyes. He squeezed his lids together and fell back.

Echoes of his greeting redoubled his misery. He couldn't have found a worse way to wake Helen if he'd tried. But maybe she hadn't heard him.

"How is your head?" he asked, again cracking his eyelids.

"Fine."

She didn't look fine. Her scramble had turned her face

stark white. Terror widened her green eyes. Grabbing the quilt had left him exposed in all his nakedness.

He pulled the sheet to his chest and forced calm over his voice. "Do you remember yesterday?"

"Of course! Don't you?"

At least her tone was snappish rather than fearful. "You are Helen Thomas, my wife." That summary was clear enough. "Why didn't you tell me you'd cracked your skull?"

"It's only a bump."

"Hardly. Knocking it made you swoon. You have a concussion, Helen. What happened?"

She shrugged. "It isn't that bad."

"Damnation, Helen! You have a knot on your head the size of a rat, topped with a six-inch gash. You need stitches and bed rest." He scowled, furious at her for being stubborn, furious at himself for drinking so much he couldn't think straight, and furious at his libido for insisting that sex would return the color to her cheeks and settle his stomach.

It wouldn't.

She slowly shook her head. "I'm perfectly fine, barring a headache. It is vital that I visit my trustees, but as you pointed out last evening, I must first acquire a decent gown. Neither errand can be postponed—we discussed this in detail over dinner. I must prevent my uncle from interfering further in Audley's operation. My tenants deserve better."

Stubborn wench! But he retained enough sense to keep that thought to himself. "I'll take care of the trustees. I have to go to the City anyway. It's foolish to risk your health by gallivanting about."

She raised her chin—just like Hillcrest. "I have no intention of *gallivanting*. I propose a brief call on the dressmaker followed by an essential visit to my bank. If you have business of your own, I will hire a hackney. Paul can accompany me, I presume?" Her tone was as uncompromising as Hillcrest at his worst.

"I will not allow you to risk—"

"Allow?" She leaned forward to glare at him. "Stop! Take a deep breath, then listen to yourself. I am not your servant. Nor am I your master. We are partners."

Green eyes bored into his. A flicker of desire cut through his fury. This was not Hillcrest. This was his wife, the woman he must learn to live with if he was to retain his sanity. "My apologies, ma'am," he mumbled. "Not my best in the morning."

"Hardly a surprise after—" She stopped to draw in her own deep breath. "I appreciate your offer, Rafe. Under other circumstances I would consider it, but I doubt that you could accomplish anything at my bank without my introduction."

Rafe bit back another objection. She was right. Any trustee worth his salt would look askance on a stranger arriving out of the blue with claims of marriage. This situation was odd enough without raising speculation that he'd abducted her.

"We'll go together, but keep the visit short. Announcing our marriage will be enough to forestall your uncle. Detailed business discussions can wait. You belong in bed." Keeping a firm grip on Satan's demons, he gingerly slid to the floor and reached for his dressing gown. His stomach turned over but didn't rebel.

"Who is Lydia?" Helen asked.

He whirled, then swallowed hard. Nothing was going right today. Yesterday's visit to Hillcrest marked a clear descent into hell. "Someone I used to know. Forgive me. I was still asleep."

She nodded, though her eyes remained wary.

He tried to reassure her. "We parted company several weeks ago. I didn't replace her."

"You needn't explain. I can hardly expect you to disrupt your life for a stranger."

"Not a stranger. My wife." He covered her hand, tracing circles on her palm in an effort to regain lost ground. Her concussion made bedding her impossible at the moment, but a day or two of recovery would give him time to gentle her—he hoped. "Marriage means more than a list of duties, Helen—at least it does to me."

Skeptical eyes moved from his hand to his face, clashing with his own.

She doesn't know you, he reminded himself. While that meant she knew nothing of his reputation, it also meant she could judge him solely on his actions, which so far were unworthy of confidence.

Yet her distrust hurt, for it reminded him too much of Hillcrest. Would she also judge without facts? Would she argue every statement he made, as Hillcrest had done with his mother? Granted, she was right about her trustees, but he needed peace and a wife he could trust.

As Rafe turned away to dress, Helen cursed herself for asking about Lydia. Perhaps her head was more scrambled than she'd thought. It was the only explanation for her *faux pas*.

There would be affairs, of course. Rafe's behavior had marked him as a rake from the first. It was unlikely that he would change. Few did. So she must abandon her dream of finding a loving, faithful husband like her father had been. But that was the least of her concerns.

She had awakened from the most lascivious dream of her life to find that the man in her bed was real, with a more magnificent body than any field hand she'd ever seen and a darkly stubbled chin that increased his aura of delicious danger. Sensuality radiated from him in waves powerful enough to knock her over. To keep from drooling when he rose, baring a straight back that tapered to firm buttocks and muscular thighs, she'd blurted out her question about Lydia.

Stupid. Wives did not acknowledge their husband's mistresses.

Dear God! She was married. Her head reeled.

Rafe shrugged into his waistcoat and turned back to the bed. "I'll have to help you dress. The maid is a daily who won't arrive for a couple of hours."

Helen nodded but couldn't pry her fingers from the quilt. She was naked. Now that he was clothed, her condition was even more embarrassing. If his eyes had retained that lascivious gleam, she might have managed, but today they radiated fury. He already regretted their hasty marriage. Or maybe it was her injury.

Last night remained hazy. What had transpired after arriving in Rafe's rooms was unclear. Which parts were memory and which lingered from her dream? Had he—

"No," he said, apparently reading her mind. "You passed out when your head hit the pillow. We'll leave the rest until you're recovered." Anger threaded his voice.

Of course, he's angry. He committed matrimony to bed you, but now he must wait.

At least he hadn't ravished her unconscious body—a surprise, considering how drunk he'd been.

"Did you fall while escaping from Christchurch?" he asked.

"No. My uncle bashed me with his walking stick. It was how he got me inside."

"Is he stupid? That is no way to win cooperation."

"No. He's desperate and venal. Bribing the vicar eliminated any need for my cooperation. Hand me my shift."

He stared as if she'd grown an extra head.

"My shift, Rafe," she snapped. "You do know what a shift is, I presume? You said you'd help me dress." The shift dangled from the corner of the washstand.

He flung it at her head. "Bribery?" He'd abandoned any hint of charm. "You can't believe that."

She gritted her teeth. "I'm not stupid, I don't exaggerate, and I refuse to be treated like a lack-wit. My uncle is determined to claim my estate, but he knows I would rather die than marry his son, so he made sure he would not need my consent."

"Why not kill you and claim your estate as next of kin? Bribing vicars is risky."

"I inherited Audley nine months ago, Rafe. I'm alive today only because killing me will not suffice. If I die, Audley goes to a benevolent society to become a school." She pulled the quilt over her head so she could wriggle into the shift, but her heart quailed. Rafe considered murder a viable way to gain a fortune. As did Steven and Dudley and Clara's husband. Gentleman's honor was a flexible code often twisted to justify satisfying men's own desires. Even her father used his oft-proclaimed protection primarily to thwart his despised brother.

"How did he find a vicar willing to break both canon and civil law? Approaching the wrong man would expose his scheme to the world."

"It wasn't easy," she admitted. "I first met my cousin a month ago when he returned from the Peninsula. I refused his hand. If I'd suspected this new plan, I could have escaped sooner." She pushed the quilt down to her neck and steeled herself to ask for her stays.

"We haven't time for modesty." Rafe's smile sent tingles along her nerves. "Get up, Helen."

"Can't you—" She twirled her finger.

Sighing, he turned his back.

Ignoring her headache, she jumped down and pulled her gown on, then slipped her stays in place beneath it, holding them up with her left arm. The gown wasn't much protection, for it gaped in the back, and the skirt bunched around her arm, but each layer made her feel better.

"I need help with the lacing."

"I know." His voice turned seductive, making her nerves tingle. Warm hands burned through the thin shift as he expertly laced her up. No maid could have worked faster. It spoke volumes about his experience.

"Relax," he murmured. "I can enjoy touching without ravishing you."

She didn't trust her voice to respond. By the time he'd fastened her gown, her heart hammered wildly. There was no hiding it, for the kisses he trailed up the side of her neck paused with his lips on her pounding pulse. His breath melted her bones.

A moment later, he calmly straightened. "What about your hair?"

She had to swallow twice before she could speak. "Have you a comb I can borrow?"

"There's one in my shaving stand. Be careful you don't open that cut again."

She touched the bump and flinched.

He lifted her hand away. Gentle fingers probed the wound. "The swelling remains, though not as extensive. There is no bleeding now, but your hair is matted. I was serious about the stitches. Even with care, it will take weeks to heal."

"It's too late for stitches, Rafe. Once a cut scabs over, nothing can be done. But as long as it doesn't start bleeding again, it should be fine." Turning, she met his gaze. "You haven't grasped the gravity of my situation, Rafe. My uncle is obsessed. He wants Audley Court more than life itself, and he will do anything to get it."

"Anything?"

She nodded. "This is not a recent problem. His lust for Audley is part of a lifelong rivalry with my father. That turned to hatred after Papa refused to cover his gaming debts."

"Many men carry grudges."

"I don't doubt it. But this has gone far beyond a grudge. He needs Audley to pay his creditors, so he convinced himself that it should have gone with the title. He's already talked the trustees into violating Papa's orders. I cannot give him a chance to do it again. Papa knew that if his brother gained control, he would milk Audley of every shilling and lose most of it at the tables. The tenants would suffer badly. I must protect them, but I can't do it lazing about here."

"I agreed to call at the bank. But once that is done, you must stay in bed. For now, be careful not to tug on the wound lest it break open. And take your time. Paul won't have breakfast out for another half hour. He has to fetch it from an inn two streets away." Rafe left the bedroom.

Helen traced the swelling. Rafe hadn't exaggerated its extent. If seeing her trustees was any less urgent, she would take his advice. But that was not possible.

At least he listened to reason, unlike most gentlemen. Her father had turned stubborn when his will was crossed. Dudley became vicious. Steven ignored anything he didn't like. Was Rafe's tolerance real, or was he humoring her?

She washed her face, then began untangling her hair— leaving it down for the night had turned it into a Gordian knot.

Had she convinced him to stay alert? Steven would be livid about losing the prize he'd long considered his own. And Dudley was more than capable of violence. If Rafe came to harm because of her, she would never forgive herself.

Defending Audley Court was *her* responsibility. Cravenly foisting it onto a stranger was unconscionable. She should not have allowed fear to push her into accepting Rafe's offer.

It was too late to back out of marriage, but she must at least prepare Rafe for the consequences. Steven never let a grievance pass unpunished. He might be satisfied with destroying Rafe's reputation, or he might consider assault.

Yet how could she start? If there was any hope of making this marriage work, she had to retain Rafe's respect. The time to mention Steven's character had been yesterday, before she'd succumbed to temptation. She should also have told him that marriage would not place Audley in his hands. He would be justly furious when he discovered the truth.

Shaking her head, she coiled her hair around the bump, pinned her handkerchief into a cap, then joined him in the dining room.

Rafe swallowed the last of his tasteless breakfast, praying that his churning stomach could keep it down. Helen was glowering at her plate. He hoped it wasn't a portent of their marriage.

He shouldn't complain, though. He'd remained silent for at least a quarter hour because the words to explain the betrothal announcement wouldn't form. Every time he opened his mouth, the curve of her neck would distract him. Or her ripe mouth, or—

He snapped his thoughts back to the job at hand. Postponing it was impossible. All of society would know about the announcement by now. He couldn't let Helen hear the tale first at the dressmaker's.

But how could he explain? Her insistence that her uncle was dangerous confirmed that she considered him her savior. When she learned his motives, her opinion would change. Already he'd tarnished the image with his morning greeting. Once he admitted that he had married to escape his father's machinations . . .

Marry the first girl I see.

In the cold light of day, that vow seemed ridiculously perverse. She would never respect him again. Worse, such bizarre behavior made him look weak. Too often, confronting Hillcrest reduced him to childish irresponsibility. No wonder the man refused his respect. If he knew even half the things Rafe had done in a fury . . .

He stifled a groan. Anger, pain, and wine had corrupted his thinking, validating most of Hillcrest's complaints. While repudiating the announcement would have caused scandal, it would not have irrevocably ruined him. Society expected him to be outrageous. The sticklers would have been appalled, but the scandal would have blown over in time. Marriage might easily land him in a worse pickle.

Alquist would have berated him up one side and down the other, and rightly so. The baron had taken him firmly in hand after that month of debauchery. Until then, Rafe had barely known the man who'd married his mother's sister, so he'd been shocked to find Alquist on his doorstep the morning after the infamous Berkeley Square incident—even today, recalling that particular stupidity made him wince.

Alquist had taught him far more than how to go on in society. From him, Rafe had learned the ins and outs of investing, the fine points of honor, and an appreciation for learning. Alquist had taught him how to control his temper, which now slipped only with Hillcrest. But Alquist's wisest advice had been caution—*Actions cannot be both hasty and prudent, Rafe. Smart men consider the consequences before they act.* It was an axiom that had saved him from many mistakes.

But yesterday had been hasty, with no thought of consequences.

Downing the remains of his coffee failed to wash away his bitterness over Alquist's death. The man had been mentor, friend, and surrogate father. Losing him was a devastating blow. Losing him to the idiotic negligence of an imbecilic stranger made it worse.

Stop sidetracking. You have to tell Helen about the announcement.

She might believe him. If her uncle was as venal as she claimed, Hillcrest's machinations would not seem all that odd. At least Hillcrest didn't resort to violence.

He drew in a deep breath. "Helen, we need to—"

"I'm afraid my uncle will—" she said at the same time.

"What?" they both asked.

Someone pounded loudly on the door.

"Who—" Helen blanched.

"We are not at home." Rafe gestured Paul to the door. None of his friends would call this early. Most would have found their beds only an hour ago.

"Not at home," said Paul.

"He'll see me." The caller's voice grated.

"I'm sorry, but—"

"Stand back, you fool! This is an emergency. His ward is missing and likely in danger."

"But—"

A loud smack sent Paul thudding to the floor. Pain stabbed through Rafe's head.

"Steven!" gasped Helen, jumping behind the table as a man burst into the dining room. His red face and flashing eyes promised violence to anyone in his path.

Rafe surged to his feet, then swayed as dizziness overwhelmed him.

Steven's jaw dropped. "You!" He advanced on Helen. "What are you doing here? Who told you Thomas was your guardian. I burned—"

"Guardian!" Helen blanched.

Rafe's jaw hit the floor. "What—"

"We'll talk later," snapped Steven, dismissing Rafe with a contemptuous glare. "Come along, Helen. I've had enough of your tantrums. Duty calls."

"Get out!" Helen ordered. "You have no business here."

"You are my business."

As Steven circled the table, Rafe pulled Helen behind him. "Leave my wife alone."

"Wife! Impossible." His face purpled. "She is betrothed to my son."

"Never," snapped Helen, escaping Rafe's grip. "I wouldn't have him if he were the last man on earth. Leave us! You've lost, Sir Steven. Audley is mine and will stay mine."

"Every word proves you need a keeper, girl." Steven sneered. "Don't you know a fortune hunter when you see one?"

"You—"

He spoke over her. "I've no doubt he plans to wed you, but you deserve better. Thomas is notorious. He is already salivating over that forty thou—"

"Never!" She glared.

"We were wed yesterday by special license," explained Rafe, fighting past his weakness to jump between them. His temper hung by a thread. He recognized her uncle now, though they'd not formally met. Steven St. James, a man of questionable honor who would think nothing of attacking a lady. Few would admit him to their drawing rooms.

"The bishop will take a dim view of such abuse of power." Steven backhanded Rafe into the wall hard enough to cross his eyes, then grabbed Helen. "Come along. We will rescue you from this bastard. The bishop—"

"Rescue?" Digging in her heels, she clawed his hand until he let go. "I'll take Rafe's rescue over yours any day. It wasn't Rafe who incarcerated me and replaced my staff."

"The trustees demanded that I correct a criminal oversight by an obviously deranged—"

"Liar!" Helen shoved, forcing him back a pace. "Papa was in full possession of his faculties when he set up my trust. You may have duped my trustees, but that ends now. Either leave this instant or I'll have you prosecuted for embezzlement."

"Embezz—"

"Exactly. Nothing you've done is legal. The trustees risk similar charges if they support you. The books prove that you've been stealing from me for months. The income listed from wool sales alone is barely a quarter of the current—"

"Quit blathering about subjects you can't possibly understand," he snapped.

Rafe straightened, shaking his head to rid it of fog. A white-faced Helen faced Sir Steven, her fists held in defensive mode.

She snorted. "Stupid, as well as venal. Granted, I was distracted while Mother was ill, but I checked the books the moment you proposed this jaunt to London."

"But they were in the safe—"

"So? Father trained me to run Audley. By the time he died, I'd been in charge for years—as anyone could have told you."

Rafe watched in fascination as Steven paled. The baronet couldn't have been more shocked had Helen turned into a toad. He must have thought her a complete widgeon.

Lust stirred once more, for she looked magnificent. Boadicea in person, crossing swords with the Romans. He'd always admired feisty females. His mother had not allowed anyone to ride roughshod over her.

"You prove yourself incompetent with every word," shouted Steven. "Nothing in those books can be twisted into embezzlement. Only a madman would believe you could run a cottage, let alone an estate. One look at your so-called husband proves your lack of judgment."

"Anyone is better than Dudley," she snapped. "As for the rest, I can hold my own with any estate manager in the land."

Steven laughed. "You are so naïve. You can't even recognize a scoundrel. Look at him, the great Rafael Thomas. A notorious gamester, a drunken libertine, and the most desperate fortune hunter in town. We thought we'd seen the last of you when we heard about Miss Pauling, Thomas, but this dishonor exceeds even your wildest exploits. You weren't satisfied with nabbing a modest heiress, were you?" he taunted. "The moment a bigger prize walked by, you grabbed her instead."

Rafe flinched, but before he could form a reply, Helen slapped Steven.

"You always did have a poisonous tongue," she said coldly. "Leave. Rafe has more honor in one finger than you can muster in your entire body."

Steven's fist snapped her head back, crossing her eyes.

"Bastard!" Rafe sprang, landing an uppercut to the chin.

Helen screamed as Steven plowed a shoulder into Rafe's chest, then pounced as Rafe fell.

"Leave him alone!" Helen kicked Steven in the side as he drove Rafe's head against a table leg. This was just what she'd feared. Steven hated to lose.

Rafe landed another blow, but the aftereffects of yesterday's overindulgence slowed him, and Steven outweighed him by at least three stone. Before she realized Steven's intent, his hands closed around Rafe's throat.

"No!" Fear lent her new energy, burning away her dizziness. She grabbed a platter of ham and smashed it over Steven's head. Two plates and a tankard of ale followed. It didn't dent his skull, but he let go of Rafe long enough to slap her.

Jameson and Paul burst in as Rafe landed a knee to Steven's groin and another blow to the head. They hauled Steven aside and pinned him to the floor.

Helen threw herself on Rafe. "Are you all right?" Her hands searched for damage.

"Fine," he croaked, shakily sitting up.

Steven twisted, trying to escape.

"See him to the street," ordered Rafe. "If he returns, truss him up and take him to Bow Street. I'll swear out a complaint for assault."

"You won't get away with this!" screamed Steven as Jameson and Paul each twisted an arm behind him and dragged him to the door. "I'll see you in hell!"

Rafe ignored him. His head throbbed, and he had to concentrate to pull air past his bruised throat, but one thought remained uppermost. Sir Steven was a bigger threat than even Helen had claimed. He had to protect her.

And not just from Steven. The son was worse. He fingered his scarred cheek, recalling another fight. At least that one had garnered admiration from his peers. Today must make him seem weak, inviting Helen to take charge. He couldn't allow that or he would face a lifetime of battles. Pulling himself together, he headed for the brandy decanter.

The moment Steven left, Helen's knees gave out. Spots danced before her eyes.

"Drink," ordered Rafe, rising to shove a glass into her hand. "You've had a shock." He drained his own.

She complied. The brandy burned all the way to her stomach, but it cleared her head. Steven had come to see Rafe. Her own presence had been a surprise.

"My guardian?" she demanded, glaring. "How interesting that you didn't mention that little detail." Her guardian would know about her trust. Rafe must have thought he'd won the lottery the moment he'd heard her name. No wonder he'd insisted on accompanying her to the bank. He expected to twist her trustees around his thumb—and might already have done so. How had he arrived so providentially outside the church?

Rafe shook his head. "I don't know where he got that idea. It's the first I've heard of it."

"Right." She swallowed more brandy.

He frowned. "I suppose it's possible. Alquist married my mother's sister. We've been close for ten years."

"But you were at his burial. You must have seen his will. And he would hardly pass the duty without warning." It wasn't logical, yet Rafe's eyes seemed honestly puzzled. Was he truly ignorant or a better actor than even Alex had been?

"I rode down to Hampshire immediately after his death," he admitted. "But my aunt's grief made mine so unbearable that I left from the churchyard. I wasn't up to facing society, so I stopped in Oxford to visit a friend. When I arrived home yesterday, my father's summons met me at the door. I was returning from Hillcrest Manor when we met."

"I don't see—"

"I didn't stay to hear Alquist's will—aside from a few books, I wasn't expecting anything. His solicitor will have sent me the details, but I wasn't here to receive mail."

"Then let's look at your mail." She stood.

His desk was in a corner of the bedroom, stacked with a mountain of cards, unopened letters, and newspapers. So he'd spoken truly on that point.

"Why would he put you in charge of his ward without discussing the matter first?" Such negligence seemed odd. Of course, Alquist had made no attempt to see her during his tenure as guardian, so perhaps he was heedless.

"How should I know?" Rafe dropped into the desk chair. "Maybe his will offered an explanation." He grabbed a stack of mail and started sorting.

Helen shrugged. The truth would come out eventually.

Until then, she must guard herself. She picked up the *Morning Post* and moved closer to the window.

"The Regent created Wellington a duke," she murmured moments later.

"Hardly a surprise."

"I suppose not, now that the war is over."

"Why don't you help me sort these? There should be something from Alquist's solicitor even if Sir Steven lied about the guardianship." His voice sounded odd.

"He wouldn't lie about something so easy to check. He expected you to know about it. He came here to demand your assistance in finding your runaway ward." Which meant that Steven had intercepted the letter notifying her of the change. She frowned. How many other letters—

"Are you sure he didn't trace you here?"

"Positive. He was shocked to see me and concluded that he'd missed at least one letter—he must have been confiscating my mail. I've received nothing from Alquist since Father died. Not even a note of condolence."

Rafe nodded. "Alquist would never ignore a duty— even an unwanted one. You can read the paper later, Helen. I need help. There are too many invitations. We must leave for the bank, but sorting this will take half the morning."

"I doubt it. Besides, that errand is less urgent now. Steven will be too busy confirming our marriage to bother the trustees yet. I haven't read a paper in months—Steven wouldn't allow it. It's a pleasure I've missed."

Rafe sorted faster, scattering invitations right and left as he searched for personal letters.

Helen turned a page. "The allied leaders will arrive next month to celebrate Napoleon's abdication, but this story gives no details. Do you know what is planned? I've been so out of touch since Father died that I'm amazed I even know the war is over."

"The details will probably be in last week's papers." He gestured to the pile.

"I'll look when I've finished this one."

More invitations slid to the floor. Rafe seemed almost

panicked in his search for the letter, but she ignored the thought, more interested in reading.

"Aha!" he exclaimed suddenly. "This must be it." A seal cracked.

But her eyes stared at the name that had leaped out when she turned the page. "My God!" Her heart crashed to the floor. "You're betrothed to Alice Pauling!" She glared. Steven had mentioned Miss Pauling. An heiress.

"No, I'm not." But his face was red.

"It says so right here. *Lord Pauling of Paulus Grange, Surrey, announces the betrothal of his daughter, the honorable Alice Elaine Pauling, to the honorable Mr. Rafael Edward Thomas of Hillcrest Manor, Surrey. Nuptials are scheduled for June the seventh.*"

"I—am—*not*—betrothed." It sounded as if he were talking through gritted teeth.

"Are you accusing the editor of the *Morning Post* of fabricating the story?" She tapped the paper. "Who is she?"

"A neighbor, but that doesn't—"

She slammed down the paper. "How dare you wed me when you are promised to another?"

"It's not like that, Helen. Sit down." He sighed.

Since he looked exasperated rather than dangerous, she complied. But her heart pounded harder than ever, worsening her headache. The day had already served up too many shocks, and it was barely eight.

"Thank you." Rafe laid aside his letter. "I started to tell you about this at breakfast."

She frowned, recalling that he'd interrupted when she'd tried to warn him about Steven.

"I've refused this match repeatedly for ten years," he continued. "Our fathers are the ones pushing it. Hillcrest submitted the announcement without my knowledge or consent."

"You expect me to believe that?"

"It's the truth. I told you about yesterday's summons. When I arrived, he announced that he'd made the arrangements despite my continued refusals."

"No father would treat his son so shabbily."

"Hah! He's hated me since the day I was born."

"I don't believe it." She raised her chin, which usually prompted men to take her seriously.

"Believe it." He glared. "He hated my mother, too. The price of his affection has always been repudiation of Mother. He's added other conditions over the years—like abandoning London. He believes it is a godless place brimming with degenerates. Since I choose to live here . . ." He shrugged.

"But that doesn't explain this." She tapped the paper. "Does he hate Miss Pauling, too?"

"Of course not, but her feelings don't concern him. He wants her dowry. Paulus Grange is a prosperous estate that would more than double Hillcrest's holdings. He's coveted it since childhood. Pauling is ill and easily swayed. Since Hillcrest abhors scandal, he expects me to avoid raising one. He refuses to accept that scandal doesn't bother me. We had a flaming row when I repudiated the match yet again."

Flaming row. Her heart sank. That was why he'd proposed. She'd appeared when he was in the throes of rebellion, something he would soon regret. So she could not rely on him.

Rafe ran his fingers through his hair. "I was heading for my solicitor's office to see if he could quash the announcement when I met you. Hillcrest will never listen. I'm tired of battles. Marriage ended the war once and for all."

"Why me?"

"You are intelligent and competent, will never turn weepy or demanding, possess beauty and breeding, and I love your hair."

His words seemed glib. How could anyone determine intelligence on five minutes' acquaintance—while drunk? How could he claim she'd be undemanding when she'd made demands from the first—*take me to Berkeley Square . . . take me to Formsby's Bank*. She'd all but begged him to save her from Steven. And while she hadn't shed tears, she'd been very close.

His eyes were the color of slate today, swirling with emotion she couldn't read. His apparent sincerity meant nothing. Alex had always sounded sincere, even the day he'd poured out his love and devotion between searing kisses and passionate caresses, swearing she was the most beautiful, most fascinating, most exciting miss in the realm. Two days later, he'd abandoned her without a word.

She could believe Rafe's fury. He harbored a stubborn streak. If Hillcrest had truly sent the notice without warning, Rafe would see red. But that didn't mean that he opposed the match, only that he wanted to make his own decisions. If Hillcrest hadn't been so heavy-handed, Rafe might have wed Alice long since. They'd known each other for years and might be deeply in love—like Clara's husband and his impoverished neighbor.

Which boded ill for the future. She did not want a man who preferred another. In truth, she wanted a husband who loved her, though she could hardly cavil on that score. She had wed Rafe solely to escape Steven and Dudley, so there was no question of love on her part, either. Yet a loveless marriage was a far cry from one to a man who loved another.

But there was no point in continuing this discussion. Rafe would deny an attachment regardless of his feelings, justifying the lie as necessary to protect her delicate sensibilities. So she must take every word with a grain of salt.

"What does the solicitor say?"

"Sir Steven was right. I'm your guardian. But Alquist never mentioned you."

"Why?"

"I've no idea. How well did you know him?"

"I met him once or twice as a child. We lived in London in those days, but callers rarely came to the nursery. He visited Audley a few times, but I was away at school." Or not allowed to mingle with house-party guests. "He did not attend Papa's funeral. And if he sent condolences, I did not see them." The situation seemed surreal. What fate had thrust her into her guardian's arms?

"He sent condolences. He would never neglect a duty, even if he didn't care, but it was not like him to leave me responsibilities without warning. Granted, he was in good health and expected to live many years, but he was a stickler for planning ahead." He sighed. "We can ponder his motives later. Are you ready to face the dressmaker?"

She nodded.

"Good." He bit his lip. "Hillcrest's announcement is bound to cause trouble, but we can minimize the scandal by addressing it after our marriage announcement appears tomorrow. I hope to wrest an apology from the editors for today's mistake, which will make washing the family laundry in public unnecessary."

"That seems reasonable."

"Thank you. So you will remain Miss St. James for today?"

She nodded. Keeping the scandal to a minimum might also keep her tarnished reputation from coming out. Something else she must warn him about . . .

Later. So many things must wait until later.

Steven's voice echoed. *Notorious fortune hunter.*

If they were to build any sort of partnership, Rafe must learn to know her first as an individual, not as an heiress. It was the only way to protect herself. Only an honest commitment to each other would keep her safe. Unless he cared, other emotions could rule—like greed. So she must do everything possible to win his heart, while praying she could trust him.

As Rafe escorted Helen downstairs, he cursed his stupidity in forgetting that Paul would collect today's paper along with breakfast. He should have hidden it until he'd made his confession. He'd known the damned thing would cause trouble.

But instead of explaining over breakfast, he'd turned coward, dawdling as he searched for words that would make his idiocy sound reasonable. Now it was worse.

He'd made a muck of marriage already. Despite his long-stated desire for an intelligent wife, he'd treated her like a widgeon.

He'd been wrong. She might be a country miss, but her eyes had gleamed the moment she'd spied the papers. She'd turned first to politics and international news, skimming the society page last. In that respect, she was much like Alquist.

Fate had chosen his wife well.

Unfortunately, his ham-fisted handling had eroded her trust. It would take time and skill to restore it. And more courage than he'd shown to date. Helen would not accept platitudes. He could only pray that he could rectify matters before she decided to take charge. She'd shown a lamentable streak of independence—fleeing Christchurch, insisting on going out despite her injuries, confronting Sir Steven head-on. It could lead to serious clashes if not checked. However alone she'd been since her parents' deaths, she now had a husband to look after her. It was time she recognized that.

Chapter Four

*H*elen paced Mademoiselle Jeanette's elegantly appointed fitting room while an assistant lengthened a mourning gown. Rafe had stayed in the carriage so their names would not be linked before tomorrow's announcement—or so he claimed. But the real reason was probably cowardice. He must have known his name would be on every tongue. He was more notorious than even Steven had implied.

It was the height of the Season, so the shop was crowded. She'd waited half an hour for an assistant to serve her—Miss St. James, newly arrived from Somerset, commanded no concessions from a prominent London establishment. Not that she minded, for the wait allowed her to bring her provincial gawking under control. She had never seen so refined a shop, with lush carpets, Sheraton chairs, and a dozen tables piled with pattern cards, dressmakers' dolls, fabrics, and trims. Servants raced in and out of the main salon, fetching fabrics and serving tea.

But today's conversation rarely touched on fashion. Rafe's scandals echoed from all sides.

"Is Miss Pauling mad?" demanded an elegant blonde of her friend as she fingered a piece of Caledonian silk that matched her blue eyes. "Everyone knows Mr. Thomas is in debt and will likely lose her dowry at the tables before the ink dries on their marriage lines. He takes after his grandfather, though his notoriety extends far beyond gaming. Remember Lady Chatsworth?"

"Chasing her naked through Berkeley Square." Her

friend giggled. "My governess nearly fainted when she discovered I knew the tale. I wish I'd been there to see it."

"Watch your tongue, Martha," snapped an older woman. "If anyone hears such talk, they will think you fast."

"But how will we know whom to avoid if we don't discuss such things?" asked the blonde, widening her eyes in faux innocence. "You must admit Mr. Thomas has caused no end of scandal. Like what he did to Lady Melthorpe."

"Come, Mama. You laugh at that tale yourself— cavorting together in the Serpentine under a full moon." Again Martha giggled. "How adventurous!"

"Until Lord Melthorpe arrived." Icicles dripped from her voice. "Forget Mr. Thomas. The man is incorrigible. Do you wish to put Lord Blakeley off? He is your best chance for an offer, so concentrate on pattern cards. You need a gown for Lady Debenham's ball. As for you, Lady Elizabeth"—she glared at the blonde—"if you must speculate on why Miss Pauling accepted Mr. Thomas, at least be honest. He has charm to spare and could talk the devil into mending his ways if he put his mind to it."

Lady Elizabeth fell silent, but the discussion raged elsewhere.

"I always knew he would court an heiress," said a dowager as she frowned over a piece of Mechlin lace. "Runs in the family. Hillcrest wed money, too. Thomases have always sought the fastest ways to expand their coffers."

"Even an heiress would think twice about allying herself with Thomas," snapped her companion. "He must have seduced her. A fortnight away from town would leave him desperate. You know what he's like."

"True. Few have his appetites. Or his temper. Imagine dueling over a courtesan! And without seconds! Disgraceful! But he's never defiled an innocent or even seriously flirted with one, which is why I keep him on my guest list. Unlike some rakes, he has scruples. Something to think about, Mildred," she added cattily. "And you can't claim she doesn't know him. They are neighbors."

Helen tried to shut out the voices, but it was difficult. They buzzed from all sides.

"—that outlandish wager last month. It was bad enough to goad Lord Creevey into making preposterous claims, but forcing him to prove them was dishonorable. Creevey was too foxed to think clearly."

"Good heavens, Margaret! You didn't think it outlandish at the time. You cheered along with the rest of us. Creevey thinks his nose is more sensitive than anyone's. I laughed myself silly when he lost."

"But a thousand guineas—"

Helen gasped. A thousand guineas could finance an opulent Season or support a tenant for years. If Rafe was accustomed to wagering such amounts, it was no wonder he was in debt.

"It's all of a piece," snapped Lady Horseley from another table. "He loves shocking us. Remember that masquerade last year? He showed up nearly naked! Bare chest. Bare legs . . ."

Helen's nerves tingled at the memory of Rafe sprawled naked in bed. Even the thought of sleeping nude was outrageous. The actuality . . .

Her face heated.

His reputation was far worse than hers—and well deserved. Unlike the lurid speculation that she had endured, society could cite chapter and verse of Rafe's misdeeds. Not that it made confessing any easier. The world weighed ladies and gentlemen on different scales.

Her heart sank. It would be hard enough to endure his courtesans and scandals—she had no illusions about her temper when insulted; it went with her red hair. But gaming boded ill for the future. Rafe couldn't touch Audley itself, but if he lost its income, he would press her to dip into her trust. Charm made him dangerous. As did pride. What would he do when she refused to cover his losses? Even the most even-tempered man could turn vicious when thwarted. And she suspected that Rafe's temper was far from even.

Was it too late to escape this travesty? They had not yet consummated the union.

But a moment's thought banished the idea. Nonconsummation had not been grounds for annulment in at least a century. Maybe longer. So her only choice was to find a compromise they could both endure, which meant abandoning her girlish dreams of love and praying they could become friends before she had to disclose her worth.

Fate must be laughing up her sleeve, for despite every caution, she'd fallen prey to a fortune hunter. But at least he would be in the same fix as Steven. Neither of them could harm her while the trust remained in force. And her husband controlled its income only while she lived. As long as she didn't trigger a temper fit, she would be safe enough. Unlike Clara.

Rafe slumped inside his carriage. His head throbbed, his throat hurt, and a bruise was spreading where Steven's shoulder had rammed his chest. So far, marriage was miserable.

He'd considered accompanying Helen, if only to silence the gossip she was sure to hear, but anyone seeing them together would assume she was Alice—or a new mistress—neither of which would help matters. Yet as his wait stretched longer and longer, he cursed his stupidity. Mademoiselle Jeannette was always overworked during the Season. Since Helen needed only one temporary mourning gown, they could have gone anywhere.

Waiting left him nothing to do but dwell on his mistakes. The carriage's folding table was too small for patience—not that he had patience for the game or cards with which to play it. If Carley were here, they could have played chess. They'd enjoyed many a match while driving to house parties over the years.

But he hadn't seen Carley since the night Alquist died.

His mind circled back to the dilemma he'd been avoiding. He feared that wedding Helen had been a grievous mistake. And like Shakespeare's Caesar, he might grievously answer for it.

Helen was an enticing wench whose sensuality could raise the dead. Intelligence crackled behind her eyes. She refused to be a victim, instead fighting for what she wanted. Fleeing that church marked her as a lady of spirit, like his mother.

On the other hand, she was apparently accustomed to

being in charge, not just of herself, but of those around her, which boded ill for establishing a harmonious union. Already she'd demanded answers and argued perfectly reasonable suggestions. While he enjoyed debate, fighting sapped so much energy that it left him limp for days. He despised arguments, having suffered too much criticism from Hillcrest. In the past, he'd endured by letting angry words slide past him, then doing whatever he wished.

But that wouldn't work with Helen. He could ignore Hillcrest's diatribes because he rarely saw the man. But he must share a house with Helen. Which meant he must either stand up to her or let her lead him around by the nose. Intolerable.

Rapping snapped his head around.

"Naughty boy," purred Lady Willingham, pulling the carriage door open. "Why didn't you tell me your plans?"

"Why should I share my private business with you?" He couldn't manage his usual smile. If Helen returned now, the fat would be in the fire.

Lady Willingham laughed as if he were teasing. "But we are such good friends, my dearest Rafe. And you will need friends. The girl must have a mentor, of course, to introduce her to the right people. A country miss can't understand London without help."

He shuddered. Not only did he not want Helen to meet Lady Willingham, he had no interest in paying the price she would expect for such service. She pursued her liaisons so aggressively that only Lord Willingham's fortune and social power kept people from cutting her. Rafe's refusal to become her latest lover had increased her determination to bring him to heel.

"My aunt will present my wife at court," he said, shifting his legs to block the door.

Fury flashed across her face, immediately banished. "I suppose she needs the distraction. As do you. Take advantage of your freedom while you have it, darling. You'll have to waste your talents until you get her with child, so this is your last chance for pleasure. I'm free tonight." Her hand brushed his thigh in blatant invitation.

He opened his mouth on a stinging set-down, but swallowed it as Helen emerged from Mademoiselle Jeanette's. Lady Willingham would laugh off a set-down. Thus there was only one way to be rid of her, short of arguing for half an hour. "What time?"

Triumph twisted her face. "Willingham leaves by eight."

He nodded. "In the meantime, I must call on my tailor."

"Until eight, darling." With a blatant caress across his groin, she left, her smile sending chills down his spine that stifled any guilt. He'd not precisely lied. And it would do the lady good to spend an evening alone.

Helen was glaring daggers at Lady Willingham. Cursing, he whisked her into the carriage—Lady Willingham was the sort who couldn't resist a last flirtatious glance before she vanished—then opened his mouth to explain.

His breath caught.

He'd thought yellow suited her, but black turned her into a red-haired enchantress. No wonder Dudley wanted her. She looked bold, dashing, and quite the most desirable woman he'd seen in years.

Which was good. Her stunning beauty would explain why they'd wed so precipitously. He could describe his recent absence from town as courtship. The friend he'd visited was practically a hermit, so he was unlikely to talk.

"I need a bonnet and black gloves," Helen said coolly. "Someone recommended Michelle's Millinery. Do you know it?"

"Of course. It is around the corner." But he cursed while she finished her shopping. Her tone would freeze the balls off a brass monkey, as his military friends liked to say. She must have overheard him arranging an apparent assignation. Or perhaps Lady Willingham's blatant flirtation appalled her. Yet he could hardly ask without making matters worse. Besides, they had other problems to address. Like her claim that she'd run her estate for years. Such behavior was so far outside the accepted range that it was bound to cause trouble.

He pondered that while they headed for the City.

In every loving marriage he'd known, the wife had

begun with a minimal dowry. Yet despite his long determination to avoid that trap, he'd wed a girl with assets. He could only pray that they didn't equal his. Steven's claim that Helen's fortune exceeded Alice's was troubling.

His fear that he'd fallen into his worst nightmare was so powerful that he almost welcomed Helen's interruption.

"Everyone is discussing you today," she said when they paused for the first tollgate.

"I expect so. My affairs have filled conversational voids for ten years—rarely with facts. Tomorrow will be worse, though at least people will have the truth by then."

"Will they?"

"The public truth, I should have said. It will be best to claim a love match, Helen. The guardianship should explain our acquaintance and halt further speculation."

"I doubt it. Most people believe that you seduced Miss Pauling because you need her fortune to pay gaming debts. Heaven knows what they'll think of me."

"Preposterous!"

"Is it? You don't keep a low profile."

Rafe scowled. "Actually, I do." Not that it helped. If anything, circumspection made the gossip worse.

"How—" She halted, dropping her gaze to her hands. "I need the truth, Rafe. It is obvious I will face more than curiosity about our marriage. If I'm to avoid looking shocked, I must be ready."

"Which stories did they trot out?" Damnation! He didn't need this. No wonder she'd glared at Lady Willingham. He'd hoped to build some trust before explaining his reputation. A futile hope, he now saw. Gossips would delight in exposing him. Short of locking her up, he couldn't protect her from rumors.

"One concerned a tryst in the Serpentine. Another involved chasing a nude lady through Berkeley Square. Or perhaps you were the nude one. It wasn't clear."

"Those are ten years old and so twisted that I barely recognize them."

"Really?"

He sighed. It was a long drive to her bank, so he

might as well talk. "My mother died just after I came down from Eton. We were very close. I couldn't handle the grief. The Serpentine incident happened the night I returned from her grave. It was hot, and I'd had too much to drink. The lake looked cool, so I went swimming, retaining just enough sense to remove my clothes first. Lady Melthorpe spotted me in the water. I hadn't expected anyone in the park at midnight."

Helen snorted.

"All right, I wasn't thinking clearly. But I hadn't expected a lady. Especially one without an escort. She'd had a row with her husband and stormed out of the house—it overlooks Hyde Park. She was tipsy enough to join me. It was completely innocent, but when Lady Beatrice drove by—she is the most malicious gossip in town—Lady Melthorpe repaid her husband by jumping me. Melthorpe arrived moments later and nearly called me out, though in the end, he accepted the truth."

She shook her head.

"As for Berkeley Square, that was stupidity, pure and simple," he admitted with a sigh. "I'd been out of control for a month, doing anything to take my mind off grief. I'd borrowed a friend's brougham—my allowance didn't cover even a riding horse, let alone a carriage— but I didn't notice that the coachman was drunk."

"You didn't notice the coachman?"

"I was eighteen. Between grief for my mother and fury at my father, there were many things I didn't notice. At any rate, he took a corner too fast and overturned. The clamshell top popped open, spilling us out. The *naked* part is a lie, though I have to admit to *disheveled*. The scandal shocked me into reform. I haven't lost control since." Except for his latest confrontation with Hillcrest, which had pushed him into marriage.

"Reform? That's not what society claims—showing up half naked at a masquerade, fleecing Lord Creevey, duels over mistresses—"

"Enough!" And he'd thought gossip at the clubs was bad. "Those tales range from gross exaggeration to outright lies. *Half naked*. My God!"

"Lady Horseley was outraged."

"I don't doubt it, but she is a self-righteous meddler

who has made it her mission to despise me—as have several of her closest friends. If my behavior seems too tame, they make up scandal. My costume was Robinson Crusoe. While it's true that I wore no coat or cravat and my breeches were tattered, it was hardly obscene. There were pirates at that ball who wore less. And one of the Aphrodites—" He shook his head, for the lady might as well have been naked.

"As for Creevey, that arrogant boasting about his sense of smell has annoyed society for years. I finally called him on it. He set the terms for that test himself—one good sniff of ten substances while blindfolded. He swore he could identify anything. The fool lost, of course."

"What did you use?" Interest replaced the challenge in her voice. A smile tickled the corner of her mouth.

He grinned back. "Obvious scents to start with—sandalwood, vinegar, rotten fish."

"Deadening his sense of smell."

"Exactly." He caught her hand, twining his fingers with hers, delighted when she squeezed. "We finished with a wool scarf and pure water. He couldn't tell the difference."

"Because his jacket was wool. Clever." She nodded. "So you won the thousand guineas."

"Twenty, actually. The rest went to the other witnesses."

"Then why do people think it was all yours?"

"I take the blame for lots of things—even duels that never happened." He grimaced, but there was no way out. "Some of it is my own fault. The gossips loved my exploits ten years ago. I was young enough so that they could cluck their tongues and forgive me. Since I settled down before they grew tired of the game, their clucking never turned to censure. But instead of accepting that month as an aberration, they decided I'd learned circumspection. So whenever they need sensational tales to relieve boredom, they speculate about my secret activities. And if I do anything to draw notice, they magnify it into flamboyant scandal. They'll never change. Accepting the truth would mean admitting ten years of delusions."

"That doesn't make sense."

"It does, unfortunately. Hillcrest rants against me, so society accepts that I'm incorrigible. Their speculation increases my notoriety, convincing Hillcrest that I am indeed a godless wastrel. His condemnation breeds new speculation. And so it goes. Year after year." He snapped his mouth shut, appalled that he was whining. He hadn't meant to go this far.

Hillcrest's public criticism had hurt far more than their private war, for it affected him every time he spotted suspicion in someone's eye or watched a new acquaintance back away after a whispered warning. He hated the man for his unjust persecution nearly as much as for mistreating his mother.

"If he hates you, why does he continue your allowance?" she asked.

"He doesn't. I've not received a groat from him in ten years."

Helen bit her lip. Rafe sounded sincere, but Alex had taught her that sincerity could be faked and that men twisted their own foibles to make them seem better. While she could accept that his reputation was exaggerated, she doubted that the incidents were as benign as he claimed—Alex had sworn that he barely knew a disreputable moneylender in Taunton, yet Helen had seen the pair retire into a private office for two hours. And her father had disclaimed any fault when his carelessness injured a footman.

Then there was the lady who had been caressing Rafe's thigh when Helen emerged from the dressmaker's. Despite his vow that marriage meant something, he'd wasted no time arranging an assignation. He might not have set up a formal mistress after releasing Lydia, but that didn't mean he was celibate.

So she must take his latest claims with a grain of salt. By his own admission, he'd been penniless ten years ago, then had his allowance cut off. Gaming was an uncertain source of income. Even imagination, skill, and intelligence could not guarantee favorable results.

Which revived her problem. Rafe was the one man in England who might know her worth to the last shilling— even Steven had only guessed at its extent. Rafe had demanded marriage the moment she'd introduced herself. *Helen St. James of Audley Court, Somerset . . . uncle wants my estate.* He might claim ignorance, but how could she believe him? The letter from Alquist's solicitor was a formality demanded by law. He would have written the same missive whether Rafe had attended the will reading or not.

The only way to protect herself was to keep her wits about her. Letting him play on her emotions must lead to trouble. Her reputation could not withstand another mistake. Nor could her heart.

"Tell me about Sir Steven," Rafe demanded, releasing her hand to pull her against his side.

She shivered as his heat penetrated her gown, but accepted the change of subject. He needed all the information she could give him if he was to adequately protect himself. And she needed time to identify his goals. This wasn't the place to admire how elegantly his morning coat stretched across his shoulders. Or recall what lay beneath his tight-fitting pantaloons.

"I already told you that he hated Papa. They grew up in London after Grandfather lost his estate. Steven's manipulation turned Grandfather against Papa, so Papa inherited only the baronetcy. Steven got everything else."

"Ouch."

She shrugged. "There wasn't much by then—a third-rate town house and a few hundred guineas, which Steven immediately lost at cards. Papa had a modest income from an investment he'd made while still in school, but he refused to support a gamester. Steven was furious."

"That fits what I know of him."

"His wife brought him a sizeable dowry, which helped for a time, and he won a small estate at the tables. But he lost far more than he won, sinking into debt. Then Papa backed a couple of ventures that paid well and bought Audley. He barred Steven from the estate, so his appearance at Papa's burial was the first time I'd seen him since childhood."

"Expecting an inheritance?"

"No. Determined to steal one. Papa left him nothing—as promised. After he set up my trust, he warned me to avoid Steven. But though he swore Steven was unscrupulous, the only vice he ever mentioned was gaming."

"You don't like gaming, I take it."

"It's dangerous." She twisted until she could glare at him.

"For some," he admitted, dropping a light kiss on her nose. "But all gentlemen play cards. A few guineas for an evening's entertainment is not evil. The intelligent ones know when to stop. The really intelligent ones don't mix gaming and drinking, for that is what leads to ruin."

She wanted to ask why an intelligent man would support himself by inflicting misery on others, but refrained. It was more important to keep him complacent so he wouldn't ask questions at the bank. To that end, she curled into his side.

"What about Dudley?" he asked, touching his scarred cheek. His voice had deepened.

"Papa despised Steven, but he feared Dudley. Even as a child, Papa never allowed him to call on us, claiming something was broken in Dudley's head. So I met him for the first time when he returned from the Peninsula last month. He is vicious, especially when drunk, which is his usual condition. I'm grateful that war kept him away."

"He was never a gentleman."

"You know him?"

"Not well, thank God." His face darkened, making his scars stand out alarmingly. "I last saw him when he was sent down from school. Is he also obsessed with Audley?"

She frowned. "*Determined* would be a better description in his case. Steven wants everything his brother had, regardless of value. He would covet Audley even if it were mortgaged to the hilt. Dudley wants money, period. Audley produces ten thousand a year."

Rafe whistled. "That's four times what Hillcrest Manor brings in."

Helen stifled a sigh. Her test had worked too well. Dudley had reacted the same way upon learning Audley's income. Avarice was a powerful force. She had nothing

with which to counter it. He might want to bed her at the
moment, but she could never distract a rake for long.

Rafe fingered his scars as Helen sank into silence.
Dudley sounded worse than ever.

The younger students had rarely crossed his path, so
their first meeting had occurred on a sunny day in April
twelve years earlier when a free afternoon sent Rafe to
the confectioner's shop for his favorite apple tart. He
arrived to find the baker unconscious and Dudley forcing
himself on the man's unwilling daughter.

After a lifetime under Hillcrest's thumb, Rafe hated
bullies. In a flash, he hauled Dudley off the girl and
slammed him into a wall. Dudley fought back. The struggle took a toll on the shop, overturning chairs, breaking
crockery, and smearing both combatants with pastries.
But the bigger, stronger Rafe was well on his way to
winning when three other students approached.

At the first sound of footsteps, Dudley grabbed a broken bottle, slicing Rafe's cheek as he twisted the jagged
edge toward his eyes. A knee to the groin jerked his
hand back, and before Dudley could slash a second time,
Rafe subdued him. But the damage had been done. Eton
sent Dudley down for the incident, but he showed no
remorse. His parting words vowed vengeance.

Now Rafe had again interfered with Dudley's desire.
Dudley wasn't the sort to let Helen's marriage interfere
with his plans.

Steven slammed into St. James House, seething from
the encounter with Thomas. His shoulders burned where
Thomas's servants had twisted his arms. The bitch's foot
had likely cracked a rib. His groin still throbbed. A
glance in the hall mirror confirmed a black eye, swollen
jaw, and scraped forehead. Thomas would pay—with
his life.

But his first priority was money.

"You're fired!" he snarled at the butler. "The staff,
too. Now."

"Sir Steven!" The butler lost his impassive countenance.

"You're wasting time. Anyone here in one hour will

be arrested for trespass and their possessions confiscated." Satisfaction bloomed as the man fled.

Helen would find a vacant house when she came to claim it. Very vacant. The epergne on the dining table would fetch a few shillings. And that Chinese vase in the drawing room, the Queen Anne writing desk . . .

He hurried upstairs to wake Dudley.

The boy was snoring. "Get up," ordered Steven, whipping the covers off. Cuts and bruises decorated Dudley's body. Yesterday's disappointment had sent him looking for trouble. He must have found it.

"Get up!" he repeated, slapping Dudley's backside. "I found Helen."

"Where?" Dudley opened bleary eyes. "The bitch needs a lesson in obedience."

"It must wait. She's married."

"What?" He leaped to the floor. "I'll kill the bastard. Helen is mine."

"Agreed, but we have to handle this carefully. Do you want to face charges?"

Dudley glared.

"Now that she has a champion, she will claim this house," explained Steven. "They could be here any minute—I left them at breakfast." Fury returned at the memory. "We can't afford a brawl. They may bring runners with them."

"Why?"

"To haul you off to prison, of course. He's already champing at the bit in his eagerness to attack you. She must have spun a wicked tale."

Dudley's face darkened. "Who is he?"

"Rafael Thomas. The man whose lies expelled you from Eton."

Dudley roared, drawing Steven's most satisfied smile. There was more than one way to wreak revenge on the bitch.

Leaving Dudley to do his worst, Steven ordered his secretary, Stone, to load the most saleable items into the baggage carriage, then headed for Helen's room. Her trunk stood forlornly in the corner.

Glass crashed downstairs—hopefully a window. Mirrors were unlucky.

This was a minor setback, he reminded himself as he rifled her trunk. Audley was his, as anyone of sense agreed. It would take a few days to deal with Thomas, but in the end, he would prevail. He couldn't afford otherwise.

For twenty years he'd lived on expectations. After Arthur's wife nearly died birthing Helen, the doctor had forbidden another pregnancy. Thus everyone had known that Steven was Arthur's heir. The knowledge had kept the duns at bay until news of Arthur's will reached London.

"Damn that bastard for cutting me out," he growled again. Canterbury should have overturned the trust. Leaving everything to a puling female was clearly mad. Yet the archbishop had refused his petition. His only chance for justice was to wed her to Dudley.

But it had to be soon.

"Arrange a meeting with Mr. Chum of Maiden Lane," he told Stone a quarter hour later. "Tonight, if possible. Tomorrow at the latest. I have a job for him. And tell Mr. Hicks I will call at three."

"I'm not familiar with Formsby's Bank," said Rafe as they passed the Bank of England and turned up Broad Street. "What do you know of them?"

"Not much," she admitted. "I've dealt with them for four years, but never in person. They've been Papa's bankers since he was in school, though, so I presume they are trustworthy. Papa was quite meticulous about business associates."

"So you have no problem with them as trustees."

"It's not much of a job." She shifted, refusing to meet his eyes, obviously hiding something. "Papa set up the trust so I would run Audley. A London banker can hardly oversee a Somerset estate."

"Not directly, but most appoint stewards."

"Who must still take orders from town. Papa felt it was better that the steward report to me."

Her voice had assumed an edge Rafe didn't like, but he stifled his pique. He needed facts before he could determined his course. So for the moment, he must remain in the background. When the carriage rocked to a halt before the bank, he let her take the lead. He would learn more from observation than from questions.

"Helen St. James to see Mr. Formsby," she said, handing her card to the doorman. "I was married yesterday and must discuss my trust."

In a remarkably short time they were ushered into Formsby's heavily paneled office. Impressive—and unsettling. Helen was an important client. The trust must contain more than just Audley. Steven's words echoed. *Forty thou*— That was as much as he had.

"I'm pleased to meet you at last, my dear," Formsby said, seating Helen before his desk. "As you requested, I've prepared all the documents for your signature."

"What documents?"

"The usual transfers, Mrs. St. James. The trust terminates upon marriage—property laws, you understand. It is merely a formality."

"The name is Mrs. Thomas," she snapped. "And my father drew up this trust so that marriage would change nothing, as you very well know."

"T-Thomas?" he stammered.

"May I present the honorable Mr. Rafael Thomas, my husband. My banker, Rafe."

"Mr. Formsby." Rafe bowed, applauding the steel in Helen's voice. She would not allow this obsequious man to ride roughshod over her.

"But—" Formsby's voice cracked. "How— Why did you throw over your fiancé?"

"What fiancé?"

"Don't deny it. I have your letter right here." He pulled a sheaf of papers from a deed box, sorting until he found the one he wanted. "Eight months ago you announced your betrothal to Mr. Dudley St. James."

"Never!" Helen snatched the letter, reddening as she read. "My God. So that explains it." She passed the letter to Rafe. "I told you Steven was devious. That is not my hand."

Rafe stared at the page. It informed Mr. Formsby that after careful consideration, Helen was convinced that Sir Arthur had allowed spite to strip his heir of property that should rightfully stay with the title. To rectify the injustice, she proposed to wed her cousin Dudley, restoring Audley to the baronetcy.

"Don't lie to me," snapped Formsby. "You wrote that. If your memory is that bad—"

"It is a forgery," she insisted. "And not a very good one, as even a cursory look must prove. I am appalled at your laxity, sir. The assertions in this letter are ridiculous. Father warned you time and again that his brother would do anything to steal my inheritance. Yet within days of his death, you appointed him to oversee the estate, granting him power to dismiss staff that had been there since Father bought the place."

"I did no such thing! You demanded his oversight because your mother was ill." He waved another letter.

"Balderdash!" Helen leaned over the desk to glare. "I wouldn't allow Sir Steven to oversee the cutting of a plum pudding. The man is venal to the core and the most avaricious schemer the world has ever seen. He has kept me incarcerated ever since you sent him there."

Rafe laid a calming hand on her arm. She would accomplish nothing if she lost her temper. "Relax, sweetheart. It seems that you are both victims of forgery. How close is that signature to yours?"

"Not very." Grabbing Formsby's quill, she dashed off four signatures on a piece of stationery.

"You are deliberately changing your hand," snapped Formsby.

"She's right about your laxity." Rafe held Formsby's gaze. "You abrogated your fiduciary responsibility, sir. Appalling in a bank manager, and worse in a trustee. How can you ignore the evidence?" He turned to Helen. "Surely he has your signature on file."

"He should." Taking advantage of Formsby's shock, she pulled the deed box closer and leafed through the papers.

A memory that had been tickling the edges of Rafe's mind suddenly returned. St. James. *You can't go wrong buying shares in that woolen mill,* his man of business had said eight years earlier. *The primary backer is Sir Arthur St. James. He has a genius for sniffing out new enterprises and rarely makes a mistake.*

Brockman had been right. The value of Rafe's shares had increased fourfold in only two years. Sir Arthur's name had garnered respect, which meant he must have amassed a fortune. Rafe's heart sank, but he would deal with that later. For now, he must support his wife.

"Summon the other trustees," he ordered as Helen laid several letters on the desk. "You have until they arrive to decide whether you are a credulous fool or Sir Steven's accomplice."

Formsby blanched.

By the time Goddard and Carstairs arrived, Formsby was shaking. All old correspondence matched today's signatures. Nothing sent in the last nine months did, though some were better approximations than others.

"We didn't know," insisted Carstairs, the trust solicitor.

"You didn't care." Rafe glared at each man in turn. "Upon receipt of that first letter, conscientious trustees would have sent a representative to Somerset to verify its contents."

Helen nodded. "Malfeasance, at the very least. You were so pleased that I'd apparently come to my senses that you accepted even outlandish claims without question. Look at this." She brandished a letter. "*I have replaced Ridley as steward, due to continuing incompetence.* Your own records show that Ridley doubled Audley's income after I hired him three years ago. How could you accept this slander without an investigation? You should have questioned my intelligence for even suggesting such a change!"

"Where is Ridley now?" asked Rafe.

"God knows. Steven turned him off without a reference because he insisted on speaking with me. He knew that Father would never have allowed Steven on the property. Since then, Steven has drained the estate accounts." She pulled out another letter. "This forgery demands that you send the quarterly trust payments to a new bank."

Carstairs blanched.

Rafe shook his head. "Another nonsensical order you didn't question."

"It was a reasonable request," stammered Formsby. "We had remonstrated with Sir Arthur many times for trusting a provincial bank. It was one of the few changes Miss St. James made that we wholly approved."

Helen snorted. "Harold's may be provincial, but Mr. Harold would never execute an order he hadn't verified," she snapped icily. "If you are typical of London bankers, then it's time to move my trust to Harold's. I cannot remain subject to such incompetence."

Rafe watched as three red-faced trustees struggled to explain their oversight. They had clearly thought Sir Arthur befuddled for leaving a lady in charge of Audley.

Any suspicions he'd entertained in that direction disappeared as he listened to her catechism. She had a firm grasp of what should have been done and a firmer grasp of who was at fault in the affair. Every time someone tried to sidestep guilt, she pounced. In minutes, their attempts to explain their behavior turned them into gibbering idiots.

It seemed that Fate had provided him with a wife remarkably close to his ideal—the backbone and vivacity his mother had displayed, Alquist's intelligence and acumen, more passion than any mistress . . .

The passion was obvious as she strode restlessly about, flinging questions at her trustees. Every turn plastered her skirt against those long, long legs, reminding him how she'd rubbed against him in bed last night. His hands recalled the weight of her breasts and the smoothness of her skin. His body tightened as it remembered her ardent explorations. If he used her passion to attach her affections, perhaps they could find a solution to her wealth—maybe endow a benevolent society with it.

But first he must win her trust. Hillcrest's damned announcement had made her wary.

You are also wary.

He frowned. He had long admired his mother's backbone and sworn his wife would also stand up for herself. Yet at the same time, he'd expected his wife to accept his decisions without complaint. Only now did he see the conflict between those ideals. And it was the first one that would cause trouble. Her determination could so easily turn against him. He could not tolerate a marriage filled with dissention. Nor could he tolerate a wife who tried to rule him. Rather than fight, he would have to live in town. Alone.

It was not the future he had envisioned, but he might have no choice.

Yet it was early days to walk away. He must give marriage a chance, though he would guard his heart against any attachment. If she turned into a tyrant, he could not afford pain.

It ought to be easy—shielding his heart had never been a problem before. But Helen was different. Already, she'd enticed him more than any female in years. So he must be very careful.

He tore his eyes from her form and concentrated on the meeting.

"Lord Alquist was quite upset about Sir Steven," Formsby was saying. "He called three weeks ago, demanding answers to the oddest questions."

"Yet you did nothing?" Helen's voice could have cut glass.

"We agreed to conduct an audit, but we've not had time to arrange it," said Mr. Goddard. He had taken over for the trust's original investment officer two years earlier and sounded so apologetic that Rafe wanted to ram his teeth down his throat—an urge that grew as he considered how many investments Goddard might be handling.

"And why is that?" demanded Helen.

"Lord Alquist's concerns seemed so bizarre that after his death, we felt it best to consult with his successor before proceeding further," said Mr. Carstairs.

"But you didn't," said Rafe shortly.

"How do you know?"

"Because I'm the successor—not that it matters. Overseeing the trust was never her guardian's job. An audit should be a regular part of your procedures. When was it last done?"

Goddard reddened. "Sir Arthur sent us copies of his annual reviews. We never needed to send a man out there."

"Actually, my father did no reviews," said Helen crisply. "I have overseen Audley since this trust was established. I put together the annual summaries for my own records. Since you never requested further information . . ."

"Well, um . . ." Goddard was clearly at a loss for words.

Helen met Formsby's eye, raising her chin high enough that Rafe tensed. "Mr. Thomas is correct. Audits are a fiduciary responsibility that you have clearly ignored for four years. But that lapse pales beside these letters. Each is in a hand that is clearly not mine yet orders changes in the trust that are outside your power to grant. Since you breached the trust conditions in blatant disregard of your sworn duty, I will expect you to restore every shilling drained from my accounts through your negligence."

"We can't—" began Formsby.

"I wouldn't finish that thought," said Rafe quietly. It was time to end this farce. "Your position is shaky already. No competent trustee would put Goddard in charge of investments."

"What?" snapped Formsby as Carstairs cringed.

"He is known throughout the investment community for his ineptitude. What return did he show last year? Two percent? One percent? Losses?"

"What with the war and the weather—" began Goddard.

"Poppycock!" snapped Rafe. "My man of business made eight percent despite those problems. Most years he returns much more. Sir Arthur would be appalled at your performance. Men show better returns by placing all money in three-percent Consols." Rafe glared at Formsby. "This smacks of deliberate sabotage. You needed something for Goddard to do, so you put him in charge of a lady's affairs, assuming that she wouldn't notice his incompetence. Your brother-in-law, isn't he?"

Goddard reddened. Carstairs looked ready to swoon. Formsby feebly stuttered.

"This meeting has lasted long enough," said Helen, rising. "I want a detailed report on trust assets within the week, Mr. Formsby. And you have four weeks to conduct a full audit and restore every shilling paid out improperly. That includes funds siphoned from my regular accounts, funds deposited in fraudulent accounts, and the restoration of any securities sold without my authorization. We will discuss further measures at our next meeting."

Formsby nodded. "The matter will be dealt with immediately. I will assign my best—"

"We will send our own representative to supervise." Rafe watched Formsby swallow an objection.

Helen nodded. "I will insist that my own man of business oversee the trust in the future. In the meantime, Mr. Goddard will buy or sell nothing without my direct authorization. Is that clear?"

Formsby and Carstairs nodded. Goddard looked like someone had kicked him.

Rafe offered Helen his arm. "Gentlemen." He escorted her from the room.

Chapter Five

"*D*o you know a good man of business?" asked Rafe, sliding his arm around Helen's shoulders as the carriage headed home.

Tremors shivered under her skin. He hoped it was pleasure at his touch, but he suspected it was fury at Formsby's obsequious condescension.

Disturbing heat swept his body as she snuggled closer. He had set himself a grim task—using passion to bind her heart while keeping his own heart free in case he failed.

She removed her hat so she could finger the bump on her head. "I know no one in London. Papa's man of business died two years ago—that was when Goddard took over the investments. Is yours really that good?"

"You're thinking about my rooms, aren't you?"

"Can you blame me? You live by gaming. Hillcrest cut off your allowance. Everyone knows people present prosperous façades to the world even when in debt. How many ornate entrance halls and ostentatious drawing rooms exist in tumbledown houses?"

Rafe cursed ten years of secrecy. "I've never bothered correcting society's misconceptions."

"Why?"

"To protect myself." He'd shared his secrets only with his mother and Alquist—he'd never fully trusted others, even Carley—but Helen deserved the truth. "I won ten thousand guineas playing cards ten years ago."

"And didn't lose it the next day?" She stared.

"Never. It meant freedom. Hillcrest was furious that I'd moved to London. He threatened to cancel my allowance unless I returned home—he's always used money as a whip."

"You don't like being threatened." It wasn't a question.

"Who does?" Hillcrest's blatant bribery attempts were worse than the demands that he repudiate his mother. He would never forgive the man for slashing his allowance after Dudley sliced up his face. Despite that the headmaster had placed the blame squarely on Dudley, Hillcrest had decided that Rafe was a troublemaker. In his opinion, the girl was merely a merchant, so Rafe should have ignored the assault. Interfering had created a scandal.

He met Helen's gaze. "I hate threats, and I hate bribes. Winning that game freed me from both. I hired the best man available to invest it and have lived on the proceeds ever since."

Helen stared, fighting to keep her shock from showing. Rafe was the most secretive man she'd ever met. Even Alex had been more open.

She couldn't figure out who Rafe was. She'd believed him when he swore his reputation was exaggerated. She wanted to believe his betrothal was false. But now he claimed to be wealthy. "Why haven't you said anything?" she demanded. "Who in his right mind pretends poverty? It has to feed the gossip about you."

"I feared Hillcrest would confiscate it. I wasn't of age."

"You are now."

He shrugged. "Old habits die hard. But it no longer matters. We'll look for a house tomorrow. Something—"

"I already have one."

"What?" Rafe cursed as his voice cracked. Her control of her fortune gave her an advantage that his mother had never enjoyed in her long war with Hillcrest. Then there was her secrecy. His mother had shared everything with him. He knew it was too soon, but he'd expected his wife to do the same. Yet every time he turned around, she shocked him with something new. "Why didn't you mention your house yesterday?"

"I knew Steven would be there."

"He has his own house."

"But he wants mine." She sighed. "We had to avoid him yesterday, Rafe. You saw how he reacted this morning. How much worse would it have been if we'd faced him with you drunk, me concussed, and no servants to lend a hand? Besides, I've no idea what condition the house is in. Papa let it once we moved to Audley. It's been vacant only a few months."

"Where is it?"

"Hanover Square. Number fourteen."

"That's just around the corner."

"I hadn't realized." She bit her lip. "I'm also not sure how suitable it is. Childhood memories often exaggerate size, yet I remember it as small. Papa could afford nothing larger when he married, but perhaps we should sell it and buy something else. The *Post* listed a house in St. James's Square for sale."

"Parker's place, most likely. The location is good, but the house is cramped and falling to bits. Yours will do for now." Though he had no intention of living in hers for long. He hadn't spent years escaping Hillcrest's thumb so he could crawl under his wife's. He would buy a house himself.

She shrugged. "Whatever. My first priority is the audit. Would your man of business have time to speak with me today?"

"Brockman?"

"If that's his name. I don't wish to make any hurried decisions, but if Goddard is truly incompetent, I need someone to oversee him until I decide what to do. All three of them, actually. I cannot understand how Papa came to trust Mr. Formsby. He was quite adept at spotting liars, yet Formsby must have lied often if Papa thought him supportive."

Rafe shook his head. "I thought he would expire from shock when you announced that you had written all the reports he thought came from your father. How did that come about?"

"Papa supervised me while he could, but his health worsened rapidly. That last year, he was too ill to do anything. Some days he couldn't muster the energy to speak."

Shouts drew her eyes to an angry teamster berating a youth whose curricle had cut him off. Or perhaps she was hiding tears. She clearly loved her father—something to envy.

He stroked her arm, ignoring the sizzle in his blood. "I'm sorry for your loss, Helen."

"Thank you."

Pushing the problem of her inheritance aside, he focused on the other fear that had been growing since leaving the bank. "I don't like what Formsby said about Alquist."

She again relaxed against his side. "His demand for an audit? I know that was outside his authority, but—"

"That's not what I mean, sweetheart. Alquist would never have made inquiries unless he suspected illegalities, which makes his death very convenient."

"What?" Shock suffused her face. Shoving his arm aside, she twisted to face him.

"Think about it," he said. "Alquist stirred up trouble. A week later he was dead."

"You can't mean Formsby killed him!"

"No." The banker was foolish, arrogant, and distrustful of a woman's ability to conduct business, yet he wasn't openly dishonest. "But Formsby must have notified you of the audit. A week was long enough to return a response to London."

"You can't believe there is a connection. Granted, Steven was intercepting my mail, but if he wished to stop an audit, he would attack the trustees."

"Not if he had any sense. It would provoke the very investigation he didn't want."

Helen frowned. "Are you sure Formsby is innocent?"

"I'm sure." He again caressed her arm, nodding in satisfaction when she leaned into his hand. "Formsby might cancel the audit once circumstances gave him an excuse, but from laziness, not concern. On the other hand, Steven must fear an audit, for it would prove theft and forgery, at the least. Yet killing Formsby would install a new trustee, who would immediately examine the records."

"And who might be less credulous than Formsby."

"Exactly. Removing Alquist would trigger Formsby's

laziness, giving Steven time to force you into marriage, thus terminating the trust."

"He knows it doesn't terminate," she said absently.

Rafe scowled at her reminder. Yet it made little difference which of them controlled her fortune. That it started as hers made it a whip. Just as his mother's dowry had been a whip.

He cringed at the way he'd worded the thought, yet it was true. And it was entirely Hillcrest's fault that his mother had been forced to wield it. Given a choice, she would have been sweet and generous, but Hillcrest's belligerence had pushed her to defend herself and her son using every weapon at her disposal.

Helen dragged his mind back to business. "There is one huge flaw in your theory, Rafe—aside from an utter lack of evidence that Alquist's death is suspicious. Steven was at Audley two weeks ago. So was Dudley. He is more likely to consider violence than Steven."

"True. Dudley acts first and thinks later. When did he arrive?" He again pulled her close.

"The fourth week in April. When did Alquist die?"

"The fifth of May."

She frowned, resting her head on his shoulder—which proved only that she was weary. She ought to be in bed. "Dudley was at Audley that day. I had to hide when he came home in his cups."

Rafe swallowed a flash of fury.

"Steven was also there."

"One of them could have hired a cutthroat."

She shook her head, tickling his chin with a wayward curl. "Absurd! Steven has no money, and Dudley has been away for years. Who would he know?"

"Well . . ." She had a point.

"The audit might have pushed Steven into bribing that vicar, but that's all it did. Marriage would end Alquist's guardianship, and Steven had already proved he could control Formsby. I'm sorry Alquist died, but you must accept that the timing was a coincidence."

"No." He couldn't trust Dudley. "Alquist's death makes no sense as an accident," he began slowly. "I should have questioned it at the time."

Helen covered his hand. "I know you were close, but

don't let grief twist memory into something that wasn't there. Accidents never make sense. That's why we call them accidents."

He nodded. "True, but don't dismiss the possibility without hearing the story."

She nodded.

"We spent that last evening playing cards at White's."

"Was he drinking?"

"Very little, but he was unusually preoccupied. Perhaps he was concerned about you. Or maybe it was something else. I didn't ask, and he didn't say. I wondered later if distraction had made him careless." He stroked her arm until she wriggled closer.

"What happened?"

"He left White's about midnight—early for London. He was on foot." Rafe swallowed a sudden lump in his throat, lifting Helen into his lap to counter the iciness forming in his stomach. It had been ten years since he'd last held someone for warmth and comfort. It felt good.

Helen snuggled into this new position, rubbing his chest as his arms closed around her.

He sighed. "Someone left an old wagon in a narrow lane a block from Alquist House. It had no brake, so he'd jammed a chock under the wheel—sloppily. It loosened, letting the wagon roll into the street. Alquist leaped aside but slipped and struck his head on the cobblestones."

"I'm sorry for your loss, Rafe, but it sounds like an accident. You know how slippery cobbles can be."

Especially when dampened by fog, but Alquist was no fool. "It doesn't make sense."

"Why?"

"Several reasons. The details were on every tongue by daylight. That in itself was normal—gossip spreads faster than the wind. But who started the story? No eyewitnesses ever came forward. Then there was the wagon. I've passed that spot hundreds of times at all hours of the day and night, but I've never seen a wagon there. It's a narrow walkway between two buildings and not meant for vehicles. Even riders don't use it."

"What did the wagon's owner say?"

"No one ever claimed ownership. Teamsters would

starve without their vehicles, so who would abandon one? And where were its horses? None were found near the scene, nor were any unfamiliar horses stabled nearby. Which leads me to wonder if it was stolen. The culprit could have used the team to escape."

She smoothed his coat. "A lord died, Rafe. That's enough to send anyone into a panic. Admitting involvement would lead to transportation, or worse."

Rafe ground his teeth, but she had a point. Even if the death was an accident, the teamster would face charges of negligence. But his gut insisted that it was no accident. "There are too many coincidences, Helen. Alquist was known for tenacity. He never broke his word, never left a job half done, never lost interest in a subject until he'd answered all his questions. If he demanded an audit, he would press until it was finished."

"Hmm." Helen frowned.

"Another oddity was Alquist's fall. The chock remained in the walkway, showing that the wagon had rolled barely twenty feet along a gentle slope. Wagon wheels on cobblestones are loud enough to wake the dead—especially at night when there is no other traffic. Even someone deep in his cups could easily have evaded it, and Alquist wasn't drunk."

Helen fingered the bump on her head.

"Exactly. I think someone struck him down, then arranged the wagon to explain his death. That same someone started the rumors to prevent awkward questions."

"But who? You think Formsby is innocent. Steven and Dudley were at Audley. No one else would care."

"What about Goddard? He is more than a credulous fool. He never quite knows what's going on and agonizes over decisions for weeks. Thus he is the last to invest in any venture and the last to recognize when one goes bad. His investments show poor returns because he waits until the opportunity is nearly gone before deciding to try it. Many men turn to Goddard when they decide to dump shares, so he pays top prices for ventures that are ready to collapse."

"Ouch." She shook her head, curling her hand around his neck. "But that would make him even less likely to kill anyone. A slow-thinking, indecisive man might consider murder, but he would still be debating the merits when his target died of old age."

"Under normal circumstances, perhaps. But even a coward will strike when cornered."

She frowned. "It's possible, though unlikely." Twisting, she met his gaze. "Intuition aside, there is no evidence of murder, Rafe. A scapegoat might mitigate your grief, but—"

"I'm not imagining this, Helen," he snapped. "Too many facts don't fit the accident theory. I have to investigate. The first step is to discover what Alquist knew. Did he suspect Steven was holding you hostage? Did he think Goddard was cheating you? His wife should know. They were very close."

"Let's call on her, then."

"Easier said than done. She remains in Hampshire."

"Hampshire is on the way to Somerset. I need to return home as soon as I arrange oversight for Formsby. Those forgeries bother me more and more. Steven is not scheming for Dudley's benefit. He wants money on his own account, so he may be defrauding my tenants."

"You must face Formsby next week to judge whether he's met your first deadline. Your orders will lack authority if you let that slide. We will use the intervening time to speak with Lady Alquist and investigate Alquist's death. I owe him too much to let murder go unavenged. And I doubt Steven will bother with Audley now that you are wed."

"Sometimes it is better to delegate authority, Rafe." She cupped his scarred cheek, kissing him lightly. "Your man of business can oversee Formsby better than I, for while I am a good estate manager, I have little training in finance. I'm sure that Formsby will whitewash any problems on this first report. I need a keen eye that can spot skullduggery. And since you have no experience in investigating crimes, you will be better off hiring a runner. Steven can hide any defalcations by ordering Audley's ledger destroyed—the new servants would obey him. Or he can create havoc for my tenants. Since I have no one I can trust to protect them, I must go in person. His obsession won't let him abandon his quest, despite our marriage."

Rafe tried to find a trick hidden beneath her words, but he couldn't think while distracted by her warmth. Nor could he refute her logic. No matter how much he feared her position at Audley, he must let her run the place. The tenants did not deserve to be sucked into a struggle for control. After a lifetime trapped in other people's wars, he knew what it felt like.

"Very well. We'll leave in the morning," he murmured, abandoning further discussion for the lure of seduction.

"Thank you." Her green eyes glowed.

Her hip pressed against a burgeoning erection. He licked her lips, then covered them. His temperature soared.

"Rafe!" she gasped as his hand cupped her breast, teasing its nipple into a hard ball.

Easy, he admonished himself as his hips flexed against her. He was supposed to bind her with passion, not succumb to his own.

But her response drove his need higher than ever. Every touch sent sparks raging through his body. Every moan heightened his need. It took all his considerable control to defer acting on the fantasies raging through his mind. He longed to toss up her skirts and take his pleasure. It had been years since he'd last coupled in a carriage.

But he couldn't. They were already in Maddox Street.

"We'll finish this later," he murmured, smoothing her gown as he forced calm over his ragged breathing.

She was too stunned to respond.

He smiled as his groom let down the steps. By the time he actually bedded her, she would be blind with desire.

Brockman had already arrived for their daily meeting. Rafe introduced him to Helen, then headed for Hanover Square, accompanied by his secretary, Barnes.

Number fourteen was on the west side, part of a brick terrace constructed shortly after passage of the Building Act of 1774. Helen was right about its size. The terrace was second-rate, according to law, so the units were a modest three bays wide and three stories high, occupied mostly by merchants. Cramped, though it would do for now.

The iron railing around the kitchen area was rusting. A glance into the area itself revealed broken steps and enough dirt to start a garden. The staff had clearly skimped on cleaning.

No one answered the front door. The knocker was down, but there should have been a caretaker.

"It's unlocked, sir," said Barnes, testing the latch.

"Damn." That could only mean trouble.

Entering confirmed his fears. The hall was littered with debris from deliberate, wanton destruction. Someone had hacked the walls and turned the banister to kindling. Shards of mirrored glass were everywhere. "I should have sent Sir Steven to Bow Street," he growled. But he'd considered Steven's attack a momentary burst of temper. The man should have come to his senses by the time he reached the street.

He'd been wrong.

Rafe glared at the destruction. If Helen had explained Steven's obsession earlier, this wouldn't have happened.

A quick tour revealed damage in every room, though not as bad as to the hall. Her trunk stood upstairs, her clothing scattered but intact. Any jewelry was gone, though, along with any money she might have had. He wondered what else was missing.

"Stay here," he ordered Barnes. "Find out where the staff is—the neighbors should know. If Sir Steven turned them off, rehire them and order an inventory. Otherwise hire new. Arrange for repairs, and I want new locks on all the doors." Steven might have a key.

"At once, sir."

"And send a note to Shipley. I'll call at four." He added details, then loaded Helen's clothes into his carriage and headed for Berkeley Square.

The familiar façade of Alquist House revived his grief. Alquist had turned a wild boy into a responsible gentleman, offering the respect Rafe had never received at home. He'd been the anchor that kept Rafe from harm. Now the anchor was gone, and that boy was again adrift.

"Good morning, Harris," he said when the butler opened the door.

"Master Rafe." Harris welcomed him inside. The spacious opulence stood in stark contrast to the ruins in Hanover Square. Alquist House was solidly first-rate, occupying a double lot deep enough for a separate servants' wing, formal garden, and mews. With eight bedrooms and its own ballroom, it was the sort of house Rafe had always wanted. But that was for later.

"I just discovered that Alquist named me guardian to his ward, but he'd never discussed the girl. May I check his desk to see if he left any instructions?"

"Of course, sir." Harris led him to Alquist's study.

The desktop was empty of its usual clutter. "Where are his papers?" he asked.

"Lady Alquist ordered everything sent to Hampshire so Rhodes could deal with it."

Rafe nodded. The secretary had been with Alquist for thirty years, longer even than Harris. His collapse at the burial meant it would be some time before he could manage. Something else Rafe must see to. There might be matters that needed immediate attention. Alquist's son was with the army in North America. Until he returned, Rafe was the nearest kin.

"I am returning to Hampshire tomorrow. In addition to instructions, I was hoping to discover what bothered Alquist that night." He met the butler's shuttered eyes. "I've never seen him so pensive. If it was concern over his ward's trustees, I need to know."

"I know nothing of that." But he shifted his weight from foot to foot in a very unbutlerly fashion.

"But you do remember something." Rafe pulled several scraps of paper from a drawer—Alquist had always jotted notes to himself.

Harris finally spoke. "A man called after he left that evening."

"Who?" Not a gentleman, or Harris would have identified him as such.

"He claimed to have an urgent message for Lord Alquist. I sent him to White's. But Lord Alquist had no time to act on that message. I fear something important was forgotten."

"Rhodes would know. Or the solicitor. Whoever sent the message would write to them," said Rafe soothingly, but his stomach churned. No one had delivered a message to White's. Rafe had spent the entire evening with Alquist. Had the caller's goal been to learn Alquist's location? "What did the fellow look like? Perhaps I know him."

"I doubt it, Master Rafe. He was only a messenger—coarse, dark, and dressed worse than a groom."

"In that case, the matter cannot have been as urgent as he claimed." The description would fit half of London, including Goddard, though he doubted the man was smart enough to effectively impersonate a servant.

Harris nodded and left him to his search.

The closing door unleashed a tidal wave of grief. Every inch of the study was dear—the chairs flanking the fire where he'd discussed everything from money to manners, Alquist's favorite walking stick propped in the corner, books, maps, a painting of Alston Place. Much of what he knew about the world he'd learned in this room. It was hard to believe he would never see Alquist again.

Tears burned his eyes. Alquist House was the only real home he'd known—the perpetual war at Hillcrest was hardly welcoming.

Unable to blink away his grief, he laid his head down and sobbed. How could he go on alone? He couldn't count on his aunt. She'd been too shattered to speak to him. Could Helen ever fill even part of the void?

Minutes passed before he pulled his tattered control in place and set to work. A quick search turned up no instructions. The notes weren't much help, either.

Audit A bks.

H to wed—why no word? Formsby must have mentioned Helen's supposed betrothal.

Send R to A. Probably Rhodes. If the "R" stood for Rafe, Alquist would have said something at White's. Apparently he'd decided to conduct his own inquiry in addition to Formsby's audit.

Inv S and D. A reminder to invite Sharpton and Diggery for cards. His friends had returned to London the day after his death.

The others confirmed Alquist's concern about Sir Steven and his determination to protect Helen—a course

that might have cost him his life. Rafe hoped the papers
Lady Alquist had taken to the country would contain
more information. Or perhaps Rhodes would know
something. Alquist might have found information that
could hold Steven at bay.

In the meantime, Helen needed jewelry. It was time
to show the world that he could properly support a wife.
The best jeweler was Rundel and Bridge, which lay on
the way to his solicitor's office.

Her half-mourning made the errand easy. He emerged
from the shop with two boxes tucked into his pocket.
One contained a stunning necklace of carved jet with
matching eardrops. The other held pearls. He would return for the emeralds that matched her eyes another day.

Helen woke to find Rafe sitting on the bed, his hand
sliding seductively up and down her arm. His touch recalled those incendiary kisses in his carriage. She
shivered.

"You should not have pressed so hard today," he said,
sounding concerned. "I can't believe how pale you look.
It's time to send for a doctor."

"No." She forced a smile when he frowned. "The day
was wearying, but I feel much stronger now that I've
slept. I always look pale because my hair is so red."
She reached back to touch her bump, then added, "The
swelling is much reduced."

"Let me see." He helped her sit, then slid behind her
to examine the wound, curving his legs around her hips.
"You're right. It's improving, with no sign of fresh
bleeding, but I wish you would see a doctor. Head
wounds are tricky, and I'm not exaggerating your pallor.
You are several shades lighter than when we met."

"And will likely remain so for several days. Mother
always swore I looked at death's door after even minor
injuries. It was especially bad the time I fell from an
apple tree. Even Papa looked at me askance—and his
coloring was as odd as mine, so he was accustomed to
it." She realized she was babbling, which wasn't like her,
but Rafe's touch scrambled her wits worse than Steven's
blow. His hands had drifted down to massage her
shoulders.

She glanced back, meeting eyes silver with heat.

"Relax, sweetheart," he murmured. "I enjoy touching you."

"And I enjoy your touch." She smiled when the words brightened his eyes even more. His fingers slipped beneath the neck of her gown.

Rafe clamped down on desire. The gentling process was progressing at lightning speed, but it was too soon for intimacy. Her face remained white even as her breathing quickened in response to his caress. Lines at the corner of her eyes spoke of continuing pain, and she'd flinched when he'd touched her head.

He should not have kissed her in the carriage, for it left him frustrated. As long as she remained injured, his purpose would best be served by keeping her aroused. But to retain his sanity, he must do so without promising his own libido satisfaction. So he lightened his touch, sliding his fingers down her arm to tease her wrists— and brush her breasts as he passed.

She instinctively arched, then leaned against him, baring her throat to his lips.

He couldn't resist.

"I retrieved your trunk," he murmured to divert his thoughts from the bottom nestled against his groin.

"Steven's gone, then?"

"From Hanover Square. Anything of value is gone, but your clothes are intact."

She turned her head to nibble his ear. "I didn't bring much—a few guineas and some trinkets. But I'm grateful for the clothes. Napping in this gown has done it no good at all. I should change for dinner."

"True." Since she couldn't reach the fastenings, his fingers jumped into action, opening the ties to bare her shoulders. His lips followed, drawing her gasp. Her lack of a maid gave him opportunities gentlemen rarely saw—and tested his control to the limit. "Paul should return with food shortly," he managed huskily, mostly to himself. His hands slid her gown lower.

She arched against him, wiggling until he nearly exploded. "The gray should be wearable. It crushes less than the others." The breathlessness with which she uttered the words raised his temperature another notch.

He had to move before his control snapped. Her innocent ardor was too tempting. Was it an act to bind him? But he dismissed the idea. She lacked the experience for such a scheme.

Extricating himself, he lifted her from the bed, letting her slide slowly down his body in a long, agonizing caress. Torture.

He added to the torture by prolonging the undressing process, touching every inch of flesh he could reach, from the upper half of her breasts to her long, long legs. By the time he settled the new gown in place, they were panting as if they'd raced to Kensington and back—on foot—and he could barely string two words together.

His hands shook as he fastened the gown. Leaving her to comb her hair, he fetched the boxes, then practiced deep breathing until he had his libido back under control.

"For you, my sweet," he murmured, hooking the jet necklace around her elegant neck. Her perfume made his senses reel.

"It's beautiful." Her eyes sparkled greener than ever as she fingered the carving, meeting his gaze in the mirror. "Thank you, Rafe. I've never seen anything so exquisite."

"Then thank me properly." Leaning forward, he kissed her.

With a moan, she twisted, throwing her arms around his neck as she sucked his tongue deep into her mouth. She was the fastest learner he'd ever met. In twenty-four hours she'd gone from a novice to a Siren capable of bringing him to his knees.

He stifled the thought, gasping, "I've pearls, too," as he nibbled his way to her ear.

"You've been busy." Her hands threaded his hair as she blatantly rubbed against him.

Need exploded so fast he was untying her gown before he realized it. She rubbed harder in a long caress that nearly blew the top off his head. Her thighs cradled his shaft. As his hands cupped her bottom to lift her against him, she moaned, driving every coherent thought from his mind. In an instant he was on the brink of completion.

He was turning toward the bed when Paul rapped on the door. "Dinner, sir."

Damnation! What the devil was he doing? He'd successfully incited her passion. Losing control of his own would negate that victory.

"We'll finish this when you are recovered," he managed, reluctantly doing up her ties.

"I certainly hope so," she murmured, then blushed.

Sucking in a deep breath, he led her to dinner. At least she no longer resembled a corpse.

Helen was grateful for his silence. She could barely form a coherent thought as she took her place at the table. Every time Rafe touched her, she went up in flames. Yet he retained complete mastery of himself—just as Alex had always done. It didn't seem fair that men could remain emotionally aloof.

Rafe was becoming more of an enigma with every passing hour. His public and private selves might be two different people for all they had in common. On a personal level, he was hot one minute, aloof the next, with too many secrets lurking behind his eyes. Was he trying to win her trust, emotionally as well as materially? Unlike Clara's husband, Rafe must convince her to share her inheritance before he could act against her.

Yet he couldn't be that devious. Surely she could not melt into his arms if he were a ruthless schemer. Or was she willfully blind? Confirming the worst would condemn her for reckless stupidity. Wedding a stranger was bad enough for anyone, but her responsibilities made it worse. What would her father say if he could see her now? After all his warnings . . .

Chapter Six

*A*lice Pauling arranged bits of ham and eggs to form a chessboard on her plate, ignoring her father's monologue. Today's subject was her wedding—as if she cared how many people attended or what Cook served. Her only goal was to escape Paulus Grange. She was tired of being told what to do and think every moment of the day.

Being an obedient daughter was boring. Pauling hated excitement, so he refused to visit London, forbade novels, and demanded that she avoid Sir David's daughters, who had acquired appalling ideas at school. And God forbid that he discover she'd read Mary Wollstonecraft's treatise on the rights of women. He expected her to embrace his own puritanical views.

Settling her betrothal in childhood had increased his stodginess. Why should he introduce her to society when Rafe could do it later? He had everything he needed at home. Not once had he considered her needs.

Lord Pauling swallowed an enormous bite of ham, chased it down with half a tankard of ale, and continued arranging her future. "You will live here, of course."

"Yes, Father." It was easier to agree, for he never listened to her anyway. But she had no intention of staying at Paulus Grange. Rafe would hardly abandon London's excitement for a dreary life in the country. She would enter society at last.

"See that Mrs. Dorsey removes the partition in the drawing room."

"Yes, Father."

"The dressmaker will arrive at two to discuss your new gowns."

Alice bit back a sigh. He'd been like this since Rafe had signed the marriage contract a week earlier. How could she survive until the wedding?

She crumbled toast over the ham and eggs.

The next three weeks would pass, just as the previous twenty years had passed. And then she would be free—except for Rafe. But she doubted that Rafe would pay her much heed. He wasn't a tyrant, and despite her father's assurances, she did not believe he impatiently awaited their marriage. If he loved her, he would have claimed her years ago.

"Eat your breakfast," ordered Lord Pauling. "You must keep up your strength. I can't supervise everything."

"Of course." She raised a bite of ham to her mouth.

"That's my girl." He smiled, then buried his nose in the *Times*.

Alice transferred the ham to her napkin. She hated ham, but Pauling insisted on it for breakfast, allowing no other meat on the table. His preferences were all that mattered.

A twinge of conscience replaced her irritation with a frown. His health was obviously deteriorating, despite his protestations to the contrary. The doctor's face had been grave after his last visit. Pauling's fainting spells must be more serious than he let on.

He'd abandoned wearing boots last year because he could no longer pull them over swollen feet. His hands weren't much better. And his eyes seemed yellow. But it was the spells that terrified her. If he stood up quickly, he passed out. It reportedly took his valet half an hour to get him out of bed by gradually elevating him with pillows—which might explain his insistence that she and Rafe stay at the Grange. Maybe he needed a nurse.

Shuddering, she picked up the *Morning Post*. Its society page was her only contact with Rafe. Hillcrest might find his scandals appalling, but she envied him his freedom. He enjoyed such an interesting life.

Her eyes skimmed, seeking the name that had been noticeably absent for a fortnight.

The Season was in full swing. Yesterday had seen a balloon ascension in Green Park. Lady Jersey had hosted a grand ball. Lord Charles Meriweather announced his betrothal to Lady Edith Chanson.

She was so used to seeking *Mr. R——T——* that she nearly overlooked the announcement.

Married—the honorable Mr. Rafael Edward Thomas, heir to Viscount Hillcrest, Hillcrest Manor, Surrey, to Miss Helen Elizabeth St. James, spinster, Audley Court, Somerset, on May 20, in London.

Alice's heart jammed her throat. "Papa," she quavered. "Rafe's married."

"What?" He shook his head. "That's preposterous."

"No. Look." She handed him the paper, pointing to the announcement.

"That traitor!" He surged to his feet, blanched to a sickly gray, then dropped like a stone.

"Papa!" She flew to his side, cursing his illness. Shaking and slapping didn't revive him.

"Briggs!" she shouted at the butler. "Send for the doctor! Where's Walden?" she added. The valet should know what to do. She hoped.

Leaning closer, she tried again. "Wake up, Papa!" Her vinaigrette had no effect. Nor did propping his feet on a chair. Why had the doctor insisted on secrecy?

Tears rolled down her cheeks. This was the worst spell yet, and she was helpless.

Rafe glared at his wife.

"I am perfectly fine!" she snapped, raising her chin.

Gnashing his teeth at her intransigence, he cursed himself for a fool. He should be more careful what he wished for. As he'd feared, a wife with a backbone was a headache. She argued every suggestion and made no bones about wanting to be in charge.

Just like Mother.

"No!"

"Yes," she insisted.

Only then did he realized he'd spoken aloud. Again he cursed.

The argument had raged since breakfast. He should have insisted that she see a doctor yesterday. Her head had to be worse than she was admitting. She'd slept badly, tossing, turning, and whimpering in pain. Yet she had again refused help. Nothing he'd said had swayed her from leaving for Hampshire, forty-five miles away.

His breath escaped in a frustrated sigh. A husband had the right to force obedience, yet he couldn't bring himself to do it. That was Hillcrest's way. So he had to rely on logic.

"Please speak with Dr. McClarren," he begged, pulling her against him when the carriage bounced, draining the color from her face. They had just passed the Hyde Park tollgate, so calling on the doctor was still possible. "He's Scottish trained and very competent. He won't do anything nasty like bleed you. If he says you are fine, I'll cease pressing."

"You'd believe him, but not me." She recoiled from his side. "It's my head, Rafe. My memory is intact. There is no sign of nausea or blurred vision or any other symptom of concussion. I slept poorly only because I'd napped for three hours in the afternoon."

"Pain stabs your head with every jolt, your eyes are fuzzy, and your cheeks are far paler than is fashionable."

Helen sighed, wondering why she was attracted to him. Her sleep had been plagued with erotic dreams and passionate memories. Yet every time she'd awakened, moaning with desire, Rafe had been hugging the edge of the bed as if he hated the thought of touching her. Now he seemed determined to bend her to his will.

She met his gaze. "Yes, my head hurts. Bruises don't clear up in a trice, and arguing is making it worse. But speaking with Lady Alquist is more important than a headache. Once she sets your mind at rest, we can proceed to Audley." And form a partnership—she hoped.

Rafe lowered his voice. "There is no need for you to accompany me, Helen. Go back to bed. I'll ride down to Hampshire and be back before you know it. Two days. Three at most. By then, your head will be fine and the journey to Audley easier."

"Rafe—" She laid a hand on his arm, trying to break through his stubbornness. "You still don't fully comprehend the danger. Steven is not a gentleman. He is an obsessed bully who cares nothing about society's rules or expectations. Throwing him out yesterday will turn him vengeful—he is not a man who ignores grievances. I don't want to stay in town alone."

Rafe's jaw dropped as he finally recognized her fear. Damn but he was blind. "Then we'll go to Hampshire tomorrow."

"No. We cannot afford to wait. Though I am convinced Alquist's death was an accident, I may be wrong, so the sooner we see Lady Alquist, the better. Would you stay in bed just because you hit your head?"

"That's different."

"No, it isn't. I am not fragile. Nor am I sheltered, weak, or flighty. This trip is necessary, so stop fussing. Tell me about Lady Alquist. Though we've met, I don't know her well."

He gave up in defeat. "Lady Alquist was my mother's younger sister. I met her for the first time after Mother's death."

"At the funeral?"

"No. Hillcrest had cut all ties with Mother's family."

She straightened, staring. "What did they do to draw such censure?"

"Nothing. It was his way of punishing Mother." He pulled her against his side, not wanting to discuss Hillcrest. "When we finally met, she was avid for news of Mother, as she'd received no letters in several years— Hillcrest again; he controlled the estate's post."

"He sounds like Steven—intercepting mail, forcing obedience to his will."

"Probably." He shook his head. "Once she satisfied herself about Mother, she insisted that I make my bows to her friends—she is so well regarded in town that she can make or break someone's Season. Her support prevented my ostracism after the Berkeley Square incident."

"You swore that tale is exaggerated."

"True, but it could have caused more trouble than it did. As for your original question, she is one of the kindest ladies I've known. While she gossips as avidly as anyone, she generally avoids exaggeration and doesn't repeat tales of questionable accuracy."

"That's good to know."

He wasn't sure what to make of her tone, which sounded relieved. So he changed the subject. "Did you leave your maid at Audley, or must we find a new one?"

"Find one. Steven turned off Tessa and the upper servants several months ago, then assigned his mistress to maid me so he could keep a close eye on my activities."

"His mistress?" His arm tightened around her. "Appalling! You shouldn't even meet such a person."

"Steven cares little for the niceties."

He cradled her head on his shoulder, watching Hammersmith roll past as he fought his temper into submission. Every new glimpse of her ordeal made his blood boil hotter. Steven must pay. And she was right. He couldn't leave her behind. Nor could he postpone his query into Alquist's death. But while he admired her spirit, he wished she would accept some limitations. She was not a man.

Her scent teased his nose.

Most definitely not a man. Her taste lingered on his tongue—haunting, demanding, chipping away his control. He shifted uncomfortably.

Helen moaned.

He turned to plunder her ripe mouth before identifying the sound as pain. Again.

"Try to sleep, sweetheart," he murmured, cursing himself for entertaining lascivious thoughts when she was injured. She needed protection more than passion just now, though temptation urged him to stake his claim. Passion would crack her wall of distrust, banish her need to contradict his every statement, and elicit the loyalty their marriage needed if it was to prosper. Postponing pleasure had never been his way.

But he must stay his hand if he hoped to bind her heart.

Reminding himself that success would atone for his current frustration many times over, he smoothed her hair, gently massaging first one temple, then the other. Her skin was soft and smooth, a perfect companion to the silky fire of her hair. Removing the pins let him enjoy the hair's texture even as it eased the pull on her cut.

A soft sigh escaped as she relaxed into sleep, leaving him with nothing to do but think.

This was his first opportunity to seriously evaluate his marriage. In truth, wedlock was little different from any other business venture. He may have skipped his usual prepurchase investigation, but proper attention to detail could still produce good returns—a willing bed partner, someone to enliven the hours when he wasn't busy and produce an heir for the future, a hostess who could aid his political aspirations. He was making progress toward claiming her heart, but it would not be fully his until he dealt with Steven. The bastard kept distracting her attention. And his. Why else hadn't he demanded to know the secrets he sensed were lurking behind her eyes?

Thought convinced him that Steven was less venal than she claimed. Her father had vilified the man since she was a child—much as Hillcrest had vilified Lady Alquist. But Hillcrest had exaggerated and even lied to perpetuate his own feud. Lady Alquist was much different from the harpy he had described.

Perhaps Sir Arthur had been guilty of the same distortions. Granted, Steven's tactics were heavy-handed, and he was clearly perpetrating fraud, but turning him into a larger-than-life bogeyman could paralyze thought and lead to improvident action.

You are no better.

Shuddering, Rafe pulled Helen closer. He didn't want to admit such folly, but his conscience was right. He'd fallen into the same trap by magnifying Hillcrest into the devil incarnate. The image was so fixed that he rarely listened to Hillcrest's words, assuming that the man had nothing of interest to say—he always acted as if he knew what was best for others. It was time to move past that childish reaction and admit that Hillcrest was human. Impossible to live with, of course, but not an ogre.

Habit pushed his sire from his mind. He would keep an open mind when dealing with other men, judging only on facts. Only thus could he protect Helen as he'd promised. She needed him badly, for she could never protect herself. It felt good to be needed.

She shifted, pressing a breast against his side. Her hand slid under his coat, re-igniting desire, then slithered toward his lap.

Easy, he reminded himself. Rest would hasten her recovery. He needed her healthy so he could complete the job of binding her.

He tried to focus on Alquist's death or Steven's threats, but as the miles passed, he couldn't keep his eyes off Helen's form—graceful curves that fit perfectly against his body, tawny lashes fanned across creamy cheeks, satin-soft hands that had clasped wonderingly around . . .

Desire built until it was all he could do to quietly hold her. Heat blazed wherever they touched as if her hair were indeed fire.

By Maidenhead, he was out of his mind. To keep from ravishing her, he rented a hack and rode the rest of the way.

Helen glanced up as Rafe spurred past the carriage window, jumped a ditch, then trotted to a pond so his horse could drink. He rode very well, which should have told her from the beginning that he had a comfortable income. A man who lived in penury would be out of practice. Nor could he afford his own horses. Caesar was nothing like this rental hack, and keeping a carriage in town was expensive. But she'd not been thinking clearly that day.

It was a relief to have some time alone. They had argued from the moment she'd awakened, raising new questions about yesterday's attentiveness. The strain of remaining so reasonable was taking a toll on him. Men expected to be in charge.

Or perhaps his temper rose from regret. Rafe could handle Steven, but he seemed genuinely afraid of Dudley, cupping his cheek whenever his name arose. Was Dudley responsible for those scars?

Rafe must be cursing their bargain by now. This marriage of convenience had already embroiled him in assault, embezzlement, and vandalism. No wonder he'd hared off on the trail of Alquist's mythical killer. Assuaging his grief by investigating the accident was safer than facing her enemies. And it gave him time to catch his breath.

Her, as well. Her marriage was nothing like her dreams, and Rafe's description of Hillcrest boded ill for the future. How had growing up under the thumb of such a man affected him? It added yet another contradiction to a character that was already complex. She wanted to believe that he was unlike other men, but she could not ignore his similarities to Alex.

Rafe's sensuality seemed more blatant than Alex's, and far more alluring, but that perception might arise from her own maturity. She recognized her response to the glint in his eye more easily than she had four years ago. Rafe need do no more than look at her to incite raging desire, but that was dangerous, for it clouded her mind. She must know who Rafe was and what he wanted before she dared risk her heart.

She fingered the necklace he'd given her, wondering yet again if it was the generous gift of a willing partner or the next move in a game to line his pockets. Alex had given her many gifts, yet in the end he'd walked away, destroying her reputation and blighting her life.

I won't hurt you, they'd both said. Was Rafe also lying for his own ends?

Her questions always circled back to her inheritance. Rafe must have known about it. At the very least, he should have recognized her father's name, for it was well-known in investment circles. Brockman certainly did. And his description of Rafe's finances raised new questions.

Rafe had begun his struggle for financial independence while still in school, cutting his expenses to the bone so he could save enough to escape his father's thumb. Amassing a fortune had changed nothing. He had continued to live frugally, hiding his income even from his friends. Ten years later, he still saved every shilling he could, hoarding worse than Midas himself. So she could not acquit him of being the fortune hunter society labeled him.

And that cast doubts on his behavior. He had treated

her as an equal, letting her take the lead with Formsby and refusing to force obedience. Most men would have been deaf to any argument, but he had listened and agreed. Many would have ignored her injury, then taken her again last night. Rafe concentrated on her recovery.

She feared that he was trying to charm her into breaking the trust. If she then died, he would be free to pursue whatever life he wanted. Her father's greatest fear had been that she would fall prey to a man who would do just that. As his strength failed, the fear had turned to obsession, prompting daily warnings and lectures.

Take care, Helen, he'd said on his last lucid day. *Beware of fortune hunters. Never reveal your worth. Find a gentleman who loves you more than life itself. Only thus will you be safe.*

He'd also urged her to judge men on their actions, not their words. It was so easy to shade the truth by choosing words that conveyed false meanings even as they seemed honest. Alex had been a master at that. It was too early to know if Rafe was another.

Yet her father's warnings seemed overblown as she watched Rafe return to the road. Surely he was honorable. Merely looking at him backed up the air in her lungs. Sunlight glinted from his dark hair. Muscles rippled along his thighs. There was no denying that he was a marvelous specimen of virility. A single glance skittered sparks along her nerves, pooled heat in her womb, and made her fingers tingle with the need to touch.

She jerked her eyes away, fearful that she might form an attachment before she understood him. Marriage made him more dangerous than Alex, who had merely broken her heart and reputation when he walked away. Rafe could leave only by destroying her. Even being locked in an asylum so he could enjoy her fortune unfettered was unacceptable. She would go mad. So she must be sure of his sincerity before investing emotion in him.

The countryside changed as they descended from the rolling pastureland of the chalk downs to a broad plain. Her practiced eye took in crops as robust as Audley's, sheep sleek from recent shearing, frolicking lambs, fat cattle, and fruit trees already setting the year's crop. Hampshire was a prosperous county.

But she was more than ready to escape the jolting carriage by the time it turned through impressive gates onto a drive lined with yews. Her head pounded. She wished Rafe had remained inside with her. His shoulder cushioned her head far better than the best-padded seat.

They finally stopped before a handsome brick manor house smaller than Audley but more welcoming. Audley's size could intimidate.

Guilt choked Rafe when the butler ushered them into Lady Alquist's cozy sitting room. She looked haggard, her puffy eyes staring vacantly at the fire.

He should have stayed in Hampshire after the burial. It was unconscionable that he'd let his own grief blind him to her need. But it had hurt unbearably to lose the man he'd considered both father and friend.

Father and friend. His feet froze. Had Hillcrest killed Alquist because the man commanded the respect Hillcrest lacked?

"Are you all right?" murmured Helen, penetrating his shock.

"Fine." A lie, but he needed time to consider the appalling idea. No matter how autocratic Hillcrest became, Rafe had never suspected him of violence. The most physical act he could recall had been shoving him into a chair on his last visit.

"Mr. and Mrs. Rafael Thomas, my lady," announced the butler.

Lady Alquist jumped, her eyes wide with shock. When she saw that Rafe was indeed accompanied, she smiled tremulously, then rushed into his arms. "My dear Rafe. What a wonderful surprise! But married? When?"

"You look better," he said warmly. He'd missed her. She was the only one left who cared for him. "We wed two days ago. I believe you know her, Helen St. James of Audley Court."

"Helen!" Lady Alquist's smile broadened as she hugged Helen, then stepped back to look up at her face. "My, but you've grown! You can't have been more than thirteen last time I saw you. We were making plans to visit when Alquist—" Tears welled, but she blinked them away. "How did you come to wed my scapegrace nephew? I'm surprised to find you acquainted. He never leaves town."

"It's a long story." Helen was also blinking back tears.

"We've plenty of time, dear." Lady Alquist gestured to the sofa. "Come and tell your godmother all about it. I've missed Fanny's letters these past months. She always had such witty things to say, especially about you. It was too bad that you were at school the last time we visited. I'd planned such a wonderful Season for you."

"Of course, but Papa's illness—"

Rafe felt as if he'd stepped off a cliff. Lady Alquist had often mentioned her goddaughter, but he'd not made the connection. Hadn't Dear Helen wed several years earlier? He was sure there had been talk of a betrothal.

"We were meaning to visit," Lady Alquist repeated as Helen sat. "Alquist was most disturbed when he heard Sir Steven was at Audley."

"As well he should have been," said Helen with a sigh. "How did he learn of it? He cannot have gotten my letter, since I received no reply. In truth, I've heard nothing since Papa died. Steven intercepted my mail."

"The nerve of the man! If only we'd known. But our first inkling that you might need help came from Mr. Haskell." She glanced at Rafe. "You wouldn't know him, dear. He mentioned meeting Sir Steven in Taunton, which surprised us very much since Steven never goes near the West Country. Mr. Haskell swore that Steven inherited Audley. Alquist immediately called on the trustees."

"That must have infuriated him," said Rafe.

"Very. I've never seen him so incensed. His description of Mr. Formsby was—" She shook herself vigorously. "He was sure that Helen's letters were written under duress. Arthur had touted her acumen often enough to convince Alquist that she was astute."

"Thank you," said Helen. "Steven didn't bother with duress. The letters are forgeries."

"Well I never—" Lady Alquist sputtered to a halt as a footman slid a tea tray onto the table at her elbow. "We knew that Steven had to be scheming—your parents feared he would try something underhanded. Very insistent about it, you know. And who's to blame them?"

She poured wine for Rafe, then lifted the teapot. "I'll never forget the day Arthur refused Steven a loan— fifteen years ago it must have been. Fanny and I were in the next room, you see, and Steven's threats penetrated the wall. Not at all what a gentleman would say, especially to another gentleman. Please forgive us for not checking sooner, my dear. We were at a house party in Yorkshire when your father died. By the time your letter reached us, it was too late to attend the burial. We should have come to Audley anyway, but it seemed an awful imposition with Fanny so ill. She would have been distressed had I seen her in that condition. And your household hardly needed another disruption."

"I understand. As would she." Helen sipped, grateful for the fortifying nature of tea. "She lingered for eight months, unable to move or speak and barely able to swallow. I prayed often that her understanding was as slight as it seemed, for it must have been awful to be imprisoned by a body that no longer functioned."

"So very true. I am thankful that Alquist went so quickly. It was a shock, of course, but at least he didn't spend years in pain like poor Arthur." She shook her head, seeming to chastise herself for raising melancholy subjects over tea. "What brings you back so soon, Rafe? I doubt you traveled all this way merely to introduce your wife—how did that come about?"

Rafe grinned. "Quite by accident. We ran into each other and decided we would suit."

"Just like that?"

"Absolutely. Fate presented me with the perfect bride at the very moment I was contemplating marriage. There seemed no reason to wait."

Helen shook her head. "He's leaving out a few details. I was fleeing Steven at the time—trying to reach you, actually. I'd not heard of Lord Alquist's death, for Steven kept the newspapers to himself. It was a shock. My condolences, my lady."

"Thank you, child."

"When Rafe learned that I had no place to go, he offered for me."

Lady Alquist raised a brow.

"She's leaving out a few details as well," said Rafe, sighing. Trying to explain that day was impossible. No matter what they said, they sounded like lunatics. "Steven was forcing her to wed Dudley. She had just leaped through a church window when we met. Marriage seemed the best way to prevent a recurrence."

"Dudley!" Lady Alquist slammed her cup onto the tea tray so hard it broke. "It is worse than Alquist feared. Steven is evil. And that son of his is worse. I haven't forgotten that he tried to blind you, dear," she said to Rafe.

Helen gasped.

"He tried the same thing on their butler two years later. Broke the fellow's nose, if you can believe it, then turned on Steven when he intervened. It was a nasty scandal—but you won't remember, for poor Catherine had just died. He'd been—"

The dressing bell sounded.

"Heavens. Is it dinner already? I do run on at times," declared Lady Alquist. "And you've yet to tell me why you are here."

"That tale can wait until morning," said Rafe, enjoying the fire that indignation raised in her eyes. Alquist's death had turned them quite flat.

Helen smiled approval, weakening his knees.

Chapter Seven

May 23

*W*hen Helen arrived for breakfast, Lady Alquist was already eating. Sun drenched the east lawn and poured through the windows, warming the yellow and cream walls. A gay ceramic rooster perched on the mantel, its colors echoing the carpet, cushions, and brightly painted plates.

Lady Alquist's eyes twinkled. "Good morning, my dear. Did you sleep well?"

Helen blushed.

Lady Alquist beamed.

Helen took her seat, searching for the words that would reveal her qualms without insulting Rafe. Lady Alquist doted on him, but she was Helen's only source of information. "I hope you can help me, my lady. Our marriage was so sudden that I know little of Rafe. He seems so contradictory. Can I believe everything he says? Some of it sounds incredible."

"What troubles you, dear?" Lady Alquist dropped sugar in her coffee and stirred.

"Lord Hillcrest. A man who would publish notice of a nonexistent betrothal must have been a horrible father. What did growing up in such a family do to Rafe?"

Lady Alquist's hand jerked, sending her spoon across the room, where it hit the wall. "He published a betrothal announcement?"

"Two days ago in the *Post*. Rafe swears he never consented, but I can't imagine a father being that dictatorial."

"That's Hillcrest." Lady Alquist absently accepted another spoon from the footman and resumed stirring her coffee. "I dislike speaking ill of others, Helen, but you need to understand Hillcrest if you are to help Rafe."

Helen blinked. "So I was right that he needs help."

"Exactly."

"Rafe claims Hillcrest has hated him from birth."

"It is more stubbornness than hatred, but it has mired them in a war that neither can win. Yet neither is strong enough to abandon the fight. Rafe has tried to retreat— and succeeded to some extent, creating a normal life for himself in town. But he will need more help than I can give if he is to be truly free."

"Why?"

"Because the battle started before he was born, so he knows nothing else. Retiring from the lists resolved nothing, though even that much accomplishment proves his remarkable character."

Helen frowned. It seemed that Rafe's depiction of his father might be truer than she'd thought. "What started it?"

"Many things." Lady Alquist shook her head, then sipped her coffee. "I was twelve when I first met Hillcrest, but the seeds of this battle had already been sown. He was horrible."

Helen shivered.

"You may think I was too young to judge," Lady Alquist continued. "But I knew. He was all of thirty and stone cold. The thought of Catherine— But I must back up so you'll understand. Hillcrest would not have entered our lives had my sister Catherine been less willful. She and Papa crossed swords almost daily. Tired of the turmoil, he finally set out to find her a husband. I don't know how he thought Hillcrest would do for a girl barely sixteen." She toyed with her cup. "He was domineering, bad-tempered, and desperate for money—his father had recently died, leaving him nothing but a derelict estate and crushing debts. It was the scandal of the year, for the Hillcrest fortune had been legendary. To find it replaced by a mortgage seemed . . ."

"Your father gave his daughter to a tyrannical fortune hunter?" Helen stared. Granted, arranged marriages had been the rule, but most fathers chose grooms who could enhance their own credit, then demanded elaborate marriage contracts to assure their daughters' comfort and grandchildren's security. It was yet another reason her father had set up the trust. He feared he wouldn't be available to negotiate the contract.

"It was a good match." Lady Alquist's dry tone belied her words, pulling Helen back to the story. "Papa was a baronet, so snaring a viscount was a coup."

Was that how people would see her? wondered Helen suddenly. An heiress who had traded her fortune for consequence? She stifled a shudder.

"Papa was adamant that it was a good match," repeated Lady Alquist. "But I never believed him—not even the day he announced it. He and Catherine had butted heads for years."

"Why?"

Lady Alquist sipped while she composed her thoughts. "Rafe will never admit this, for he worships his mother, and I would deny it to anyone outside the family, but much as I loved Catherine, she was perverse. If our governess called us to do sums, Catherine would insist on needlework. If ordered to remain upstairs, she would barge into the drawing room, but if invited to join guests, she would refuse. She was headstrong and willful to a fault—especially with Papa. I would like to believe he thought Hillcrest could settle her, but at best, he didn't care. And I suspect he accepted Hillcrest's offer to punish the daughter he had never understood."

"Dear Lord," murmured Helen, more thankful than ever that her parents had loved her.

"I've made her sound unbalanced, I fear." Her face registered frustration. "She wasn't. She was inquisitive and very bright, with a zest for life few people manage. Her only fault was her refusal to accept what Papa termed *her place*. Rafe inherited her best traits, along with a dose of her stubbornness. But at least he listens, uses logic, and is willing to concede an argument if evidence proves him wrong."

She nodded. "I take it Catherine wasn't."

"No. She accepted Hillcrest to escape Papa, but she soon learned that he was just as autocratic. She'd expected a gay life in London, but he took her directly to his estate. Catherine was furious. If she had been older . . ." She shrugged. "I don't know all the ways she fought, for while her letters were filled with complaints, she said little on her own account. But I do know that neither of them ever compromised."

"So she lost."

Lady Alquist nodded. "Men have all the real power, and they wield it at the first sign of trouble. Papa refused to intervene—oh, yes, within the month, she begged him for help. But he'd washed his hands of her." She shook her head. "The next time I saw her was three years later at Rafe's christening—he was such a darling baby, and well worth the scold."

Helen raised her brows.

"I slipped away from school while your mother covered for me." She giggled. "Such a to-do when they found me gone, but I had to see Catherine. Her letters had grown quite frantic. Mostly a hum, though. Hillcrest might be cold and autocratic, and he never gave in to her demands, but he treated her well enough otherwise. She had her gardens and hothouse as well as adequate food, clothing, and shelter. With a little effort, she could have built quite a congenial life. But she refused to give in on the least point. It made me fear that Rafe would be caught in their struggle for power. And so he was."

At least this explained Rafe's stubbornness. It hadn't all been wine. Like both parents, once he got an idea into his head, he refused to give it up—marriage, pampering her wound, investigating Alquist's death . . .

He was occasionally susceptible to logic, though. Or seemed to be. Only time would tell if he was pretending so she would drop her guard.

Lady Alquist accepted more coffee. "As for Hillcrest, you need to know that he is incapable of any strong emotion except fury. Some people cannot love, though it is an easily disguised fault. Emotional displays are disparaged in our class."

"So Mother claimed when we discussed my Season." Helen pushed her plate aside.

"Dear Fanny." Lady Alquist smiled. "She never quite mastered ennui."

"I know. She told hilarious stories about your school days—giggles during deportment, pranks on the dancing master—"

"Ah. I'd nearly forgotten the dancing master—such a short little man. Even at fifteen, Fanny towered over him. How he hated it when we crowded round to pelt him with questions. Fanny was especially adept at tying his tongue in knots. Laughter was so easy for her." Her smile faded. "But not for Hillcrest. I don't think the man has laughed once in all the years I've known him. Nor is he capable of love. Because Rafe was Catherine's from birth, Hillcrest rejected him. By favoring his mother, Rafe neglected his duty to his father, so he had to be punished. Catherine's attempts to protect him made matters worse."

"But she has been dead for ten years."

"In body." Lady Alquist sighed. "But her spirit lives on. Rafe won't repudiate her, which keeps the battle alive. And Hillcrest prefers that. He sees any retreat as surrender. So he keeps fighting. In his eyes Rafe has become Catherine and thus must return home and dutifully accede to Hillcrest's demands—including that he wed Alice Pauling, since that was the last battle before Catherine died."

"Surely Rafe could end the war by conceding something."

"I doubt it. Only complete victory will satisfy the man. So much of his character is tied to the battle that he would cease to exist without it. Sad."

"Very. And Rafe seems just as stubborn."

"Not quite. He sees nothing dishonorable in retreat. Living in London lets him ignore Hillcrest entirely. As a result, his character is more balanced."

In public perhaps, but that was only a façade. She was beginning to recognize the fury and frustration seething inside him—not that she had any idea how to subdue it. What would happen if he turned it on her?

But beyond that was her fear that he would become the same sort of husband as Hillcrest—children usually resembled their parents. An instinct to command rather than discuss had already surfaced more than once. Or he might fall back on his London persona, with all its attendant lies and secrecy. She needed more. Love was unlikely, but they could at least attain honest cooperation—she hoped.

Lady Hillcrest shook her head. "Set it aside, Helen. Rafe will never subject you to the indignities his mother suffered. He will make you a husband at least as dear as Alquist." She sniffed. "I was so fortunate to find him. And marriage was so joyous that I made sure dear Fanny was happy, too. I introduced her to Arthur, you know."

"So she said." But talk of happy unions revived an earlier fear. She met Lady Alquist's eye. "You claim Rafe's confrontations with Hillcrest are a habit he can't break because he knows nothing else. So did he refuse Alice because he wasn't interested or because Hillcrest demanded the match?"

Lady Alquist flinched, dropping her cup on the floor. Her face twisted in distress. "I don't know, Helen. He has always sworn disinterest, but I truly don't know. Refusing Hillcrest's demands is automatic, I fear." She shook her head. "Why do you ask?"

"He makes a romantic tale of whisking me to the altar because he recognized his perfect wife. And that tale is essential for town if we are to avoid scandal. But in truth, he was drunk as a lord and reeling from his latest battle over Alice. For years he has been obsessed with securing his financial independence. I have a fortune."

But Lady Alquist was already shaking her head. "Rafe would never wed a fortune, not after watching his parents quarrel over money every day of his life. Catherine threw her dowry in Hillcrest's face in every battle, reminding him who had rescued his inheritance and delivered him from poverty. She demanded concessions in return, which he never allowed. Money, even more than power, fueled their feud. Hillcrest tried to control Rafe with money, too. So Rafe learned early on that money was essential, but only if it was indisputably his own. He claims Hillcrest created his own hell by wedding a fortune and has long sworn that he would never accept a wife who had a dowry. If he'd known about your inheritance, he would have fled as far and as fast as possible."

"If? He's my guardian."

"But Alquist never told anyone about your trust. You would have been hounded by fortune hunters. Even Arthur hid much of his wealth lest Steven become more importunate. Alquist was amazed when he learned the extent of your inheritance."

Helen nodded, relieved. If Lady Alquist was right, she must banish the instincts implanted by her father, which wouldn't be easy. "Tell me about Rafe," she begged. "Good and bad. He is reluctant to discuss his past, and I've no one else I can ask."

"You've heard the rumors, I take it."

Helen nodded.

"Ignore them. Most are exaggerations of incidents that happened ten years ago. If Hillcrest didn't keep them alive by decrying Rafe at every opportunity, they would have died long since."

"That's what Rafe said."

"Listen to him. Gaming was his way of escaping Hillcrest's financial blackmail, but he quit after winning a large sum just after Catherine died. He's parlayed that windfall into a respectable fortune."

"I wonder how the loser felt."

Lady Alquist waved a hand. "Naturally, he was unhappy—the loss put him deeply in debt. And though it was his own fault, he still bears a grudge and vies with Rafe at every opportunity. Some men never grow beyond childish spite. He started half the rumors—like that idiocy about dueling over the fair Lydia. All nonsense, of course, but he has never accepted responsibility for his own stupidity."

Lydia? Helen clenched her fists under the table.

"Forget the rumors, Helen." Lady Alquist was still prattling. "They arise from envy of a man who lives life to the fullest. Rafe ignores them. After growing up with Hillcrest's censure, society's exaggerations don't faze him."

"He sounds more like his mother than you claimed."

"They are very like. But their differences are important. Catherine held no real convictions. She would fight tooth and nail, but her goal was to defeat her opponent, not uphold any particular belief. If Hillcrest had exhibited the least sense, he could have controlled her easily, for she always did the opposite of what he demanded. In contrast, Rafe knows what he wants. His arguments support his principles. His behavior conforms to his code of honor. Thus he never lies, never cheats, and never harms others, even when doing so could benefit him. He enjoys debate, but if logic convinces him he is wrong, he will admit it."

"Thank you."

Not that she accepted the statement in its entirety. Every gentleman she knew lied in the name of honor or to protect his family and reputation. Even her father had lied when necessary to achieve a goal. Rafe would be no different. And while he displayed many characteristics she admired, when it came to Hillcrest, he doubtless fought with the same blind determination as his mother. That battle was so engrained that it superseded logic. Even Lady Alquist could not tell whether he loved Alice.

High stakes could also prompt uncharacteristic behavior—as Steven's recent excesses proved. Her fortune had driven Steven far beyond his usual reckless gaming. She feared it was large enough to tempt even a man who decried wedding money, for she was one of the wealthiest individuals in England. Killing her once the fortune was firmly in his hands would prevent it from ever becoming a bone of contention. Rafe had expressed surprise that Steven had not done just that.

So she must remain wary. Lady Alquist had long ago chosen sides in the Hillcrest war, planting herself firmly behind her sister and Rafe. That must color her perceptions.

If only she could peer into the recesses of Rafe's mind. So far he was tiptoeing through the early days of marriage, unwilling to press her. But a stubborn man could not maintain that posture for long. Worse, he had never known a loving family. Could he learn, or would she find herself in the same barren household his mother had known?

*   *   *

Having eaten early, then gone for a ride, Rafe headed for Alquist's study. Rhodes was visiting his brother, so it would be some time before they could talk, but the casket of London papers sat on a table beneath the window.

He pulled out three past-due accounts that must go to the solicitor. Invitations. Condolences. Information on a potential investment. Notes on a speech Alquist had planned for Parliament. A report on the spring planting. Pleas for contributions from three benevolent societies. A preliminary report from a Bow Street runner—

Rafe stared. The report concerned Steven and Dudley. *Inv S and D.* Not invite. Investigate. "My God."

"What?" asked Helen, entering the study.

Rafe looked up. Her face held more color today, but her eyes remained wary. It hurt. Yet perversely, her distrust did nothing to diminish his desire. Winning her trust was a stimulating challenge. He clasped her hand, raising it to his lips in a courtly gesture that deepened the roses in her cheeks. An answering heat pooled in his groin, but he thrust it down, determined to give her another day to recover so he needn't think about her head. He could manage one more day.

Maybe.

"Alquist was investigating Steven and Dudley," he said, forcing his mind back to business.

"It was a reasonable step, undoubtedly arranged after meeting Formsby. He must have recognized Formsby's weaknesses and feared Steven might be stealing me blind. Alquist never trusted Steven."

"I didn't realize they were acquainted."

Her eyes widened in surprise. "Surely you know Alquist's grandmother was a St. James. He and Papa were second cousins. Alquist sided with Papa after Grandfather died, which drew Steven's fury. They have been enemies ever since."

"Arthur! Damn. I never made the connection." Stupid. But he and Helen had not been properly introduced. She'd all but fallen out of the sky, with no link to the world he knew, at least none his drunken mind had noticed. Since then, he'd been too busy to consider how she related to that world.

"What connection?"

"Alquist often mentioned his cousin Arthur, but never by rank." The memory triggered another one.

Cousin Arthur died, Alquist had reported over wine several months earlier.

My condolences, Rafe replied. *He sounded like a fine man.*

And much like you. He is another who built a comfortable income from nothing. He'd gazed into the fire for several silent minutes. *He named me guardian to his daughter. She's a cute little thing—or was when last I saw her.*

Quite a responsibility. Rafe grinned at the image of Alquist raising a little girl with golden curls.

Not really. She'll remain with her mother. Another long pause. *But I'll have to name a successor. You would be perfect.*

Rafe had shrugged, which Alquist must have taken for assent. By morning, he'd forgotten that conversation. Alquist had been barely fifty and in excellent health. Even a child in the nursery should have been settled long before he passed on.

"Alquist's cousin," he murmured, shaking his head.

Helen nodded. "Mama and Lady Alquist attended Miss Harris's Select Academy for Young Ladies—as did I. Mama would not have met Papa without Lady Alquist's introduction, for he rarely went about in society in those days."

"How is it that you know so little about Alquist if he was family?"

"Adults rarely include children in their affairs," she said with a shrug. "So though Alquist often called on Papa in London, I remained upstairs. When he visited Audley, he and Papa were so engrossed in talk, they forgot I existed. The same was true for Mama and Lady Alquist, though as my godmother, she usually paid a brief courtesy call to the schoolroom."

Rafe grimaced. He had often wished Hillcrest had allowed Alquist to visit, which could have provided that positive influence in boyhood. But now he saw how pointless that would have been. Alquist would not have taken an interest in his wife's young nephew, and even slight childhood acquaintance might have diminished the attention Rafe had received as an adult.

It was time to change the subject. "Alquist did mention your guardianship."

"Really?"

He grimaced at her patent disbelief, then repeated the conversation and his impressions.

"He does seem to have made light of the matter. But he and Papa were more like brothers than second cousins. Perhaps he was grieving."

"Perhaps."

Helen sighed, recalling her father's tales. He and Alquist had always been close—they'd been born only a month apart and attended school together. A joint investment had paid well, making Arthur independent of his father. They had often shared financial information after that, benefiting both of them. So Alquist must have felt Arthur's death keenly.

"What did the runner report?"

"Steven owes several moneylenders and dozens of tradesmen. His estate is worthless—it was never more than a minor shooting box before he won it. Both it and his town house are mortgaged for more than their value."

"So he is in worse straits than I knew. We will have to be careful."

"We will." When he tried to say more, she laid a finger across his lips, snapping his libido to attention. Helen's mouth, with its ripe lips and sparkling teeth, moved several times before he realized she was speaking. "What?" He licked her finger.

"Did Alquist's papers contain anything else of interest?"

"Not yet."

"Then you'd best look." But instead of leaving him to his work, she settled into his lap and traced his lips. "That's why we're here."

"True." He sucked her finger into his mouth.

"Are you trying to distract me?" Reclaiming her finger, she ran it through his hair.

"What do you think?"

"That your reputation as a rake is well deserved." Helen shifted, smiling as he hardened against her hip. As long as he wanted her, they remained equal. "We came here to find out what Alquist knew."

"Which I will do as soon as you kiss me." He covered her mouth.

Her bones turned to mush. Rafe was even better at distraction than Alex. Each kiss drew her further into the sensual world she'd yearned to join since the first time Alex had led her into the shrubbery. Rafe was a master of the sensual arts, eliciting more response with his tongue and teeth than she'd believed possible.

Not that she objected, for she needed distraction. Describing how close her parents had been to the Alquists had shredded a long-held delusion by reminding her how focused they'd been on each other. She'd clung to the image of her close, loving family since the day Alex had left, but in truth, she'd been a distant second in both parents' hearts. She'd had nurses and governesses and school, but she'd wanted more. Dreamed of more. Unlike her classmates, who believed that love was a vulgar emotion suited solely to the lower classes, she had grown up surrounded by love—but rarely its recipient. So she'd eagerly awaited the Season that would produce a man who could fill the empty places in her heart.

Another delusion. Love played no role in her marriage despite the heat that sizzled from Rafe's lips. So she must protect herself. Men were adept at using pleasure to mask their secrets and bind women to their wills. She must become equally adept.

She shifted, satisfied at the effect the motion had on his manhood. At least he wanted her physically. If she could reduce him to mind-numbing passion, he couldn't take advantage of her.

Chapter Eight

A quarter-hour later Rafe reluctantly set Helen on her feet when someone rapped on the door. "Enter."

The butler ignored their flushed faces and heavy breathing. "Lady Alquist requests that you handle these, sir." He proffered a salver piled with letters.

"Of course."

"What are they?" asked Helen when they were again alone.

"Probably business letters—Alquist's secretary is away just now." He pulled her back into his lap, despite knowing that another kiss might snap his control. "Where were we?"

Helen stared glassily at the desk and tried to think past the sensual fog encasing her mind. Rafe's kisses were potent. She needed time to strengthen the shields around her heart. "Lady Alquist was telling me about your family."

Rafe stiffened.

"She mentioned that your grandfather lost his fortune. What happened?"

"Gaming, but Hillcrest never speaks of it." He brushed her breast.

He was trying to avoid discussing his family. But she had to understand him before taking this further, which meant learning about the people who had molded him. "She mentioned that your mother cared for the gardens."

"Yes." His face softened into a smile she'd not seen before, one unrehearsed and utterly without guile. "She adored color and spent most of her time adding masses of flowers to the park. She had a knack for mixing colors you'd swear would clash, yet in her hands they seemed vibrant." Again he brushed her breast. "You mentioned hiding from Dudley the day Alquist died. Was that a common problem?"

His abrupt change of subject was further proof that he didn't want to talk about family, not even the mother he'd adored. But perhaps she could elicit openness by being open herself. "Dudley considered us betrothed, though I'd often refused him. When he was sober, he behaved himself, but I rarely saw him sober. For the most part I avoided him, but twice he cornered me. The first time, I knocked him down and escaped. The second time, he passed out before he managed more than ripping my gown."

Rafe growled.

"Did your mother have interests beyond the garden?" she added, returning to her own questions.

"No. Hillcrest wouldn't let her leave the estate." He started to rise, but relented when she traced his brows. He was a rake to the bone, responding with alacrity to any touch—as was obvious to anyone sitting in his lap. "Let's talk about something else, Helen. Mother has been gone for ten years."

She nodded, though his assertion was a lie. Lady Hillcrest would not be gone until her husband and son ceased fighting over her.

Rafe rubbed her arm. "What do you know about Dudley? The runner didn't learn much."

"Hardly a surprise. He's been out of the country for years. Papa considered him vicious, but he never mentioned details. Dudley doesn't care a fig for me or for marriage, but since wedding me will line his pockets, he is willing to do so. He needs money badly."

"So he stayed at Audley until he could force you."

She frowned. "Not exactly. Steven actually restrained him from forcing me. If Dudley had had his way, he would have dragged me to London a month ago. He hates the country and was dangerously tense by the time we left Audley. It didn't help that Steven treated him like a recalcitrant child."

Rafe nodded. "I know how that feels."

"But in Dudley's case, it is deserved. He is stupid, credulous, and uneducated. He plans to sell Audley the moment we wed so he need never leave London again. Despite my explanation of how the trust works, he thinks marriage would hand him everything, but he couldn't touch more than the income." That hadn't come out right, but before she could soften her words, Rafe dumped her on the floor, slamming a fist on the desk.

"I won't accept even the income!" he spat. "Do whatever you want with it. Hoard it, use it, throw it away. But if you spend one shilling on me, I'll—" He whirled to glare out the window. His hands trembled with his effort to regain control.

Helen retreated to the fireplace, appalled at his outburst. Her first impression was that Lady Alquist was right. He didn't want her inheritance. Yet his reaction was so shockingly emotional that it seemed contrived. For some reason Rafe was beating her over the head with the notion that he was not a fortune hunter, which revived the possibility that he was. Gentlemen never displayed real emotions.

Alex had exploded into similar outrage the day she'd spotted him sneaking into the house during one of their games of hide-and-seek. Abandoning her hiding place, she had intercepted him on the terrace, only to have him angrily order her away. He'd sworn that being seen together would damage her reputation—a ridiculous charge since everyone at Sir Montrose's house party had watched them slip away together a dozen times. After he left, she had wondered if he'd used his attentions to cover secret assignations with someone else—a wife, perhaps?

Rafe finally returned to his seat. "Forgive me, sweetheart. That was uncalled for. Going through Alquist's papers has put me on edge."

She didn't believe him, but this was no time to argue. Nor could she continue discussing family, so she nodded, running her hands along his shoulders, then moving behind him to massage his neck. Touching him was becoming a habit. "What will you do about the runner's report?" She nodded toward the desk.

Rafe sharpened a pen, kicking himself for his outburst. Too much pressure was building in his head, but this wasn't the way to relieve it. He had vowed to ignore the subject of money until he figured out how to handle it. But fury had exploded before he'd even suspected its presence. Somehow he had to get rid of her fortune—without leaving her bitter.

The precise movements necessary to create a decent point tightened his control. When he again spoke, his tone was acceptably calm. "I hired a runner to look into Alquist's death. I know you don't think it's possible, but this report strengthens my fear that Steven or Dudley is responsible, so I'll have the runner resume Alquist's investigation."

"A good idea. Even if his death was an accident, we need to know more about Steven and Dudley."

"It was no accident. I'm more convinced than ever that he was murdered." And Steven was the most likely killer. That he was Alquist's cousin changed everything. Helen was not just Alquist's ward. She was family. Alquist would never condone Steven's plans, so he had to die. But Helen wasn't ready to hear that. No matter how much she hated Steven, he was family, too.

Helen paced to the fireplace and back, cupping the back of her head as if to confine pain—she was obviously hurting more than she would admit. The glow raised by their kiss had faded, leaving her cheeks paler than when she'd reached the study.

Picking up the report, she sank into a chair. "Suggest that the runner interview Mr. Garrison Waddell. He had a run-in with Dudley six years ago. Sir Harold Atchison might also help. And Lord Bromley."

"What happened?"

"I don't know, but Papa mentioned them. He had many correspondents and often shared news with us, especially when he was irritated with Dudley."

Rafe wondered if Dudley had been instrumental in sending Bromley to the country on a repairing lease.

"A thorough investigation will prepare us for the next confrontation," she continued, tapping the report. "If he is this deeply in debt, he can't afford to abandon his obsession."

"I agree. Even if someone else killed Alquist, Steven and Dudley will remain threats."

"Do you still think Goddard did it?"

"Or Hillcrest."

"Hillcrest!" She sprang to her feet. "Why would he kill Alquist?"

"He's hated him since the day we became friends—longer, really. The charge that he led me into dissipation replaced an earlier one that he encouraged Mother's intransigence—Lady Alquist often urged Mother to visit them in London." Hillcrest would never accept that Alquist had prevented Rafe from destroying himself.

"Irritation doesn't drive a rational man to murder." She shook her head.

"I don't consider him rational."

She covered his hand. "Investigate to set your mind at rest, but I will not believe that even a madman would consider that just cause for death."

"Perhaps not." Sighing, he pulled out a sheet of stationery. A quarter hour later, he sealed his letter, then pulled Helen into his arms. He needed her warmth to dispel the chill of picturing Alquist murdered. It was jolting to realize how quickly he'd come to crave her. He must be more careful. "I wish we could count on Steven to stay in town. But desperation might push him to pillage Audley so he can flee the country. We'll leave first thing in the morning," he murmured into her ear. "You were right. The only way to protect Audley is to be there."

"No." She pulled back far enough to see his face. Steven's fleeing England was the best solution. And it expanded her options. Rafe was so reticent about his family that she could only understand him by seeing them together. And he was so good at inciting passion that she must do it before he snagged her heart. "Audley is important, but it must wait a few days. If Steven steals enough to flee the country, I will rejoice. It's more important to call on your father."

"Absolutely not!" Shocked, he whirled away.

"Are you ashamed to introduce me as your wife?"

"Of course not!" He glared at her. "But I refuse to set foot in his house. I can't escape being his heir, but I won't subject you to one of his fits."

"Rafe." She paused to find the words. His fury increased her determination. If he needed help, as Lady Alquist claimed, she must meet his father. "Hillcrest might be the greatest ogre imaginable—"

"He is."

"—but that doesn't change that he is your father. You also owe Miss Pauling an explanation. Whatever your own feelings, she expected to wed you. It is bad enough that she learned the truth from a newspaper. You cannot pretend she doesn't exist."

"She won't have seen the announcement," he insisted, pacing the room. "She buries herself at Paulus Grange, rarely seeing anyone. With Pauling ill, they have no callers at all."

"Not even your father?"

He paused with one foot in the air. "Hillcrest is hardly a guest. He spends as much time at the Grange as he does at home. He already considers the place his."

"And you expect him to say nothing? He might rant at your insult, or he might calmly cancel the wedding, but he cannot ignore our marriage."

"You don't know him. He cares nothing for others. I doubt her situation will cross his mind—she is merely one of his pawns. Besides, he is so determined to win, that he might kill you so he can continue his scheme. I don't want you hurt."

She strode to the window and back. "I can look after myself, Rafe. A man as devoted to duty as Hillcrest won't harm even an unwelcome guest."

"Devoted to duty?" He laughed mirthlessly. "Hillcrest demands duty of others but cares nothing for it himself. Do you know how cold he is? When Mother contracted lung fever, he refused to summon a physician. She thrashed in agony for a week, calling repeatedly for me, but he allowed no one to comfort her. I didn't even know she was ill until her death announcement appeared in the paper a full week after her burial."

"My God." All blood drained from her face. She had to grip a chair to remain on her feet.

"I learned later that he taunted her the entire week, claiming that I was too busy pursuing frivolity to visit a dying woman. He swore that I had denounced her as a failed wife and mother and had cut her from my life. She died with his lies in her ears. So don't ever tell me that Hillcrest understands duty. I know better. The man is cold, calculating, and utterly selfish."

Helen was at his side before she even realized she'd moved. No wonder he'd gone mad. Gripping his arms, she stared into the desolation and pain swirling through his eyes. "Don't let hatred poison your heart, Rafe. It will devour the good until you become just like him. Do you want him to win this war you've been fighting?"

"No. But I won't subject you to his malice. Nor will I enter his house again."

"Then we will stay at an inn. But you must make peace with Alice. I cannot believe that *you* consider her a pawn."

"She knows I—"

"What she knows is irrelevant. You owe her an explanation to her face. She is a real person with real feelings. It is not her fault that your father plotted against you. She is as much a victim as you and must already pay the price of being jilted."

He flinched, confirming that he'd not looked beyond his own quarrel.

She nodded, gratified that he was capable of understanding. Whatever doubts remained about Rafe's feelings, she could not allow another woman to suffer as she had suffered after Alex walked away. Betrayal was the ultimate weapon, for it left emotional destruction in its wake. And questions. Thousands of questions. How many nights had she cried because she didn't know what she'd done to kill his love? Might that same flaw drive Rafe away?

She stifled the old pain and focused on making him understand. "A man can recover from a jilt, Rafe, but a woman pays forever. It doesn't matter if the betrothal was false," she added, speaking over another protest. "The world believes you jilted her. Shunning her will make it worse. Everyone will assume she is a fallen woman. They will speculate about her liaisons—how many men did she entertain? When? Where? Who? Even why. They will whisk their children out of her path lest she corrupt them, and will drop her from their invitation lists. Every libertine for miles will sniff at her door, seeking his share of her favors. Only by showing your respect and demonstrating your support can you quash such talk."

He clenched his fists. "Very well. We'll go to Hillcrest. But you won't enjoy it."

"I didn't ask to enjoy it." It was clear that she wouldn't. If Rafe was telling the truth, she would meet an abusive lord, an angry lord, and a hurt girl. None of them would welcome her. But only seeing them with Rafe would answer her questions. All she could do was pray she could live with the results. If Rafe had lied about Alice, Alex's defection would seem benign. And if he was covering more than an abusive father, she might yet regret this marriage.

Rafe scrubbed his hands over his eyes, furious that he'd conceded the argument. It made him look weak. But what else could he have done? She was right, damn her. "We need to tell Lady Alquist about our suspicions. Do you know where she is?"

"She was headed for the morning room when I left her."

"I'm not looking forward to this."

"Nor I, but she's strong. We'll face her together."

Helen's back burned where Rafe's hand steered her into the sunny morning room, reminding her of his incendiary kisses. But this was no time for lust.

"You look rested," Rafe said when Lady Alquist looked up from her needlework.

"You don't," Lady Alquist replied teasingly.

Helen's face again heated. She wished they were holding this meeting in the drawing room rather than this cheerful space. Formality would feel more appropriate.

But the subject could not be postponed. Joining Lady Alquist on the couch, she watched Rafe straighten a pair of vases, a clock, and two candlesticks on the mantel while searching for the least painful opening. "I've been sorting Alquist's papers."

Lady Alquist bit her lip. "Are they so disturbing?"

"In a way. He was more concerned about Helen than you implied."

Lady Alquist relaxed. "True. We meant to visit Audley, as I mentioned last evening. Steven was always incorrigible, even as a child. The tales Alquist told of those days—" She shook herself thoroughly. "It is best to let past cruelties die. Suffice it to say that we feared Steven's hatred of Arthur would extend to Arthur's family."

"It does," confirmed Helen. "Steven is determined to own everything Father had, regardless of value. He will let nothing stand in his way."

Rafe gestured her to silence. "Alquist demanded an audit, then hired a runner to investigate Steven and Dudley."

"I didn't know about the runner." Lady Alquist frowned. "But he was very uneasy that last week. He even complained about eyes boring into his back, as if some malevolent force was watching him. If Steven had been in town—but he wasn't, and Alquist never saw anyone."

"Perhaps he was right," said Helen, squeezing Lady Alquist's hand. *Eyes boring into his back.* Rafe's theories seemed less absurd than before. "Rafe believes the accident was odd. He makes a strong case that it was staged to cover a blow to the head."

"You mean murder?" Lady Alquist's voice squeaked as the color drained from her face.

"Perhaps," said Rafe.

"B-but who? Steven?"

"We don't yet know."

A tear slid down Lady Alquist's cheek. "I couldn't believe he had been careless. It wasn't like him." She swiped her handkerchief across her eyes. "Find the truth, Rafe. I must know."

"I'll do everything possible, though we may never—"

"I have to know." Her voice cracked. Excusing herself, she fled.

"It may take more than one runner," murmured Helen, shaken.

"We'll hire them all if we have to," Rafe choked. "She shouldn't have to go through this. An accident is hard enough to accept . . ."

He was speaking of himself as much as of Lady Alquist. Rising, Helen gathered him into her arms. "We'll find out what happened, Rafe. Grieve for him, but don't let anger blind you."

"I thought I'd accepted it." He pulled her closer, for comfort rather than passion. "But the pain on her face . . ."

And his, though she didn't say it. Instead, she held him, absorbing his tremors as he fought to hide the desolation wracking his soul. It would have been less disturbing had he broken down and cried. The control that could stave off such deep-seated grief confirmed how wretched his childhood must have been.

Helen was gratified when Rafe carried his port to the drawing room after dinner. Lady Alquist had not eaten with them, and Helen hadn't wanted to spend the evening alone. Passing much of the afternoon in a dark room to rest her head had given her too much time to brood—about Steven, about Rafe, even about Alex, who had again invaded her dreams. She must find a way to eradicate him. Surely Rafe's passion should have done so by now, for he'd taken her far beyond anything Alex had done. Or did shielding her heart keep Alex close?

She frowned.

"Lady Alquist will be fine," Rafe assured her, sipping as he stared into the fire. "But she's been through a lot these past weeks."

"I know. Adjusting to sudden change is always difficult. I castigated Fate for months after Mother's apoplexy. If I'd learned that someone had deliberately struck her down, I'm not sure I could have managed."

"You would have."

She raised her brows.

"You're strong. How else did you escape Steven?"

"I had no choice."

"Of course you did—to go or to stay. Many ladies would have stayed and made the best of things."

"Why?" His assertion startled her, for she had never considered any alternative but escape.

"Because they have been taught since birth that men are the only gender capable of rational thought. Because they prize conformity and reject contention. Because fleeing into a rough part of town would expose them to terrifying dangers. But Lady Alquist is much like you. Murder is a shock, but she will rally by morning." His voice cracked.

"Don't think about it, Rafe. Alquist would not welcome your pain. He would likely suggest that you concentrate on other things for a time. It will clear your mind. So tell me more about your mother. You mentioned that you were close."

He stiffened, but finally inhaled deeply and spoke. "She protected me from Hillcrest's temper, though doing so deflected his ire to her."

"Was he violent?" She needed to know what to expect.

"No. He can be fearsome when angry, but he never struck anyone, even Mother." Rafe joined her on the couch, stretching his legs out before him. "His tongue can blister ice, though. I did what I could to protect her, but it was never enough."

"Hardly a surprise," she murmured, stroking his hand. It turned, clasping hers in his powerful grip. "No child can successfully counter a determined adult."

He raised his brows. "I never thought of it in those terms."

"Of course not. She probably considered you her savior, welcoming your efforts. But such support cannot confer invincibility. How old were you when you first stood up for her?"

"I don't recall. Young, though. I'd found her in tears in the folly—she often spent afternoons there to escape Hillcrest."

"What happened?"

"He'd again denied her to a caller—Lady Pauling that day." He frowned. "Lady Pauling died when I was eight, so I suppose I was five or six at the time. But such petty cruelty infuriated me even then. It was Mother's right to make and receive calls. And how could he object to Lady Pauling when Lord Pauling was his closest friend? It was absurd!"

"So you confronted him."

"For all the good it did." He snorted. "He berated

me for interfering, then confined me to the schoolroom for a week and forbade Mother from visiting. She was appalled, though knowing I supported her made enduring her isolation easier."

Helen squeezed his hand.

"I could never keep Hillcrest from hurting her," he concluded. "But at least I proved him wrong—he claimed that she was an unlovable ogress and a cruel mother." His voice softened as he related other times he'd protested his mother's isolation, her persecution, her humiliation at being denied activities that were her right as a viscountess. Once he started, the words flowed so fast they tripped over one another. Agitation drove him to pace, scuffing the carpet and slapping the mantel every time he passed, his tone wavering between fury and pain, his demeanor that of the child he'd been.

Helen fought down her growing anger. Lady Alquist was right. Rafe had been trapped in his parents' war. His mother had deliberately encouraged his confrontations with Hillcrest by holding him up as her champion and applauding every effort. Loyalty was a desirable trait, but when it came to his parents, Rafe's logic faltered. He had been schooled since birth to see his mother as a saint and his father as the devil incarnate. Such engrained blindness overlooked Lady Hillcrest's manipulation and ignored that she had provoked as many battles as her husband. Had the woman showered Rafe with love only if he stood up for her?

She couldn't ask. Couldn't even hint. They might be wed, but her bond with Rafe was fragile at best. If faced with a choice between his wife and mother, he would choose his mother without a second thought. His fists were white as they fought to contain his fury at how Lady Hillcrest had suffered.

"At least she is finally at rest," she said when his recollections faded into silence. "Nothing Hillcrest does can hurt her now."

"He is twisting her memory."

"But that cannot hurt her. You know the truth, which is all that matters. And Hillcrest's persistence makes him look unbalanced. No rational man wastes time fighting a ghost."

"You have an odd view of life." He returned to the couch, sliding his arm around her shoulders to draw her against his side.

"Did Hillcrest always punish you for supporting her?" she asked, resting her head on his shoulder. She would rather watch his face but suspected he would not talk if she was looking.

"Always. He hated anyone who stood up for her."

"What about your other meetings with him. Surely you didn't discuss your mother every time."

"I can't remember a meeting that didn't include her. He summoned me only when he was furious. Since her blood flowed in my veins, every misdeed was her fault. Thomases never cause scandal. They are prudent, logical, and don't display emotion."

"I presume he delivered such tripe without anger?"

He chuckled. "Interesting point. I've never seen him any way but choleric. But I was too busy protecting myself to call him on it." He sobered. "All my most vulgar behavior was her fault. He tried every possible way to defeat that breeding, but I was perverse enough to cling to those parts of me that came from Mother."

"Hardly a surprise. You inherited stubbornness from both parents."

His hand gripped her shoulder painfully. "Mother wasn't stubborn. She was brave in the face of unspeakable cruelty!"

Silence stretched as Helen considered his words. Hillcrest's tongue had inflicted deep wounds, eroding Rafe's confidence by denigrating his worth. Even his mother's praise for his support could not counter his sense of failure. The damage would be worse if Rafe suspected deep inside that his mother had engineered those confrontations. Lady Alquist was right that he needed help. Even his London reputation had to hurt, despite his dismissal of the gossip. Anyone with his background would be sensitive to criticism.

She snuggled closer. "Was there anything else Hillcrest criticized besides your support of your mother?"

"I don't want to discuss Hillcrest tonight."

The heat in his eye told her what he would rather

address. Already it was too late to continue her probing. He was very good at deflecting conversation from topics he wished to avoid—a skill undoubtedly learned from years of battles.

She fought that melting sensation, trying to concentrate on how she reacted to her touch. But he was too adept. His kisses burned logic to a crisp. His hands untied her intentions along with her gown and stays, baring her to the waist. When his fingers rolled a nipple between them, she sank into a sensual haze and was lost.

Rafe could no longer remember why he'd decided to wait another day. Helen insisted that she was recovered. She melted the moment he touched her. Her wariness had dissipated, leaving her as eager as he.

Her fingers removed his cravat and unbuttoned his waistcoat, trailing fire in their wake. The eagerness with which she stripped off his shirt turned his bones to jelly.

As she brushed his chest, he moaned, "Touch me. More."

Fingernails rasped across his nipples, sending shivers to his toes.

He pulled her up to straddle his lap so he could kiss her breasts, nipping and sucking until she cried for more. His lips smothered the sound, then surrendered to the ecstasy of her mouth. She'd learned much about kissing in the last three days. By the time she pulled back to nibble his ear, he was shaking with need.

But he had to retain control, and not only to protect his heart. This was her first time. Unless he made it good for her, she might lose her enthusiasm.

"Rafe?" she gasped when he paused.

"Relax, sweetheart. Enjoy." Her nipples stood up, wet and hard from his earlier ministrations. Laying her down, he sucked a breast deep into his mouth while his fingers skimmed up her leg, drawing her skirt to her knee, her thigh, her hip . . .

She moaned, eagerly parting her legs so he could touch her core. Trembling, she arched into his hand.

He nearly exploded.

"Rafe!" she screamed as he slipped a finger inside her tight, tight passage.

His control trembled, but he forced his need down. He had to bind her with passion before he could relax his guard. It was the only way to protect himself.

His finger withdrew, then thrust again, drawing new moans. Circling his thumb to increase her pleasure, he kissed her long and deep.

Her gasp stole his breath.

"Don't fight it. Let it come," he murmured huskily, increasing his speed as he slid a second finger into her heat.

His shaft pressed painfully against his pantaloons, begging for release. But he had to prepare her so he could enter without pain. His own pleasure could wait a few minutes longer.

Maybe.

His tongue delved deep into her mouth, mimicking his hand as she bucked against him. "Come on, sweetheart. Let it out."

She shattered, clamping so hard on his fingers that he nearly followed her into oblivion. He swallowed her screams, reveling in their sweetness, for they were genuine, untutored, gloriously free.

Now! demanded his libido as her climax subsided. *Need her now!*

He flexed against her thigh even as his fingers fought the buttons that would free him.

Go upstairs, ordered his conscience. *The drawing room is no place for lovemaking. Not when you are a guest. You didn't even lock the door.*

But he would never make it that far. A moment's delay would drive him mad. He needed—

Helen's fingers pushed past his fumbling hand to stroke his straining shaft. Fire swept over him, shattering the last vestiges of his control. Buttons scattered—

A door slammed.

Helen froze. "Let's go upstairs, Rafe. The butler will be here any moment to bank the fire." She pushed against his chest.

He stared, fighting free of the fog encasing his brain. How could she remain so calm when he was out of control?

Out of control. He stiffened. He had vowed to remain

aloof until he was sure she could not rule him. Yet only minutes after she'd insulted his mother—she wasn't stubborn; Hillcrest had forced her to defend herself—he was rutting on her like a lust-crazed animal.

He was losing his mind. His only hope was to stay away from her until he had himself firmly in hand.

"I shouldn't have pressed you so soon. You are still too pale," he announced. "Get some sleep, Helen. I want you to enjoy lovemaking, which will be impossible if we must constantly fret about your head." Tomorrow he would be back in control, for the inevitable confrontation with Hillcrest was sure to deaden all desire.

"What's wrong, Rafe?"

"Nothing," he managed, lacing her up. "Go to bed. Tomorrow will be another long day. The roads between here and Hillcrest are not the best."

Biting off another protest, she left.

He donned his clothes and headed for the study, clasping his hands at hip level to hide the missing buttons.

What the devil was wrong with him? Tonight's loss of control exposed a problem he should have recognized sooner. Gentlemen showed a stoic face to the world, never revealing surprise or pain or fear or any other emotion. Yet for three days, his sensibilities had run rampant—furious temper, unbridled lust, anger, grief, guilt, shock . . . He'd broken down and cried. Then nearly done it again—with an audience. Since meeting Helen, he'd been so off balance that he barely recognized himself.

Something about her scrambled his wits. And not just sensually. Only three days after vowing never to return to Hillcrest, he had agreed to introduce his wife to his father.

But what else could he have done?

A long gulp drained a glass of brandy.

Helen was magnificent. Touching her incited enough heat to burn him to a crisp. What passion she would bring to his bed!

Even better, she argued like a man, her reasoning cogent and logical. There were no threats, no tears, no hysterics. She stated her case firmly and remained in control despite his reluctance. Her defense of a girl she clearly distrusted had put him to shame. She could not have been more eloquent if she'd been defending herself.

Much like his mother.

Or was she?

He frowned, appalled at the disloyalty implied by even asking the question.

He had always admired his mother for standing up to Hillcrest, but her arguments had often been barbed—not that he could blame her. Hillcrest could drive a saint to sin. Only insults had any chance of penetrating the man's thick skull.

Yet Helen didn't employ such tactics. Not even against Steven. Nor did she gloat when an opponent conceded defeat. She'd actually said *I may be wrong*—and meant it. Neither of his parents had ever uttered those words. She almost made his mother seem cruel.

He shoved the thought violently aside. Helen was destroying more than his control. Her innuendoes were warping his mind. He could not allow it to happen again. His past might not be comfortable, but his mother's innate goodness had allowed him to accept it and put it behind him. If that turned out to be a lie, he would fall apart.

His hand shook as he refilled his glass.

Helen. Concentrate on tomorrow.

Her determination was bound to cause trouble. In retrospect, he should have found another way to protect her. Marriage left him in an untenable position. His mother's need for his support had kept her firmly on his side. But Helen needed only temporary assistance. What would happen when Steven was vanquished—assuming they survived Hillcrest?

He sobered. He had vowed to protect her—a vow he took seriously. Despite her verve, Hillcrest would hurt her. His tongue was adept at probing sore spots, exploiting weakness, and slicing confidence.

Yet she was right. Honor demanded that he do what he could to help Alice. Hillcrest certainly wouldn't, and Pauling would soon be gone. Only fortune hunters would court a girl with a tarnished reputation. She deserved better.

Hillcrest's scheming had ruined an innocent. Rafe would recover, thanks to Helen. His marriage would be a nine-day wonder, but the scandal would soon blow over. By the time they returned to London, society would welcome them.

But Alice would face censure. The apology he'd wrested from the newspapers wasn't enough. He had to protect her.

Chapter Nine

May 24

*H*elen clung to Rafe's arm with both hands as the carriage approached Hillcrest Manor. It didn't help her nerves that he was more tense than she. He'd been silent for the last hour, shrinking deeper into himself with every passing mile. His confidence had collapsed, turning his face white and hunching his shoulders until he resembled a frightened child.

Fury stiffened her spine. No father should mistreat his son so badly. She must help him break free. But helping him would be impossible until she cracked the wall he'd built between himself and others, which he was defending with all his might.

She still wasn't sure what had happened last evening. He'd been well on his way to bedding her when he'd suddenly pulled back, announced that she was too pale, and packed her off to bed alone. He'd been furious, though not at her. When she'd tried to ask what she'd done wrong, he'd refused to discuss it. Shades of Alex, who had left without telling her why.

If Rafe was one of those men who avoided anyone who seemed ill, he would have to adjust. She was naturally pale. And the sooner he accepted that, the better.

Her plan was simple. Remain by his side to keep Hillcrest civil, then join him in bed, consummating their marriage to forge the next link in their partnership. It was time he accepted that she was not a fragile flower.

She'd learned enough from Alex and from her encounters with Rafe that seducing him should be easy. He was as susceptible to stroking as she was, and a rake of his reputation must be frustrated enough by now to respond to any overture.

Anticipation heated her cheeks, but she forced her mind back to business. Before they could go to bed, they must face Hillcrest.

The Manor's grounds looked stark despite the warmth imparted by the setting sun. The house seemed equally gloomy, rising from an unadorned hilltop like a wart. Cold gray stone. Flat façade lacking either gothic arches or Palladian pediments. It fairly shouted repulsion and would better fit barren Dartmoor than the prosperous countryside near London. Hillcrest's housekeeper would never face curious travelers seeking a tour. Growing up in such uncompromising surroundings could explain Hillcrest's rigidity. But what had it done to Rafe? His insouciant-gentleman act covered deep sensitivity.

"I thought you said your mother loved flowers," she said, forcing Rafe from his long abstraction. "This is the most barren estate I've ever seen."

"Hillcrest's revenge." His voice cracked. "The house was always plain, but when I was a boy, the grounds were lush with greenery. The rose garden was more than a century old and renowned for its variety, and Grandfather's Italian garden was the envy of the neighborhood." He pointed to a second hill. "The folly sat on that rise, with a commanding view of the park. There was a lake, fallow deer, a small maze . . ."

"What did he do?" She stroked his arm, but he had retreated to the past and didn't notice.

"Mother spent hours with the head gardener planning improvements that turned the park into a showplace. The moment she died, Hillcrest destroyed everything she'd touched. And not just outside. The house is more austere than a monk's cell these days, and just as gray."

Helen shivered. Despite Lady Alquist's warning, she hadn't realized how deep Hillcrest's antagonism ran. Was it hatred or wounded pride? Had he spent thirty years lashing out because poverty had forced him to beg?

But it was too late to turn back. A footman opened the door as the carriage rocked to a halt. "You made it, Master Rafe," he said, smiling. "I knew you would. His Nibs couldn't hold back the announcement this time."

Rafe's head snapped up as he stepped onto the drive. "What announcement, Ned?"

Ned looked shocked. "You didn't know? Lord Pauling is dead. The interment is tomorrow morning. But why are you here, then?"

"To introduce my wife."

Ned gaped as Helen alighted from the carriage.

"Helen, this is Ned," said Rafe, sliding a possessive arm around her shoulders. "Ned is the only servant you can trust. His warnings saved me from grief too many times to count."

"I'm glad someone kept an eye on him," said Helen lightly as Ned's wrinkled face turned red. "It's a pleasure to meet you. Thank you for helping to raise a fine gentleman."

"I didn't—" Ned's face grew redder.

"You did," said Rafe firmly.

Ned pulled himself together. "Welcome to Hillcrest, Mrs. Thomas." He bowed deep enough for royalty, then lowered his voice. "Beware, sir. His Nibs is in rare form today. If he's not expecting you, I doubt you'll find welcome."

"He'll be in rarer form by the time we finish," vowed Rafe. "Perhaps you should busy yourself in a cellar or attic. He'll not welcome your letting us in."

"He would take out his anger on a servant?" whispered Helen as Ned slipped away.

"It's been known, though to give him his due, he is generally fair to servants—when not in a temper. New employees quickly learn to gauge his moods. We can still leave," he added hopefully. "I don't like exposing you to his spite."

"Enough, Rafe. Duty demands that you introduce me. And now there is a burial to attend. Miss Pauling will be doubly hurt." Losing her father and her betrothed in the same week might have driven her to despair.

Gripping Rafe's arm, Helen urged him up the steps.

A man's voice boomed from inside. "Why is that door

open, Mason? No more callers! The ghouls have no proper feeling. They come only to gloat at my misfortune."

"B-but, my lord . . ." sputtered the butler, gesturing as Rafe and Helen crossed the threshold into an entrance hall that differed from a working class boarding house only in size—plain wood floor, painted walls, and a flat plaster ceiling. Two chairs and a pier table were the only furnishing. A candle sat unlit on the table next to a small mound of calling cards and a cane.

The setting sun streamed through the open door, illuminating a gray-haired man standing three steps up a broad staircase. His face turned purple, bulging the veins in his neck. "I knew your word was worthless," he said coldly. "But returning was a waste of time. Be gone with you. I don't allow criminals under my roof."

"Marriage is hardly a crime," said Rafe lightly, though his voice trembled. "People commit it every day."

Helen swallowed hard. Rafe was falling apart before her eyes. His arm shook beneath her hand as his shoulders slumped. Was it Hillcrest he feared, or something else?

Hillcrest gripped the banister. "You murdered Pauling!"

Rafe said nothing.

Helen dug her fingers into his arm, trying to break the spell. His reaction was appalling.

Her efforts seemed to help, for he straightened. "Only four days ago, you swore he was at death's door, sir. It is no surprise to find him gone."

Hillcrest glared. "You fool! They gave him three months, but you stole that. One glance at your cursed lies killed him." His voice broke.

"I never lie!" Rafe choked, blanching.

Hillcrest gripped the banister. "How dare you contradict me? You've lied every day of your life, just like your bedamned mother—refusing to admit your transgressions, spouting false charges against me, ignoring every duty expected of you. Why was I cursed with such a . . ."

Helen quit listening, too concerned about Rafe to attend to Hillcrest's dramatics. She could feel Rafe retreating mentally. Why didn't he stand up to Hillcrest?

He was an intelligent, agile debater with charm enough to convince the devil to repent, according to society.

Hillcrest was clearly insane. Far worse than Lady Alquist had intimated. His treatment of Rafe was inexcusable. Common felons received more respect than he accorded his son. Her anger built until her fingers again bit into Rafe's arm.

He flinched, but pulled himself up to address Hillcrest. "This rant is pointless and only demonstrates how little you know me. I value truth above all else."

"Hah! What does a hedonistic wastrel know of truth? First you kill my one true friend. Then you come to gloat over my pain."

"I didn't know he'd died until just now—"

"Get out! And take your whore with you."

Helen gasped as Hillcrest leaped from the stairs. She hadn't expected the confrontation to turn physical. Even Rafe claimed his father wasn't violent. But murder blazed in the man's eyes. She stepped forward to provide a buffer.

Hillcrest raised a fist.

Rafe thrust her behind him. "Apologize, Hillcrest," he snapped, shaking off his lethargy. "I'll not tolerate insults to my wife."

"This jest has gone far enough," snarled Hillcrest, shoving Rafe aside so he could drag Helen toward the door. "The farce is over, bitch. I don't know how much he paid you to impersonate a bride, but your job is done."

"You—" began Helen.

"Unhand her!" Rafe twisted Hillcrest's fingers from Helen's arm. "You are making a fool of yourself."

"Don't touch me." Hillcrest jerked free. "Throw the doxy out, Mason, then summon the rector. The only way to salvage our reputations is an immediate wedding."

Helen stepped between them. "Is he always delusional, Rafe?" Effort kept her voice light.

Rafe matched her tone, looking more like himself. "I fear so. He thinks nothing matters but his own selfish whims. Stay out of this, Mason," he added, glaring until the butler backed into a corner. "Helen, though I'm ashamed to acknowledge this madman, he is my father. My wife, Hillcrest. Live with it."

Hillcrest sputtered for a long moment. "My God!" he finally managed, backing a pace. "I'd hoped she was an actress, but you actually married the first girl you saw. Of all the idiotic things you have done, this takes the cake. How could I have spawned such a ne'er-do-well?"

Helen froze. *Married the first girl you saw.* Was that why he'd offered? No wonder Hillcrest was appalled. What hope did a marriage conceived in fury and wine have of success?

Yet she couldn't believe Rafe was irresponsible. Lady Alquist would have spotted such a flaw. And fretting over the why of their marriage was less important than addressing their future.

". . . care for nothing but yourself!" shouted Hillcrest. He was well into a more vehement diatribe than before. "You cost me the best friend a man could have."

Rafe's scars slashed white across his red face. Clearly temper had banished his earlier fears. "If anything, it was your own greed for the Grange that killed him, Hillcrest."

"How sharper than a serpent's tooth—"

"Don't quote that drivel to me. You never wanted a son, grateful or otherwise. I was merely a prize for you and Mother to fight over."

"You are too worthless to be anyone's prize." Hillcrest growled, reaching for his walking stick.

Shock flared in Rafe's eyes.

Helen knocked the stick aside, too aware of the damage it could cause.

"You've destroyed Alice," Hillcrest continued. "She's been in tears for days."

Rafe glared. "Of course, she's in tears. Her father is dead. Did you even tell her he was ailing?"

"She cries for you!" shouted Hillcrest. "You broke her heart with your callous—"

"Balderdash! I've repudiated that connection for years—as you well know. If—"

Helen stopped listening, wishing she'd not insisted on coming. Rafe's childhood had been worse than she'd feared. The confrontation was illuminating, but at what cost?

Rafe made no attempt to be conciliatory. When he listened at all—which wasn't often—he argued every statement. If that was his usual defense against opposition, it would be impossible to reason with him.

"You have legal and moral obligations to Alice," insisted Hillcrest, pulling her attention back to the confrontation. "She is the perfect—"

Rafe laughed rudely. "Perfect? Why? Because she doesn't tell you what a blithering idiot you are? Alice is the most insipid female I know. She hasn't two thoughts to rub together and can't make the simplest decision for herself. An infant needs less oversight. There is nothing about her I find attractive. Five minutes in her company is enough to drive me mad."

Helen snapped her mouth shut. Rafe might turn stubbornly passive when lectured, but some topics triggered outbursts emotional enough to make most gentlemen cringe. Yesterday it had been her fortune. Today it was Alice. Was he trying to convince Hillcrest or himself? Either would oppose the other just to be contrary—a lesson Rafe had learned from his mother.

"You are cruel, indeed," said Hillcrest through gritted teeth. "You take pride in hurting her, don't you? You killed her father, her love, her dreams of family, her—"

Rafe released a weary sigh. "I have repudiated this match a thousand times, yet you refuse to look beyond your own greed. Did your marriage teach you nothing? Mother's dowry wasn't worth forcing oil and water to mix."

"I am sick to death of how you twist Catherine's memory to justify your perversity." Hillcrest sprang.

Helen pulled Rafe from his path. "He's trying to goad you, Rafe. Ignore him."

Rafe inhaled deeply. "Twisting memory is your habit, Hillcrest," he finally managed. "I've long marveled that Pauling considered you a friend when you've fought so long and hard to destroy his daughter."

"Destroy his daughter? I would have made her a viscountess. What more could she want?"

"A husband who respected her."

"Pah! All a female needs is a title she can flaunt before the neighbors."

"If you believe that, then you are more delusional than I thought. Rank will never atone for a husband who despises her. Not that it matters. I am no longer available. Wed her yourself if you think she needs a title—though I doubt she would have you."

"Arrogant fool! How can you think marriage is more than a breeding contract? Alice has the breeding to be a viscountess. You could get her with child, then never see her again if that's what you want. Duty demands obedience to your father."

Helen couldn't believe her ears.

"You forfeited my allegiance when you rejected me," snapped Rafe, scowling. "My life is mine, to live as I please."

"So you wed the first whore who propositioned you," growled Hillcrest. "Pitiful. I'll cut you from my will and smear your name from the Channel to the Highlands. You'll be laughed from your clubs for blackening your blood and barred from your favorite brothels because you can't pay."

Helen stiffened.

Rafe pulled her against his side. "Your threats ceased working long ago, Hillcrest. I don't need your money."

"Nor do I," added Helen. It was time to end this confrontation. Rafe was ready to collapse. He held her more for his own support than to protect her, sagging so heavily she could barely stand. Hillcrest held a huge advantage in this war, for his purpose was to rule. Rafe sought recognition, which left him vulnerable to cruelty.

Hillcrest snorted. "Drop the pretense, girl. My secretary went to London yesterday, so I know all about you. Everyone is laughing because a scheming whore tricked this drunken idiot into wedding her."

"I can't imagine why. My breeding is the same as your wife's."

"Another liar. But it's over. I won't pay a groat to buy you off."

"You need a new secretary," said Rafe shortly. "Yours is as delusional as you are. My wife is a lady."

"Hah! She is still pulling the wool over your eyes. Not

that it matters." His chin rose as he glared at Helen. "Using a false name invalidates any marriage. Forget about a life of ease, girl. I won't tolerate a harlot in the family. My fortune will go to a benevolent society. He hasn't a groat of his own, so you'll find yourself back on the streets before you know it."

Hillcrest's determined insults were the last straw for Helen's temper. Raising her chin, she glared. "I didn't believe Rafe when he declared you a fool, but he's right. You haven't the brains of a flea." She shook off Rafe's arm and advanced, shoving Hillcrest in the chest, amazed to find him an inch shorter than she was—his belligerence made him seem larger.

"I told you she was a vulgar baggage," chortled Hillcrest. "Maybe now you'll listen to older, wiser heads." He spat in her face. "Peddle your wares somewhere else, girl."

She rammed him into the banister, then scraped the spittle onto his coat. "Do you honestly believe I care about your money or this pitiful estate?"

"Pitiful!" he sputtered. "Hillcrest produces two thousand a year."

"Paltry." She shook her head. "My estate brings in ten, and my investments return four times that. And that is after expenses."

"A Cit!" Hillcrest exclaimed, horrified.

"No. The heir of Sir Arthur St. James. I could buy this place a hundred times over—not that I'd want it. This has to be the most unattractive house I've ever seen."

He straightened. "A pretty tale, but females haven't the wit to handle money. I doubt you'd recognize decent land from waste."

"You think so?" Her voice sharpened. "If those fields we passed near the gates are yours, I'd say you were the one lacking wit. They are obviously on a two-year rotation, an agricultural plan discredited years ago. Changing to a three-year rotation would improve your yields by at least a quarter. But since the cattle and sheep look healthy, your claim of two thousand a year means you probably control about four hundred acres."

"Rafe told you that."

Helen ignored him, hardly pausing for breath. "Now Audley Court covers two thousand acres, including four villages, fifty tenants, and the most fertile land in Somerset. I've run it for four years—and done very well, despite the depredations of weather and war. We doubled the yields by adopting modern methods."

Rafe's head spun as she listed crops, animals, and local businesses. Hillcrest's jaw hung.

"But most of my fortune derives from investment," she continued over Hillcrest's new attempt to interrupt. "I own controlling shares in three import companies and housing crescents in London, Birmingham, Bath, and Exeter. Then there are minority stakes in two coal mines, a woolen mill . . ."

Rafe stared. Helen knew to the penny what should be in her trust. The sums were staggering—and made his heart drop further with every word. He had assumed from Steven's rant that her trust was worth forty thousand. Instead, it returned forty—with Goddard in charge, for God's sake—so it had to be worth at least half a million. Probably more. She was right. His own fortune and Hillcrest's were paltry in comparison. How could they ever get along when she wielded such a weapon?

His mind boggled. No wonder Steven was obsessed. And here she was acting the fishwife as she slapped Hillcrest in the face with her fortune—just as his mother had always done.

He shook his head over his phraseology, which couldn't be right. His mother had been a saint, pushed beyond endurance by the unfeeling monster she'd married.

Helen gestured, pulling her pelisse tight across that generous bosom. Despite his growing terror of her wealth, lust stirred. She looked magnificent in a temper. And she'd achieved more than he or his mother had ever managed. Her barrage of figures had turned Hillcrest to stone.

Rafe drew her into his arms. "There is no point in continuing," he murmured, rubbing her back. "He's deaf. Let's go."

"No." She pulled herself together. "We've come this far. Let's finish our business. It is nearly dark, and you still have to see Alice. We will spend the night and attend Pauling's interment in the morning."

"Spend the night?" Hillcrest shook himself and glared at Rafe. "If you must. But you will leave tomorrow and never return. Hillcrest Manor will be an empty shell by the time you inherit it. I'll make sure of that." He left them standing in the hall.

"This way," said Mason.

"Go with him," said Rafe. "I need air."

Helen nodded, grateful for the respite. She needed to think. Losing her temper had been a mistake. Rafe now knew the extent of her trust. She'd seen his glazed eyes. He couldn't be more shocked if her head had sprouted snakes like Medusa's. Whether he despised it or coveted it, her inheritance would clearly cause trouble.

Several servants whisked out of sight as she followed Mason to a guest room. Her face heated. Losing her temper in front of Hillcrest's staff was embarrassing. She hoped it didn't cause new trouble for Rafe.

His rift with Hillcrest was worse than she'd expected. Even Lady Alquist underestimated the problem. If this was usual—and she had no reason to think it wasn't—Rafe might never learn to live in harmony with others. Those who faced constant battles knew nothing but fighting. She could only pray that his willingness to compromise was real. If not, they were doomed.

Rafe stumbled out to the terrace, so many thoughts crowding his head that he felt drunk.

He'd jumped blindly into his worse nightmare—a wife who must be one of the wealthiest individuals in England, who held absolute control over her fortune, and who wasn't afraid to wield that fortune to win an argument.

His eyes stung.

There was no way he could live with her. Either he would spend every day in battles worse than his mother had endured or he would turn into a cipher, meekly following orders while his own persona shrank into nothingness.

Intolerable.

He fled to the end of the terrace, keeping his eyes on

the flagstones so he couldn't see the desolation that had replaced his mother's gardens.

Every instinct urged him to return to town immediately, yet he'd never broken a vow in his life and didn't want to start now. He'd vowed to restore Alice's reputation, to protect Helen from Steven, to take her *for richer or poorer* . . .

The words of the marriage service, unnoticed at the time, now made his skin crawl. But he could satisfy the vow from a distance.

You can also achieve the rest from afar.

He considered the possibility, then relaxed. It was the perfect solution. By returning to town, he could eliminate society's suspicion of Alice—he no longer cared if the truth tarnished Hillcrest's reputation—then watch Steven and Dudley so they couldn't harm Helen. She could go home and look after her tenants. Running her empire would keep her too busy to bother him.

Approaching footsteps whirled him around. His snarl turned to a frown when he identified Alice. "What the devil are you doing here?"

"I live here now. Lord Hillcrest is my guardian."

Married the first girl you saw.

Helen paced her depressing bedroom as she reviewed Rafe's actions from the moment she'd run him down four days ago. But she couldn't believe that he had acted solely from drunken fury. He had been far too attentive, touching her whenever possible, as if he couldn't get enough of her. His eyes brightened whenever she joined him. There had to be an element of genuine interest driving him, which gave them a starting point toward creating a partnership. It might not be easy, but at least it was possible.

Relieved, she set aside her fears over her marriage. The London rumors were a more urgent problem. Hillcrest's secretary would not have fabricated such stories even to support an employer's prejudice. Hillcrest might have exaggerated the details, but not by much. So the tale had to be on every tongue. But why would society believe that someone had stolen her identity solely to trick Rafe into mar—

Rafe's shout penetrated the window. Angry fragments followed. "—how could you . . . marriage . . . you know I . . ."

Fearful that Hillcrest had again accosted him, Helen parted the curtains and looked down at the terrace. Darkness had fallen, but light from a window illuminated Rafe leaning against the balustrade. A petite blonde laid her hand on his chest—one of the females who had listened to the confrontation in the hall. As Helen watched, Rafe pulled the girl into his arms and kissed her. Tension flowed from his shoulders.

Not a servant.

Shifting his hold, he led her onto the lawn, pulling her against his side in the same protective, possessive gesture he used with his wife—and with Lady Alquist, she realized, cursing. It was likely a habit he employed with every female he met, and thus meant nothing. His head bent to the girl's in earnest conversation.

Helen watched until they disappeared around the corner of the house, then collapsed into a chair.

Betrayed. Again. That had to be Alice.

So it had all been a lie. Even his caresses had been a rake's lies. He couldn't go near a female without touching her, holding her, flattering her. He needed affection and adoration, and did everything possible to elicit them. But it meant nothing. Except with Alice, whom he'd known all his life.

Tears welled as Clara's fate flashed through her mind. Despite his claims, Rafe must also love the girl next door. He might protest the match out of habit—he'd likely never accepted a Hillcrest suggestion in his life—but that didn't mean he opposed it. As for Alice, she'd been furious, but his explanation had satisfied her.

Sealed with a kiss. Now they were off planning—or perhaps celebrating. Alice must know that Rafe could charm women into anything. He was a composite of every seductive wastrel her father had warned her against. Had he opposed this visit because he feared she would discover the truth? He'd grabbed the first opportunity to slip away and meet Alice in private.

Horrified, she recalled his truncated comment when

she'd told him that Alice deserved an explanation. *She knows I—*

What did Alice know? That he loved her? That he would wed her in a few weeks or months? That his sudden marriage was a temporary setback in their plans, but worth the wait?

"I should have known better." Tears streamed down her face. "Never trust a charmer. They care only for themselves."

The pain worsened. Why did she attract cads? Alex. Dudley. Rafe. Had her mother been right that only helpless, fluttery females won men's respect?

She was too tall to appear helpless and too independent to try. Nor could she fake naïveté or indecision. Her only asset was her fortune, which she'd stupidly disclosed. That must have won Alice's agreement. Rafe had offered to lay it at her feet if she exercised patience. Though Clara's husband had succeeded in weeks, Rafe must know it would take longer—he had to break her trust—but he would be confident of success. After all, she melted at his every touch.

Locking the door, she buried her head in a pillow and cried for all she'd lost. Alex had stolen her reputation, isolating her from friends until her parents had remained her only confidants. Their deaths had left her utterly alone, but with a purpose to sustain her—until Steven stole both her purpose and her independence. Now Rafe had stolen her last hope of building a loving family for the future.

She had no one. Yet surrender was impossible. Steven still threatened her dependents. Somehow, she must protect herself from Rafe while defeating Steven and defending Audley.

Examining her options convinced her that she could not turn back the clock. For better or worse, Rafe was her husband. Marriage was forever, tying them together until death.

On a positive note, Rafe could not harm her while she controlled her trust. As long as she refused to break it . . .

He would be furious, of course, and would do his best

to coerce her. So she must guard her heart more assiduously than ever. Forming an attachment could give him a lever against her.

She must also keep Rafe's true nature from Lady Alquist. Learning that her beloved nephew was a dishonorable cad would add to the grief she already suffered. And to no purpose. He honestly cared for his aunt, so her illusions hurt no one.

Helen frowned. Could she have misconstrued that scene on the terrace? Lady Alquist knew Rafe far better than she did.

She reviewed every nuance but could find no other explanation. His easy intimacy surpassed what even lovers revealed in public. He must be pressing every advantage to bend Alice to his will. His relief when Alice accepted his plan had been palpable.

So her best course was to use Rafe to stop Steven and Dudley, then pray that time would produce a compromise they could live with. Alice would have to find a new beau, and Rafe would have to accept his marriage. Beyond that, she couldn't see, though it was more than likely that Rafe would resume his London life, leaving her at Audley.

In the meantime, she needed time to retrench. Merely looking at him quickened her breath and made her fingers itch to explore his hard muscles and silky hair. But desire left her susceptible to his blandishments and vulnerable to searing pain when next he betrayed her. It also interfered with her logic, so seducing him must wait until she could control her emotions. She would not avoid her duty to provide his heir, but letting him dazzle her with passion could only lead to trouble.

Rafe's hand shook as he closed his bedroom door with a soft click. He wanted to slam it, but he wouldn't give Helen the satisfaction of knowing how much she'd riled him.

Locked out.

He should never have brought her here. As he'd feared, Hillcrest's tirade had turned her against him. She wouldn't even answer his knock.

And it's your own fault.

He tossed his coat over a chair, then frowned as he untied his cravat. For the first time in his life, he examined a confrontation with Hillcrest through impartial eyes. What had she seen?

Two angry men throwing insults at each other.

Two dogs fighting over a bone so worn it had long since given up all nourishment.

Two squabbling children.

His knees collapsed, dropping him into a chair. All his life he'd yearned for respect, praying that Hillcrest might finally treat him like an adult. Yet how could he expect it when he turned into a sullen child at every meeting? It made him look weak. Even Helen had retained enough control to counter Hillcrest's tirade with logic.

It was time to give up on Hillcrest. Since childhood, he'd believed that walking away would betray his mother and brand him a coward. But Helen was right that his mother was beyond caring. Let Hillcrest exert his petty tyranny over the manor. It no longer mattered. Only Helen's respect mattered now, so he would forget Hillcrest and build a new life elsewhere.

He mulled Hillcrest's latest diatribe as he stripped off his clothes—he'd been too furious to think about the charges earlier. Hillcrest's depiction of Helen bothered him, for it could not be the product of Hillcrest's warped imagination. Thus it must be real, which made it dangerous.

He had vowed to protect her. Sending her home while he went to London was cowardly and would seriously undermine his claim of a love match. As his wife, she deserved his support. So they had to stay together while he exposed the London rumors. Only when her reputation was safe could they address the problem of her inheritance.

Chapter Ten

May 25

*W*ind whipped through the churchyard, ripping leaves from the trees and petals from the flowers planted on several graves. Clouds boiled overhead, promising rain to disguise any tears and wash away any regrets. It was the perfect day for a burial.

Clutching her skirts to keep her legs decently covered, Helen watched Alice as men slid Pauling's body into the family crypt. The girl was beautiful—blonde, petite, and fragile as a porcelain doll. Hillcrest remained at her side, ready to catch her if she swooned.

Helen's chest tightened. She'd been a fool to jump into marriage knowing nothing about Rafe. How could he not love sweet Alice? The girl was every man's ideal wife—and everything Helen was not.

You're jealous, whispered her conscience.

Never! She stiffened. Jealousy implied an attachment, but she did not know him well enough to be attached. *Married the first girl you saw.* No man of sense would consider uttering such a vow, let alone acting on it. Irresponsibility was no basis for marriage. She would have been better off eloping with any of the fortune hunters her father had turned away.

Rafe rested his hand on her back, but she stepped out of reach. He'd been furious to find her door locked last night and had been trying to charm her ever since. She couldn't let him succeed. Pain left her too susceptible.

Hillcrest pulled Alice against him, letting the wind wrap his cloak about her.

Rafe stiffened.

That was jealousy. His eyes hadn't left Alice since she'd stepped from her carriage. Every time Hillcrest brushed against her, Rafe tensed. Despite challenging Hillcrest to marry Alice himself, he clearly hadn't meant it.

Hillcrest whispered in Alice's ear.

Rafe growled.

She nearly warned him to keep his jealousy hidden, but she didn't trust his control. He seemed on the verge of another temper fit. Arguing in a churchyard would shame them both.

Alice laid a lily atop the shroud, then accompanied Hillcrest to her carriage.

"It's over," said Rafe, taking Helen's arm. "We can leave." Hillcrest had made it plain that they were not to return, not even to share the customary funeral meats. "Thank you for insisting we come," he added as they picked their way toward his carriage, which was the last one in line. The other mourners were already pulling away. "Pauling was a decent man. Not overly bright, but he did his best."

"There are worse epitaphs," said Helen noncommittally.

"Like Hillcrest's." Rafe opened the carriage door. "The best description is, *A petty tyrant who forced his views on everyone he met.*"

Helen ignored his bitterness. "We need to—"

"We need to return to London," Rafe said, speaking over her.

"No!"

He shook his head. "You heard Hillcrest. There are rumors reviling you."

"Which we cannot remedy just yet. No one knows me, and no one will believe you."

"Absurd! I am a gentleman. Gentlemen don't lie."

"Think, Rafe. The tales claim you were duped by a scheming courtesan who stole my identity, passed herself off as an innocent, then pressed for marriage after you drunkenly seduced her. Considering your reputation, who will believe your denials? And since no one in town knows me, they won't believe me, either. Keeping Steven away from Audley is more important than the rumors—and requires that I study the estate books."

"You don't understand society. Once gossip takes hold, it is impossible to eradicate," insisted Rafe. "You will forever be suspect. Do you want to face cuts? Society is brutal to anyone who breaks the rules. Our only hope is to nip this tale in the bud."

She could write a book about society's brutality, but she refused to let him distract her. "Once Lady Alquist vouches for my identity, there will be no gossip. As soon as Steven is under arrest, she can inform her friends about her goddaughter's marriage to her nephew. Her introduction will settle the matter in a trice, banishing these rumors for all time."

"Why wait?"

Sidestepping a windblown newspaper, she cursed gentlemen's one-track minds. "Steven must have started the story, probably by decrying that a prostitute appropriated his niece's good name. He will be furious if Lady Alquist discredits him. I won't put her at his mercy. We have not acquitted him of ordering Alquist's death."

"You are overreacting," he said stubbornly. "No gentleman would harm a lady. We need to show ourselves in town. One day should do it. Then we can leave for Audley."

"No." She scowled. A man could laugh off his gaming and would actually preen if thought a rake, but no man liked being called gullible. And Rafe was more sensitive than most.

Yet she feared that more than concern for his reputation underlay his insistence. His eyes had followed Alice's carriage during their entire exchange. If Alice had given him some errand to town, he might use the rumors as an excuse to execute it.

It was time to remind him whose priorities took precedence. "If you insist on returning to London, I can't stop you, but I am going to Audley. I owe it to my tenants to protect them, and I owe it to Papa to carry out his last wishes. Stopping Steven was uppermost in his mind."

Alice's carriage disappeared over a rise. Rafe glared. "A wife's duty is to obey—"

An angry voice spun him around as Hillcrest dragged Ned behind a crypt.

"I don't countenance traitors!" Hillcrest snapped, loud enough to be heard throughout the village. "You knew I had barred entrance to that wastrel, yet you allowed him inside. Be gone with you. There will be no reference. Mason will send your things to the Green Bottle."

Ned blanched.

"Stay here," Rafe ordered as Hillcrest strode to his horse and sped away.

Rafe was gone before Helen could reply, but she wasn't about to meekly follow orders. *Obey*, indeed! She set out after him.

Rafe caught up with Ned near the church and pressed a letter into his hands.

Helen frowned.

"Alice . . . help . . ." The wind drowned the rest.

Helen tripped over a root, falling against a gravestone. ". . . protect . . . Alice . . . Hillcrest . . ."

She rubbed her shin. Rafe was arranging for Ned to look after Alice—and probably carry out her commission to London, too. When he passed over a heavy purse, she trudged wearily back to the carriage. Rafe might accompany her in body, but his spirit was clearly elsewhere. Finding a compromise they could live with had seemed possible last night. Now she wondered. But she had to try.

Alex Portland slowed as he rode into the village of Hillcrest. Another hour and he would be home. The war was over, his last assignment complete. He could finally retire.

At least this mission had been a success. He glared at the Green Bottle, recalling two wasted weeks in its wretched taproom. All for naught—because of Lord Hillcrest.

On the thought, the viscount burst from the churchyard, nearly running him down.

Alex swore.

"You!" hissed Hillcrest, dragging his horse to a halt. "I told you never to show your face here again. We don't need scoundrels hereabouts. We're peaceful folk."

"Meddlers, morelike," snapped Alex, giving tongue to the fury he'd fought for two years. Doffing his hat, he nodded in a parody of a bow. "Allow me to introduce myself. The honorable Alex Portland, third son of the Earl of Stratford and chief investigator for His Majesty's Home Office. Your high-handed meddling cost England thousands of lives. If it had been my choice, you would have been arrested for treason." He shoved his hat in place as a gust of wind tried to rip it from his hand.

"How dare—" sputtered Hillcrest.

"Take your posturing elsewhere." Alex scowled so fiercely that Hillcrest backed his horse into a wall. "By waylaying me that day, you let the French courier I was following escape."

"But— He said you were a highwayman!"

"*He?*" He pressed his horse closer, forcing Hillcrest into a post. "Was it Harriman?"

Hillcrest nodded.

"And you never questioned why he complained to you instead of the magistrate."

"It was my land!"

"Fool! Harriman was the traitor I was seeking. Duping you protected his mission—he knew you were too stupid to question his tale. If you'd consulted the magistrate, you would have learned the truth. Instead, you jumped me, letting the courier escape and prolonging the war at least a year. It took us another six months to identify Harriman and execute him."

"I—"

Alex cut him off. "Go home. Stop interfering in things you don't understand. And the next time someone runs to you with a tale, investigate before accepting it. I've never met a more credulous idiot. You accept even ridiculous charges as gospel." He pushed his horse to a canter, leaving Hillcrest behind.

Damn, but he hated that family. Hillcrest had precipitated the worst failure of his career, and the son was an even bigger thorn in his side.

"Rafael Thomas." The name was bitter on his tongue.

Thomas had nearly destroyed him ten years earlier, fleecing him of every penny he had and more. Ten thousand guineas stolen by a pariah who wallowed in idle pleasure while worthier gentlemen risked life and limb defending England from those who would destroy it.

Fury raged so hotly he could barely see. By the time he controlled it, the village was out of sight, so he slowed to a walk. But he couldn't slow the bitter memories.

Thomas had done more than rob him. He'd turned his family against him by spreading lies about his character, then added new humiliation by blackballing him from Hasley's club. The last straw was stealing his mistress, then accusing him of fighting a duel over her. The incident had nearly cost Alex his position at the Home Office.

He suppressed echoes of Sidmouth's dressing-down—the Home Secretary had scoffed at claims the tale was false.

It was done. Thomas wasn't worth a moment's thought. Only the future mattered now. His last assignment was complete. Ten years of service would end next week, allowing him to marry, set up his nursery, and embark on a new life. His betrothed was waiting.

Green eyes wavered before him, smiling beneath a crown of auburn curls. He passed Hillcrest Manor's gatehouse without seeing it, sunk in memories of her sweet kisses.

"That's him," growled a voice as two horses burst from a copse.

The movement shattered Alex's reverie.

"Damnation," he gasped, ducking a club. He'd let down his guard too soon.

Spurring his horse to a gallop, he fumbled in a pocket for his pistol. He always carried one when traveling, but he'd not kept it ready today. Napoleon's abdication should have sent French supporters into hiding.

His shot missed. "Double damnation!"

The men surged closer, one on either side. Their horses were fresh, while his had already traveled fifteen miles today.

The blond again swung his club, missing when Alex hauled his horse to a stop. But before he could wheel for the village, they were on him, dragging him to the ground.

He elbowed the dark man in the jaw, then landed a blow to the blond's stomach and a kick to his groin. But he was outnumbered. As fists slammed into his body, he could only curl up and protect his head.

"Why?" he choked through the bile churning into his throat.

" 'E said t' make ye suffer afore we killed ye, Mr. Thomas."

The dark man laughed.

I'm not Thomas, Alex tried to scream, but no sound emerged. Darkness descended. He'd never see Helen again.

Helen stared through the carriage window as they left the churchyard behind, biting her lip as she searched for an appropriate opening. Since returning to the carriage, Rafe's demeanor had again changed, reviving yesterday's attentiveness. It had to be an act. Somehow they must move beyond such posturing.

The problem was how to convince him to take her seriously—and guard herself while doing it. His glib tongue could make black seem white. Charmers could glide through life without paying penalties. Like Alex. He'd never suffered a moment for abandoning her.

Now she was wed to another charmer whose words contradicted his deeds. She glared at Rafe. Look at him sprawled across the opposite seat as if he hadn't a care in the world. Wind-tossed hair. Loose cravat. One foot propped in the corner.

He appeared dangerously virile.

She forced her gaze outside, watching the last cottage slide past.

"I'm sorry you had to endure Hillcrest's vicious tongue," Rafe said, breaking the silence.

"It was enlightening—*married the first girl you saw.*"

"Damn him!" he cursed. "It wasn't like—" He shook his head. "Well, maybe it was a bit, but not really. I mean—"

She watched him flounder, astonished. No glib tongue here. He seemed honestly embarrassed. Which he should be. Who in his right mind would set out to wed the first girl he saw? "Am I supposed to be flattered?"

"I wasn't serious. I never intended— And you weren't the first anyway."

"Ah. Just the first with acceptable breeding."

"No. Damn it, Helen!" He ran his fingers through his hair. "That was a stupid taunt made in the heat of the moment that meant nothing. Forget it. Steven's lies are more important. They could ruin you."

She shook her head at this proof that his sudden attentiveness had been an act. He hadn't set aside his earlier argument and might plan to drive straight to London despite her objections.

"They will, Helen. We need to counter them."

"Steven's lies can't hurt me."

"Of course, they can."

"No, he's attacking the schemer who borrowed my identity and plans to dispose of you the moment she gets her hands on your fortune."

"What?"

"Think about it. Steven still wants my inheritance, but Dudley can't wed me while you're alive. The rumors will explain your disappearance and absolve me of any complicity. Forget them. Once we expose him, no one will believe his tales. In the meantime, going to London could put you in danger. Our sudden journey to Hampshire may already have saved your life."

Rafe's mouth hung open. Closing it, he swallowed. "That is the most idiotic suggestion I've ever heard. You can't possibly believe it."

"Why? It's an obvious conclusion based on the evidence we have."

"You are twisting facts for your own ends."

Appalled, she stared. "Will you stop treating me like you do Hillcrest? Arguing for the sake of arguing is childish. I swear, you'd declare grass was blue if he proclaimed it green."

"Nev—" He snapped his mouth shut.

"Take a deep breath and think, Rafe. If you can find a flaw in my logic, I will listen. Otherwise, we must avoid town."

His fists whitened, then gradually relaxed. "Very well."

She nodded. "We haven't had much time to discuss our marriage, Rafe, but this demonstrates that we should. I know you don't want to turn into your father, and I certainly don't want to tu—mimic him." She nearly compared herself to his mother, but snatched the words back in time. "To avoid that, we need to work out the details of our partnership."

"Partners?" He dropped his foot to the floor, leaning forward to glare. "How can a man be partners with a woman? I never heard of such a thing. You're my *wife,* for God's sake."

"Hillcrest would never discuss things like a rational man," she agreed. "Especially with his wife. But many couples work together—the Alquists, for example. And my own parents."

He paused. "Alquist told his wife things," he admitted at last. "But she knew her place."

Helen fought back a sharp retort, reminding herself that Rafe's childhood had been one long battle. He might hate Hillcrest, but he had absorbed many of the man's beliefs. "They discussed all important problems before making a decision."

"How would you know? You swear you rarely met them."

"Because my parents were the same—Alquist and Papa were as close as twins. Didn't you discuss problems with your mother?"

"Of course not! She had enough trouble of her own."

Helen's heart quailed. This would be more difficult than she'd expected. Sharing was hard enough to learn when young. "Everyone needs a confidant, Rafe. In a marriage, each partner has his own duties. But carrying out those duties is easier if they solve problems together. For example, when I first took charge of Audley, I discovered that the steward was hidebound and lazy. It hadn't mattered before, because Papa made all the decisions and saw that they were carried out. But I needed a man who understood agriculture. I discussed the situation with Papa and Mama. Together we decided that I should replace him with Ridley."

Rafe stared, a red haze forming before his eyes. It had been bad enough when she'd announced that she would go to Audley whether he accompanied her or not. Now she expected to have a voice in everything he did. She was trying to take over. "Do you actually believe I should consult you before making decisions?"

"For important ones. That doesn't mean you have to listen to my advice, of course, though I might see details you miss. Just as you have perspective I lack. Papa always said . . ."

He let the words slide past. She was just like Hillcrest—finding fault, expecting him to obey, demanding control of his life. He wouldn't do it. He hadn't escaped Hillcrest's thumb just to crawl under hers. Even a fortune didn't give her that much power.

"Must you argue everything?" he snapped at last.

She glared. "I am not your mother, Rafe. I never argue just to be perverse. But this is a serious matter. We must find a compromise we can both live with."

Compromise? Did she really think he was stupid enough to believe she would settle for anything less than total surrender? A small concession here, a tiny indulgence there, and before he knew it, she would be firmly in charge.

He opened his mouth to explain the facts of life, but shouts cut him off. Glancing out the window, he yelled, "Stay here!" then flung open the door and leaped down.

"Wha—" Helen leaned out as the carriage jerked to a halt.

Two men were systematically beating a third. Rafe's flying tackle knocked the larger one aside. But before he could land more than a single punch, the smaller man abandoned the victim and attacked. He was wiry and quick. Rafe might be powerful, but he didn't stand a chance against two opponents.

The coachman had his hands full with the team, and Rafe's valet and groom were far ahead with the baggage coach. Cursing, Helen grabbed the carriage pistol and jumped down. If Rafe had any sense, he would have taken it himself.

Rafe was on his feet and giving a good account of himself, but he could not hold off two bruising fighters for long. Leaning into the wind, she raced closer, seeking a clear shot.

A knife flashed.

She fired.

The blond fell, clutching his leg.

"Idiot!" Rafe grunted as he punched his smaller opponent's shoulder. "Get back in the carriage."

"Your gratitude needs work," she snapped as Rafe knocked the highwayman off balance. Leaving him to finish the job, Helen turned to the victim.

He was an unconscious mass of torn clothing and bloody bruises, curled into the tiniest ball he could manage. His breath whistled out in a long groan. Gently prying his arms from around his head, she rolled him onto his back.

"Oh, my God. Alex!"

His arm flopped to the ground, revealing a swollen face covered with blood from a gash across his forehead. Disreputable clothes made him look scruffier than the highwaymen. But he was undeniably Alex Portland.

Tears slid down her face as she catalogued his injuries. This wasn't his first fight. He'd acquired a ragged scar across his left cheek that made him look grimmer than before. Other scars showed through rents in his clothing.

So much pain.

How much different he'd looked in Sir Montrose's ballroom—an elegant stranger bowing before her, his smile sending excitement tingling down her back. His touch when he'd lifted her hand to his lips had melted her knees. Within moments, she'd fallen under his spell, for he'd been the first blazingly masculine gentleman she'd met.

Another whistling groan returned her attention to his battered face. This was no time for memories, good or bad. He needed help. What quarrel could trigger such a vicious attack?

Ripping the lowest flounce from her petticoat, she pressed it to his forehead.

Chapter Eleven

*R*afe hammered another punch against the highwayman's jaw, but the man had the constitution of an ox. Nothing seemed to faze him.

It didn't help that milling tactics were useless against this pair. He was considered a bruising fighter at Gentleman Jackson's Boxing Saloon, but the rules of gentlemanly battle meant nothing to rough-and-tumble street brawlers. By the time he'd realized his error, they were moving in for the kill. If not for Helen—

Something shifted to his right. Whirling away from his opponent's fist, he sidestepped the hand trying to trip him, then slammed the toe of his boot into the blond's wound. The fellow screamed, clutching his thigh as he rolled away.

With that threat removed, Rafe concentrated on the remaining bandit. The man's quickness balanced his own longer reach, but reach should prove superior in the end—as long as he kept his wits and did nothing stupid. He couldn't leave Helen at the man's mercy. Blocking an uppercut, he aimed a kick at the fellow's groin.

Helen shifted to shield Alex's face from windblown grit, heaving a sigh of relief when his eyes flickered open.

"My Helen of Troy," he murmured hoarsely. "I must be dead."

"No, but you might have been."

"My dearest love," he murmured.

"Be quiet so I can stop this bleeding." *His love?* That

gilded tongue hadn't changed a bit. "Can you move your arms?"

He flexed fingers, wrists, and elbows.

"Good. How about your legs?"

"Hurt."

"Broken?"

"Uh-uh."

"How bad are your ribs?"

"Fine."

She doubted it. He winced with every breath. But at least the bleeding was stopped.

"Oomph!" grunted Rafe behind her. The fight still raged. Two blows landed in quick succession.

Alex struggled to push himself up.

"Don't sit yet," she ordered, holding him down. "You'll swoon if you rise too quickly."

A horse screamed. The coachman was fighting to keep the team from bolting. So far, he was winning, but the approaching storm and smell of blood were turning restlessness into panic. She could see the offside leader trembling from fifty feet away.

A body hit the ground. Not Rafe. One fear gone.

"Don't move," she told Alex. "I have some ointment that will help that cut." Rafe had been applying it to her head.

He gripped her hand. "Stay!"

"I'll be back in a moment, Alex." Her assurance relaxed him into semi-consciousness.

Rafe had the highwayman pinned to the ground, but the man was still squirming. "Bring me the rope from the boot," he grunted as she passed.

She nodded, a barrage of questions hammering her head. Who had Alex betrayed this time? Or had he turned to theft or piracy? His crimes must be bad to attract such vicious retribution. His clothes hinted that he'd fallen far down the social scale.

By the time she returned with rope, water, and Rafe's remedy box, Alex had pulled himself up to sit, white-faced, against a tree. "I can't believe it's you," he murmured as she washed blood from his face. "I was on my way to fetch you."

"Why?" She shook her head. "Forget it. You'd just lie again."

"I'm sorry."

"For what? Disappearing without a word? Ruining my reputation?"

"I never meant—"

"I'm sure you didn't."

"I planned to come back that night," he swore.

"Good intentions don't count, Alex. It's too late." She slathered salve on his cut, then ignored his flinch as she ripped another flounce from her petticoat to wind around his head.

"Helen."

"Be quiet. Talking will restart the bleeding."

The villain landed a kick as Rafe bound his arms, drawing a curse.

Alex jerked his head around. "My God," he choked. "Don't tell me you've taken up with Thomas! When you said ruined, I didn't— You were supposed to wait for me. You can't have turned mistress to that rakehell!"

"How can you believe I'd be any man's mistress!" Her fingers dug into his arm.

"Then why are you with him? Don't you dare claim you just happened to be passing by."

"Of course not. He's my husband."

Alex blanched. "He can't be. There's been no announcement."

"Certainly there was. Four days ago."

"How— Why— But you love me!"

Helen shook her head. "You walked out four years ago without a word, Alex. Why would I pine for a scoundrel?"

"You knew I'd be back. We couldn't wed until it was safe."

"Safe?"

"Don't pretend ignorance, Helen. You knew my position came first."

"What position? You said you were a London gentleman. That's hardly dangerous."

"I—" He shook his head. "I can't believe you jilted me."

"Are you mad? *You* jilted *me*. You didn't even say good-bye. *I'll be back in a moment, Helen*. Then you slipped out the window and disappeared. What was I to think when you failed to return?"

"You knew I loved you. We'd talked about marriage often enough."

"Really?" She brushed his hands away. "Oh, you were free with hints and half-promises, but you never offered and you never wrote. That is not the mark of a serious suitor."

Alex gaped. "Your father accepted my suit that afternoon. I would have proposed that evening if duty hadn't interfered. But I knew he would keep you safe until I could return."

"Duty?"

"I work for the Home Office and was in Somerset investigating a suspected traitor."

"Who?"

"Sir Montrose."

Helen laughed. "That is the most idiotic suggestion I've ever heard. He is—"

"You needn't defend him. We proved him innocent. But at the time, things looked black. He had a brother in the Foreign Office and a cousin at Horse Guards, and wrote regularly to both. Information from both offices turned up in France after passing through Sir Montrose's hands."

Helen shook her head, but it explained the games he'd played that year, like his favorite, hide-and-seek, which had always ended in torrid kisses that made her forget how long she'd been alone. She'd been his excuse to slip away. All those times he'd hurried off to collect a gift from his room, he'd really been searching private papers. And his lengthy delays before discovering her hiding places had covered spying. He'd used her.

"We learned the truth that last night," he continued. "When my assistant signaled me, I meant only to take his report and return to you, but he'd found our traitor—Sir Montrose's secretary, working with secretaries to the other men. A courier had already collected the latest information, so the only chance to recover it was to leave immediately."

"You could have let me know."

"There wasn't time."

She opened her mouth to protest—poking his head through the window would have taken no more than a moment. But his face spoke volumes. He had expected her to throw a tantrum.

The insult hurt. Even at her worst, she'd been understanding—as he should have known. Not once had she protested his actions, not even the day he'd left her in the maze for three hours.

Yet beneath the pain was relief, and a growing joy as the weight slipped from her heart. She hadn't driven him off. He'd used her, callously and deliberately, then left when he no longer needed the cover she offered. But it wasn't her fault. Never again would she wrack her brains trying to figure out why—or fret that Rafe might detect the same flaw and abandon her, too.

"We barely reached the coast before the tide turned, Helen," he swore now. "Five extra minutes would have ruined our chances. We didn't even have time to collect local officials to help, which proved unfortunate. There were more of them than we'd expected. Though we won the skirmish, it took me three months to recover from my injuries."

"What happened?" Shock drove recriminations from her mind.

"Broken leg, cuts." He stroked his cheek. "By then, I'd realized that marriage would endanger you as long as the war continued—the French might have attacked you to punish me. They have no honor. I knew Sir Arthur would keep you safe in the meantime."

"Alex—" She picked up the salve and slathered another cut on his arm. "Father never said a word about any offer. He was as furious as I that you'd left without notice. And as hurt. You must have known that your disappearance would raise doubts about my virtue. I've been a social pariah ever since."

He blanched.

"Furthermore, you said nothing about duties that might take you away at a moment's notice. Even with us you continued your pretense. And however honorable your disappearance, nothing excuses your silence. We did not hear a word from you."

"I wrote!"

She shook her head. "I don't know what fantasy you've woven to cover your perfidy, but you cannot have made your intentions clear. A formal offer would have saved me untold grief. I don't know what you think you said, but there was nothing that made Papa believe your intentions were honorable."

"Don't fall into hysteria, Helen," he said soothingly. "Parents rarely share business decisions with daughters."

"Balderdash!" She didn't care if she sounded childish. He was treating her like an infant. "Not that it matters. I am wed, which makes this entire discussion moot."

"But you shouldn't be," he insisted. "And to Thomas, of all people. He's the wildest rake in London and can never make you happy. How long have you known him?"

"Five days."

"Five days!" He straightened. "How could you wed a stranger?"

She stepped back. "That's my business, Alex. You lost any say in my life when you walked out on me. And don't tell me again that you had no choice. There is always a choice. You didn't even send condolences when Father died."

He had the grace to look abashed. "I'm so sorry, Helen. I didn't know."

"That was nine months ago."

"I was away from town. Except for an occasional week, I've been gone for a year. But I was too busy when at home to catch up on the news." Grabbing her hand, he pulled her down beside him. "I'm sorry, Helen. What happened?"

"You knew he was ill."

He nodded.

"It was terminal." Dust swirled past, giving her an excuse to blink away tears.

"My condolences, Helen. It must have been awful for you." His finger brushed her cheek. "How is your mother holding up?"

"She died last month."

"Dear Lord! I swear I didn't know."

His concern cracked her last layer of composure. Sobbing, she let him pull her against his shoulder, accepting the comfort she'd needed for so long.

"Ahem." Rafe's cough cut through her grief.

Alex kissed the top of her head, then released her and smiled at Rafe—nastily. "Congratulations, Thomas." His tone could have cut glass. "You're a lucky man. Helen is the most caring woman I've ever known. A veritable angel."

Rafe glared. Why did the victim have to be Portland? The man had hated him for ten years, gleefully grasping every opportunity to annoy him. He'd long suspected Portland of starting the most vicious rumors.

Now the man would have a new complaint. Rafe hadn't missed the intimacy between him and Helen. Nor had he missed Portland's fury that Rafe again had what Portland wanted. Would he retaliate for Lydia by seducing Helen? She seemed willing. He wished he'd been close enough to hear their conversation.

"How badly are you hurt?" he asked brusquely, pulling Helen against his side in a show of possession that tightened Portland's mouth.

"I'll live." Portland struggled to his feet, using the tree to keep from being blown over.

"I'm not so sure of that." Rafe tightened his hold so Helen couldn't lend a hand.

Portland grimaced. "The worst is a wrenched shoulder and bruised ribs, but both will heal." He slowly rolled the shoulder. "Thank you for stopping. They caught me by surprise."

"In broad daylight?" asked Rafe.

"I was lost in thought and not paying attention." He glared at Helen.

"That's not what I meant. Highwaymen prefer darkness to reduce the chance of being caught by passersby."

"Oh." Portland frowned. "But these are assassins, not highwaymen."

"So I was right." Helen struggled against Rafe's arm. "What did you do this time, Alex?"

"Nothing! You can't think—"

"What happened?" demanded Rafe, shifting Helen to his other side.

Portland pointed toward Hillcrest. "They broke from that spinney as I rounded the gatehouse—it probably looked like I came from the estate. They thought I was you."

"My God!" Helen quit struggling and met Rafe's eyes. "Steven."

"So it would seem, sweetheart." He returned his attention to Portland, who was leaning weakly against the tree. "Did they say why they were after me?"

"No, but their orders were to make your death long and painful."

"We can't let him get away with this," snarled Helen. "It's bad enough he's after you, but to hire a pair of cutthroats stupid enough to attack anyone who looks like you . . ."

"We don't look alike," protested Rafe, so shocked he let her pull free.

"Of course, you do." Hands on her hips, she glared at each in turn. "I noticed it from the first—same height, same build, same coloring. Alex has even acquired a scar since we last met. Your features are different, of course, but not in a way Steven could easily describe. His men would be at Hillcrest seeking a tall, dark man with a scar."

Rafe's head was spinning so fast he nearly keeled over. Helen had looked at him that day and seen Portland. No wonder she'd traced his scar, the most noticeable difference she knew. But if she loved Portland . . .

He'd been furious when she'd locked him out last night, but he'd thought it was distrust raised by Hillcrest's diatribe. Now he knew better. She had finally admitted that fear and injury had driven her to wed the wrong man. Again that memory tickled his mind—Dear Helen's canceled Season, followed by hints that she'd found a beau in the country. Portland was often away from town. So why hadn't they wed?

"Who wants to kill Thomas?" Portland asked Helen.

"Besides you?" Rafe grimaced.

"My uncle, Sir Steven," said Helen, glaring at Rafe before moving back to Portland's side. "Or possibly his son Dudley—*long and painful* sounds like him. They want my inheritance, but Rafe stands in the way."

"You've had a worse time than I thought," he said sadly, raising her hand to his lips. "We need to hide you somewhere safe until the danger is over."

"I'll take care of her." Rafe scanned the sky as thunder rumbled in the distance. "The first step is to find out who hired this pair. Helen, hold the team while the coachman collects the other horses." They had finally calmed, so she could handle them. "I don't want cutthroats inside the carriage, so they'll have to ride."

Helen started to protest, but thought better of it. Rafe was being as autocratic as Hillcrest—and as unwilling to listen. The air was thick with tension that had nothing to do with the storm.

She understood his fury. He and Alex obviously hated each other—which must make his bruises more painful; he'd risked his life to rescue a man he despised.

But he was right to insist on action rather than talk. Aside from the worsening weather, Alex needed a doctor. The sooner they finished with the highwaymen, the sooner he would see one. Rafe, too. That fight had inflicted more than bruises. He was favoring his left leg.

Your fault.

She stumbled as dizziness swept over her. Her conscience was right. This attack was her fault. By dragging Rafe into her family squabble, she'd not only endangered his life, but Alex's and Lady Alquist's as well. Steven was eliminating anyone who opposed him.

Which meant that Rafe's instinct had been correct. Alquist's death *was* murder. Hiring that runner had signed his death warrant. Steven had known that nothing would stop him. She was family, not just a legal obligation. Even ending his guardianship would not have halted his investigation. So Steven faced ruin. A baronetcy would not protect him from transportation if his defalcations came to light.

Rafe waited until Helen was gone, then glared at Portland. "Keep your hands off my wife," he hissed. He might have doubts about his marriage, but he would never disclose them to his worst enemy.

"Why are *you* angry?" snapped Portland, ramming one fist into Rafe's chest and the other into his stomach.

"She's my betrothed. The wedding is supposed to be next week."

"Liar!" He wouldn't believe it. Helen had sworn she knew no one in London.

But Portland hadn't been in London. And she'd started some sort of confession just before Steven burst in during breakfast.

"I can't believe you found another way to ruin my life." Portland again swung, missing as Rafe sidestepped. "Weren't you satisfied with fleecing me and—"

"I never fleeced you!" Rafe landed a punch of his own. "You are the one who drank yourself into oblivion and insisted on one more game."

Portland wasn't listening. "Now you've stolen my wife. Damn you to hell!"

"She is *not* your wife!"

"Why the devil did she turn to you, anyway?" growled Portland. "If Sir Steven was causing trouble, she should have gone to Alquist. Sir Arthur swore Alquist would be her guardian if anything happened to him."

"Alquist is dead." He advanced, glaring. "I'm her new guardian."

"But—" Portland flinched as he backed into the tree. "When?"

"Three weeks ago." His voice cracked, increasing his fury.

"Damn! If only I'd been in town."

"Enough of this, Portland. Helen is my wife. Period. You can help me question your attackers, or you can sit down and catch your breath. But stay away from Helen."

Portland released a long sigh that drained the last vestige of belligerence. "I'll help. I take it personally when people try to kill me. And I've dealt with men like these before."

Ten minutes later, Rafe's patience was nearly gone. "Who hired you?" he demanded for the hundredth time.

"I told ye, nobody!" Arnold had finally revealed his name—if it was his name—but he refused to divulge anything else. "We was riding along, peaceful-like, when this bruiser jumps out wit' a barker. *Yer money or yer life,* 'e says, all menacinglike. I don't got much to give, so when I seed a chance, I tackled 'im—protecting meself, I was."

"Where's his barker now?" asked Rafe.

"Dropped it, 'e did. Aside the road. It's there somewheres. Find it. You'll sees how it were."

Rafe snorted. Leaving Arnold to his lies, he pulled Portland aside. "He swears you pulled a pistol, so he had to defend himself."

"I did pull a pistol—after Barney tried to smash my head with a club." He nodded toward the blond. "Too bad I missed. I could have subdued one opponent."

"Probably." He hated to admit it, but Portland was in better shape than he was. Portland's injuries would have laid him out cold. His own lesser ones made staying on his feet difficult. But he couldn't waver. He would not give Portland the satisfaction of seeing him collapse— or the opportunity to make off with Helen. "Any luck with Barney?"

"Some. They were hired three days ago, though he doesn't know by whom. A broker handled the deal."

"Broker?"

"Brokers fill temporary jobs—some honest, some not. Barney won't name the fellow, but I can find him. There are only half a dozen brokers who frequent the area where they met."

"How do you know—"

Portland lowered his voice. "You're out of your depth, Thomas. I work for the Home Office recovering stolen information. Many French couriers frequent the stews."

"You track spies?" Hillcrest's charges taunted him. *Worthless . . . useless . . . wastrel . . . a gentleman's primary duty is to get an heir.* He'd always consoled himself with the nobility of defending his mother, but next to Portland's record, he felt a fool.

"I used to, which is why we couldn't marry sooner. Now that the war is over, I'm retiring." He glared. "Anyway, once I identify the broker, I'll find out who hired him." He nodded toward the attackers. "Barney swears they were supposed to rob you and teach you to mind your own business, but I don't believe it. You're heir to a title. Every runner in England would be after them once you spoke your piece. But Barney won't confess to attempted murder. He'd hang. What he's too stupid to realize is that whoever hired him can't let him live."

"So tell him. Maybe that will shake some information loose."

"Like what?"

"Who else was hired? Steven can't seriously expect to find me at Hillcrest. Everyone knows I avoid the place. Posting Barney and Arnold here was a contingency plan. The smart assassins will be waiting near Audley."

"Or in town."

"Another possibility—we left four days ago."

"You spent four days with Hillcrest?" His voice rose in astonishment.

"Of course not! We needed to speak with Lady Alquist. I believe Alquist was murdered." He might hate Portland, but a Home Office investigator was the ideal ear for his suspicions.

"Why?"

Rafe explained, adding, "This attack adds credence to my theory."

Portland swore. "I can't believe Helen didn't tell me about Steven."

"Forget Helen." He glanced up as the first drops of rain hit his face. "Where should I take this pair? Squire Hawkins is the nearest magistrate. Or should we go to London?"

"The squire. He's a good man." He paused. "Were you headed for town?"

"No. For Audley. But this attack—"

"Changes nothing. Helen will be safer in the country. I'll take care of these two, then investigate Steven and Dudley. Don't argue," he added, when Rafe tried to protest. "I am used to following such trails. And I know London's shadier neighborhoods better than you ever will. You won't learn anything useful in brothels, Thomas."

Rafe clenched his fists, but it was true that he knew nothing of London's underworld. And Helen had been right, damn her hide. Returning to town might kill him. Yet he didn't want Portland poking about in his business. Nor did he want to lead Helen into the danger he feared awaited them at Audley.

"Steven is probably waiting for this pair's report," said Portland, noting his indecision. "He won't stir until he is safe, so you needn't fear Audley. Now that you're warned, you can avoid further ambush. No one will attack you while Helen is nearby. They need her unharmed."

Rafe nearly snarled at the suggestion that he hide behind Helen's skirts.

"I need to help," Portland added. "For Helen, because I wasn't there when she needed me. For you—you saved my life, and I always pay my debts. And finally for Alquist. He was a good man. I must see his killer pay. Trust me. This transcends our differences."

"Because of Helen."

"I love her. You can't change that." He jerked his head toward the coachman, who was returning with three horses. "Help me tie this pair to their cattle. I'll take it from there."

Rafe couldn't afford to refuse Portland's help. Oddly enough, he did trust him in this. His own efforts would be better spent protecting Helen and Audley. But he couldn't leave just yet.

"I'll accompany you to the magistrate. Don't kill yourself being a hero, Portland. I doubt you can sit a horse."

Chapter Twelve

*H*elen flinched as Rafe slammed the carriage door in her face. He was furious—as was she. When he and Alex had squared off, she'd been appalled. Hadn't they taken enough of a mauling from the attackers? How could they turn on each other?

Now she knew. Rafe may have schooled his voice, but Alex had not.

Fleeced.

Rafe's fortune derived from Alex's gaming losses. Lady Alquist was right. Alex still bore a grudge about that game.

But Rafe's fury must extend beyond having risked his life to save his worst enemy. Whatever his reasons for wedding her, he hadn't expected it to kill him.

The carriage lurched into motion. Rafe rode Alex's mount, leading the highwaymen's horses. Alex's voice rumbled from the box.

Knowing about Alex's mission did not mitigate the pain he'd caused. He'd been a man of the world who should have understood that abandoning her after raising expectations would destroy her reputation—at that point, a gentleman would only flee if he learned that she took frequent lovers. So she was ruined. People cut her and forbade contact with their daughters. The only men who called wanted Audley, not her.

He hadn't changed. Using duty to excuse his behavior was being deliberately obtuse. And utterly selfish. Had he even once looked beyond his own desires?

Thunder crashed, releasing torrents of rain as the carriage halted before a small manor. Servants rushed out to cluster around Rafe's prisoners. One of them finally opened her door.

"Welcome to Hawkins House," he said, shielding her with an umbrella. "Mrs. Hawkins will be pleased if you would join her while the gentlemen conduct their business."

Two hours later, Rafe silently handed Helen into the carriage, fearful that a word would unleash a tantrum. She was strung tight as a bow. He wanted to believe it was shock, but he knew better. Fury emanated in waves, aimed squarely at him. Not until they pulled away did he relax.

Too soon.

"Why did you lock me out of that meeting?" she demanded.

"There was no reason to put you through another ordeal. The day has been—"

"No reason?" she spat. "It's my uncle and my problem. I shot that man, for heaven's sake. How can you claim no reason?"

"Helen." He tried to catch her hand, but she jerked away. "Helen," he tried again. "Calm down. You are nearly hysterical, which isn't like you."

"I am *not* hysterical," she snapped. "I'm furious. I should have met with the magistrate. You were too busy defending yourself to take in details, so my testimony is important. Did you tell him about the knife?"

"What knife?"

"The blond was pulling a knife when I shot him. That's why I aimed at him instead of the other. It's an important point, for it explains the shot. But your high-handed orders kept that fact quiet. How dare you leave me with that stupid woman and her disgusting tonics?"

He gave up. "Maybe I was wrong, but you were in shock. Shooting a man is not easy."

"No, it's not, but shock does not excuse ducking responsibility. You had no right to lock me out."

"Agreed. Write Hawkins a letter."

She glared, but it was a reasonable suggestion. He

wasn't about to turn back. If she contradicted his own tale, they would be here all day sorting out details.

He couldn't believe she was upset because he'd protected her from Hawkins. The squire considered women weak, meek creatures unable to comprehend serious matters. If Helen claimed responsibility, Hawkins would suspect her of lying to cover some dastardly deed. He might even give credence to the claim that Portland had attacked two innocent travelers.

He tried to explain, but she cut him off. "If Mr. Hawkins is that credulous, I'm amazed that you left Alex with him. He needs a doctor and reliable nursing. That woman will kill him with her potions."

"He's fine."

"He's not. He was unconscious when we arrived. His ribs—"

"If he needs attention, I'm sure he'll seek it when he reaches London." Her concern infuriated him almost as much as her arguments. And the effect she was having on his libido made it worse. How could he lust after a termagant? Surely he should prefer someone anxious to please him. Yet her spunk hardened him faster than any seductive caress.

"London!" she shrieked. "He can't sit a horse long enough to reach London. This storm will likely give him lung fever if he tries." She rose as if to jump out and return to the house.

"Sit down! Portland is perfectly capable of looking after himself. He's an investigator for the Home Office, for God's sake."

"That doesn't make him invincible! It took him three months to recover the last time."

Rafe clenched his fists. "If he needs care, which is debatable, he will do better in town anyway. The only doctor around here is as likely to kill him as cure him. I wouldn't send a rabid badger to the man. Mrs. Hawkins and her tonics are far better."

She opened her mouth, but he cut off her next objection. "We cannot offer him a ride unless you wish to postpone your arrival at Audley by at least a day. It is already well past noon and this rain is turning the roads to quagmires. We'll have to travel half the night if we hope to arrive tomorrow. And even then we won't catch up with our baggage until morning. London traffic would add several hours to the journey."

"I still think we should help him. Riding will aggravate his injuries."

He ignored an urge to pull her into his arms. "Trust me, Helen. Portland knows far better than you how to manage injuries. You will be better off resting. No matter how necessary that shot was, you cannot harm another with impunity. Sleep. You need it."

But suggesting that she sleep was a mistake, he admitted soon after she closed her eyes. Silence gave him too much time to think—and yearn.

Helen looked more delectable every day, yet it was increasingly clear that she didn't want him. Portland swore he loved her. It looked as though she loved him back.

He cursed.

What perverse fate had placed her in jeopardy when her betrothed was unavailable?

Hillcrest's tirade had forced her to admit what she had thrown away by giving in to Rafe's pressure. He might bear a mild resemblance to Portland, but they were nothing alike. Hillcrest's criticism always hurt, but most of it was true—he was indeed a wastrel, prevented by Hillcrest from helping with the estate yet barred by custom from doing anything else. Even his dream of a seat in Commons would never happen because his ideas made finding a sponsor impossible. So he had to admit that Portland was the better man. While Portland had heroically risked his life to defend England from spies and traitors, Rafe had risked nothing more than the French pox by warming an endless procession of beds. His only goal had been to avoid Hillcrest's plots. He couldn't even take credit for his fortune, which had been won by luck and quadrupled by Brockman.

What a sad commentary on his life. His mother would have been appalled. Portland was right to despise him.

But no more. He had hidden behind a false image long enough. It was time to prove he was a man, not a fribble. And his marriage was the best place to start.

Already it was vastly different than he'd expected, but

honor demanded he uphold his vows—starting with the protection he'd promised. So far he'd acquitted himself poorly, first exposing Helen to Hillcrest's sharp tongue, then leaping blithely into battle with men who would have ravished her the moment they'd defeated him. And his attempt to protect her from Hawkins hadn't worked, either. She'd been furious at his lack of respect. Had he taken credit for shooting Barney in a pitiful attempt to bolster his own showing?

Determination faded as his faults paraded through his head. What did he think he could do for her? Helen had already saved his life and his reputation. He'd never met a female less in need of protection. So what the devil was he supposed to do with himself while she ran her estate, oversaw her trust, and calmly shot any highwaymen who wandered by? She was making him feel more insignificant with each passing hour.

He sank deeper into his seat, stretching his left leg to relieve its growing pain. Barney had done something to it in that first mad rush. And Portland's unexpected blows weren't helping any. One had landed on the bruise Steven had inflicted.

A soft moan drew his eyes to Helen, curled up on the opposite seat.

She'd been right about one thing. Somehow they had to come to terms. He could no longer accept the idea of leaving her at Audley while he returned to town. Every time Portland disappeared, he would wonder if the man was calling on her.

Intolerable.

So they had to live together, which meant she must relinquish some of her power. If she wouldn't trust him, then she must turn Audley over to the steward so she could accompany him to town. He needed to work harder at finding a sponsor if he ever hoped to win a seat in Commons—he wasn't ready to abandon his political aspirations, and waiting for Hillcrest to die so he could sit in Lords was too frustrating.

But before he could decide how to win her cooperation, he must learn more about her affair with Portland. And to do that, he must appease her temper, then phrase his questions so they sought information without challenging her.

By the time she woke, he had his plans in place and his temper under control. "Do you play chess?" he asked, hoping the game's ritualized warfare might drain her belligerence.

"Not well." She smoothed her skirts, drawing his gaze to her legs.

"I've little else to offer in the way of entertainment," he said, forcing his eyes up. "Shall we try a game?"

She shrugged. "Why not?"

He set up the traveling board, waiting until the game was well under way before speaking. "Thank you for helping back there. Where did you learn to handle a pistol?"

"Mama."

"Your mother taught you?" He'd expected her to name Portland—especially in light of Portland's claim that his position put her in danger.

She nodded. "Grandmother was nearly killed by a highwayman when Mama was twelve. She was so furious that her coachman had forgotten the blunderbuss he carried for just such a contingency that she demanded Grandfather teach her to shoot and install pistols inside her carriage. She then taught Mama, who in turn taught me."

"I would not have believed a lady could control the recoil," he said, absently moving a pawn.

She frowned at the pistol, which he'd returned to its holder. "Yours is considerably larger than the ones I learned to shoot, but ladies are not helpless, Rafe." She turned back to the board, grinning when she spotted his newly exposed knight. Her queen snatched it up.

"Botheration." He hadn't been paying attention. The day's events had shaken him more than her. But at least he'd succeeded in relaxing her. It was time to seek answers. "Why didn't you tell me that you and Portland were betrothed?" He moved another pawn.

"Betrothed! What gave you that idea?"

"The words, *She's my betrothed,* as he punched me in the stomach."

She trapped his castle in a corner. "He lied. He's good at that."

His heart leaped, but he thrust it down. Helen was too aware of Portland to deny the connection. And while Portland exaggerated on occasion—like turning a few heated words into a duel when he trumpeted the tale in public—the man was a gentleman born.

"How long have you known him?" Rafe asked, trying to sound calm.

"Four years." Her voice broke.

"Four years," he repeated. So Portland was the suitor Lady Alquist had mentioned.

"It's also been four years since I've seen him," she snapped. "You, of all people, should know him well enough to disbelieve his claims."

"Men don't claim betrothals that don't exist."

"Hillcrest did—or was that another lie?"

Rafe drew in a deep breath, returning his attention to the board. "Hillcrest is my father. You saw for yourself that he's mad. And Steven is venal," he added when the name hovered on her lips. His statement had been ill-worded under the circumstances. "But why would Portland lie about your betrothal?"

"Why does Alex lie about anything?" She sighed. "Four years ago he spent time with our neighbor. You know what happens when a new face arrives in the country—picnics, routs, dinners, even a ball. So I saw him often. But when his business was done, he left. I've not heard from him since." She turned to the window to hide suddenly bright eyes.

Portland's voice echoed—*I love her . . . she's my betrothed*.

Pain exploded through his chest. Nothing had gone right since Alquist's death. He stared at the chessboard, trying to regain his composure, but the pieces all looked alike.

For years bored wives and avid courtesans had clamored for his attention. None had sought more than light diversion and the cachet of sharing his bed—he was well known for discrimination—yet they'd puffed his pride, convincing him that, at least in this arena, he was out of the ordinary.

Now he knew better.

He'd experienced much rejection, but it had never before been personal. Hillcrest hated anyone who supported his wife. The strictest matrons decried his false reputation. Portland attacked him to shift blame from his own stupidity.

Now two women in two days had turned on him. Him. His core. His essence.

Alice's words had plagued him since she'd cornered him on the terrace last night. *When I saw your marriage announcement, I was filled with joy . . . you terrify me . . . your size . . . your intensity . . . your interests.*

He'd been shocked, insulted, and so furious that he'd nearly tossed her through a window. Why hadn't she protested years ago? Only remembering that he had found a better wife in Helen had kept his temper under control long enough to warn her against Hillcrest, who was so obsessed with owning the Grange that he might force her.

That had led to the first serious talk they'd ever held, one that transformed his hatred to pity. Helen had been right to call Alice a victim. She deserved recompense for the harm inflicted by his family. Hillcrest would never pay, which left it to him.

But while Alice had pricked his pride, learning that Helen loved another shattered it.

He absently moved his bishop as he fought past the emotion fogging his mind.

He had to seduce Helen away from Portland. She was *his,* no one else's. Whatever problems they would face—and he feared they would be massive—they must find a way to work together, which meant convincing her that he was her perfect husband.

Her rescue gave him a starting point. She could so easily have let him die. After all, she'd not known Portland was the victim. Remaining in the carriage with a pistol to fend off attack could have freed her from her rash marriage. Her impulse to follow him had to have been concern for his welfare—unexpected considering her coolness since reaching Hillcrest. And her request for a partnership might have been honest, not a ruse meant to bring him to heel.

"Check," said Helen, sliding her queen through the opening he'd stupidly left.

He cursed, inching his king behind a pawn. "So Portland visited Somerset four years ago."

"Sir Montrose hosted a house party." She frowned, then again moved her queen. "Check. Why the inquisition, Rafe? Alex lied. He lied to me. He lied to you. He lies so often, he can no longer tell truth from fiction."

"He's an honorable gentleman." His defense of a long-standing enemy shocked him. But despite their differences, Portland was a better man than he was.

"Hillcrest is also a gentleman." Helen crossed her arms and glared.

"What?" Her movement drew his eyes to her bosom.

"For pity's sake, Rafe, birth is no guarantee of behavior. No one would deny that a viscount is, by definition, a gentleman, yet Hillcrest lied about your betrothal. So how can you claim Alex is truthful because he was born a gentleman? You can't have it both ways." She turned back to the board.

At least anger brought color to her face. "Very well, Portland lied," he said soothingly, removing her queen with his remaining knight. It wasn't likely, but argument would not achieve his purpose. So he would drop the subject of Portland and display interest in her affairs instead. Ladies loved talking about themselves.

"Check," said Helen, moving a castle.

Devil take it! He'd missed that move. Again he slid his king out of danger. Running away, just as he'd done most of his life—retreating into his head, moving to London, ignoring any unpleasantness . . . But no more. "Could you tell from that glance at the books whether Steven interfered with the spring planting?"

"No."

"How bad will it be if the crops are late?"

"We'll manage." When he tried to ask how, she continued talking over him. "Don't worry about Audley, Rafe. Discussion is pointless before we see what he's done. In any case, Audley is not your concern."

The rebuff slapped him in the face. She was dismissing him as useless—just like Hillcrest did. "You are my wife, Helen. Everything you do is my concern. And you will likely need help. No matter how long you've run Audley, I doubt that you know everything."

"I have to know everything," she snapped. "If I don't, I fail."

"Helen." He reached across to take her hand, but she jerked it aside. Somehow, he'd irritated her again. "I'm not trying to interfere, but you suggested we discuss our concerns. I can guarantee that the tenants don't tell you everything—because you are a lady."

"You would like to believe that, wouldn't you?" Her eyes flashed green fire. "You'd like to walk in and take over. Well, forget it. Audley is mine and will stay mine."

"I never—" He paused, drawing in a deep breath while clenched fists contained his growing fury. He hadn't meant to start a fight—and certainly not one that invited her to rub her damned fortune in his face. Only last night he'd sworn to manage his temper. "Audley is yours. I have no interest in it. But like it or not, most men do not enjoy taking orders from a lady."

"Perhaps." She made an obvious attempt to relax. "But this is not the time to discuss it. Wait until I study the books." Her tone told him hell would freeze before she revived the issue. "Check and mate," she added, moving a bishop, then turned to stare out at the rain.

He growled, irritated at his bad play. He should not have suggested chess when his mind was mired elsewhere. This had not gone as he'd envisioned. He was tied to a woman who loved another, and he had no one with whom he could discuss the problem.

Grief welled, nearly blinding him. Grief for his mother, who had respected him and loved him unconditionally. Grief for Alquist, who had willingly discussed any topic, but never forced him to accept advice and never revealed his confidences to others. With Alquist gone, there was no one trustworthy left. Even Lady Alquist was not completely safe. Her tongue ran away with her when she was in the throes of gossip.

He had vowed to remain faithful to his wife, which should be easy. Helen was beautiful, passionate, and desirable, setting his blood on fire with every glance. She was spirited, intelligent, and capable, which was what he'd always wanted in a wife.

No wonder Portland loved her.

Rafe's spirits plummeted. He'd bedded scores of bored wives who cared little for their husbands. Would Helen be any different—especially if Portland pressed? Even if Portland had lied about loving her, he might dance attendance on her to repay Rafe for Lydia.

He flinched. That vow of fidelity would destroy him unless his wife was equally faithful. The only way to keep her from straying was to attach her affections. So he was back where he'd started, trying to control her with passion. It seemed to be his only skill.

Tonight he would drive all thought of Portland from her mind. She'd melted beneath his touch before. He'd make sure tonight was even better. Once he enslaved her, she would admit that he could provide everything she needed—home, family, passion, and a partner in her business ventures.

His libido approved the plan. It longed to trace the curl framing her ear, lick the bones accented by her jet necklace, peel her gown away so he could touch her breasts. Lust welled until he no longer cared about anything but branding her as his.

Two more hours, he reminded himself as the sun set. They had to reach Hungerford tonight or they would never make Audley tomorrow. But at Hungerford, they would have the privacy he needed to enact the fantasies swirling in his mind.

Yet it didn't work that way. By the time they reached Hungerford, he was too stiff to move.

Chapter Thirteen

May 26

$\mathcal{A}$s the sun cleared the horizon, Helen opened her eyes. It had not been a good night.

Rafe's leg had collapsed as he'd stepped down from the carriage, pitching him to the ground where he lay gasping and holding his ribs.

"Idiot!" she'd snapped an hour later when the Hungerford surgeon finished strapping him up. "Whatever possessed you to sit in a bouncing carriage for ten hours with badly bruised ribs?"

"They were all right until those last ten miles," he'd snapped back. "I'm complaining to the Surveyor General. The company responsible for that stretch of turnpike is not doing its job."

"The road wasn't that bad," she'd murmured soothingly. "You just pushed yourself too far. You should have asked Mrs. Hawkins for one of her remedies."

That had earned her the blackest scowl she'd ever seen. Rafe had fallen silent, though it was obvious that he remained in pain. If anything, binding his ribs made it worse.

But that had not been her only problem. The surgeon had dressed Rafe after treating him so he could join her in the private parlor for dinner, not realizing that Rafe had no valet to help him undress. He was too sore to do it himself. Thus Helen had to lend a hand.

Her cheeks heated as she recalled the ordeal. She

couldn't afford to risk her heart, so she'd set out to strip him as quickly as possible. Which turned out to be slow indeed.

She hadn't realized how enticing broad shoulders could be when clad only in very thin cambric. No one had warned her that untying a man's cravat made stroking the adjacent jaw irresistible. And how could she avoid meeting that molten silver gaze without seeming missish?

Steeling herself for another look at his chest hadn't kept her knees from trembling, even though bandages covered half of it and bruises the rest. He had leaped into battle with no thought for his own safety, his only goal to uphold justice. Such a man demanded respect.

Helen carefully slid out of bed, moving slowly so she would not wake Rafe. He needed rest, for he'd awakened often during the night, moaning in pain.

Alex's fault. The only damage inflicted by the highwaymen had been a twisted knee, and while ten hours of inactivity had let it stiffen, it should be right as rain in a day or two. It was Alex's assault that had done the most damage. She'd like nothing more than to break something in return. Alex had no right to be angry.

Shaking her head, she forced her thoughts to her real problem.

Rafe would wake soon and demand that she help him dress. If he truly needed help, she wouldn't mind, but she suspected that he was exaggerating his infirmity to seduce her. There was no reason why he couldn't at least fasten his own pantaloons. His hands certainly had no problem gripping her waist. Or teasing her breasts. Or . . .

Again her face flushed, and not just because her own fingers had brushed far beyond his buttons. Despite his pain, he'd fondled her and pulled her against his manhood while he ravished her mouth. If his ribs hadn't protested, he would surely have taken her.

She wasn't ready for that. It was lowering to admit that with Rafe, her usually rigid self-control faltered, leaving her susceptible to his wiles, which could only lead to trouble.

Rafe shifted, again groaning.

He could not manage the twelve hours it would take to reach Audley. Yesterday's ten hours had nearly incapacitated him. But if he could tolerate half the distance, they could at least catch up with the baggage coach and his valet.

"Come here, sweetheart." Rafe struggled to sit up. "I'll fasten your gown, then you can loosen this bandage. That sawbones is mad. I'll never recover if I can't breathe."

"I'm sure the binding is necessary to—"

"Helen." His tone froze her tongue. "Come." His gaze slid down her throat to settle on her bosom. Her nipples surged to attention, sending heat raging through her body.

Cursing, she went to him.

Sir Steven stared at his secretary, noting the nervous fingers, the lowered eyes, the stooped shoulders. Stone was bringing bad news.

"Well?" he asked, not inviting him to sit.

Stone cleared his throat twice before speaking. "Our men were arrested." He shifted his weight to the other foot.

"Fools!" snapped Dudley from the corner, making Stone jump. "I warned you not to trust outsiders. We should have handled it ourselves."

"What happened?" Steven ignored Dudley's outburst—the boy had always been too quick off the mark; Steven couldn't wait to get a grandson he could raise to be a proper gentleman. Stone's news was hardly a disaster. He had anticipated the possibility and made sure no one could connect him to the assassins. "Out with it," he added when Stone again cleared his throat.

"As ordered, the men waited outside Hillcrest's gates. When a horseman matching Thomas's description emerged from the estate, they attacked."

Dudley grinned in anticipation.

"As ordered, they beat him thoroughly," continued Stone. "But instead of dragging him into the trees first, the idiots remained on the verge. Thus they were spotted by a passing carriage. Its occupants subdued our men and revived the horseman."

"So he still lives." Steven's tone sent Stone back a pace.

"But battered," put in Dudley.

"Thomas and his wife were in the carriage," said Stone hesitantly. "Thomas shot one of our men and captured the other."

"The horseman?" asked Steven over Dudley's curses.

"A Mr. Portland, sir," said Stone miserably. "Third son of the Earl of Stratford. He is with the Home Office and has personal ties to Home Secretary Sidmouth."

It couldn't be worse. "Tell me, Stone. When did this attack occur?"

Stone blanched. "Midmorning."

"Then why did I not hear about it yesterday?" he roared.

Stone drew himself up. "I did not realize anything was amiss until our men failed to return to the inn last night. We agreed that I was not to follow them about. It has taken hours to amass the information, for I dared not ask questions."

"What's done is done." Steven managed a calmness he didn't feel. "We must accept it and move on."

Stone straightened. "Which will be difficult. Portland is not stupid. Nor is Thomas, despite his reputation. The men will not remain silent. It was a mistake to involve them—"

Steven glared. "And if one of us had been caught?"

"—and a mistake to linger over Thomas," continued Stone, cutting Dudley, who had insisted on the beating. "If we had shot him as I recommended, there would have been no interruption, and the job would be done."

"With the wrong man dead," sneered Dudley.

"Hardly. Would *you* have confused Portland and Thomas?"

"I wanted the job, as you well know," snapped Dudley in return. "But he—"

"Enough!" Steven slapped both hands on the desk to restore order, then motioned Stone to a chair. "We must plan the next step. Does Thomas remain in Surrey?"

"No. He was leaving when he chanced upon Portland. But he did not return to London. His rooms remain empty, as does the Hanover Square house."

"He's headed for Somerset, then. This time, we'll take the direct approach. We can travel openly to Audley. And if we hurry, we can reach it before news of Thomas's arrival spreads beyond its gates. The staff will deny seeing him. Society thinks he was duped by a bawd, so no one will look for him at Audley anyway. Helen will wed Dudley immediately." Without Thomas to support her, she wouldn't dare oppose his commands. How the devil had she known he was her guardian? "We'll leave within the hour," he added, shooing them out. It was time to end this farce once and for all.

Rafe stared out the carriage window. Yesterday's collapse had embarrassed him down to his toes, as much because he should have expected it as from the injury itself.

He'd tried to milk his condition to keep Helen close, but that hadn't worked, either. Every time her body responded to his touch, her mind retreated another step, until she'd flung a wall of ice between them.

Portland's fault. She longed to be free so she could return to her love.

Pain stabbed his ribs with the admission, for it made his situation worse. Like it or not, they were tied together for life. It had been bad enough when she'd started laying down rules. Now she was trying to escape.

The future looked grimmer than ever. Unless she forgot Portland, her distrust and dissatisfaction would grow. Which meant Rafe must guard his heart even more vigilantly.

He had never wanted a marriage of convenience. Such a passionless arrangement could not satisfy him. Yet he could not blame Helen. It was his own drunken stupidity that had landed him in this fix.

He should have listened to his mother the day she'd held forth on choosing a wife.

"You will one day marry," she'd begun without warning a fortnight before her death.

"Not Alice!" he'd snapped.

"Of course not." She patted his hand. "Marriage means more than dowries, or even breeding. You will have to live with your wife forever, so choose well."

Relieved that she would back him against Hillcrest's latest insanity, he'd ignored her discourse on the traits necessary for a congenial marriage. Only her final words had penetrated.

"Promise me, Rafe. Fidelity is important, though the concept is out of favor in our class. Sow whatever oats you must before you wed, then remain faithful to your wife. Promise."

Her intensity had surprised him, but he'd readily agreed, unwilling to bring more strife into her life. "I promise."

That vow bound him still, though he was beginning to question her purpose. Was making it easier to withstand Hillcrest's pressure what she'd really wanted?

The question sounded disloyal, but he couldn't ignore it. Hillcrest had first suggested wedding Alice a week earlier. Lady Hillcrest had opposed the idea. Extracting that vow had made sure Rafe would also reject it—how could he wed so insipid a miss after vowing fidelity?

Helen's voice echoed—*argue just to be perverse . . .* She'd hinted that Lady Hillcrest was as stubborn as her husband, caring for nothing beyond forcing her will on him. Something deep inside feared Helen might be right, which meant his mother's lecture on matrimony had been a ploy to assure his continued support.

No! The very thought was abhorrent. And completely untrue. She had meant to protect him—she'd known he could never be happy with Alice. Her support provided the armor that deflected Hillcrest's barbs. And the affection she'd showered upon him once he made his pledge had been born of relief that she needn't fear for his future.

The carriage bumped to a halt to change horses, pulling his mind from the doubts that plagued it more each day. His mother was beyond Hillcrest's cruelty now, as was he. Thinking about the past served no purpose. It was more important to seduce Helen.

To prevent his leg from freezing again, he gingerly climbed down, then paced the stable yard to loosen his knee while grooms buckled new teams in place.

By the time he returned to the carriage, he had settled on a strategy. Serious seduction must wait until they reached Audley that evening, for he couldn't stay focused while rough roads battered his ribs. In the meantime, he could gather information—with more finesse than he'd shown yesterday.

He waited until they were out of town before speaking. "Tell me about your house. I'd like to know what to expect."

She frowned. "It is huge—four wings enclosing a large courtyard—which makes upkeep difficult, as every owner can attest."

"Expensive?"

"Very. And we haven't even tried to maintain everything."

"Tell me about it."

She relaxed into the corner of the seat. "The oldest wing was an ostentatious Tudor manor with state apartments large enough to accommodate Henry VIII's entourage—the builder was one of Henry's advisors. But his fortunes declined under Queen Mary, forcing his heir to sell the estate. The new owner wanted to add three short wings to create an Elizabethan 'E,' but managed only a 'C' before his purse ran dry. By the time his grandson sold Audley, poor maintenance left the Tudor wing unlivable, and the second Elizabethan wing was nearly as bad—they must have cut corners in its construction, for it deteriorated rapidly. Rather than restore them, the new owner closed the courtyard with a Palladian wing taller and broader than the Tudor section. But his grand vision outstripped his purse, leaving his heirs deeply in debt. Papa bought the place twelve years ago. He refurbished the Palladian wing and repaired the better Elizabethan wing so he could accommodate large house parties. The others remain derelict."

"But Steven could enter if he decides to come here?"

She nodded. "He was fascinated by the house from the moment he arrived, exploring it every chance he could. I often found him poking about in odd corners."

"What about Dudley?"

"Dudley explored nearby taprooms and gaming establishments, but cared little for the estate. He spent his few hours at Audley sleeping off excess wine."

Rafe stared blindly at the passing scenery. Audley

Court was larger than he had imagined. "What about the staff?"

"Most of the underservants have been at Audley for years. Steven replaced the upper staff. But as servants dare not oppose their superiors, I can't trust anyone."

"I don't understand how he turned off your staff. It's your house."

"I made a mistake," she snapped, lowering her gaze to the hands twisting in her lap.

Startled, he softened his tone. "Everyone makes mistakes, Helen. It's part of living." He covered her hand. "What happened?"

"I was so concerned with Mother that I left the supervision of everything else to my butler, housekeeper, and steward."

"You trusted them."

"Yes. But they couldn't fight Steven. That letter he forged from Formsby gave him more authority than I initially realized, and he passed on numerous orders he claimed came from me. Before I knew it, his own servants were in charge, and no one would talk to me."

"So we have a staff we cannot trust and a house that might already shelter an enemy."

"That sums it up. I can't believe I was so stupid." She retrieved her hand, turning to stare out the window.

"Not stupid." He stroked her hair, trying to soothe her distress—and remind her she was his. "You were wracked by grief and effectively alone. No one functions well under such conditions."

"That's no excuse. Papa put me in charge. He expected me to keep Audley safe and prosperous. He depended on me, but I let him down."

"Relax, Helen. You—"

"Relax? How can I relax? The staff distrusts and despises me. God knows what the tenants believe. I've neglected them terribly and deserve their contempt. And what about the villagers?"

"Stop this, Helen. Hysteria won't help." He gripped her shoulders, forcing her to meet his gaze. But inside, he cursed. He should have realized that Steven's takeover had stripped her confidence. Assuming male responsibilities would have already left her susceptible to doubt—too many men would question her competence. Her spirit was badly battered. A husband she didn't trust would add to the problem and might explain why she clung so tightly to duty.

He should have fetched a copy of Sir Arthur's will from the Doctors Commons archives before leaving London. Granted, there ought be one at Audley, but Steven might have destroyed it. Was there any local authority who might know the truth?

"Who was your father's solicitor?" he asked.

"Mr. Fielding. He has offices at Lincoln's Inn."

"London." He should have known.

"Papa saw no reason to change advisors after we moved to Audley."

Cursing, he sought some way to bolster her confidence. Facing Steven would be hard enough without fretting whether she would fall apart.

"Arthur would never have entrusted you with Audley unless he believed in you," he began, again catching her hand. He wasn't sure that was true—Arthur hadn't had much choice—but calming her was vital. "Alquist often marveled at his cousin's instincts and perspicacity."

"But his mind died before he did, Rafe. Though I denied the truth to outsiders, Papa could barely function that last year, and his periods of confusion started much earlier."

At least she trusted him enough to share a family secret. Perhaps he could build on that. "Tell me about him," he urged, pulling her against his side. "From Alquist's tales, he sounds a most unusual man."

Helen relaxed and began to talk.

Alice paced Hillcrest's drawing room, wondering where to start looking for a companion. As Rafe had pointed out, she could not stay at Hillcrest without one.

An even bigger problem was her meekness. Hillcrest had easily intimidated her at dinner last night. His idea of a perfect female was one who never intruded on his thoughts. But if she remained silent, she might spend the rest of her life in this cheerless house. Hillcrest would never take her to town without a battle. So she must learn to stand up for herself.

Rafe's charge that she was insipid, timid, and naïve had hurt, but he was right. Though she'd triumphed in scores of fantasy confrontations, her actual record was grim.

Mason appeared in the doorway. "Mrs. Everly to see you, Miss Alice."

"Who?"

"She *says* she is your companion." His butler's demeanor slipped, producing a disapproving frown.

"Send her in." But she cringed. Any woman Hillcrest had summoned would never do. Selecting a chair, she tried to look formidable.

"Mrs. Everly," Mason announced. A nervous middle-aged woman hovered behind him.

Alice gestured her to a seat, all the while castigating herself for expecting a battle-ax. Hillcrest would not allow a woman of strong character under his roof. "I'm afraid you have me at a disadvantage," she said, keeping her voice firm. "I hadn't expected you."

Mrs. Everly nodded. "Yes, I was told that the position was subject to your approval."

"By whom?" She perked to attention.

"Mr. Barnes." When Alice said nothing, she clarified. "Mr. Thomas's secretary. He called at my employment registry yesterday."

Rafe? She relaxed. Rafe knew how domineering Hillcrest was, and how obsessed with obtaining the Grange. Until he'd raised the subject, it had not occurred to her that Hillcrest could now claim it only by wedding her himself.

But she would never have believed Rafe would actually find a companion for her. It belied everything she knew about him.

Five minutes extracted Mrs. Everly's background, references, and a note from Mr. Barnes explaining the employment terms he had negotiated. Another half hour convinced her that she and Mrs. Everly would suit quite well. Lady Sherwood, her most recent employer, had been active in London society, often taking Mrs. Everly on morning calls and to other affairs. Such experience would aid Alice's come-out.

Alice gave Mrs. Everly the room next to hers, then

headed for the library to inform Hillcrest that she had hired a companion. There would be no better time to lay aside her meek subservience.

"How dare you bring a stranger into my house?" he demanded the moment she entered his dismal room.

His fury struck like a fist. She wanted to run, but Hillcrest treated life as a war. One victory, and he would never relent. Straightening to her full five-feet-two, she locked gazes. "I need a c-companion, my lord. I c-cannot live here without one."

"Ridiculous. I am your guardian."

"B-but not a relation." She gripped the door handle to stay upright. "P-people will talk, sir. We cannot seem improper."

"Impro—" Veins bulged purple at his temples.

For an instant, she feared he would collapse like her father, but he'd been far angrier when Rafe had appeared with a wife. "Improper," she repeated, taking the chair he hadn't offered—her knees could no longer support her. "P-people see what they wish to see—scandal. My reputation cannot sustain further damage. Mrs. Everly will make a p-perfect companion."

"Hah!" He rose to tower over her. "Females can't think. A decision of such import is beyond you."

Spots danced before her eyes. Only imagining him as her husband gave her the strength to continue. "P-please sit down, sir. A gentleman cannot rise while a lady remains seated."

To her surprise, he sat. Did he actually apply manners to himself? Her small victory steadied her nerves. "Mrs. Everly will do more than protect my reputation," she continued softly. "She will prepare me for London."

"You can't visit that hellhole!" His body vibrated, but he remained in his chair.

"I must find a husband, sir. If you don't wish to go, then I will find another sponsor. In the meantime, I need instruction in the ways of society. Mrs. Everly will do quite well."

"Absolutely not!" He pounded on a table.

His violence unleashed a temper she'd never before lost. "If you insist on being perverse, sir, Mrs. Everly and I will repair to Paulus Grange. I would rather raise eyebrows by setting up my own establishment than forgo the perfect companion."

"But—" He sputtered for nearly a minute before continuing. "If you must have a bedamned female hanging on your skirts, at least examine the options. Don't hire the first floozy who raps on the door. What do you know of her? She might intend to rob me."

"Hardly." She repeated Mrs. Everly's history. "I have examined her references closely and find them impeccable."

"You can't have contacted an agency this quickly," he protested.

"That is true. I've hardly had time to think since Papa died. Rafe's secretary handled the initial interviews."

"Rafe? If the woman claims he sent her, then you know she's lying. He is a dishonorable cad, an uncaring wastrel who never looks beyond the desire of the moment, a self-centered—"

"Wrong!" For a moment she thought he would expire from shock. "I spoke with him two nights ago, sir. He was furious at your disregard for my reputation. This is his way to make amends."

"But that isn't like him at all."

"How do you know?" His bewilderment confirmed her suspicions. "You are so busy maligning him that you never observe him. Isn't it time to discover what sort of man he truly is?"

"I know very well what sort of man he is."

"Then why does this surprise you? Why did you ignore his refusal to wed me? Why do you condemn him every time you open your mouth? Mrs. Everly finds him generous and caring. No one has seen anything deserving censure in ten years."

"Where there is smoke, there is fire, and the newspapers reek of smoke. Not a week goes by without new tales."

"Forget that old adage," she dared. "Society sees smoke long after the flames have died. People love scandal and look for it everywhere. If their expectations are foiled, they are quite happy to speculate—it gives them something to do. But that does not mean the tales are true."

"How can you defend him after the way he treated you?" He again pounded the table, an intimidation tactic he must use often.

She nearly quailed, but giving up might cost her Mrs. Everly. "How can you cling to your hatred when evidence proves you wrong? Rafe is a man, not a substitute for your wife."

"How dare—"

"I dare because everyone knows about your long feud—your public arguments made you laughingstocks. I dare because I won't remain here if you try to draw me into your battle. Lady Hillcrest is dead. Perpetuating the past by attacking Rafe serves no purpose. He is not responsible for events that occurred before he was born. Lay that feud to rest."

"Enough!" he roared. "He took her side. He—"

"Only because you forced him to choose sides."

"Are you really so coldhearted that you would champion the man who jilted you?" he demanded.

She sighed, shaking her head in disgust. Hillcrest was the most pigheaded, impossible man she had ever met. She could not afford to retreat, yet entering his war would nullify standing up to him. She tried a simple fact. "Rafe did not jilt me. On the rare occasions when we met, he made his disdain clear. It was you who insisted that a betrothal existed."

"Pauling—"

"No. Father had nothing to do with it. We will not discuss it again."

"How dare you imply—" he sputtered. "A girl your age should know her place. No gentleman—"

"I do know my place, sir. It is you who ignore your place. You call yourself a gentleman, but no gentleman would blacken his son's name merely to score points against his wife. How can you brand Rafe a jilt over a betrothal he refused? Don't you understand what you demanded? Wedding me would have forced him into debauchery worse than the most exaggerated tales. How else could he have tolerated your injustice?"

He gasped.

"You cannot change a man's character by force," she continued, clasping her hands to control their shaking.

"Rafe is too full of life to accept the rustication you enjoy."

"He would have settled down."

"Not until he'd withered and died. Lay your dreams aside, sir. If demanding he wed me was meant to expand Hillcrest's coffers, then Rafe has done better without your help."

"If you believe her."

"I do. And you will, too, if you send your secretary to London with orders to collect facts. Rafe is not stupid. He knows his wife's godmother very well and has heard many tales of her over the years. He told me that meeting her in person was like meeting an old friend. When your secretary returns, I will expect your apology. Without it, I will move back home and petition the court to appoint a new guardian."

His face purpled. Again he leaped up to tower over her, trying to intimidate her into submission.

She concentrated on sitting still, though every instinct sought flight. Even reminding herself that he'd never been violent couldn't lessen her fear.

But he finally resumed his seat.

"I appreciate that, my lord." Rising, she headed for the door. "I must thank Rafe for sending Mrs. Everly. You might do the same. And you owe him an apology."

"No."

She paused with her hand on the latch, but his raised hand halted her reply.

"You are headstrong to a fault and too willing to think well of people you don't know. The only way to remedy that is to prove you wrong. We will leave for Audley in the morning."

What had she done? She swallowed hard. This was not at all what she wanted. "Only if you keep an open mind, sir. I won't subject Rafe to another of your tirades."

"So be it. I've nothing to fear. You will admit your mistake and accord me proper respect in the future."

That sounded ominous, but Alice knew she would win no more concessions today. She would have to see that he kept that grudging vow.

Chapter Fourteen

*H*elen tensed as they stopped at yet another inn to change teams. She needed to get out of this carriage so she could breathe. Rafe didn't even have to speak to seduce her.

He'd moved to the opposite seat after lunch, but escaping his wandering hands and the brush of his thigh didn't relax her, for she couldn't keep her eyes from straying to his form. His presence filled the carriage, suffocating her with awareness until her heart pounded and her lungs gasped for air. His every glance tightened her nipples and pooled moist heat between her legs. Each twitch of his fingers raised memories of their wedding night. If only she hadn't passed out. She'd been willing—nay, eager—to carry out her duties. But no more.

She grimaced. Part of her still longed for his touch, but knowledge had added a layer of fear—of the pain an attachment would cause if he left; of the pleasure he offered, for it threatened her control; of failing to meet her father's expectations. Until she banished those fears, she could not bed him. Yet only trust could banish them.

And that was the rub. How could she trust him after seeing him with Alice? She couldn't even ask about that kiss, for his denials would mean nothing.

"Come inside," Rafe ordered, flinging the door open. The words conjured images of beds until he added, "We will have a bite to eat and refresh ourselves."

"We can eat at Audley. We'll be there within the hour."

"Helen." He shook his head. "Think. Do you really want to face Steven on an empty stomach?"

Reality crashed back. "You expect him to be there, don't you?"

"No, but he might be. So you must be strong. Come inside and eat. You will feel better for it, and it won't delay us more than a few minutes."

He was right, but she resented that he could remain so calm while his eyes seemed to strip her, turning her legs to mush and melting her mind. It was more proof that he cared little for her.

A servant entered as they were washing up in the Blue Boar's private parlor.

"Tessa!" gasped Helen.

"Miss Helen!" Tessa's tray wobbled, spilling tea and ale.

Rafe rescued it.

Helen hugged Tessa. "My God! Are you all right? What are you doing here? I've been so worried about you. Steven swore you'd taken a better post, but I knew you'd never leave without a word."

"I take it you know each other." Rafe leaned against the mantel, arms crossed.

Helen jumped. "Of course. Tessa was my maid—one of the servants Steven turned off. Tessa, my husband, Mr. Thomas." The name rolled easily off her tongue.

"Married! I hadn't heard."

"We wed last week. But why are you here? Surely with your training you could do better than serve at an inn." And not a very good inn at that. They had left the turnpike several miles earlier.

"I'm lucky to have this post, Miss Helen," admitted Tessa. Her eyes flattened. "Without a reference, I mean. Sir Steven vowed he'd have me up for theft if I went near another lady. I didn't steal nothing, sir!" She appealed to Rafe.

"Of course you didn't," he agreed. "We know he turned you off because you remained loyal to your mistress."

Helen nodded. "Frankly, I need you back, Tessa. I have no maid at all just now."

"Really?" Hope lit her eyes.

"Of course. You are a very good maid. And you can hardly enjoy working here."

"No, ma'am. It's a rough place and not what I'm used to. Serving's the least of what they expect of me."

"That's over now," said Rafe soothingly. "You can be sure I'll hold Sir Steven accountable for what you've suffered."

"Th-thank you, sir." Tessa burst into tears, turning toward the corner to hide her emotion.

Helen laid a hand on Rafe's arm. "You mean she had to—" Her whisper died before she could put her fears into words.

He nodded, pulling her close. "Don't question her. A girl without family or position has no other choice if she wants to survive. And she's pretty enough to draw interest. With time, she will put it behind her, but she will be fragile for a while."

Helen agreed. Females were helpless without men to protect them. Even her own supposedly secure position hadn't kept Dudley from trying to assault her. But Rafe's tolerance was a surprise. She hadn't expected compassion from a rake. It was one way he differed from Alex, who had never noticed servants, let alone imbued them with humanity.

She met Rafe's gaze. "How could Steven turn her off, knowing he was condemning her?"

"I doubt he wasted a moment's thought on her— which is yet another insult for which he must atone. The upper classes have many privileges, but they also have responsibilities. One is to care for those dependent on them." Tessa was wiping away the last tears with her apron, so he returned to business. "Where is your room? I'll collect your things."

"Leave them," she said, sniffing. "There is nothing here I value. McGee will know if you go upstairs. He won't let me leave without a fuss."

"In that case, we'd best depart. Wrap up the food, Helen. We'll eat in the carriage."

"Here," said Helen, settling her shawl around Tessa's shoulders to cover her ragged gown. "And take my bonnet. Go with Mr. Thomas. I'll follow with our dinner."

*   *   *

"Have you heard anything about Audley since you left?" Helen asked Tessa half an hour later, seeking a diversion to occupy her mind. Rafe had shared her seat since the Blue Boar, sending sparks along her nerves whenever a bump brushed him against her. The corner of her mind that wanted more was already whispering that Rafe was not like other men. She should trust him and seduce him. Yet the corner still reeling from Alex's betrayal countered that Rafe had too many secrets and would use her to achieve goals that didn't include her.

"A little." Tessa's response made Helen jump, for her thoughts had moved far afield. "Rose's parents live near the Blue Boar, you might recall. She visits them on her days off. We met twice. She swore you were betrothed to Mr. St. James."

"No, though Sir Steven wished it. He wants Audley."

"Everyone believes he owns it," said Tessa. "I tried to set them straight, but McGee accused me of putting on airs. I needed the post. Even at its worst, the Blue Boar is better than the workhouse."

"Why would people believe Steven's claims?" Rafe asked Helen. "Surely they know about your father's will."

A good question, she conceded. Inheritance news made prime gossip, especially when a will left everything to a daughter. Not that it would have surprised anyone. Her father had described his intentions for years.

"Damn," she murmured, suddenly sick.

"What?"

"There was no formal will reading. Mama's collapse threw everyone into a tizzy. The doctor was sure she would die any minute. When Mr. Fielding's clerk arrived—Mr. Fielding was too ill to travel—we spoke privately at her bedside. I told him to pay out Papa's bequests to the servants. Everything else was in the trust and required no immediate action. But within the week, Steven replaced everyone who had known Papa's intentions. Probate was in London."

"So no one actually heard his words." Rafe frowned.

"Exactly. How could I have been so stupid!"

Rafe squeezed her hand. "Sir Steven claims that Audley is his?" he asked Tessa.

"Yes, sir. And he has run it for so long that no one questions his right. He explained that Sir Arthur had arranged Miss Helen's marriage to Mr. St. James to assure her security."

"That would prevent questions," conceded Helen. Many neighbors would have applauded his apparent change of heart. They had paid lip service to her authority while her father lived, but she'd known she would face battles once he was gone. In her concern for her mother, she'd forgotten that. "What else has Sir Steven been doing?"

"He doubled the rents, then turned off old Quigley when he couldn't pay."

"Oh, no!" Helen stared. "Are you sure? The books show no increase."

"Positive. Quigley stopped at the Blue Boar on his way to his cousin's house in Devonshire. That must be six months ago now. He said others will have to leave, too, unless the crops bring in more than usual this year."

Helen clenched her fists. Steven must have kept two ledgers, setting up to cheat Dudley.

"That's all I know about it," said Tessa. "Quigley was that upset. He could barely talk."

"We have to make sure he's all right," Helen murmured.

Rafe nodded, covering her hand in a gesture of comfort.

Rafe stared as Audley Court loomed against the setting sun. Even Helen's description hadn't done it justice. His fears roared back, choking him.

The drive circled the building—its current entrance was opposite the gates—winding through an elaborate park of open vistas, woodland, lake, and formal gardens. They passed the original Tudor manor, whose crenellated walls remembered medieval unrest while large windows anticipated more peaceful times. The Elizabethan wing dropped crenellation for ornate stone latticework, and boasted even larger windows with diamond-shaped panes. But the Palladian wing was breathtaking. A double sweep of steps cradling an ornate fountain led to an elaborate columned portico. Pilasters framed beautifully proportioned windows topped by elaborate pediments. Intricate cornices crowned warm stone walls.

Pure elegance.

And it belonged to Helen.

He stiffened his spine. They needed to address her wealth, and soon. His mother's fortune had been a festering sore between her and Hillcrest. He felt as though he were walking on eggs trying to solicit loyalty while avoiding any mention of her inheritance. It couldn't last.

A servant opened the carriage door as it rolled to a stop. "Miss Helen!" he exclaimed, smiling in delight. At least someone seemed genuinely pleased to see her.

"Robert. Is Sir Steven or Mr. St. James in residence?"

"No, ma'am. Nor are they expected."

"Excellent. They must never again be admitted. See that the trunks are taken upstairs. Mr. Thomas will use the green bedchamber next to mine."

Robert circled the fountain and disappeared through the servants' door. Two footman emerged a moment later and headed for the baggage carriage.

Rafe followed Helen up the sweeping staircase, catching his breath when they entered a double-height marble entrance hall. Pilasters marched down either side, framing alcoves displaying oversized Greek statues. Columns across the end drew the eye to a split staircase leading to the next floor. Scenes from the Greek classics covered the ceiling.

"There you are, Nalley," said Helen to a nondescript man in a wrinkled coat standing near the stairs. "This is my husband, Mr. Thomas. Our butler, my dear."

"Husband?" Shock twisted Nalley's face. "He c-can't be. You are b-betrothed to Mr. St. James."

"Nalley!" She pinned him with a frigid gaze. "You are a victim of lies. There was no betrothal. I own Audley Court. My uncle and cousin took advantage of Mother's illness to insinuate themselves into the household, but they have no rights here."

"But—"

"If you wish, we can read Papa's will. There is a copy in the archives."

"That won't be necessary, Mrs. Thomas."

Rafe wondered. More than shock had lit those dark eyes. Was it fury? Why?

"Good," said Helen. "Now that you know the truth, I will expect your loyalty. If either Sir Steven or Mr. St. James returns, you will deny them entrance."

"Yes, ma'am."

"Summon the staff. They must meet their new master."

"Of course." But Nalley's eyes grew darker with each command.

Rafe suspected they would need a new butler.

He watched the thirty indoor servants closely as Helen introduced him. Signs of laxity were everywhere—stained aprons, smudged liveries, soot-stained hands. Attitudes ran from pleasure through wariness to open hostility.

"The staff will be a problem," he said when Helen showed him to his room, an elegant guest chamber larger than the master's room at Hillcrest.

"I know. Even those who have been here for years are confused. I never dreamed that Steven might tell people he owned Audley. No wonder they turned against me so quickly."

"Where are the archives? I'd like to see Sir Arthur's will."

"The muniments room. You don't think—"

"I think we need proof of your claims," he said, pulling her close. "Victims of lies will be slow to believe a new story."

She nodded.

"I wish we could turn everyone off." His hand stroked her back.

"Impossible." She glared. "Where would we find replacements? This isn't London. The next hiring fair isn't until June. Besides, how can we turn off servants who have done nothing wrong? Many of them were born on the estate. I refuse to act like Steven."

"I wasn't recommending such a course. I was merely contemplating the danger of sharing a roof with so many potential enemies. Nalley isn't the only one disgruntled by our arrival. Vince and Charlie look more like bully boys than footmen. And Mrs. Lakes is the most disapproving woman I've ever seen. She makes Hillcrest seem congenial."

Helen swept her hand across the mantel, frowning when dust smudged her glove. "She is not overly competent, either," she concurred. "Perhaps Tessa can discover if she is causing trouble among the maids. I agree about Vince and Charlie, but if we turn them off arbitrarily, what's to stop them from attacking the tenants or slipping back to murder us in our beds? It would be better to catch them red-handed, so they have no complaint."

Rafe shivered. "In the meantime, we must be careful. It will be days, if not longer, before the last of Steven's lackeys shows his colors."

Helen nodded, then headed for her own room.

What the devil was he doing here? Rafe wondered as he watched the sunset fade beyond the formal gardens. Audley Court was intimidating. Despite living in substandard rooms for a decade, he had never felt as insignificant as when he'd stood in Audley's entrance hall. It didn't matter that a viscount's heir ranked higher than Sir Arthur and much higher than the baronet's daughter. He didn't belong.

Yet he had no choice but to remain, for abandoning Helen was impossible.

He shivered, fearing he was becoming attached. But surely it was only lust. Anything more would leave him vulnerable. Not that he could further his campaign tonight. Seduction must wait—a painful decision, for he'd watched the heat grow in her eyes all day, helped by suggestive gestures and pointed glances at her lips, her breasts, her . . .

He fought his lust into submission. Their immediate problem was safety. Nalley's belligerence made standing guard essential, despite his aching ribs. He and Jameson would alternate watches, but he would have to sleep when not on guard.

If only they could use the master suite. It was easier to defend than the guest rooms, but it had not been cleaned after Helen's parents' deaths.

This was a bad time to have servants they couldn't trust.

                     *   *   *

Helen dismissed Tessa, then stared into the grate while she tried to order her thoughts. Tessa had been agog to find her married—they reverted to friendship when alone—and had demanded every detail.

"So you can see my problem," Helen had said after describing the last week. "I'm terrified that he will use his sexual expertise to make me sign over my trust."

"Nonsense!" Tessa set the brush down and started braiding Helen's hair. "I watched him in the carriage. He wants you, I agree. But *you,* not your fortune."

"That's his rivalry with Alex. Each covets what the other has."

"No." Tessa paused, then inhaled deeply. "I've seen many men since leaving Audley, Miss Helen. And I've learned to read faces—lust, anger, celebration, and more. Mr. Thomas isn't comfortable, but he *is* protective, and he wants you very badly. Don't turn him away."

"I won't," she'd said, not quite meaning it. She wanted nothing better than a week alone to think before making any decisions.

Tessa had left then, leaving Helen to brood. Was the girl right?

It was possible. Tessa had seen much of the sordid side of life before entering service at age sixteen. Now she'd endured more—and survived, which she could only have done by anticipating trouble. So she probably could read faces, even aristocratic ones.

The admission lightened her heart, though wariness remained. When Rafe joined her tonight, she would listen to his answers and try to believe.

Chapter Fifteen

May 27

T he next morning Helen slumped at her dressing
table, her head in her hands. Tension throbbed in
her temples. Why had Rafe avoided her last night?

After his many pointed glances in the carriage, she'd
expected him to bed her—had welcomed the idea. Her
emotions had been so chaotic in the past week that she
needed to soothe at least some of them. Lust was a good
place to start. Perhaps relieving it would clear her head.
So she'd prepared to meet Rafe.

Needlessly.

He'd not even stopped to bid her good night. When
she'd finally found the courage to go to him, she'd found
his room empty.

It was mortifying to realize that she'd needed more
than intimacy from him. The staff's cold suspicion and
her fear that Steven might appear at any moment left
her craving Rafe's warmth. But he'd offered nothing.
What was he up to now?

"I knew your head was bad," exclaimed Tessa from
the doorway. "You can't hide pain from me. Here." She
produced headache powders and a pot of tea.

"Thank you, Tessa." It was stupid to hide her pain.
As soon as their horses were ready, she and Rafe would
call on the tenants. A pounding head would make the
excursion unbearable.

She closed her eyes, sighing as Tessa massaged her

temples. "Did you learn anything new from the staff?" she murmured.

"Not as much as I'd hoped. Mr. Nalley and Mrs. Lakes insist I was turned off for theft. The staff follows their lead."

Helen cursed under her breath.

"But I learned some'at from Rose." Tessa expanded her massage to the forehead.

"What?"

"No matter what you say, Mr. Nalley and Mrs. Lakes consider Sir Steven their master—you'll have to replace both of them, like as not. Sir Steven vowed vengeance on anyone who opposed his orders, so no one dares speak up in your favor. He won't toss troublemakers out without a reference this time. There'll be heads broke."

Helen and Rafe had discussed the staff problem over breakfast—it had already been apparent that service would be grudging while Nalley remained. But turning off those acting from fear of Nalley or Steven was unfair.

In the end, they'd sent Robert to London for copies of the will and the trust documents—the estate's copies had disappeared. Robert had served as underbutler for several years and would replace Nalley when he returned, but she hoped the rest of the staff would settle once they saw the evidence for themselves.

In the meantime, they would have to live with tepid water, slow service, and other annoyances. But at least she and Rafe had managed the discussion with no hint of argument, which boded well for the future.

"There's more," continued Tessa. "Sir Steven told the neighbors that Sir Arthur came to his senses last year and apologized for the childish dispute that had caused their rift. He changed his will and summoned Sir Steven to Audley, but died before he arrived."

"That's preposterous!" The outburst sent knives slicing through her head. "Father was too weak those last months to write, and his mind barely functioned. Half the time he didn't recognize anyone. There was no way he could have corresponded with Steven. Nor would he have tried."

"You know that, and I know that." Tessa busied herself setting the room to rights. "But the last time the neighbors saw him, he was mentally alert. You kept his senility a secret, so no one understood his condition. Many men make peace with their enemies before the end."

Helen nearly choked. It sounded all too plausible.

She'd been afraid that revealing his fall into senility would call his judgment into question, casting new suspicions on her ability to run Audley. And it was a valid fear. Without his seeming support, many would have refused to do business with her. But it was unfortunate that it had given Steven an opening.

"In your favor, people find Sir Steven obsequious, and they loathe Mr. Dudley," continued Tessa. "And not just for his arrogance. He mauled the butcher for interrupting an assault on his daughter. Missy escaped with her innocence intact—she's contracted to Tom Freeman, by the way—but Mr. Mortimer's leg will never be the same. Mr. Dudley snapped it like a twig."

"I'll call on him," she promised. But her heart sank. How many other crimes had Dudley and Steven committed against her people?

"Be careful in the village," added Tessa. "Mr. Dudley and Mr. Smith are fast friends."

Helen cursed, though she should have expected it. The blacksmith had been a problem for years. Perhaps Rafe could discover what he'd been doing in recent months. It was the sort of help he'd offered. He could enter taprooms and other places a lady could not.

"Find my habit, Tessa. The horses should be here soon."

But they weren't. Helen had been in the estate office for half an hour before Rafe returned from the stable. "Nalley neglected to order horses," he reported. "My coachman is overseeing their preparation now. I'll fetch you when they arrive."

Helen smiled. Nalley was making it easy to replace him.

Rafe barely kept his temper in check as he dismounted in the stable yard eight hours later. Helen didn't wait for his help, but jumped down on her own.

"Walk with me," he commanded when she turned

toward the house. "We need to talk, but not in front of the staff."

"Can't this wait? My head hurts, and I have to finish examining the books."

"No." He led her to the far corner of the rose garden while memories of the estate tour flogged his mind. Rooting out Steven's influence would be harder than he'd thought. Ignorance, prejudice, and inertia combined to make everyone wary. Nine months had accustomed them to Steven's rule. Even those who hated Steven would be slow to change.

The day had both humiliated and humbled him as he'd escorted Helen around a larger domain than he'd imagined. It wasn't just Audley's value that gave him pause. His mind hadn't translated her diatribe at Hillcrest into an appreciation of Audley's vastness—four dozen tenants, villages, weavers, cheesemakers, a mill, a pottery . . .

His head ached. She knew more about every enterprise than he did.

He'd sworn that he preferred competent, intelligent women to the conformable widgeons he usually encountered in society. Debating ideas with his mistresses had always increased his enjoyment of the subsequent bed games.

But he'd never lost one of those debates, he admitted grimly. His love of books meant he knew more and understood more than any of his friends. Even his mother had rarely bested him in a battle of wits. He was beginning to fear that Helen might.

A sobering thought. Why was obtaining the wife he'd claimed to want so chilling?

Her voice echoed: *You'd declare grass was blue if he proclaimed it green.*

Hillcrest insisted that ladies must obey orders and never contradict their husbands. But if Rafe sought independent, intelligent women because Hillcrest abhorred such creatures, could he claim to be independent? Had he—horrible thought—made sure that none of his carefully selected mistresses possessed enough wit to debate him as an equal? Such chicanery would gratify his need to flout Hillcrest while maintaining his own superiority.

The idea was so troubling, he thrust it aside. They had

more pressing problems. Steven had poisoned everyone against Helen. Despite her vow to return the rents to normal and refund last year's increase, the tenants remained suspicious. Few believed she had the authority to institute change. And everyone looked at him askance. Standing aside while Helen conducted business made him appear weak, eroding his credit in the eyes of Audley's tenants. If the neighbors reacted the same way, he would become a laughingstock.

But even that was not his most pressing problem.

They had stopped in the nearest village to speak with the butcher, who was recovering from a run-in with Dudley. As they'd emerged from his shop, a mob had surged forward, led by the blacksmith. Helen was clearly the target, and not because she owned Audley.

The charges still rang in his ears—*whore . . . corrupter of children . . . thief . . . poisoner . . .*

Rafe had gotten her safely away—despite years of Luddite rabblerousing, most of the villagers still hesitated to physically cross class boundaries, so he'd had to subdue only Smith. But he needed answers.

Chills wracked him as he examined the last week in light of these charges—her seductive caresses outside Christchurch, her uninhibited response to his touch, the speed with which she'd mastered the arts of lovemaking, the secrets he could see lurking behind her eyes. Was she experienced? So passionate a woman might well have yielded to temptation, and she'd been betrothed to Portland.

Suspicion nearly choked him. He didn't want to believe the tales, but he could not afford to ignore them. And not just on a personal level. If even one was true, he would never find the backing to stand for Commons. Who could trust a man who had jumped into marriage with a wanton? Or worse, a killer?

"What the devil was that all about?" he demanded, seating Helen on a bench, then standing over her so she had no escape.

She didn't pretend to misunderstand. "Smith has been a problem since Father bought Audley," she said, shaking her head. "Friendship with the previous owner gave him airs above his station, but the sale canceled his entrée into the gentry. Though Papa admired his artistry as a blacksmith, he didn't invite him to dinner. Smith has been sullen ever since."

"So twelve years later he risks transportation by attacking you? It won't wash, Helen. What did you do to draw such ire?"

"Nothing!" She surged to her feet, glaring into his eyes. "I've never even heard half of those charges. They are ridiculous!"

"What about the other half?" His heart sank, though he kept his voice steady.

"Baseless innuendo."

"It must have had a cause, Helen. Even my reputation had a starting point."

"But not everyone is to blame for their reputations, Rafe. I told you Alex was here on business—not that we knew of his ties to the Home Office. We thought him just another guest at Sir Montrose's house party." Bitterness tinged her voice. "Pretending to court me gave him an excuse to remain after the house party ended, but it also convinced everyone that he was serious about offering. So when he left without a word, everyone believed it was my fault."

"I see."

"I might have countered the gossip if I'd been paying attention, but the next day we learned that Papa was dying. With Alex gone, he had to train me to run Audley, which meant I didn't get out socially for weeks."

Rafe flinched. It would have seemed as if she were hiding in shame.

"By the time I realized what people were saying, my unladylike interest in the estate had added new stains to my reputation, turning me into a pariah."

"For a time," he agreed, grabbing her arm when she started to turn away. "But people should have discovered the truth by now. Even the most sensational rumors eventually die if there is no evidence to support them. And this sort of thing rarely interests villagers anyway."

She flinched as if he'd struck her, then shoved his hand aside. "That might be true if I were male, but females never get second chances—not that you seem to care. You are as contrary as your mother and as gullible as your father. I can't believe you would accept the demented ranting of a mad blacksmith over your own wife. Alex would never be so stupid. He knows I'm honorable."

"Helen, I—"

"Enough. Go soak your head in the horse trough. I have work to do." She stormed off, leaving him frozen, mouth agape, heart in his toes. He'd just witnessed an exhibition of the adage, *the best defense is a good offense*. Rather than answer another question, she'd gone on the attack. Were there worse secrets she was hiding?

But it was choosing Portland as her weapon that hurt the most. His feet felt like lead blocks as he made his way to his room.

"I need information," he told Jameson when the valet answered his summons. "The villagers are vilifying my wife. I must have facts if I am to protect her."

"I can't—"

"You must." He could see that Jameson believed the stories. But without knowing the details, he could never find an innocuous explanation to offer the gossips. Whatever the truth, he had to protect her. His political future wasn't the only thing at stake. Scandal of this magnitude would tarnish any children they produced.

Jameson sighed. "Very well, sir. But it will not be easy. No one trusts me because I belong to you. Nalley is threatening to turn off anyone who serves you."

"I'll have him up on charges if he tries. But his antagonism will encourage others to vilify Helen, so you should learn the worst quite easily."

Jameson nodded.

But Rafe's heart sank. They might yet have to turn off the entire staff. The current situation could not continue.

"Mr. Portland started the trouble, as you might expect," Jameson reported two hours later as he brushed lint from Rafe's evening coat. "He ran tame here four years ago. According to Frank—the head footman—he was closeted with Sir Arthur for two hours that last afternoon, discussing marriage settlements. That evening he and Miss Helen disappeared together. She returned an hour later—alone. Mr. Portland has not been seen since."

That matched her story, though she continued to claim there had been no betrothal.

Jameson continued. "Most regard him too highly to believe he seduced her, so the consensus is that she confessed earlier indiscretions, forcing him to withdraw his offer. Her fury when he defected—she vowed to rip his heart out—was so unladylike that it reinforced the image of a vulgar harlot."

So whatever Portland's true intentions, Helen's heart had been thoroughly engaged. Humiliation might drive her to disclaim a betrothal, or Portland might exaggerate their understanding to annoy a long-standing enemy, as he'd done with his duel claim. It would provide a new tale to set London on its ear—Rafe had again shamelessly poached from Portland.

But Portland's intentions didn't matter. Rafe needed to know whether Helen's heart remained engaged and how badly she'd been compromised. At least everyone agreed they'd parted years ago, so he needn't fear she was carrying Portland's brat.

"Miss Helen was immediately cut from local society," continued Jameson. "She might have recovered if she'd remained in the drawing room, but plunging into estate management confirmed that she was no lady. The lower classes didn't care, though—except the blacksmith, who hates her family. She turned her back on the neighbors and concentrated on Audley."

Rafe nodded.

"It was Sir Steven who maligned her to the estate dependents, reviving and exaggerating the earlier tales. Mr. Dudley added to the scandal when he accused Miss Helen of poisoning Sir Arthur to cover the theft of items she'd given to various paramours. Presumably, Lady St. James discovered her crimes, which triggered her apoplectic fit. And when a village girl disappeared last month, he hinted that Helen had arranged for her abduction and sale to a London brothel to repay the girl for competing for a lover's affections."

"Absurd!"

"As you say, sir. But proving it will be difficult. Sir Steven and Mr. Dudley never visited Somerset during Sir Arthur's life, so few know their characters. And Smith has been very active in keeping anger on the boil."

"The tenants will accept the truth when we expose Steven and Dudley as liars and thieves."

He hoped. But he knew too well how difficult it was to correct false impressions. *Where there is smoke, there must be fire* was the motto of the gossips. He had to expose Steven soon or Helen would be ostracized by society. How was he to cope with a wife who loved another and whose reputation made his own pale? He had no evidence that the original tales were false.

Or had he?

Frowning, he headed downstairs for dinner.

Helen's impassioned defense of Alice and her insistence that he salvage Alice's reputation hinted that she knew the pain of unjust accusations. *Everyone will believe she is ruined . . . speculate . . . how many men did she entertain, when, where, who, even why . . . whisk their children away lest she corrupt them . . . every libertine for miles will seek his share.* Unlike the locals, Rafe knew Portland was capable of casually harming others, so Helen might well be innocent. Now all he had to do was prove it.

Audley's drawing room was as elegant as the entrance hall. Intricate paneling in subtle shades of green framed paintings and niches containing urns or busts. The patterns of the ornate plaster ceiling were repeated in the carpet. Green velvet draperies fringed with gold framed windows overlooking the park. Green-veined marble accented the twin fireplaces and topped half a dozen pier tables. Satinwood chairs sported green and gold upholstery.

Rafe paced to the window and back, letting his feet sink into the lush carpet, then exchanged glances with the cherubs dangling from the cornice—Sir Arthur had retained Adam's style when he'd refurbished. Ten minutes passed before the sound of approaching footsteps pulled his eyes to the door.

Helen looked lovely in a lavender gown trimmed with black—Tessa must have been busy, for he was sure that gown had been trimmed out in pink only two days ago. He stepped forward to take her hand, but the sounds of arguing stopped his greeting.

She rushed away. He followed.

"Of course, Mr. Portland is welcome," Helen was saying as Rafe reached the entrance hall. "He is a family friend. Put him in the red room, and set another place for dinner."

Nalley glared, but closed his mouth when he spotted Rafe.

She smiled at Portland. "I'm delighted to see you, Alex, though I won't say you look good. You don't." His injuries had bloomed into spectacular bruises. "Come in by the fire. You needn't change for dinner. It's just us."

"Thank you, Helen." He kissed her hand. "In truth, I can't change. I've outdistanced my luggage by half a day."

"You rode?" Helen gaped. "You must be ready to collapse. I can't believe you even tried such a stunt. I know very well your ribs are worse than Rafe's. Sit down, for heaven's sake." She tugged him toward the drawing room.

"Please." Rafe set aside pique. If the man had ridden *ventre à terre* to Audley, the news must be grim. But it would be better to hear it away from Nalley's prying ears.

"Thank you." Portland ushered Helen into the drawing room.

Rafe shut the door firmly behind them. "Be careful what you say," he warned. "The butler, housekeeper, and an unknown number of others seem loyal to Sir Steven."

"That does not surprise me."

They pulled chairs close to the nearest fire. Helen poured brandy for Portland and adjusted the fire screen so he was comfortable.

"You can't have been in town long," said Rafe, suppressing irritation at Helen's fussing.

"Long enough to see the investigation off and running." Portland stretched his legs. "The initial reports are troubling. The broker who hired Barney and Arnold is dead. His body was plucked from the Thames three days ago. It had been there awhile."

"He died before the attack?" asked Helen.

"Yes. And the directions given to Barney for collecting their remaining fee were false."

Rafe nodded. "Steven is severing all ties to the incident."

"Brutally dishonorable. But this means someone must have been watching Barney and Arnold—how else could Sir Steven know if they succeeded? That man may have carried the news to Sir Steven—or he may have followed you here," Portland finished.

"I doubt it," said Rafe. "I would have noticed."

Portland looked skeptical, but let it pass. "The broker's death means we can't officially connect Sir Steven to the attack. But we uncovered several investment frauds that involve him."

"Fraud sounds exactly like him," said Helen. "Father always claimed he would do anything for money."

"Why did no one notice fraud earlier?" asked Rafe.

"They did, but the perpetrators appeared to be other men—Mr. Rawlings, Mr. Bixly, Mr. Underwood, and so on. Only recently did anyone speculate that Sir Steven might be behind all the schemes," said Portland.

"I see."

"That news is not yet public, though. Your marriage occupies the gossips, Thomas," continued Portland maliciously. "I won't bore you with the details, but the rumors are ugly. Their only purpose can be to explain your ultimate death."

"I suppose you mean the courtesan stories," said Helen.

Portland scowled. "I traced them back to Lady Willingham, who is working hard to blacken your name. But I suspect she obtained the tale from Sir Steven."

Rafe flinched. So this was how she was avenging his cut. She must have gone to Steven the moment she read about his marriage.

"Supposedly you fell victim to a schemer—everyone agrees you were drunk at the time," he added smugly. "Rumor suggests that the girl did away with you when she discovered that you can't touch your father's fortune. You disappeared from town, which supports the charge."

Rafe relaxed. "Since I'm alive and well, people will dismiss the tale as soon as I return."

"I already took care of that." Portland turned back to Helen. "I admitted long friendship with your family, my dear, then mentioned seeing you in Surrey only that morning, duly wed to Thomas. A few judicious questions focused attention on Sir Steven and his motive for denying your nuptials. That's when Lady Roxbury told me that Sir Steven had defrauded Roxbury."

Rafe ground his teeth. Portland had quashed the gossip better than he could have done, for their long enmity added veracity to his support.

"As for the fraud," continued Portland. "That case was one of a dozen failed enterprises in which Steven invested."

"No one is that unlucky," said Rafe.

"Or that stupid," added Helen. "Where would he find the money for a dozen investments? He's been destitute for years."

"Exactly." Portland sipped brandy. "He used different men to promote each scheme. It was the disappearance of those men that usually tipped the investors that fraud was involved. We've not tracked any of them, so they were probably using false names."

Or were no longer among the living, but Rafe didn't say that aloud. He wasn't sure Helen was ready to think of her uncle as a habitual killer.

Portland swirled brandy in his glass. "He was canny enough to change the pitch each time—transport ventures, building ventures, import ventures, a silkworm farm . . . But each scheme operated the same way. Roxbury was caught by Courtney's Passenger Canal Company."

Rafe's stomach churned. He'd suggested buying shares in that one himself. Thank God Brockman had convinced him to pass. The idea of losing money to Steven made him sick, giving him a better understanding of how Helen must feel.

"What happened?" asked Helen.

"Sir Steven always poses as an investor," answered Portland. "He attends a meeting at which the company managers explain their goals and prospects. Steven's enthusiasm is so infectious that when he rushes to buy some of the limited shares available, others follow, fearful of missing so marvelous an opportunity. Ultimately, the venture fails and the managers disappear, leaving Sir Steven ruing losses along with everyone else."

"And no one suspected?" asked Helen.

"Plenty of legitimate ventures fail," said Rafe. "I am more surprised that society didn't notice Steven's run of misfortune."

"He was careful. Courtney's was the first scheme he'd floated in town. Until then, he'd preyed on country gentry, choosing a different county each time. But Roxbury was the wrong man to cheat. He wanted more than the shares themselves. He planned to buy land along the canal route and build housing for those who worked in the City but longed for clean air. When he checked the leases for the canal rights-of-way, he found they were forged. The principals immediately disappeared amid rumors that they'd fled to America. Roxbury had no real evidence against Sir Steven, but his scrutiny convinced Sir Steven to abandon such schemes."

"So what is he doing now?" asked Rafe.

"We aren't sure—aside from selling Lady Bounty's estate."

"What?" demanded Rafe. "She would never sell the Haven."

"Of course not, but Sir Steven needed a loan—no moneylender will speak to him. Since he expected her to stay home until she completed mourning, he sold her estate with the proviso that she could remain in residence another three months and with enough contingency clauses that she could change her mind and refund the deposit. But he'd forgotten that Lady Bounty is a prodigious correspondent. News reached her immediately, bringing her to town to find out what was going on. The victims are known swindlers—Mr. Hicks and Mr. Tilson—who don't take kindly to being duped. They are determined to make Sir Steven pay."

"So where is he now?" asked Helen.

"I don't know. That's why I'm here. Hicks sent two bully boys to avenge the Bounty fraud. They won't care if bystanders are hurt when they find him."

"How close are they to catching him?" asked Rafe.

"Sir Steven is being cautious. Creditors are camped at his London house and his estate. My men tracked him to Kensington—he moved to his mistress's cottage."

"Maude Cunningham," confirmed Helen.

Rafe smiled. "She was Helen's maid for eight months, which allowed Steven to keep a close eye on her."

"Ah." Portland shook his head. "When the Bounty sale collapsed, Steven disappeared. There is no sign of him on the turnpikes, but he would take side roads to avoid tolls, if nothing else. He collected only two hundred guineas from Hicks so must watch his purse."

"What about Dudley?"

"He left town with Sir Steven and Mrs. Cunningham, but he was not with them earlier. I don't yet have a complete report on his activities, but he broke Ottley's jaw the night you were wed." His glance begged forgiveness from Helen for such frank speaking.

"I'm not surprised," she said. "Whenever he is frustrated, he breaks something. That time I knocked him down, he smashed a mirror and two chairs," she added, meeting Rafe's eye.

He nodded, recalling her tale of Dudley's assaults.

"Dudley lost five thousand before the fight with Ottley," added Portland.

"Ouch."

"More debt."

"Exactly. Caristoke holds most of the vowels. His father is the Earl of Pembroke," he told Helen. "*Not* a man to cross. Unless Dudley pays, he will find himself barred from every club and gaming hell in England." Portland finished his brandy. "So Sir Steven and Dudley both need money badly, especially if they plan to live abroad. Sir Steven can't stay in England now that so many investigations are under way."

"I doubt that he knows about the investigations," said Helen. "But we already expected him to come here."

Rafe frowned. The news wasn't good. One explanation for Smith's cockiness was that Steven and Dudley had already arrived.

Nalley interrupted to announce dinner.

When Rafe reached the sitting room after eating—he'd remained behind to chastise Nalley for poor service—Helen and Portland were circling the courtyard, arm in arm, heads close together. The French window muffled their voices, but it was clear that they were intimate. She might have sworn to cut out his heart four years ago, but that display of temper hadn't mitigated her love. It had survived separation and forgiven whatever fight had parted them.

He turned away when Portland bent to kiss her, unable to watch. The seduction was starting already, a seduction that must lead to infidelity. He would never be able to trust her out of his sight—or in it, for that matter. If she spent her time dreaming of Portland . . .

Pain sliced his chest, exposing the truth. His feelings had moved beyond possessiveness into genuine caring. How ironic that she wanted nothing to do with him. He'd happened along when she was too injured to think clearly. Now she was trapped in marriage with the wrong man.

The future looked grim.

He'd seen what happened when strong-willed adversaries wed. His parents had fought every day of his life, never conceding even trivial points. Their marriage had been an endless struggle as Hillcrest demanded absolute obedience and Lady Hillcrest begged for the same freedoms other ladies enjoyed. That her dowry had rescued Hillcrest from ruin had made his tyranny harder to bear.

Rafe shivered. He might not be penniless, but Helen's fortune dwarfed his. They must live on her estate. She had already refused to discuss its affairs. And she was in love with another man.

His eyes burned.

He couldn't endure a marriage like his mother's. Now that he'd seen proof of Helen's preferences, he must set her free. Any other course would drive him mad.

As she opened the door, he melted into the shadows.

"Get some sleep, Alex," she was saying as they entered.

He nodded and left.

Helen remained, frowning. Her eyes were dim, her shoulders slumped. Her predicament clearly made her unhappy.

She finally released a long sigh and headed for the hall.

"Shut the door, Helen," Rafe said, stepping forward. "We need to talk."

She jumped but complied. "Steven is more dishonorable than I feared," she said, moving near the fire, which took her farther from his side. "And more desperate because of it. Why did no one suspect fraud sooner? He must be losing fortune upon fortune at the tables."

"As long as he covered his losses, no one would question where he found the money. Gentlemen don't pry into one another's business. And most of London believed he was heir to Arthur's title and fortune."

"I can't understand why Alquist didn't dispute that notion."

An interesting question, Rafe conceded. But this wasn't the time to explore it. If he was going to free her, he must do it before he turned coward. "I have been considering our situation, Helen. In retrospect, I shamelessly forced you into marriage, a dishonor for which I must apologize. Now that you are recovered from Steven's blow, you must regret my insistence. Thus I won't oppose a petition for annulment. Your concussion may give you grounds, for it rendered you incapable of clear thinking. The bishop might consider that incompetence under the law."

She stared, as if not believing she could be so lucky. Then her chin rose, twisting her face in fury. "I hadn't thought you a coward, Rafe, but if that's what you want, I will write to my solicitor in the morning." Her voice cracked. Clenching her fists, she fled.

Shocked, he poured a hefty glass of brandy. He hadn't expected anger. And how could she call him a coward for offering what she so patently wanted? It didn't make sense. What the devil did she expect of him?

*   *   *

Helen stumbled into her room and threw herself on the bed. Tears streamed down her face, despite her best effort to quell them. Rafe's voice still echoed in her ears. *Shamelessly forced . . . annulment . . .*

He must believe Smith's charges. She had hoped that her explanation would clear the air, but she hadn't even apologized for not warning him. Why would he believe her now?

Or perhaps Lady Alquist was right. Rafe feared repeating his parents' mistake. Having seen Audley for himself and verified the size of her fortune, he was running. It would explain why he'd avoided her last night. He'd wed her in a fit of pique and come to regret it.

Yet his timing was suspicious. Alex had dragged her outside to swear undying devotion, then Rafe demanded an annulment. Had Alex convinced Rafe to step aside?

The idea that they'd discussed her over port and come to terms was enough to put her off both men. She was not a scrap of meat for two dogs to fight over.

But she could hardly hold Rafe against his will. A lifelong war with Hillcrest had taught him to reject any bonds. If she refused his demands, he would fight back as least as hard as he fought Hillcrest.

Chapter Sixteen

May 28

*V*oices woke Helen shortly after dawn. Angry voices outside her bedroom door.

"This is bigger than your puny mind can comprehend, so you need my help," hissed Alex. "You haven't any idea of how to protect Helen."

"And you do?" Rafe laughed. "Your idea of protection was to abandon her."

"I didn't abandon her!" snapped Alex. "If I hadn't stayed away, my enemies might have attacked her. Do you think I enjoyed the separation?"

"So you left her to Steven's mercy." Rafe's voice hardened. "Forget the past, Portland. It is gone. I appreciate your help in town, but that's as far as it goes. You can leave after breakfast. I'll send you any evidence that might help you prosecute Steven and Dudley."

"I won't leave until Helen is safe."

"The only danger to Helen is from you. You've made your position clear enough. It wouldn't surprise me if you let Steven kill me so you can protect Helen by wedding her."

"You can't believe that!" Alex sounded appalled.

"I wouldn't trust you to accompany me down the stairs without tripping me."

"Imbecile!" snapped Alex. "It is you who can't be trusted. Who stole my mistress the moment my back was turned? Who undermined an investigation by black-balling—"

"I did *not* steal Lydia," snarled Rafe. "I don't poach. She swore you had parted company."

"Hah!"

"True. She tried to seduce me at Cavendish's masquerade. I balked, but you'd been away for weeks, so when she claimed to be free, I believed her. The moment I learned otherwise, I threw her out. I hate liars."

"An odd declaration coming from you. Your damned duel story nearly cost me my position."

"*My* story! That was *you*."

"It was not."

Helen pulled a pillow over her head in a futile attempt to muffle the voices. So much for her theory of cooperation. Imbeciles! Both of them!

Fury washed over her. How dare Alex claim to love her, then attack Rafe over a shared courtesan? And how dare Rafe demand an annulment, yet vilify Alex for loving her?

Not that this argument meant he cared. He hated Alex enough to argue anything he said—just as Hillcrest did.

"For the last time, I never claimed a duel!" shouted Alex.

"Then who—" Rafe paused. "Lydia. It must be."

"How do you figure that?" scoffed Alex.

"Use that brain you're so proud of, Portland. Lydia wants jewels and fancy clothes and a big house, but to gain them she must become the most sought-after courtesan in town. You kept leaving without explanation—"

"I could hardly share crown secrets with a whore," said Alex stiffly.

"But your behavior convinced her she couldn't hold you, which is as good as a public cut to the demimonde. To avenge your negligence, she seduced the man you hated most. When I threw her out, she invented a duel to make herself seem fascinating. It worked. Fishbein is showering her with gifts to keep her in his bed."

Alex growled.

"We're both well rid of her," Rafe declared, moving toward the stairs. "You should . . ."

*   *   *

By the time Helen reached the breakfast room, she was angry enough to shoot both men on sight—not that it would do any good. Rakes bedded anyone who tempted them. Once the attraction wore off, they moved on.

Which explained Rafe's demand for an annulment. Whatever moment of lust had prompted his offer was gone. Staying with her put him in danger.

Alex's motives were just as suspicious. He, too, was a rake. Dancing attendance on her antagonized Rafe, but it wasn't real. He was free to needle Rafe as much as he wanted, because she could no longer demand he wed her. Neither of them actually wanted her.

She examined them as she took a seat. They looked more alike than ever today. Both sported black eyes and bruises that emphasized their scars. Both wore corbeau jackets and fawn pantaloons—Alex's luggage must have arrived. Both were arguing when she walked in, but immediately pasted on false smiles. They were interchangeable, as last night's dream suggested.

It had started with the game of hide-and-seek she'd played so often with Alex. Their games had always ended in hot, openmouthed kisses and urgent yearnings for more. The dream provided more as he untied her gown, letting it drift languidly to the ground. Her petticoats had followed. Stays. Shift. She'd stripped him in turn, reveling in sunlight reflecting from the hard planes of his chest, in his questing hands and hot mouth, in—

But it wasn't Alex who laid her on the soft grass. Nor was it Alex who drove her insane with pleasure. Rafe's eyes blazed like molten silver. She touched him, marveling as she stroked steely muscle covered in velvet and satin. His tongue—

She'd awakened, moaning, with every nerve tingling. But the transformation of Alex into Rafe still shocked her. Of course, Alex had never touched her intimately, so the dream had probably re-created what she knew. But it left her unable to look either of them in the eye.

Not that Rafe noticed. He concentrated on his food, ignoring her.

Alex, on the other hand, welcomed her warmly, with impossibly effusive praise. That he continued his flirtation after she'd slapped his face proved that his purpose was to annoy Rafe. So he couldn't know about Rafe's annulment demand.

She toyed with sending him back to London, but they needed his expertise. And she might need other help if Rafe left to pursue his annulment. He was sullen enough today that she had to consider the possibility. Leaving him to his megrims, she cut off Alex's fulsome compliments.

"Nalley may be more than Steven's loyal servant." She leaned close, keeping her voice soft in case the butler was listening at the door.

"What do you mean?"

"Steven is not perpetrating fraud by himself. Nalley may be helping him. He often slips away to meet disreputable men."

"How do you know?" Alex frowned.

"Tessa learned that one of the housemaids meets a groom on the sly." She shook her head. "I will have to talk to her. Sneaking about sets an awkward precedent for the younger girls."

"Turning her off is the usual punishment," said Alex. "Sly girls make bad servants."

"That sounds too harsh—" began Helen.

"Very," put in Rafe unexpectedly. "Talk to them. I'm sure you can find an equitable solution. You've no idea what Steven's policies have been."

"Condoning lax behavior undermines discipline." Alex glared at Rafe.

"Punishing anyone without first learning facts is deplorable," countered Rafe. "Servants are as entitled to friendships as their masters."

"I will deal with the staff," said Helen before they could come to blows. The proprietor of the Plate and Bottle wanted to retire, so she needed a couple to take over the inn. "At the moment, I'm more concerned with Nalley. He slips away frequently, and always appears furtive. Rose never knows where he'll pop up. There seems to be no rhyme or reason to his meetings."

Alex nodded. "Being predictable is the best way to be caught."

"Did Rose describe any of the men Nalley meets?" asked Rafe.

The question surprised her, for his curiosity and support stood at odds with yesterday's suspicion and demands. "Scruffy, but that could mean anything. It has been going on for months, though. And it might connect with Steven's affairs."

"I will look into it." Rafe glared Alex into silence. "But not today. We have more pressing problems at the moment." He turned to Alex. "You mentioned forged canal documents last night. Have other forgeries turned up?"

"Not to my knowledge, but I've more information on the assassins—my valet brought an updated report from my office. A Mr. Stone was seen near Hillcrest several times in recent days, which ties the attack to Sir Steven. Stone is his secretary and suspected of forging the canal documents. He is currently in France—possibly arranging for Sir Steven's arrival."

"Unless he is fleeing a sinking ship," said Rafe, shrugging. "You can add the forgeries Steven sent to Helen's trustees to the charges against him, by the way."

"And the one he gave me. I should have realized Stone wrote them," said Helen with distaste. "Steven's hand is illegible."

"What forgeries?" asked Alex.

Helen explained.

"You can collect the actual letters from Formsby," said Rafe pointedly.

"My staff will see to it."

Helen interrupted to prevent another argument. "What are the plans for today?" She kept her eyes on Rafe, wondering if he meant to leave. An annulment would negate his promise of protection. Prudence would dictate a swift departure in the interest of personal safety.

Rafe shoved his plate aside. "We need a better defense. The house is far too vulnerable."

Helen nearly swooned to realize he wouldn't abandon her. Her reaction surprised her, but a moment's thought made her admit that her morning pique had ignored per-

tinent facts. Rafe and Alex were far from interchangeable. Merely looking at Rafe sent her heart racing. That
no longer happened with Alex, and last night's kiss had
turned her cold. Rafe might behave questionably at
times, but he'd never actually betrayed her.

Alex nodded. "Defense is important, but any plan
must include the grounds." He turned to Helen. "It is
impossible to guard every entrance in a place this size,
but sentries can tell us if anyone approaches."

"How many servants can we trust?" Helen met
Rafe's eyes.

"Considering Nalley's antagonism, I dare not approach the indoor staff, and I've not met the grounds
staff. But the stable hands are sound—they are thrilled
to discover the truth, for Steven and Dudley abuse
horses. My coachmen and groom can arrange the
watches. How many came with your carriage, Portland?"

"My coachman, a groom, plus three couriers—I must
stay in touch with my office. One courier will leave
shortly, but the others can stand guard." He turned to
Helen. "Show me the grounds. I've forgotten the exact
layout."

"I need you to show me the house," said Rafe. "I've
not had time to explore even this wing, let alone the
others."

"Take Tessa. She knows Audley as well as I do, but
she's less familiar with the grounds." Helen stifled regret—she needed time alone with Rafe—but it couldn't
be helped. "I'll ask Frank to order horses," she added
to Alex. "We will leave in twenty minutes." But a new
thought occurred as she rose. "What if I give Steven
enough money to establish himself in France or Italy?
Would he leave?"

"No." Rafe shook his head. "He is too obsessed to
admit defeat—which is how he would describe flight. His
instinct will be to avenge his losses. I ruined him by
wedding you, so I must die. You stole his inheritance,
putting you in equal danger."

"He can't be that mad."

"Don't underestimate him, Helen. The more I learn
about him, the more convinced I am that he is like Hillcrest. Rather than accept blame, he will look for a scape-

goat—you. He will not leave England without first punishing you."

"You're wrong, Thomas." Alex turned to Helen. "Sir Steven is selfish, greedy, and willing to do anything for a fortune. But he is not mad. He severed his ties to Barney and Arnold. He does not know we are investigating his frauds. The runner you hired is stirring suspicions over Alquist's death, but no one yet connects it to him. So if he takes possession of Audley, he can pay his creditors, placate Hicks and Tilson, and live wealthily ever after."

"But we will be ready for him," she said steadily.

"Not you. Thomas is right that you are in danger, Helen, though his logic is twisted, as usual. All this rubbish about forced weddings is ridiculous. Sir Steven will kill you, then claim Audley as next of kin."

She snorted. "Impossible. He is not my heir."

"He will kill Thomas first, my dear. Then where will you find an heir? I presume you revised your will, Thomas."

"Of course."

"I—" Her blood ran cold. "I never revised mine." Effort brought her panic under control. "Not that it matters. The trust has its own beneficiary in case I die intestate. Steven knows that. It's his reason for pushing me on Dudley."

"But Stone is a forger," said Rafe. "It is mere speculation that he has broken with Steven. What is to prevent Steven from producing a new will? He might even disband the trust first, removing another set of people who could ask questions."

She frowned. "Do you really think he will kill us both?"

"It is the logical solution. After Christchurch, he must know you will never obey him. Wedding you to Dudley requires that he control both of you." Rafe shook his head. "So why not cut Dudley out completely and take everything for himself?"

"There is no point in arguing his intentions," put in Alex, shoving his plate aside. "We must expect the worst, which means planning the best defense."

"Right." Rafe rose.

Alex escorted Helen to the door.

* * *

Rafe glared after them. He shouldn't be surprised that she'd chosen to accompany Portland over him. But he was. Also angry and hurt.

Tightening his fists, he stormed out and summoned Tessa, furious at himself for caring what Helen did, furious at Portland for daring to touch her, furious at . . .

He fought his fury into submission, then whisked through the Tudor wing, paying close attention to the floors and stairways. The dust was undisturbed.

"This wing sends chills down my spine," said Tessa shakily. "It's haunted, you know. Rose's beau seen figures in the windows, and he swears there was torches and music one night, like we was having a ball."

"A house this old is bound to have ghosts, but they mean us no harm," he replied calmly as they climbed to the top floor to check the connecting door to the Elizabethan wing. "How long have you served Helen? You can't be much older than she is."

"I was sixteen when Sir Arthur bought Audley. He emptied the parish workhouse to staff the place. Lady St. James's maid trained me to look after Miss Helen."

Rafe frowned at a wall. Water stains marred the plaster. He must ask Helen if the roof had been repaired.

"Tell me about Mr. Portland." The question invited new fury, but he needed answers. Despite claiming that Portland was an untrustworthy liar, Helen grabbed every opportunity to be with him. If both he and Portland were in peril, would she even notice her husband?

"There isn't much to tell," Tessa hedged. "He was Sir Montrose's guest four years ago."

"I know Portland was courting her," Rafe said gently. "But I need to know her mind now." He'd offered the annulment, praying she would refuse but expecting her to accept. Instead, she'd exploded in fury, then fled— almost as if she hurt. She hadn't yet written to her solicitor, but had turned all her warmth on Portland. Was she making sure of her welcome before casting her husband aside?

"She married you." Tessa's tone terminated the subject.

He tried another tack. "How much opposition did she face when she took over Audley?"

"I don't know. Miss Helen has always kept her own counsel."

No one had entered the Tudor wing from this end, so he moved into the unused Elizabethan wing and dropped his questions. Tessa was too loyal to Helen to reveal anything, and her nervousness reminded him of her recent ordeal.

None of the stairs in this wing had been used, either, nor had feet traversed the hallways. If Steven was in the house, he had to be in the new wing.

But further search was pointless. Without dust to reveal footprints, Steven could dodge out of sight and shift unnoticed into rooms already searched. Rafe would do better to prepare the master suite for immediate occupancy.

Helen stared at the study wall, indecision stalling her quill.

Regardless of Steven's intentions, she needed a will. She did not support some of the benevolent societies her father had designated as residual beneficiaries.

He had never expected her to retain control forever, of course. Many of his lectures had covered ways to tell if a gentleman was honest. Leaving her in charge had meant to discourage fortune hunters, but he'd intended that she break the trust once she found a decent husband. Like all men, he'd never believed her his equal.

And maybe he was right. She'd bungled things badly since his death, wallowing in grief until she couldn't think straight. Steven had easily outmaneuvered her.

"Stop agonizing over the past," she ordered herself firmly.

The easy letters were done—notes to Lady Alquist and her trustees outlining her evidence against Steven, then swearing that she would never, under any circumstances, leave so much as a farthing to him or Dudley or anyone associated with them. Any will that included such provisions was a forgery.

But the final letter was more difficult. It was addressed

to Mr. Fielding and announced her marriage to Rafe. Now she must add the instructions for preparing her new will, which meant naming her beneficiaries.

Minor bequests were simple. Five hundred to Tessa. Smaller sums to other servants. A hundred to her old nurse. It was the rest that gave her pause.

Though her family tree was sparse, Steven and Dudley were not her only relatives. Others included the St. James spinsters—her grandfather's sisters. That was all she knew about them, for they had backed Steven in the family quarrel that had disinherited Arthur, and now lived on his estate. She feared Steven would confiscate anything she left them, but she made a note to check their circumstances.

Another she'd not met was Alquist's son, though he had a fine inheritance of his own, so needed no assistance. Then there was Lucas St. James, steward to a Yorkshire squire—or so he'd been the last she'd heard. He was another she must check on. Her father had been conscientious about his role as head of the family. That position was now Steven's, but he would do nothing to uphold it.

She shook her head, irritated that she kept sidetracking. Her immediate problem was naming her main beneficiary.

Rafe was the expected choice. Yet Alice and his demand for an annulment complicated her decision. As did his similarity to Alex.

Alex was a liar who considered her a credulous widgeon, as every comment during their morning ride had proved. He might also be a fortune hunter—after losing everything to Rafe, he could hardly have recouped on a government salary. And he treated her like a fragile imbecile, becoming irritated if she questioned his assumptions.

He'd always been like that, she realized, though it hadn't bothered her four years ago. It was she who had changed, replacing drawing room conversation with agricultural discussions, and feminine pursuits with estate management. Her interests were broader, her outlook more serious, her arrogance gone—or so she hoped. In short, she could take care of herself and her dependents without help. But Alex clung to his belief that she remained that silly, conformable miss who had followed him about like a besotted puppy.

She cringed, but the image was apt. Censure and loss had awakened her to the realities of life. Alex's reactions proved that he, like most gentlemen, did not accept the change, nor did he approve of it.

But Rafe did.

She had been concentrating on all the wrong things, she realized in disgust. Rafe and Alex might seem alike, but while they shared many surface characteristics, underneath they were very different. Rafe had treated her with respect from the beginning, even when he was the worse for wine and thought her a courtesan. Recognizing her competence, he'd allowed her to conduct her business and had taken delight in how she'd handled Formsby.

When she tried to imagine any other man in that role, she shuddered.

Rafe also debated like her equal, conceding when she was right and accepting her apologies when she was wrong. He never used those apologies against her and continued protecting her from Steven despite wanting to end their marriage.

Rafe had more in common with her father than with Alex. Each had overcome a parent's opposition, struck out on his own, then turned a modest gain into a comfortable fortune. Each showed empathy for victims because he had experienced the condition himself. Each respected anyone with intelligence.

Alex didn't. Nor would he have made a good husband even four years ago. His precipitous departure had saved her from a ghastly mistake.

She needed a man who accepted her unconventional training, who listened to her ideas, who treated her as a partner rather than a possession.

In short, Rafe.

But he demanded an annulment, said her conscience.

Had he?

She frowned, trying to remember his exact words.

She'd been so shocked that the meeting remained fuzzy. But he'd been surprised at her fury. Had he expected her to leap at the offer?

Now that she thought about it, his behavior was odd. If he truly wanted an annulment, why was he still here? Remaining at Audley might cost him his life. If he had stayed to pursue justice, then his reputation was as false as Lady Alquist claimed. Or perhaps he cared for her, at least a little. The idea warmed her heart.

You love him.

She cursed, but it was true. Her defenses had been too weak to lock him out, which would explain that dream. The false love had finally been replaced by the true. One that offered greater depth and far more excitement.

Rafe might still leave, she admitted—love could be one-sided. But at least this solved her dilemma. She would bequeath him everything.

Exhaling in a long sigh, she finished the letter and sealed it. Perhaps she was blinding herself, but it was done. If Rafe turned on her, she would accept it. Recognizing her love had showed her how much she needed him. Life would be empty if he left.

If only she'd trusted him earlier. Her nights would not have been as lonely.

Closing her eyes recalled his hands, his taste, his smell, his passion . . .

Her body tingled with awareness the instant he entered a room. She felt his every glance. His presence could protect or threaten, but it never went unnoticed. She would not let another night pass without him.

Chapter Seventeen

"**S**et Lady St. James's personal effects in the blue room for now," Rafe told Tessa and Rose. "Mrs. Thomas can decide what to do with them later."

He was supervising the turnout of the master suite, a short wing separated from the rest of the court by an ornate door, with rooms forming a "U" around a private corridor. That no spring cleaning had been done was another black mark against Mrs. Lakes. She had turned out Steven's suite the moment he left for London, but she'd done nothing to the rest of the house, not even the weekly airing of unused rooms that was necessary to keep mold at bay. No one had entered the master suite since Lady St. James's burial.

He crossed back to his own chambers. The master's bedroom must reflect Sir Arthur's taste, for it was the only room in the Palladian wing with Gothic décor. Screamingly Gothic, as expressed by dark paneling festooned with ornamentation. Its crowning glory—if one liked Gothic—was the fireplace wall of elaborately carved wood. Intricate trees supported and surmounted the mantel. Birds of prey swooped toward rabbits and other small animals cavorting in woods and meadows. Two deer raised their heads, ready to flee. A boar thrust vicious tusks from behind a shrub. The high relief meant viewers had to stand well away to keep from snagging their clothing on legs, wings, antlers . . .

Portland was watching Vince and Charlie roll up the bedroom carpet. Rafe had insisted on using the pair so he could keep a close eye on them.

"That mattress needs cleaning, too," Portland was drawling as Rafe entered. "And probably restuffing."

Charlie glared, but draped it over the carpet roll.

Rafe fanned dust from his face. The breeze from the open windows had not yet dissipated the cloud raised by pulling down the draperies. "We're making progress, I see."

"Slowly." Portland paused until the footmen were gone. "Those two are the poorest workers I've ever encountered."

"Deliberate, I suspect. Have you spotted anyone outside?" They were keeping one eye on the grounds. The master suite overlooked formal gardens that could not be seen from the stables. Posting sentries during the day might draw unwanted attention.

"No, though I can't watch every second. The carpet is back in your study, by the way. Where do you want the furniture?"

"I haven't thought about it." He led the way through his dressing room.

The study walls were dark green with cream moldings picked out in gold. Beating had uncovered intricate patterns in the red, green, and gold carpet. Low bookcases flanked the fireplace. A decent painting of Audley hung on that wall with a lady's portrait across from it.

"Lady St. James?" he asked, spotting the resemblance to Helen.

Portland nodded.

Rafe hefted one end of the desk. "Let's put it there." He pointed to a spot near the window. None of this was his job, but if he relied on Vince and Charlie, Christmas would arrive before the work was done. Nor could he trust Nalley or Mrs. Lakes to supervise.

Portland lifted the other end. "I owe you an apology, Thomas."

"What?" Rafe nearly dropped the desk on his foot.

"You are not the wastrel I thought."

"My reputation does obscure truth at times."

"Why?"

He set the desk in place and adjusted its angle. "Two people have worked hard to maintain it—you and Hillcrest. Neither of you looks beyond your own conclusions even when contradictory evidence stares you in the face."

"You dare compare me to that lunatic?" Portland's face darkened. "I just dressed him down for that very fault."

"What did he do to you?"

"Interfered with my surveillance of a French courier, prolonging the war by allowing campaign strategies to reach Napoleon."

"That sounds like him. Judge first, and don't bother asking questions later."

Portland moved a chair nearer the fireplace. "Maybe I *was* guilty of misjudgment. Losing that card game put me in a bind—my father refused to cover my vowels, sending me to the moneylenders. It took me three years to recover. It was easier to blame you than admit I'd had too much to drink. And watching you squander my funds—"

"Never." Rafe shoved a marble-topped pier table against the wall. "I invested nearly all of it. The income now exceeds my expenses several times over."

"My God." Portland abruptly sat. "Have I misjudged everything then?"

"Probably. I've never acted against you despite your continuing slander."

"Not even Hasley's?"

Rafe shook his head. "I can't be sure, since the vote was secret, but that black ball was probably dropped by Sir Thomas Kettering. He'd been muttering against you for days, gifting me with his diatribes since everyone knew we were at odds."

Portland swore. "I should have known—would have, had I thought about it. I'd bought the town house he'd bid on a week earlier. He hates losing."

Rafe refrained from another comparison to Hillcrest.

"I've been a fool," admitted Portland. "About everything. Especially Lydia. If she'd gone to anyone but you I wouldn't have minded, which she undoubtedly knew. Her prattling had become a bore by then, but I was away too often to care. It is like her to scheme to increase her consequence. I never should have taken on an intelligent mistress. They are too much trouble."

"Yet you claim to love Helen, who is the most intelligent woman I know."

"Hardly. In any case, she knows her place."

Rafe stared. But before he could comment, Vince and Charlie returned, stifling personal conversation.

Helen summoned Tessa to post her letters in the village, then headed upstairs to talk to Rafe. They needed to discuss the future. Did he want out of this match? Why had he kissed Alice? What concessions would keep him by her side, and could she live with them?

She trembled. Love left her more vulnerable than ever. Yet there was little she could do to entice him if he didn't want to stay. Giving him Audley and her trust might elicit promises, but love that could be bought wasn't worth a groat. Rafe had to accept her as she was. If he couldn't, then seeking that annulment was their only course.

She mounted the stairs, then halted when someone rapped loudly on the front door.

"What now?" she muttered, turning around. It wasn't proper for the lady of the house to answer the door, but she didn't trust Nalley.

What if it's Steven?

She paused. Between them, Steven and Nalley could easily overpower her. Rafe and Alex were too far away to hear her screams. Would Steven abduct her while others eliminated Rafe?

Nalley's voice banished that fear. "Mr. Thomas is not at home."

"Nonsense!" Helen rushed down the stairs.

Nalley whirled so fast he nearly fell. "Mrs. T-Thomas."

"It is not your place to decide whether we are receiving," she said coldly, then turned to the groom seeking entrance. A crested carriage stood in the drive. "Who is calling?"

"Lord Hillcrest, ma'am," he said stiffly.

A curse nearly fell from her lips. What was Hillcrest doing here? Had he found a way to dissolve her marriage? Maybe he was unbalanced enough to arrest Rafe for killing Pauling.

Ridiculous, she reminded herself. Reining in her imagination, she smiled. Whatever Hillcrest's purpose, he was here. Which gave her an opportunity to soften his antagonism. She would not repeat his lack of courtesy. "We are delighted to receive his lordship."

Her smile disappeared the moment the groom turned away.

"Frank, show Lord Hillcrest to the library." The footman was standing behind the statue of Apollo. "Order refreshments, then tell Mrs. Lakes to prepare a bedchamber. Nalley, come with me." She stepped into the dining room.

The confrontation was short and nasty, but she felt lighter as she headed upstairs. One problem gone.

Hillcrest's arrival would postpone any discussion, though. Rafe was every bit as stubborn as his father. If she summoned him to the library, he would likely refuse. So she must personally convince him to meet Hillcrest— and do it without letting Alex or the servants overhear.

Rafe was installing a bolt on her bedroom door, while Alex worked on the bathing room. It was a crude measure but would prevent anyone from slipping in at night. The master suite's internal doors had no locks.

"Did you post your letters?" asked Rafe.

She nodded. "Let Alex finish that. We need to talk."

Rafe raised a brow, but set down his tools and followed her to his study.

"What's wrong?" he demanded once the door was shut. "Do you want me gone now that you are seeking an annulment?"

"I will *not* seek an annulment," she snapped, then reined in her temper before she could demand whether he would. An argument would make it harder to gain his consent to see Hillcrest. "I turned off Nalley."

He frowned. "I thought we agreed to wa—" He ran his fingers through his hair. "Why?"

"He refuses to obey orders, delights in irritating us, and threatens any servants who serve us. But the last straw was again denying entrance to a caller. There's no telling how many others he might have turned away."

"Didn't he learn that lesson after Portland's arrival?"

"No." She laid her hand on his arm. "He claims that

Steven hired him, so only Steven can change his orders. I informed him that Steven's estate is in Lincolnshire, so he must continue his service there, then delegated David to help him pack and escort him to a carriage. David was listening at the door and was nearly bursting with delight when I summoned him, so we can trust him."

"You had no choice." He pulled her against him. "But I fear what he might do."

She opened her mouth to agree, but he stopped her with a kiss. In moments, she was wrapped by his hard and obviously aroused body. Her last coherent thought drained away. This was what she wanted. Needed. She loved him with all her heart. And he still wanted her, despite everything. They would find a compromise they could both live with. Soon.

She threaded her fingers through his dark hair, reveling in the texture of fine silk. Rafe's hand slid up her back—

Alex cursed as something crashed against the door.

Rafe's curse was pithier. "We'll finish this later," he promised, panting. "Who did Nalley turn away now?"

"Wha—" She shook herself to restart her brain. "Lord Hillcrest. He wishes to see you."

"No." He shoved her away.

"I put him in the library."

"Why the devil did you allow him in the house?" Rafe's fists whitened. "I don't care what he does at Hillcrest Manor, but I won't allow his war into Audley. Send him packing. And don't ever try to manipulate me with kisses again!" He strode to the window.

"Damn you!" Helen followed. "I would never be stupid enough to use kisses against a rake. You started that."

"Maybe," he conceded, but his face remained grim.

"Rafe, please." She touched his arm. "Come downstairs. I know you despise him, but ignoring him lowers you to his level. You must extend our hospitality."

"Why, for God's sake? He hates us. He only came here to stir up trouble."

"You don't know that." She grabbed his head and

forced him to look at her. "The man traveled two days to speak with you. You will do him the courtesy of listening."

"Why? So he can tell me what a worthless wastrel I am—for the ten thousandth time? So he can castigate me for not following his orders? So he can put words in my mother's mouth she would never have uttered in yet another attempt to bring me to heel?" By the time he finished, he was panting, and not from passion. His scars stood out against a red face.

Helen smoothed his cheeks with her thumbs. Rafe would never be free until he put this war behind him. But running didn't work. He must meet Hillcrest and remain calm. Only proving that Hillcrest no longer ruled him would give him the confidence to move ahead. "He would not have traveled across England to say that, Rafe. Did he ever chase you down in London?"

"No." He bit his lip.

"Yet he lived barely an hour away. He could have disrupted your life at any time by showing up on your doorstep or spreading his vitriol in the clubs."

Fury faded until his eyes again shone with intelligence. And surprise.

Helen pressed her point. "His errand must be important to draw him away from Hillcrest. Perhaps he heard the truth of that attack on Alex and fears for your life."

Rafe snorted.

"Or maybe he took your advice and married Alice."

He flinched.

Ignoring his reaction, she doggedly continued. "But whatever he wants, you should show him the courtesy of listening. I know you don't want to," she added when his face darkened. "But refusing is a infantile gesture that serves no purpose. You are above that, Rafe. Do you wish to spend the rest of your life playing petulant child to his domineering parent? You will never be free of him until you withdraw from his war. He and your mother were strong-willed people who refused to compromise. But their differences are not your concern. This is *your* house, so you can set the rules. You needn't fight unless you want to, so show him how a true gentleman behaves. Let him have his say without losing your temper. Invite him to spend the night. It may not change his mind, but you will feel better for it."

"Very well." He glared. "But only if you come with me. I won't face him alone."

"Thank you." She kissed his cheek, then headed for the door.

Rafe's head swirled as he approached the library. Why had Helen kissed him? That light peck contained none of the passion of their earlier embrace. Was it acknowledgment of good behavior—like patting a dog for not peeing on the carpet? Despite her denials, she was using feminine wiles to coerce him into meeting Hillcrest. Even her response to his kiss might have sought to bend his will.

It was working. He couldn't ignore her request. He needed her too much. Her refusal to seek an annulment had sent his heart soaring—not that it meant she cared. She might have decided that Portland's adoration was more exciting in small doses than as a daily diet. Rafe couldn't imagine anyone wanting to live with the fellow. The man was a bore.

He was also a blind fool.

Since tendering his truce an hour earlier, Portland had talked incessantly, mostly about Helen. He'd even accused Rafe of forcing her to stay at Audley instead of letting her retreat to a safe haven. As if Rafe could force her to do anything . . .

But one thing was patently obvious. Portland might claim a betrothal and swear eternal love for Helen, but he didn't know the first thing about her. He considered her weak-spirited, fragile, and incapable of understanding anything more complex than a hand of whist. In his view, she had been tossed into an impossible situation by a mad father, but was bravely trying to cope.

"Absurd!" Rafe had snapped. "I daresay Helen knows more about estate management than you do. I know she is more competent than I am or want to be. And I've never met anyone, male or female, who is as calm in a crisis. You would be dead if she hadn't shot Barney."

"*She* shot him?" Portland's shock was palpable. "That's not—"

"She did." He'd glanced around to make sure the servants were out of earshot. "I pulled Barney off you, but Arnold attacked before I could subdue him. They were moving in for the kill when Helen arrived. Without her, we both would have died."

Portland had hemmed and hawed, then changed the subject. Rafe wondered if he'd put the incident clean out of his mind. He seemed determined to see Helen as a shrinking violet who needed his protection and guidance.

"You said you would talk to him," said Helen at his elbow.

He realized that his feet were rooted to the floor outside the library.

"Relax, Rafe," she murmured, tightening her hand on his arm. "He can't attack you under your own roof without making himself look a fool."

"Your roof."

"That doesn't matter. Let's see what he wants."

Inhaling deeply, he pushed the door open.

The library occupied the short wing under the master suite, with windows on three sides overlooking the formal gardens. Shelves rose head high between them. Above the shelves, intricate medallions depicting Greek classics alternated with paintings framed with gilt.

Hillcrest stood opposite the door, frowning at a shelf. A cough drew Rafe's eyes to the front window, where Alice gazed out at the garden, flanked by terrestrial and celestial globes.

Alice? His stomach clenched. If Hillcrest had forced Alice into marriage, Rafe would never forgive himself.

When Helen's subtle shove steered him behind the desk, he sat, grateful for its authority. It gave him an edge he rarely enjoyed when facing Hillcrest.

Helen headed for the window. "What a pleasant surprise, Miss Pauling. Your groom did not mention that you had accompanied Lord Hillcrest. Welcome to Audley Court."

"Thank you, Mrs. Thomas. We are pleased to be

here." She drew a woman forward. "This is my companion, Mrs. Everly."

Rafe studied the woman while Helen and Alice exchanged comments on the weather and their respective journeys from Hillcrest. He'd urged Alice to find a companion who could protect her. She'd done well. Mrs. Everly carried herself like a lady. Intelligence gleamed in her eye along with more confidence than was common in companions. She might even hold her own against Hillcrest.

He was trying to decide if he'd met her—she seemed familiar—when a shadow moved across the desk. With a start, he realized that Alice had abandoned Helen and now stood before him.

"Thank you for sending Mrs. Everly to me," she said softly. "I know you didn't personally select her, but without your secretary's help, I wouldn't have known where to look. Mrs. Everly is wonderful."

He smiled. "She makes an excellent first impression. Is everything else all right?" He glanced at Hillcrest.

"We have come to an understanding."

Her voice held so much satisfaction that Rafe stared. This wasn't the cipher he remembered.

"Your marriage changed my life, Rafe—for the better," she confirmed, reading his face. "It forced me to assess my needs, decide how best to achieve them, and stand up to Lord Hillcrest. That turns out to be less difficult than I feared. He relies on intimidation, but is unwilling to back his threats with force—which makes them rather hollow—and since he knows only how to give orders and reject demands, logic confuses him." Her eyes twinkled.

"Good for you." He pressed her hand, amazed that animation made her likable. Even her coloring seemed more vivid today. She would draw eyes in town from those who sought sweet fragility. "Tell me, how did you convince him to bring you here? He allows no one to sway his opinion, especially a female."

"Actually, this is his excursion, not mine. But I will let him explain."

Sliding her hand from his, she rejoined Helen and Mrs. Everly. In moments, Mrs. Everly had both ladies laughing. It snapped a memory into place—a rout last Season where Lady Sherwood's companion had sent three bucks into gales of laughter with a tale of two dogs meeting in the park.

Barnes had indeed done well. Mrs. Everly was not the usual downtrodden companion. If she had even a minuscule jointure, she would be a welcome member of society. Her breeding was as good as Helen's, but her family was destitute.

Hillcrest approached the desk. "Alice informs me that she, too, opposed the match."

"That is correct." His heart sank. The betrothal was dead and buried, yet Hillcrest continued to harp on it. Helen had been wrong. Hillcrest was so incensed to have lost a battle that he'd hunted his quarry down to continue fighting.

"It would have been a good match," he insisted.

Rising, Rafe planted both palms on the desktop and glared. "What is your point, sir? Times have changed. Even today's royals have some say in who they wed. The Regent may have accepted Orange for his daughter, but anyone with eyes can see she loathes the man. And rightly so. He's a toad. There are so many other princes who would better suit that I fully expect her to throw Orange to the wolves and look elsewhere. Scandalous, to be sure, but better than sharing the throne with a lout."

Red spread across Hillcrest's face. "Yes, well . . . Alice swears that I owe you an apology, and I have come to agree. She claims that I know nothing about you. In thinking it over, I have to agree with that, too."

If he hadn't been braced on the desk, Rafe would have fallen. He was sure that his pounding heart had obscured words, twisting Hillcrest's meaning. The man never backed down. Nor did he admit fault.

"So I apologize," choked out Hillcrest. "I will do what I can to mitigate any damage to your reputation."

Had hell frozen over when he wasn't looking? Rafe could feel Helen's stare and hear her begging him to be gracious. The words stuck, but he managed, "Thank you, sir."

"So . . ." Hillcrest's gaze shifted as if seeking something to say.

Rafe relaxed. "You are doubtless weary. It's a long drive from Surrey. Helen will show you to your rooms. We eat in two hours."

Hillcrest nodded in relief.

"This way, my lord," said Helen, stepping in to cover further awkwardness. "Miss Pauling, Mrs. Everly." She led them from the library.

Rafe collapsed, too shaky even to pour brandy. What had just happened?

Impossible as it seemed, Alice had succeeded where he had failed. She had forced Hillcrest to accept reality. How had she—a negligible female—managed it?

But on second thought, that was precisely why she'd succeeded. For ten years, Hillcrest had championed her as the ideal woman. Faced with a scold, he'd had to choose between admitting he'd misjudged her and recognizing that times had changed while he wasn't looking.

He had chosen the lesser of two evils.

Yet that spark of hope was again kindled. All his life Rafe had yearned for Hillcrest's approval. Such a little thing, for he could not believe that he was evil incarnate. But Hillcrest had steadfastly refused.

Stop this! he ordered himself.

Hillcrest had extinguished that hope too often to allow it to rise yet again. The man could abandon their battle only by admitting that it served no purpose. But Hillcrest hated to lose. Even his wife's death hadn't stopped the fight.

Don't fall into the same trap. By locking him out, you become as hardheaded as he.

His conscience was beginning to sound like Helen, but it was right. If he ignored this overture, he was no better than Hillcrest. Though dropping his defenses would likely lead to new pain, he had to try.

Helen wished they had a larger crowd for dinner. The antagonism between Hillcrest and Rafe was so thick it was visible. They'd kept it under wraps during their brief meeting in the library, but dinner would last two hours, with port to follow. Would Alex provide a buffer, or would he fan the flames to annoy Rafe?

The drawing room was bursting with tension when she arrived.

"I hope the rooms are to your liking," she said, joining Hillcrest and Alice by the fireplace. Rafe was entertaining Mrs. Everly near the window. Alex had yet to appear.

"Lovely, thank you," said Alice. "Your home is beautiful, Mrs. Thomas."

"Quite impressive," agreed Hillcrest.

She nodded graciously, accepting a glass of sherry from Frank, who was acting as butler until Robert returned. "I can offer a tour tomorrow, if you like. Of this wing only, though. Much of the house in uninhabitable. Father hoped to restore it, but his health failed before he could realize the dream."

"Will you take that on?" Hillcrest fingered his glass.

"I don't know. We will conserve it, of course. I replaced the roof a year ago to halt water damage in the Tudor wing. But I doubt we will ever need enough space to justify restoration." She caught Rafe's eye and willed him to join her group. He delighted her by complying.

"Your wife offered us a house tour," said Alice.

"You should enjoy that. This wing was updated only ten years ago. Pay particular attention to the bathing chamber in the master suite and the lift system between the kitchen and butler's pantry. You might wish to add such conveniences to the Grange." He switched his gaze to Hillcrest. "Mrs. Everly informs me that Alice will come out next Season."

"She thinks it necessary." He obviously didn't agree.

"And so it is." Helen nodded. "How else is she to find a husband?"

"If I might make a suggestion," said Rafe carefully. "Alice must have a female sponsor. Without one, she cannot be presented at Court and won't receive the proper invitations."

"If you are suggesting your wi—"

Rafe interrupted. "Lady Alquist would be perfect. She is a fixture in society, highly respected, and on good terms with the best hostesses. Introducing a young lady will keep her busy, easing her return to town now that

Alquist is gone. And her support will erase any lingering suspicion of Alice.''

Helen stifled a gasp. Was he trying to start an argument? While pressing Hillcrest's sister-in-law into service made perfect social sense, Hillcrest blamed her for his wife's intransigence.

"But—" Hillcrest's protest halted when Alex appeared in the doorway. "Good Lord! What happened to Portland?"

Leaving Rafe to explain, or not, Helen crossed to welcome him.

"Sorry I'm late," he murmured.

"Perfect timing, actually," she replied. "I'm counting on you to temper any arguments."

"Then you will be disappointed. Hillcrest and I nearly came to blows at our last meeting."

"Alex . . ."

"I'll be a gentleman, but I can't speak for him. He is an arrogant ass."

"Does the man have nothing but enemies?" But they'd moved too close for him to respond. "Miss Pauling, this is Mr. Portland, third son of the Earl of Stratford. Miss Pauling is Lord Hillcrest's ward, now that Lord Pauling is gone."

Hillcrest interrupted before she could present Mrs. Everly. "This is the last place I expected to see you, Portland."

"But then, you know so little about me." His tone could cut glass.

"So it seems." Hillcrest met his eye. "Upon reflection, I found your comments informative."

"I apologize for any rudeness," said Alex.

"It was necessary." Hillcrest dropped his gaze to the carpet. "I would not have listened otherwise."

Rafe's eyes bugged out. Even Alex seemed surprised.

"I knew your father at school," continued Hillcrest, shaking his head. "Quite a scapegrace, as I recall."

Alex laughed. "Still is on occasion." He launched into a tale of the family's last Christmas gathering.

Rafe drew Helen aside. "Alice has bewitched him."

"Be glad. When Alex told me they'd nearly come to blows, I feared the evening would end badly."

"Believe me, I am very glad. But I'm also amazed. Look at him." He nodded toward Hillcrest as the man laughed. "In twenty-eight years, I've never seen him smile, let alone laugh."

Alice joined them. "I'm so glad this is working. I was terrified that coming here would make matters worse. Even after he saw the size and magnificence of Audley Court, I wasn't sure he would believe you."

"We are grateful," said Helen.

Alice blushed, then turned to Rafe. "Over dinner last night, I accused Hillcrest of knowing nothing about you. To prove it, I declared you were interested in politics. So if he asks, don't be surprised."

"How did you know about that?"

"I didn't. Are you truly interested?" She laughed.

"Yes, for all the good it does me." He turned to Helen. "Hillcrest will live forever, and no one will sponsor me for Commons."

"Reformer?" She smiled when he nodded. "Then you must know Mr. Bigelow."

"Of course, though I've not seen him in some time. I heard he was ill."

"Very. He is retiring, which will leave his seat open. Talk to the landowner in his borough. There's only one."

"How do you—" He stared. "Audley?"

She nodded as Frank announced dinner, then mentally kicked herself. Offering to fulfill his dream seemed too much like a bribe. *I don't like threats, and I don't like bribes . . .*

She hoped her rash words would not hand him another grievance.

Chapter Eighteen

*H*elen led Alice and Mrs. Everly to the drawing room for coffee. Dinner had gone better than expected, though two hours of tension left her limp. Alex had carried most of the conversation, often including the entire table in his comments to cover the deafening silence elsewhere. Without him, suspicion and lingering antagonism might have erupted into argument.

Her own plans risked raising acrimony, but this might be her only opportunity to question Alice about Rafe. She had tried to push the past aside, yet the memory of him kissing Alice lingered. Loving him wasn't enough. She must lay her distrust to rest. It grew from her own defects, not Rafe's—her parents had warned her so often about her faults that it was difficult to believe anyone could want her.

"You must have been horrified to discover that Mr. Thomas had wed me," she said baldly as she poured Alice's coffee.

"Surprised," admitted Alice. "But also glad."

"Glad?" She added sugar to Mrs. Everly's cup, then poured her own.

"Your marriage set me free." Alice frowned. "May I speak plainly?"

"I would prefer it. My position is odd." Telling the truth was the only way to exact truth in return. "I know very little about Mr. Thomas. And much of what I know seems contradictory. Your betrothal, for example. I first heard about it after we were wed."

"Because it did not really exist." Alice sighed. "I was told from birth that we were betrothed. When I was old enough to realize what that meant, I protested. I rarely saw Rafe and didn't much like him. Frankly, his reputation terrified me."

"That's rather strong."

"Perhaps, but it's true—which is why I was glad he wed you. Not until I talked to him at Hillcrest did I realize that Father had lied from the beginning." Tears sprang to her eyes.

"Why?"

"I have spent days trying to understand what happened." Alice accepted a handkerchief from Mrs. Everly. "The facts are simple enough. Rafe first heard about our supposed betrothal ten years ago. He repudiated it, but Hillcrest did not tell my father."

"But he would have learned the truth the first time he mentioned marriage to Rafe."

"Rafe never visited Paulus Grange, and I'm not sure Papa would have raised the subject if he had." She sighed. "Much as it pains me to admit it, Papa was completely under Hillcrest's thumb. I loved him dearly, but he was a weak man incapable of standing up to the least opposition. So Hillcrest dictated his thoughts, directed his affairs, and made all his decisions for him. He has run Paulus Grange for years. I doubt if Papa even realized it."

Helen nodded.

"I was too meek to argue," Alice continued grimly. "Only now do I understand that I was at the end of a chain of tyranny."

"What do you mean?"

"What do you know about Lady Hillcrest?" Alice countered.

"Quite a bit. Her sister is my godmother."

"Ah. Then you must know about the war." She paused to sip coffee. "The Hillcrests fought over everything, and not just in private. Their battles were notorious and so fierce that few would invite them to social affairs. They could not occupy the same room without arguing, and they forced everyone nearby to choose sides." She shuddered. "Neither of them ever won. She

might have been satisfied to not lose, but Hillcrest
needed victories. He found them by controlling Father.
The more frustrated he grew at home, the more demanding he became at the Grange. Eventually Father
ceased questioning any pronouncement. Whatever Hillcrest wanted, Father provided—down to choosing my
governess and dictating my course of study."

"If Lord Pauling was that weak, why couldn't you control him?" Helen refilled her cup.

"His weakness wasn't obvious, for he relieved his own
frustrations by controlling me—this began long before I
was born. He originally enslaved my mother, but she
died before my first birthday. By the time I was old
enough to question his edicts, meekness was so engrained that I could rarely ask more than a timid question, then retire—shaking in fear—when he chastised me
for forgetting my place. I now realize that Father was
parroting Hillcrest when he described that betrothal. He
had never actually spoken to Rafe about it. The match
would not have worked, so I am grateful that he wed
you. It leaves me free to take control of my future."
She smiled at her companion. "Mrs. Everly is already
preparing me for London. After twenty years of seclu-
sion, I can't wait to experience its excitement for
myself."

Helen relaxed as the conversation turned to the delights of the Season. Rafe had spoken truly. He was
more honest than any other man she knew, including
her father.

Hope kindled for their future. Her father may have
been right to question other men's motives, but she
could no longer apply his suspicions to Rafe.

The moment she was free of hostess obligations, she
would retire. In the privacy of the master suite, she and
Rafe could finish their discussion and consummate their
bargain. Her body tingled just thinking about it.

Rafe drained the last of his port and rose, signaling
the end of the longest dinner of his life—though in truth,
the meal had gone better than expected.

Portland was halfway to the drawing room before
Rafe reached the door.

He nearly snarled. The man was far too eager to reach Helen's side. The pair had laughed together often during dinner, offering a chilling contrast to his own stilted exchanges with Alice and Hillcrest. It was time Portland accepted that Helen was married. There would be no gallant swains in her future.

He nearly jumped out of his skin when Hillcrest laid a hand on his shoulder, halting his escape. "May we talk privately?"

Refusing would make him sound like a petulant child—Helen's charges had echoed mockingly all evening. Perhaps she would think better of him if he faced down Hillcrest. But he wasn't about to sit through another tirade. "Would you care for a game of billiards?"

Hillcrest nodded. Silence marked their trek to the billiard room.

The table was a mess, probably destroyed by Dudley. Rafe rolled a ball back and forth while Hillcrest chose a cue.

Hillcrest seemed oddly hesitant. Half the game passed before he broke his silence. "Why did you wed Helen?"

A question? Rafe paused, unwilling to admit that he'd been too drunk to think past that angry vow. "She was in trouble and met the qualifications I sought in a wife."

"A fortune and estate?"

"No." His cue slipped, sending the ball sideways. Leaving the table to Hillcrest, he poured wine. "Helen is intelligent, independent, and passionate about injustice. Her fortune means nothing. I have my own. And though Audley is a fine property, I've little interest in it. Helen will continue to oversee its operation—much better than I could." He added that last to needle Hillcrest, who hadn't even let his wife supervise the household staff. But Helen was right. He shouldn't fight.

Hillcrest miscued. "Your own fortune? You've nothing but what you make gaming."

"Not true." Rafe studied the table. That bud of hope urged him to be open. This was the first time in his life that he had spent more than two minutes with Hillcrest without anger, the first time Hillcrest had sought information. They might never have another chance to clear the air. Which meant abandoning barbs.

He potted a ball and moved to line up the next shot. "Rumors rarely bear more than a passing resemblance to truth."

"But you do frequent the tables."

"So does nearly every gentleman in London. Clubs are the best place to transact business and keep abreast of current events—as you would know if you ever came to town."

"I've been to town often."

"Not in the last thirty years."

"No."

Rafe opened his mouth on a cutting remark before noticing Hillcrest's fight for calm. He forced his jaw shut, refusing to be the first to lose his temper.

"I spent as much time in town as anyone for a decade after I came down from school," Hillcrest admitted as Rafe lined up his next shot.

Rafe flinched, missing the ball entirely. Shock was interfering with his game. "Why do you hate town, then?"

"Catherine had extravagant tastes. Her dowry was large, but would not have covered frivolous spending. I needed to keep her home while I rebuilt my grandfather's fortune."

Rafe whipped around so fast he stumbled. Had Hillcrest actually admitted that he'd abandoned town to punish his wife?

Hillcrest's raised hand stopped his angry response. "We will not discuss that quarrel," he said firmly. "It had nothing to do with you."

The enormity of the admission buckled Rafe's knees. He groped blindly for a chair. "Why now? Why cast aside twenty-eight years of demanding my blind obedience? I can't believe you would do that for Alice."

Hillcrest reddened. "Portland."

"But Portland hates me."

"Why?"

"Long story. What did he do to bring you here?"

Hillcrest fiddled with the cue while he studied the table. "I didn't know his name until I ran into him after Pauling's interment. He berated me for interfering with a Home Office investigation two years ago. I didn't know—"

"What happened?"

"I had him picked up for vagrancy. He'd been hanging about like a highwayman."

Rafe shook his head. It was so typical—acting without asking a single question.

"He called me the foulest names," continued Hillcrest. "When Alice made similar complaints the next day, I realized Portland was right. I must investigate my assumptions. So I am asking for information. You cannot deny your reputation as a gamester."

"No, and it is true that I play often. But I rarely wager deeply, and I avoid cards unless my head is clear. For that reason alone, I win far more than I lose. But it has been ten years since I've relied on winnings to pay my tailor."

Hillcrest caught his eye for a long moment. "Why? You get nothing from me."

"Because you use money like a whip, attaching strings to every farthing," Rafe snapped before drawing in his anger. He inhaled deeply. "My reputation arose from one high-stakes game ten years ago. I won ten thousand—from Portland—then hired the best man of business I could find to invest the purse. He multiplied its value many times over. My fortune now equals yours."

"But—" Hillcrest's voice cracked. "Why did you say nothing?"

"I tried," said Rafe quietly. "But you never listen."

"How dare you imply—"

"Don't!" Rafe strode to the window, tugging the curtain aside so he could stare across the moonlit park. When he could speak calmly, he returned to the table. "Every meeting since the day I was born has been a confrontation. I haven't the energy to fight tonight."

Hillcrest shut his mouth.

Rafe followed suit, fearful that another word would provoke a battle. This meeting had no rules that he knew. He stifled pique that a witless female and his worst enemy had penetrated Hillcrest's thick skull, while he—

"Alice accused me of confusing you with your mother," Hillcrest said slowly.

"It would be best if we let Mother rest in peace," said Rafe just as slowly.

"Perhaps, though I must explain one point. Our argument was not one-sided, Rafe. I may be guilty of demanding that she comport herself more modestly than other ladies, but she never let me forget for a moment that her dowry saved me from ruin. If I can offer one piece of advice—don't let your wife's wealth stand between you."

"I won't." He couldn't choke out another word. Helen's voice echoed through his mind. *As contrary as your mother . . . treated you as her savior . . . argue for the sake of arguing . . .*

She was right. His mother was not the saint he'd supposed. She had been as instrumental in maintaining the war as Hillcrest, fighting with equal cruelty, equal determination, equal unfairness. Every fight had been waged using personal attacks and ugly insults. Even normal conversation had included barbs.

Pain flared as two truths slammed into his head. His fear that Helen would try to rule him grew from watching his mother's constant quest to rule his father. And his mother was another who had considered him a pawn. Love had been there, but so had manipulation. Each parent had tried to bind him—his mother with love, his father with duty. But each had sought the same goal—commanding his allegiance against the other. Had his support faltered, she would have turned on him, for her love was always strongest after he'd defied his father. If he could forgive her, he must also forgive Hillcrest.

The anger drained away. Hillcrest had been trapped in a battle he could never win. Unable to compromise, he had fought on, pigheadedly demanding the same concessions over and over again. Pitiable, but not evil. And not Rafe's problem.

The weight of years slipped from his shoulders, leaving him lightheaded. Love did not need weapons or manipulation. Only trust.

Hillcrest studied the table in silence. "What other exaggerations does gossip make?"

Rafe picked up his cue for the next shot. "Nearly everything."

"Surely you can't claim you live like a monk!"

"No." He potted the next ball. "But I've done nothing

worthy of comment in ten years. Yet gossips needs rogues to titillate and shock their delicate sensibilities. I let them cast me in that role at age eighteen. Since they refuse to abandon that perception, they speculate on what I'm hiding."

"Even the worst gossips lose interest after a time."

"Not when my father makes a career of denouncing me." He hit the ball so hard, it bounced out of the pocket.

"I see." Hillcrest bit his lip, then sank four balls in a row, ending the game. When he straightened, he'd abandoned the subject. "You claim Helen is in trouble. How?"

Rafe reset the table. "Her uncle resents that she inherited her father's fortune. Sir Steven is utterly unscrupulous. So far he has forged documents to divert trust payments into his own pocket, incarcerated her so she could not seek help, intercepted her correspondence, and demanded that she wed his son. When she wed me instead, he sent men to kill me."

"What?" Hillcrest dropped his cue. He stared at Rafe's black eye and scraped forehead as if seeing them for the first time. Had he thought his blow at Hillcrest had caused them?

"They mistook Portland for me," explained Rafe. "We look alike from a distance."

"So that's what happened."

"Exactly. The attack occurred outside Hillcrest's gates. The Home Office is now on the case, as well as the runner I hired. Sir Steven is guilty of defrauding dozens of men—"

"How?" demanded Hillcrest.

"Phony investments, mostly. I nearly fell for his damned canal scheme—would have if my man of business hadn't talked me out of it."

"Not Courtney's Passenger Canal!"

Rafe nodded.

Fury twisted Hillcrest's face. "Damn! The bastard took me for two thousand guineas."

"My condolences. But that's not his worst sin. I believe he murdered Alquist."

"Why?"

"Alquist was Helen's cousin and guardian. When he learned that Steven was at Audley, he started investigating Steven's activities. So Alquist died. I have runners looking for evidence."

"Where is Sir Steven now?"

"Probably headed here."

"To kill you himself?"

Rafe shrugged. "Or steal enough to support him in France—he cannot stay in England. By remaining at Audley, you make yourself a target," he added.

"Surely the staff can deflect him."

"I doubt it."

Rafe abandoned the game, gesturing Hillcrest to a chair. For the first time in his life, they were equals rather than enemies. He laid out the entire story.

"So we can't rely on the staff," he concluded. "Helen turned off the butler, but there must be others. And who knows how many servants might turn a blind eye from fear of retribution?"

"This place is huge."

"And it has far more entrances than I can watch."

"I will take a turn on guard, as will Crawford," said Hillcrest, naming his valet. "What about grooms?"

"Those we can trust are posted about the grounds. And I dare not leave the stables unguarded. I wouldn't put it past Steven to burn them out of spite."

"Mine can help there, too."

"Thank you. Why don't you retire?" suggested Rafe. "I'll wake you for your watch."

Hillcrest nodded, then excused himself and headed upstairs.

Rafe let out a long breath as he returned the cues to their case. Hillcrest would never be as close as Alquist had been, but perhaps they could get along. Even an hour ago, that had seemed impossible.

Helen frowned when Alex entered the drawing room alone. Where was Rafe? And Hillcrest?

Rafe had not wanted Hillcrest in the house. If her insistence subjected him to another tirade, she would never forgive herself. But there was nothing she could do at the moment.

Alex soon distracted her by turning the full force of his charm on Alice. Helen couldn't deflect him without abandoning Mrs. Everly. The woman was happily chattering. Helen didn't have the heart to stop her.

But she seethed. Alice's infatuation was clear—the rosy cheeks, the wide-eyed stare, the flirtatious glances across her fan. She was hanging on his every word, acting as if he were a scrumptious confection set before a starving mouth.

Helen cringed. If she had looked that sappy-eyed four years ago, it was no wonder everyone believed she had given him everything.

Warning Alice would serve no purpose. If someone had told her Alex's charm meant nothing, she would have angrily ignored the words. And Alice was less worldly than she'd been. Bereavement also made Alice susceptible to flattery.

So she must separate them. Swallowing the suggestion of whist that had hovered on her tongue, she announced, "We keep country hours at Audley. I'm sure you are longing for bed after your journey, so I will bid you a good night." As the others left, she held Alex back.

"What?" he demanded.

"Don't toy with Miss Pauling," she ordered shortly. "She is too vulnerable right now."

"I don't see that it's any of your business," he snapped. "An unwanted guest who . . ."

"Enough, Alex. Wanted or not, Miss Pauling *is* a guest. You are a blatant flirt highly skilled at fascinating young girls—I'm not sure you entirely realize it. But I won't have you hurting someone under my roof. I'll see you castrated if you damage another reputation."

"I never meant to hurt you, Helen." He ran one hand through his hair as he paced to the fireplace and back.

"But you did." When he tried to speak, she cut him off. "We will not argue fault again. Nor will we discuss your supposed devotion. Frankly, you know little about the woman I am today. Nor do you know anything about Miss Pauling."

"Right on both counts, Helen."

His agreement knocked the wind from her sails.

He smiled. "It is well that I was called away that night,

for we would have been at each other's throats inside a year."

"Very likely. You used me to mask your investigation, then decided marriage was an suitable payment. I would have accepted your offer so I could escape another year in the country. But neither reason is adequate."

"Miss Pauling seems quite like the girl I thought you at the time. But I doubt she is hiding an independent nature behind that sweet face."

"Such thinking is dangerous," she warned him, recalling Alice's disgust that she'd meekly submitted to her father's orders all those years. "She is stepping into the world for the first time after living under a tyrannical father's thumb. Even Rafe is surprised at how much she's changed since Lord Pauling's death—and he's known her for twenty years. She hasn't yet decided what she wants, but that uncertainty makes her vulnerable. She needs time to settle before being targeted by a charming rogue."

"Never a rogue."

"I disagree. At the very least, you are damnably careless. Miss Pauling is barely a week into mourning, and not just for her father. Make sure of your own intentions before you take this any further. If you attach her affections, I'll see you wed so fast your head will spin."

He raised his brows.

"As I said, you are careless. You spread charm without thought, but this isn't London, where ladies assign no more meaning to flirtation than to an exchange on the weather. I won't tolerate your hurting another girl the way you hurt me. And don't talk to me of betrothals," she added when he tried to protest. "If you think carefully about your conversation with Father, you will likely find that you left your intentions rather vague. I think even then, you knew we would not suit."

His eyes flashed.

"If you think Miss Pauling might, then wait. In three months, she will be out of deep mourning. You can call at Hillcrest Manor and see if the spark remains. But for now, stay away from her." She turned on her heel and left.

Chapter Nineteen

*H*elen finished reviewing lockup procedures with Frank, then started upstairs to find Rafe. The knocker pulled her back to the hall. Stepping into the shadows, she waited while Frank answered the door.

A murmured exchange ended with Frank saying, "Please wait, sir. I will see if the gentleman is receiving." He shut the door, then spotted Helen. "A Mr. Riley to speak with Mr. Portland."

At ten in the evening? "Mr. Portland said nothing about expecting a caller." It might be a hoax. Nalley knew Alex was here, so Steven might also know. A courier would have identified himself as such. But she couldn't be arbitrary. "Seat him in the alcove. I will inform Mr. Portland."

Frank looked puzzled, but complied.

She found Alex and Rafe outside the master suite. "A Mr. Riley is downstairs. Do you know him, Alex?"

"He's my assistant. If he came in person, he likely has urgent news."

"Then I'll bring him to the library." Maybe Steven had been arrested.

Rafe was pouring wine when Helen ushered Riley into the library.

"Terrence!" Portland gripped his assistant's hand, taking in his appearance in a swift glance. "You must have had a hard journey."

"No worse than yours, I'll warrant."

"Have you supped?" asked Helen.

"In Taunton, ma'am." Riley accepted wine from Rafe. "You are kin to Alquist, I believe."

"My wife is. My connection is to Lady Alquist," said Rafe. "I've not heard from London in two days. How goes the investigation into his death?"

Riley drained his glass. " 'Twas murder, all right. The scandal drove your marriage from every lip."

"Good," said Helen.

Riley turned to Portland. "Several gentlemen saw Alquist walking home that night. None noticed a wagon, but two remembered a pair of rough strangers hanging about—the same pair who attacked you, sir. Alquist's butler identified Arnold as the man who called at the house. He is quite upset about revealing Alquist's whereabouts."

"I will write to him," murmured Rafe. Reticence might have postponed the attack, but Alquist would have died anyway.

"Barney is cooperating in exchange for transportation instead of hanging," continued Riley, sending a glance to Portland that Rafe easily interpreted. The government would promise anything to obtain information because Barney's wound had turned lethally septic—hardly a surprise if Hawkins had let the local doctor treat him.

Riley turned to Helen. "Sir Steven's secretary hired them to kill Alquist. Society is up in arms over the news. Stone crossed to France, so it may take some time to find him, but we suspect he was acting on Sir Steven's orders, so I have a warrant for Sir Steven's arrest."

Helen puffed out a relieved sigh.

"Good work," Rafe managed.

"Where is Sir Steven?" asked Portland.

"He may have passed through Bath last evening. A carriage containing two men and a woman was spotted. The occupants spoke to no one, so I cannot prove they were Sir Steven's party, but I dispatched word to London. The duke is pressing, which is why I came myself rather than sending the warrant."

Portland raised a questioning brow.

Riley sighed. "The Duke of Oakwood is determined

to apprehend Dudley St. James. I have a warrant for him, too."

"Why?" asked Helen.

"Oakwood's grandson was found in a ditch last week, badly mauled," Riley began.

"Not Carley!" exclaimed Rafe. Lord Carley was his closest friend.

Riley nodded. "He'll recover, though a night outdoors did him little good."

Portland frowned. "Why did you say nothing when we last spoke?"

"I didn't know it connected with this case, sir. Carley was delirious for days and unable to give a coherent statement until after you left."

"So Dudley attacked him?"

"Carley was dicing in a hell on Jermyn Street the evening of the twenty-first. His winnings included five hundred in vowels from Dudley, who followed him outside, robbed him, then carried him to Hampstead Heath. After beating him nearly senseless—while cursing Carley's dastardly friends—he left him in a ditch to die of exposure. It's a marvel Carley survived. If not for two children out for a morning romp with their dog . . ."

"My fault," choked Rafe. "That was the day he learned of our wedding." He met Helen's troubled gaze. Vandalizing her house hadn't mitigated his fury. "He knew Carley and I have been close since school. I won his wife. My friend won his purse. It was too much." When Helen laid a comforting hand on his arm, he covered it, drawing strength.

"The least insult sends him into a frenzy," confirmed Riley. "I checked his service record, as you ordered," he added to Portland.

"And?"

"There isn't one."

"But Steven said—" Helen shut her mouth.

"Where has he been?" demanded Rafe.

"On the Peninsula, supposedly at hand to fill field vacancies—a common way to enter the officer corps without buying a commission," he added to Helen. "But he soon discovered lucrative diversions."

"Such as?" Portland frowned.

"Providing military personnel with girls, food, and cattle—most of it stolen. Aiding deserters. Brawling with officers, some of whom swore he'd robbed them."

Rafe shook his head. "So why is he desperate for money?"

"He shares his father's weakness for gaming, as well as his poor luck," said Helen. "In his month at Audley, he lost consistently."

Portland pursed his lips. "Steven's best course is to flee to Canada. Is it possible that he's headed for Plymouth?" The Devonshire port served many vessels plying the Atlantic.

"Perhaps." Riley frowned.

"But stopping here to pad his purse is likely, whatever his destination," said Rafe. "I doubt he has enough to cover his passage. He is hardly the sort to sign on as an indentured servant, so until we hear otherwise, we must expect him to show up with at least two men on his heels."

"We have respectable numbers," Portland reminded him.

"When we are all awake." He turned to Riley. "Sleep. You can take the third watch."

Helen left the men arranging watch schedules. One look at Rafe had stopped her offer to help. He might tolerate many of her oddities, but he would not approve of her standing guard—which did not deter her from making her own preparations.

In the gun room, she unlocked her father's pistol cabinet and examined the contents. Her mother's muff pistol would be best—small and easy to handle. It was inaccurate over any distance, but within the close confines of a room . . . And its foldaway trigger made it safe under a pillow.

She snapped open the case. Her mother had left half a dozen balls. Loading it, she slipped it into her pocket. It was best that the servants not know she was armed.

"You're late." Steven glared as his partner entered the schoolroom.

"I had to hire a horse in Taunton," said Nalley sullenly. "The bitch turned me off."

"Why?"

"You sent word to bar all callers. Easy enough to do—or should have been. But she has a knack for being in the hall whenever someone arrives. I didn't notice her until it was too late." He shrugged.

"Who called?"

"Lord Hillcrest."

Hillcrest? Steven smiled. Perfect. Just perfect.

For days he had wracked his brains for a way to kill Thomas without drawing suspicion—after initially embracing his courtesan tale, society had dismissed it, so he could not afford any connection to the death. The highwayman attack would have been perfect if the idiots hadn't blundered. An accident was difficult to arrange, for Thomas left the house only with Helen.

He'd toyed with letting Smith attack—Dudley swore the man would do anything for money—but he feared Smith would double-cross him if Thomas offered more. Or Smith might kill them both. But the grieving widow must write a new will before dying, and that would take time. Stone still hadn't reached Audley, though the man had promised to follow as soon as he identified Hicks's agents.

Steven forced his thoughts back to business. Hillcrest's arrival made eliminating Thomas simple. Everyone knew the viscount loathed his son. Jilting Miss Pauling had embarrassed him. Temper had sent him here to seek retribution. People would shake their heads when Thomas died in the resulting confrontation, but no one would be surprised.

"Are you sure Hillcrest remains here?" he asked Nalley.

"Reasonably. She ordered a room made up for him."

"Which one?"

"I don't know. Perhaps the room Thomas was using—they moved into the master suite."

"They did?" Steven frowned. "They must expect trouble."

"I doubt it. Charlie and Vince swear Thomas is staking his claim to Audley."

But Steven wasn't so sure. "Did anyone see you return?"

"No. A groom was taking the air, but I was already in the rose garden when he passed."

Taking the air? Thomas was setting outside guards who could swear that no one had approached during the night. So Hillcrest would bear the blame. The confusion when Thomas's body was discovered would allow him to leave undetected.

"Maude and Dudley are in the governess's room. Help her keep Dudley under control. I'll call you when it's time."

As Nalley hurried away, Steven sank into thought. Slipping into the master suite would be easy enough. A knife was silent. It could be left in Hillcrest's room to be found in the morning.

Helen glanced up when Rafe opened the connecting door between their bedrooms. "Is the watch schedule set?" She laid her brush on the dressing table and rose.

He nodded. "Portland and his man Tweed are on now, then Hillcrest and Crawford." He paused. "Thank you for insisting I welcome him."

"I take it you survived the evening?" she dared, joining him.

"We came to terms."

"Wonderful!" She threw her arms around his neck. "I'm so glad, Rafe."

He pulled her against him, nuzzling her hair. "I couldn't have done it without you, Helen. You were right. We'd fallen into a ritual of hate and antagonism, but that's over."

"Are you friends, then?"

"Maybe. I still disagree with many of his ideas—"

"Hardly a surprise for a reformer," she murmured into his ear.

"Right. But we've laid Mother to rest." His hands pulled her closer.

She wanted to talk. But his manhood was prodding her stomach, so talk could wait. Turning her head to meet his lips, she slipped a hand between them to stroke.

He tensed, then crushed his mouth to hers and plundered. Her heart soared. His response was fiercer than ever.

Excitement and dizziness banished further thought, letting her mind float free on a wave of pure sensation. Not until he laid her on his bed did she realize he'd lifted her.

"Alone . . . at last." He sprawled, half atop her, deep kisses punctuating his words. He untied the neck of her nightgown and pushed the fabric down.

"Yes!" She tugged off his coat and waistcoat, then pulled his shirt over his head, sorry to lose contact with his talented hands for even a moment.

"Mine," he murmured, drawing a nipple between his teeth.

"All yours," she agreed. "Forever."

He froze. Silver eyes bored into hers. "You mean that? You don't love Portland?"

"Of course not."

Rafe pinned her hands over her head, reining in passion so he could think. "This is important, Helen. If you don't love Portland, why did you insist on riding out with him this morning? Tessa knows the grounds as well as you."

She met his gaze without flinching. "I knew Tessa would be safe with you, Rafe. But Alex cares nothing for servants. I can't trust him to respect a pretty maid."

Rafe shook his head. Not once had he considered that explanation. "You really don't care?"

She tugged a hand free to cup his scarred cheek. "You may look alike on the surface, but inside, Alex is arrogant, autocratic, and intolerant. You care about the world and the people in it—as individuals, not just as names attached to duties. I prefer people who care."

His heart swelled with joy. "I need you, Helen." Kicking off his shoes, he tugged off his pantaloons, delighted that she took advantage of her freed hands to help. This time there would be no interruptions. Guards, locks, and bolts kept the world at bay. Free of clothes, he pinned her to the bed. "I haven't slept for days for wanting you . . . going mad . . . unable to think . . ."

Helen's bones turned to water as he poured out his need in desperate snatches between bone-melting kisses.

His hands were everywhere, filling her soul and sating hunger she'd not recognized. Alex had needed an excuse to slip away. Her father had needed someone to take over his affairs. Her mother had needed a nurse. Only Rafe had ever needed *her*.

She moaned, rolling so she could explore his body. Touching him banished her loneliness. His passion promised more joy than she had ever dreamed possible.

Rafe trembled, gasping as Helen's caresses sent fire through his veins. Her fingers explored every inch of his skin, filling his head with color and light and sound until it nearly burst.

He returned the favor, reveling in her passion and in the knowledge that she was his alone. He couldn't get enough of her, feasting until he was incoherent. His pounding heart left him dizzy, but nothing could stop him from feeding his all-consuming need.

He'd feared that urgency would force a frenzied coupling, but as she matched him stroke for stroke, he discovered a newer, greater need to savor, to explore, to share the joy overflowing his heart. She savored in turn, licking and biting until sparks blinded him and tremors shook him from head to toe.

"Need—" He groaned, positioning her under him.

"Now!" she panted, eyes blurring as she gripped his hips with her legs.

He eased past her barrier, then plunged.

She was perfect. So tight, so hot, so passionate that if Steven burst in with a band of armed ruffians, he would not notice.

All control splintered. Nails scored his back as he pounded into her, no longer able to wait. Not that it mattered. She was as desperate as he, bucking and moaning as she fought for release, her hair a blazing halo framing her face.

"Rafe! Aaahh!"

They exploded together in glorious ecstasy.

"Heavens," she murmured when her breathing finally steadied. "I'd no idea."

Nor had he. Lovemaking had never been as powerful. He tried to speak, to say something witty or seductive or even thankful, but a week of frustration and night watches left him too limp. "Go to sleep, sweetheart," he finally managed, pulling her against him.

"In a minute." When his arm tightened, she added. "I need to use the commode."

"Ah." He kissed her ear, then sank into oblivion.

Rafe jerked awake as the door squeaked open, then relaxed. Helen was returning. He started shifting to make room for her on the bed, but suddenly froze.

Helen's door didn't squeak. None of the master suite doors squeaked.

Wide awake, he stealthily scanned the room. He'd not lit lamps, so it was too dark to make out more than vague shapes, but one of them was moving. A second shadow separated from the deeper shadow beyond the fireplace.

An eternity passed before his brain identified his peril.

"Help!" he shouted as the shadows rushed toward the bed. "Portland! Tweed! Attack!"

He scrambled toward the table where he'd left a pistol, but the tangled covers pulled him up short.

A blow landed on his hip.

"Bastard!" he choked, smashing a fist into the man's head.

Steven grunted.

"Die, Thomas!" Dudley's knife slashed downward, missing Rafe by an inch.

He had a better chance with Steven. His lunge ripped the sheet and plowed his jaw into a fist. Shaking away the pain, he slammed his own fist into Steven's body.

"Ooomph!"

A second blow struck Steven's thigh, but the man remained standing. Instead of striking back, he shoved Rafe toward Dudley.

Rafe's foot lashed out, knocking something to the floor. Before he could follow through, Steven pinned him to the bed.

Dudley's teeth flashed as the knife descended.

Helen had just fastened her dressing gown and snuffed the last candle in her room when a squeak echoed through the open connecting door. Rafe's bed? She'd

not noticed it earlier, but passion could deafen her to a
trumpeter in full fanfare. Making a mental note to have
the estate carpenter check the frame, she collected the
pistol from her dressing table and—

"Help! Portland! Tweed! Attack!"

"Rafe!" Helen raced to his room as a series of dull
thuds erupted. Moonlight filtered through a crack in the
curtains, creating faint shadows. Figures grappled on the
bed. The far one swung a dagger.

She fired.

Rafe screamed in pain.

A figure crumpled to the floor.

"Rafe!" Cursing herself for shooting an unidentified
shadow, she rushed forward.

"Bitch!" Steven charged.

She slammed the pistol into his face, clawing for his
eyes with her other hand.

He smashed her aside. A fist landed in her stomach.

"Beast!" As she fell, her kick connected with his knee.
He toppled against the bed table. Lamp oil and glass
exploded in all directions.

Curses joined Rafe's groans.

She needed a weapon. Hoping to find a shard of glass
big enough to be useful, she ran her hands over the
floor. Her fist closed over a dagger.

"You asked for this," growled Steven, hauling her to
her feet.

She slashed.

Bellowing in pain, he knocked the knife away, then
grabbed her throat and squeezed.

Rafe fought past the pain in his shoulder. Helen
needed help. She could never defeat Steven alone. Staggering from the bed, he hooked an arm around Steven's
neck and punched him in the kidneys.

Steven twisted. A stray elbow sent sparks darting
through Rafe's eyes, but he held on. He couldn't let the
bastard hurt Helen. Fury rammed his knee into Steven's
groin. When his grip prevented the man from doubling
over, he kneed him a second time, then a third. But he
was fading fast.

Shouts sounded in the hall. Fists pounded the door. A shadow lurched around the bed.

Rafe cursed. He was too dizzy to hold off Dudley, too. But it was Portland.

Helen staggered to the window the moment Steven let go. Pulling down the curtains flooded the room with moonlight. She whirled . . .

Three men grappled near the bed. Grunts and the thud of fists smashing into flesh filled the air. Even with the moonlight, she couldn't identify individuals until Steven collapsed. The others resolved into Rafe and Alex.

Thank God!

With relief came the shakes. Blood covered Rafe's torso. Horrified, she barely noticed Alex swoon atop Steven's body.

"My God, Rafe." She rushed to his side. "Lie down. How bad is it?"

"Shhh." Rafe pulled her into his arms. "You saved my life. Your shot deflected his knife and saved my life."

"And you saved mine. Now get back in bed. You're bleeding."

"Need to tie—" He groaned, swaying.

"Down, Rafe." Shoving him back, she wiped away the blood, and gasped. More welled from a gash on his shoulder.

She pressed the wadded sheet against the wound.

"Are you awake?" she demanded. His eyes were shut.

"Just dizzy."

"So you should be." She pressed harder.

"Open up!" shouted Hillcrest, pounding on the door.

"Hold this while I let him in. He sounds frantic."

Rafe nodded. "We need light. Bind everyone. Can't afford a new attack." Someone moaned, punctuating his words. "Might be more down there." He gestured toward the hole near the fireplace where a stag had pivoted into the room.

"One thing at a time, Rafe." She made sure he was exerting enough pressure, then headed for the door.

Hillcrest stared. "My God! Are you all right?"

"What happened?" demanded Alice, stepping around him. "Oh, no! Mr. Portland!" She flew to Alex's side.

Riley followed.

Pounding footsteps whirled Helen around as Tweed charged through the hole and skidded to a halt. "Mr. Portland!" he gasped.

"Enough!" Helen clapped her hands, drawing all eyes. "Who is on guard in the hall?"

"I locked the door," said Riley.

"Return to your post," she ordered. "There may be others, and they may have keys. Tweed, where does this passage go?"

"That bookroom near the library, ma'am."

"Is anyone else down there?"

"Charlie, Vince, and Nalley, but I tied them securely."

"Good. Light the lamps here, then wake Frank. He must send David to guard the bookroom, then summon a magistrate—Sir Montrose is the nearest."

He nodded, the tinderbox already in his hand.

Light illuminated the carnage.

Hillcrest knelt over a gasping Dudley. Alice was mopping the reopened cut on Alex's forehead. Rafe still clutched the sheet to his shoulder.

"Bind Dudley," she ordered Hillcrest.

"No point. He's dying."

Her stomach lurched, but she forced her feet forward. Her shot had torn Dudley's chest. Blood pooled heavily on the floor. Gone was his habitual sneer and the fury that threatened everyone in his path. All that remained was the pitiful shell of a dissipated wastrel.

"Bind Steven, then. He may wake at any moment. I don't think we did him serious damage."

As Hillcrest moved away, Rafe pulled her down beside him.

"Don't think about it, Helen," he murmured. "You had no choice. If you hadn't shot him, I would be dead."

"I know. But I wish there had been another way." Shaking off her growing dizziness, she renewed the pressure on his shoulder.

"He brought this on himself by scheming to steal your inheritance. Don't waste time mourning him."

"I won't."

Steven awoke, cursing.

Hillcrest finished tying him, then returned to the bed, shaking his head over Rafe. "How bad are you hurt?"

"It's only a scratch," vowed Rafe.

"Nonsense." Helen turned to Hillcrest. "Dudley stabbed him. Do you want some brandy?" she added to Rafe.

"No."

Hillcrest lifted the sheet to peer at the wound. "The bleeding is nearly stopped, but you need stitches."

"I can treat him," said Tweed from the doorway. He clutched a small box in one hand. "Mr. Portland also needs stitches." He turned to Helen. "A groom is fetching the magistrate, ma'am. And David is on his way to the bookroom."

"Thank—"

A woman's scream burst from the passage. "Johnny! You killed my brother!"

Hillcrest rushed to block the opening, but Maude knocked him down, then gasped when she saw Dudley.

"Dudley!" She caught his shoulders and shook. "What have they done to you?"

Dudley's throat rattled one last time, then went silent.

"No! No! Wake up!"

"It's no use, ma'am," said Hillcrest, pulling her up. "He's gone."

"Gone? Gone! That bastard!" Tearing from his grasp, she kicked Steven viciously in the side. "I told you to leave England while we had the chance. I told you this would never work. But you never listen to anything! Idiot! Ten times an idiot!" Another kick landed.

"Shut your mouth, Maude," gasped Steven.

"Restrain her," Helen ordered Hillcrest. "I want him alive to stand trial."

"Murderer!" shrieked Maude, hopping over Steven to kick his other side. "You killed my brother!"

"Nonsense." Steven's eyes widened when Maude scooped a pistol from the bed table. "Put it down, Maude. Nalley was fine when I came up here. If anything happened, blame them." He nodded weakly toward Rafe.

"Liar! He's dead. Your fault. Everything is your

fault." She cocked the pistol. "We should never have listened to you."

Hillcrest tackled her as she pulled the trigger. Helen covered her ears. The basin on Rafe's shaving stand shattered, raining china fragments on Alex.

Riley raced in from the hall.

"Watch out," cried Helen as Maude twisted from Hillcrest's grasp. "She's a hellcat."

Riley tackled her. Hillcrest helped drag her to a chair.

"You'll pay for this," she screamed at Steven. "Bastard! Johnny dead. My baby dead. You'll rot in hell." She broke into gusty sobs.

"Baby?" asked Rafe.

"She was Dudley's nurse, then stayed on as Steven's mistress. But I had no idea Nalley was her brother." She wondered how Nalley had died.

Riley tied Maude while Hillcrest applied a gag. Blessed silence fell. Hillcrest collapsed on the other chair and closed his eyes.

Alex gestured to Riley. "Make sure David is in the bookroom, then return to your post. I don't want anyone else in here."

"Let's see that shoulder." Tweed nodded to Rafe. "Hold him down, ma'am. They always move at the worst times."

Helen nodded. She was beginning to feel unreal. "I hope you have lots of thread. Sir Steven's arm also needs attention."

"Let him suffer," growled Rafe.

"I won't let him take the easy way out by bleeding to death."

Helen was so dizzy that Rafe was holding her up instead of her holding him down. But by the time Tweed bandaged his shoulder, she'd caught her second wind.

Hillcrest and David moved Dudley and the prisoners to the bookroom, then remained there to stand guard. Helen sent Frank downstairs to await Sir Montrose. Riley went to check with the sentries. They must remain on duty in case the bully boys were on Steven's heels.

"Finished," said Tweed, rising from Alex's side.

"Good. Put him to bed until Sir Montrose arrives. You need sleep, too," she added to Alice.

Rafe shook his head as everyone filed out. "Your face is a mess."

She glanced in the mirror. One eye was turning purple, and a bruise marred her cheek. But it was small price to pay for victory.

Her gaze returned to the secret passage that had nearly been so costly. "I never knew that was there, Rafe." Tremors shook her hands, rapidly spreading to engulf her body. She clung to a bedpost as her knees weakened.

"I know. I wish I'd thought to look for one, but this wing is too new for priest's holes and such."

"I'm sure the former owner said nothing to Father. He would have mentioned it."

"Forget it, Helen."

"I can't! You almost died because I didn't know about this."

"You saved my life, Helen. That's all that matters. Even if you should have known—which I don't accept for a moment; this is not an ancestral property, for God's sake—we all make mistakes. I've made more than my share and would never blame you for being human." His nose twitched. "This place reeks of blood. Let's move."

"Of course." She stepped up to help him, but he was already sliding to the floor.

"Watch out!"

Too late. He landed on a piece of glass and fell against the fireplace wall. Antlers gouged his hip, breaking the skin when a prong broke off.

"Rafe!"

Cursing, he grabbed a hawk to restore his balance. Its wing twisted, pitching him to the floor.

"Are you all right?" She dropped to his side.

"We've got to get rid of that damned wall." He grimaced in pain.

"You've made a start—though this isn't the first piece that has snapped." Even in candlelight, she could see a dozen repairs to the slimmer projections.

"The bird must be the latch for the secret passage."

"It's on the wrong side of the fireplace."

"What the devil?" He stared. A hole had opened in the tree's canopy, revealing a niche. Inside was a canvas bag, four boxes, and a sheaf of papers.

Chapter Twenty

*H*elen was still reeling from the contents of the bedroom safe when Sir Montrose arrived. The bag contained hundreds of gold coins, more than she'd ever seen at one time—banknotes had replaced coins as war expenses and smuggling drained the country's bullion faster than reduced exports could replenish it.

The boxes held sapphires, emeralds, rubies, and diamonds in exquisite settings. Sir Arthur's illness had cancelled most entertaining, so Helen had forgotten about her mother's best jewelry.

But it was the papers that staggered her. Even Rafe seemed shocked.

Sir Montrose began his inquiry by examining the bodies and the slashes in Rafe's bed. He then adjourned to the library with Helen, Rafe, Alex, and Riley.

Rafe shared Helen's couch, letting Sir Montrose commandeer the desk. One arm circled her shoulders, keeping her close—contact he couldn't forgo, so the world might as well get used to it.

"Are you certain Sir Steven was involved?" Sir Montrose demanded ponderously. "Attempted murder is a very serious charge, Thomas. Dudley, I can understand. You are not the first to complain about him. But perhaps Sir Steven was trying to stop him. He has been a valuable addition to Somerset and—"

"You are another victim of his lies," said Rafe, interrupting. "Before you continue, you should read Sir Arthur's will." He handed over the copy they had found in the niche.

Sir Montrose's eyes widened as he read. "But he swore—"

"Lies," said Helen calmly. "Steven knew before he came here that Father had left him nothing. He took advantage of Mother's illness to incarcerate me, turn off every servant who knew the truth, then claim my inheritance for himself. But that was a temporary measure, for many outside of Somerset knew the truth. To make his theft permanent, he demanded that I wed Dudley. He had already prepared the way by forging letters to my trustees. They would not have questioned another letter requesting that they release my inheritance to my new husband."

Rafe described Steven's thefts from the trust, then passed copies of the trust documents to Sir Montrose. Another protracted silence ended with Sir Montrose scowling.

"Our marriage foiled that plot," continued Rafe. "Yet Sir Steven refused to give up. He still hoped to complete his original scheme, but that required killing me. This wasn't his first attempt." He nodded at Alex.

"I might have known you were involved, Portland." Sir Montrose glared. "You always bring trouble."

"No. I follow trouble. Thomas is no more responsible for inciting Sir Steven to murder than you were for your secretary's treason." When Sir Montrose subsided, he described the first attack, then Riley reviewed the Home Office's findings in the death of Lord Alquist and produced the arrest orders.

Sir Montrose paled. "He killed a lord?"

"He will strike at anyone who thwarts him."

The magistrate shook his head. "Describe tonight's business again," he ordered. "You were asleep, Mr. Thomas."

Rafe reviewed the attack from the opening of the secret panel until Helen fired the fatal shot.

"She had no choice," Sir Montrose agreed, then turned to Alex. "You were on guard?"

"Tweed and I had the first watch," said Alex. "When

I heard someone creeping downstairs, I woke Riley to cover my post, then took Tweed with me to investigate."

Helen hadn't thought to ask how Alex had found the secret passage.

"There was light and voices in the bookroom," he continued. "I was about to dispatch Tweed to collect reinforcements when we heard a loud creak. Dudley laughed, then said, *I told you I found a better way in.*" He and Sir Steven ordered the others to guard their backs. That's when I realized they had opened a secret passage." He cleared his throat. "We had to attack immediately. With the doors bolted upstairs, the passage was our only way into the master suite."

Rafe squeezed Helen's shoulder in apology. The bolts he'd installed for protection had nearly killed them.

"Nalley, Vince, and Charlie were in the bookroom. They had us outnumbered until Mrs. Thomas's shot distracted Nalley long enough for me to penetrate his guard. He fell, striking his head on the andiron. I helped subdue the others, then raced upstairs. Thomas was grappling with Sir Steven when I arrived. You know the rest."

Sir Montrose shook his head. "So much blood. And all because Sir Steven was greedy."

"It was more than greed," said Helen, snuggling closer against Rafe's side. "If money had been his only concern, Dudley could have wed a Cit. And it was more than his feud with Father. He was driven by fear. Father had proof that Dudley was not his legal heir."

"But—"

Rafe passed more papers to Sir Montrose. "Statements from the midwife, from Steven's wife, and from a housemaid. Steven's wife birthed only one child, a stillborn daughter. The delivery left her unable to conceive, though she remained in robust health otherwise. Steven was furious."

Alex gaped.

Helen sighed. "Maude had borne him a son only two days earlier. He swapped the babes, then threatened the witnesses with death if any of them revealed the truth."

"Passing off a bastard is a serious offense." Sir Montrose frowned.

"There's more," continued Helen. "Maude was married at the time, so Dudley was legally her husband's heir. Mr. Cunningham died in a mysterious accident the following day. Maude swore their son died with him, buried Steven's girl with her husband, then joined Steven's household as Dudley's nurse. Steven's wife was packed off to an asylum, where she has lived ever since."

"So it was Helen's legitimacy as much as her fortune that Steven wanted," finished Rafe.

"But if Sir Arthur had this evidence, why did he never use it?"

"I don't know." Helen met his eyes. "He collected evidence of other frauds as well, yet never disclosed one. Perhaps he was protecting the family name. Or maybe he planned something else. His reasons died with him."

"What evidence?" asked Alex, leaning forward.

"More than you'll ever need." Rafe handed him the remaining papers. "Proof of fraud, theft, forgery, and a host of other crimes. Dates, places, accomplices, victims. Sir Arthur documented everything. He must have had someone watching Steven's every move." Until a year earlier. The reports ceased four months before Arthur's death.

Alex and Riley bent over the pages.

Sir Montrose pulled himself together. "The next assizes is not for three months. But since many of these crimes took place elsewhere, this matter would be better dealt with in London."

Alex glanced up. "An excellent decision. My men can escort the prisoners there tomorrow."

Sir Montrose relaxed. "In the meantime, I must interview them for my report."

"I will join you," said Riley. "The others need sleep."

"Thank you." Helen grabbed Rafe and led him upstairs before he could protest.

By the time they reached the master suite, Rafe was sagging.

"Lie down," said Helen, steering him toward her bed. "Your face is white as a sheet."

"Mostly shock over your father's papers." But he complied.

"I wish he'd told me about them." She paced before the fireplace. "If I'd known what a scoundrel Steven was, I would have been more alert. I can't believe Father didn't trust me."

"I've been thinking about that since we found them. It wasn't a matter of trust, Helen. He didn't want to further tarnish your name by revealing Steven's crimes. You had enough problems because of Portland."

"But—" She shook her head. "Why collect the information then?"

"Insurance. You said Steven demanded money."

"Several times."

"Arthur probably kept him under control by threatening to release his evidence if Steven bothered his family. He may have bought an estate far from London to keep Steven at a distance—Lady Alquist said Steven never visited the West Country. And I'm sure your mother knew about these. The papers were close at hand in case she needed them after he was gone."

"Of course." She leaned weakly against the fireplace—a simple marble surround without a stag or hawk in sight. "He reminded her on one of this lucid days near the end. *Keep Steven away*, he told her as I was entering the room. I paid little heed, since he was always warning us against his brother. But he must have been alluding to the evidence and charging her with the responsibility to use it."

"Exactly. She could continue the intimidation. Once Steven gave up or died, she could have destroyed the evidence to protect the family name in the future."

"But she collapsed at his deathbed. The few times she tried to speak, we were unable to understand a word. Steven must have realized that I knew nothing when I let him inside. So he put his own plans in motion, then searched the house for the evidence. Even if he couldn't find it, the marriage plot would keep me and Audley under his control."

"True, but I doubt you understand his full purpose even now," said Rafe slowly.

"What?"

"He could have forged your will nine months ago, then arranged an accident. But he wanted more than your inheritance. He needed to punish you for daring to stand between him and the fortune he needed, and he questioned Dudley's breeding—after all, Cunningham had accepted the boy. What better way to take care of both problems than to get a son on Dudley's wife himself."

"My God!" She staggered toward the bed.

Rafe pulled her down beside him. "You're safe now, sweetheart. He'll never hurt you again."

"Or you." A sob clogged her throat. "I was so s-scared, Rafe. I thought I'd killed you." She gestured toward the connecting door. "I saw a flash and fired. When you screamed, I was sure I'd shot you. All I could see was shadows. It was irresponsible to fire under those conditions." She burst into tears.

"It's all right, Helen." He stroked her back while she cried against his good shoulder. Her breakdown was one last proof that she didn't love Portland—as if he needed one after she'd ignored the man passed out at his feet.

His head rested against hers. "I will never consider that irresponsible, sweetheart. You did the best you could in a situation that would have sent most ladies into a swoon. It's time to accept that you are not perfect—nor is anyone else."

"Am I that bad?"

"Not usually, but you accept blame for too many things that are not your fault."

"Perhaps. I suppose it started when Father handed Audley into my care. A female must be twice as able as a man to garner respect. I couldn't afford even the tiniest mishap."

"I can ease that for you, if you'll let me," he said cautiously. "Not that I want to take over. My own interest lies in standing for Commons and—"

Her fingers covered his mouth. "I would appreciate your help, Rafe. You were right that tenants can't reveal everything to a female, but I was too terrified of fortune hunters to listen."

"Never a fortune hunter, Helen. Your inheritance intimidated me, for it made our marriage seem too much like Mother's." He again stroked her back. "But it was not Mother's money that stood between my parents. It was how she chose to use it. You would never consider it a weapon."

"No. I see nothing noble in fighting."

"Nor I." He shifted so he could see her face, wincing as pain sliced down his arm. "While I enjoy a good debate, I am sick to death of the warfare my parents enjoyed. I will never subject you to that."

She nodded. "We were both influenced by our parents. Papa taught me to doubt men's words, for he was convinced that every suitor wanted only my fortune—an assessment easy to believe in light of Mama's lectures about the handicaps I must overcome to be acceptable in town."

"What?"

"I'm too tall, too outspoken, with bad coloring—"

"Nonsense. While some men may prefer insipid misses like Alice, I have always loved striking Originals—as do many others."

"Thank you." She snuggled closer. "At any rate, I learned to evaluate everything through his distrust."

"I understand." His voice caught as she again bumped his bandage.

She tried to pull away. "Let me up, Rafe. I'm knocking your shoulder."

"Stay. I need you in my arms. It's the only way I can face the world."

"Then why did you demand an annulment?"

Curses paraded through Rafe's head—harsher than he'd ever uttered in his life. He'd made a hash of too many things lately. "Watching Portland kiss you made me realize that I could not live with a wife who preferred another."

"I don't—"

He stopped her protest with a kiss. "I know that now, but I was still laboring under false assumptions yesterday."

"Which should have ended when I slapped him," she snapped, shaking her head.

"You did?"

"Of course. I don't enjoy being mauled—except by you."

"I wish I'd seen it." He pulled her closer, then answered her raised brow. "I couldn't bear to watch."

"Why?"

Her husky voice cracked his last barrier. Only honesty would do if he expected honesty in return. "Because I love you."

"And I love you, Rafe—which is why I know I never loved Alex. It's such a different feeling."

"Very." He nuzzled her neck while his fingers untied her gown. "You're overdressed, my love."

"Are you sure? Your shoulder—"

"—doesn't matter." He flexed his hips to prove it, stroking her thigh with his eager shaft.

"I see." A seductive smile lifted her mouth. "Then you are also overdressed. If you stand up, I can take care of that problem. After all, we wouldn't want you pulling that shoulder."

"True." He slid to the floor, taking Helen with him.

"Any healer would remind you that exertion is bad," she purred, pushing his hands aside so she could unbutton his waistcoat. "You mustn't do anything energetic."

Air whooshed from his lungs as she slowly removed his clothes, exploring his flesh with fingers and lips. Shaking with love, he returned the favor, easing her out of her gown and stays. Her petticoats drifted to the floor, revealing a body flushed and ready. He kept his touch light, teasing her to greater heights than before. And himself as well.

When dizziness overwhelmed him, he returned to bed to join her in an explosive celebration of life that left them breathless, boneless, and bursting with joy.

But his body pulsed with more energy than even a shattering climax could dissipate. As her hand drifted from his back to his thigh, he hardened within her.

"Mmm," she sighed as he slowly flexed. "Is it always like this?"

"Only with someone you love." He nuzzled her neck, brushing a palm across her breast. Her scent tickled his nose, banishing the ache from his shoulder. "You make me feel like the lustiest of the ancient gods. Strong. Invincible. Utterly insatiable."

He kept his thrusts languid, coaxing her into renewed readiness. Holding back stoked his own flames hotter. Passion sizzled, prodding every hair on his body to attention—as if lightning were about to strike. Each quiver rippling her satin skin drove his heartbeat faster.

Helen drifted on a sea of pleasure, scarcely able to think as Rafe caressed her inside and out. Even her most lascivious dreams hadn't prepared her for the joy of his lovemaking. His voice whispered in her ear, urging her excitement higher. Sparks skittered under her skin. Not until brushing his bandaged shoulder evoked a groan did she remember.

"You need rest, Rafe."

"Not as much as I need you." He thrust harder, deeper, drawing her gasp. "There is no pain. Only pleasure—a greedy lust for more. I'll never have enough of you."

She bit back a moan. "But your shoulder—"

"Is fine." A kiss stopped another protest. "Never tell a rake he is too wounded to make love, sweetheart. Not even a reformed rake. I'll be at least a week dead before I stop needing you." Laughter threaded his voice.

She subsided, relinquishing the reins to his practiced hands. Tension mounted as he drove deeper. Blood roared through her ears. Sensations built, whirling, colliding, and overrunning one another until she could no longer identify sources. Deep kisses turned her brain to mush.

"More," she gasped. "Faster. Harder. Can't stand—"

"Easy, love. Savor the moment. This time will be even better."

His body begged for release, but he couldn't end it yet. Touching Helen was the greatest thrill of his life. They were more powerful together than apart, a single entity that could accomplish anything.

He held her trembling on the edge, his gaze trapped in the passion swirling through her eyes. Sweat slickened his skin as he fought to prolong the pleasure. Tension built, clawing with need, burning white-hot to the point of pain. But not until she climaxed, screaming his name, did he finally let go, plunging into the abyss to share the final ecstasy as the world shattered in a blaze of light. United. Complete.

He would never be lonely again. . . .

Rafe had no idea how much time passed before he could summon the energy to open his eyes. Another climax like that would kill him. Perhaps Helen was right that he needed rest.

"Are you alive?" he gasped, pulling out.

"Barely." She curled against him, taking care not to jostle his shoulder. "What about you?"

"Never better." He kissed her. "Go to sleep, love. We have much to do come morning."

"Like writing to my trustees."

That wasn't high on his list, but news of Steven's arrest might make them more cooperative.

"We have to break the trust," she murmured.

"No. Audley is yours. I meant it when I said I didn't want it. The responsibility would interfere with my own pursuits." He no longer cared about her fortune. They would argue, of course, for they were passionate people, but the weapon would be logic, and the confrontations would end in agreement—and probably lust. His shaft twitched in expectation, but he willed it down.

"I will enjoy managing Audley, but you need to own it." She shifted closer.

Wide awake, he pulled back to stare at her. "Why?"

Green eyes stared back. "You want a seat in Commons."

"Yes, but—"

"Audley has a seat, but only if someone votes for you."

"I don't see—"

"Rafe. There is only one landowner in this borough. Not a single shopkeeper has enough assets to qualify. So I'm it, but females can't vote. The trust makes no provision for filling vacant seats."

He shook his head. She was right. Without a male landowner to cast a ballot, the seat would be filled by Parliamentary appointment—of a Tory. But he could not take advantage of her newfound trust. "Think about it for a few days, sweetheart."

"If you insist, but I won't change my mind. I'd rather you handled the investments anyway. And I trust you."

"As I trust you. Now and forever."

"I'm glad. Now go to sleep."

He pulled her against him, turning her so his shaft nestled against her buttocks and his hand cupped a breast. Her hair brushed his face, enveloping him in her scent.

How had he been so lucky? Fate was a mysterious force, sometimes rewarding the most appalling stupidity.

As dawn broke, he settled another kiss on his perfect wife and closed his eyes.

Allison Lane

"A FORMIDABLE TALENT...
MS. LANE NEVER FAILS TO
DELIVER THE GOODS."
—*ROMANTIC TIMES*

Emily's Beau

0-451-20992-3

Emily Hughes has her sights set on one man:
Jacob Winters, Earl of Hawthorne. But her
hopes are dashed when she discovers that Jacob
is already betrothed. She will have to forget
Jacob and marry another, which is just what
she plans to do—until one moonlit kiss changes
everything.

Also Available:

Penguin Group (USA) Inc.
Online

Your Internet gateway to a virtual environment with
hundreds of entertaining and enlightening books
from Penguin Group (USA) Inc.

*While you're there, get the latest buzz on
the best authors and books around—*

Tom Clancy, Patricia Cornwell, W.E.B. Griffin,
Nora Roberts, William Gibson, Robin Cook,
Brian Jacques, Catherine Coulter, Stephen King,
Ken Follett, Terry McMillan, and many more!

**Penguin Group (USA) Inc. Online is located at
http://www.penguin.com**

PENGUIN PUTNAM NEWS

Every month you'll get an inside look at our upcom-
ing books and new features on our site. This is an
ongoing effort to provide you with the most
up-to-date information about
our books and authors.

Subscribe to Penguin Putnam (USA) Inc. News at
http://www.penguin.com/newsletters